George Gilfillan, Charles Churchill

The Poetical Works of Charles Churchill

George Gilfillan, Charles Churchill

The Poetical Works of Charles Churchill

ISBN/EAN: 9783337162597

Printed in Europe, USA, Canada, Australia, Japan

Cover: Foto ©Andreas Hilbeck / pixelio.de

More available books at **www.hansebooks.com**

THE

POETICAL WORKS

OF

CHARLES CHURCHILL.

With Memoir, Critical Dissertation,
and Explanatory Notes,

BY THE

REV. GEORGE GILFILLAN.

THE TEXT EDITED BY CHARLES COWDEN CLARKE.

EDINBURGH: JAMES NICHOL.
LONDON: JAMES NISBET AND CO.   DUBLIN: W. ROBERTSON.
LIVERPOOL: G. PHILIP & SON.
M.DCCC.LXIV.

CHURCHILL—HIS LIFE AND WRITINGS.

In Churchill we find a signal specimen of a considerable class of writers, concerning whom Goldsmith's words are true—

"Who, born for the universe, narrow'd their mind,
And to party gave up what was meant for mankind."

Possessed of powers and natural endowments which might have made him, under favourable circumstances, a poet, a hero, a man, and a saint, he became, partly through his own fault, and partly through the force of destiny, a satirist, an unfortunate politician, a profligate, died early; and we must approach his corpse, as men do those of Burns and Byron, with sorrow, wonder, admiration, and blame, blended into one strange, complex, and yet not unnatural emotion. Like them, his life was short and unhappy—his career triumphant, yet chequered—his powers uncultivated—his passions unchecked—his poetry only a partial discovery of his genius —his end sudden and melancholy—and his reputation, and future place in the history of letters, hitherto somewhat uncertain. And yet, like them, his very faults and errors, both as a man and a poet, have acted, with many, as nails, fastening to a " sure place" his reputation and the effect of his genius.

Charles Churchill was born in Vine Street, Westminster, in February 1731. He was the eldest son of the Rev. Charles Churchill, a rector in Essex, as well as a curate, and lecturer of St John the Evangelist, Westminster. As to the attainments of the poet's father, we know only that he was qualified

to superintend the studies of the son, during the intervals of
public tuition. At eight years of age, he was sent to Westminster School, and placed under the care of Dr Nichols and
Dr Pierson Lloyd, where his proficiency in classical lore was
by no means remarkable; nor did he give any promise of the
brilliance which afterwards distinguished his genius. At fifteen, he stood as candidate for admission to the foundation at
Westminster, and carried it triumphantly. Shortly after,
having by some misdemeanour displeased the masters, he was
compelled to compose, and recite in the school-room, a poetical
declamation in Latin, by way of penance. This he accom-
plished in a masterly manner—to the astonishment of his
masters, and the delight of his school-fellows—some of whom
became afterwards distinguished men. We can fancy the
scene at the day of the recitation—the grave and big-wigged
schoolmasters looking grimly on—their aspect, however, becoming softer and brighter, as one large hexameter rolls out
after another—the strong, awkward, ugly boy, unblushingly
pouring forth his energetic lines—cheered by the sight of the
relaxing gravity of his teachers' looks—while around, you see
the bashful tremulous figure of poor Cowper, the small thin
shape and bright eye of Warren Hastings, and the waggish
countenance of Colman—all eagerly watching the reciter—and
all, at last, distended and brightened with joy at his signal
triumph.

At the age of eighteen, he stood for a fellowship in Merton
College, but without success—being defeated by older candi-
dates. Shortly after, he applied for matriculation at the
University of Oxford, but is SAID to have been rejected at
his examination, in which, instead of answering the questions
proposed, he broke out into satirical reflections on the abilities
of his judges. From Oxford he repaired to Cambridge, where
he was admitted into Trinity College. Here, however, his
stay was very short,—he was probably repelled by the
chevaux-de-frise of the mathematics;—and in a few weeks he
returned to London, disgusted at both universities, shaking
their dust off his feet, and, perhaps, vowing vengeance against
them—a vow which .he has kept in his poetry. In his

"Ghost," for instance, he thus ridiculed those forms of admission—

> "Which Balaam's ass
> As well as Balaam's self might pass,
> And with his master take degrees,
> Could he contrive to pay the fees."

Penniless, and soured by disappointment, Churchill returned to his father's house; and, being idle, soon obtained work from the proverbial "taskmaster" of all idle people. Having become acquainted with a young lady, named Scott, whose father lived in the vicinity of Westminster School, he, with true poetic imprudence, married her privately in the Fleet, to the great annoyance of both their parents. His father, however, was much attached to and proud of his son, and at last was reconciled to the match, and took the young couple home. Churchill passed one quiet domestic year under the paternal roof. At its termination—for reasons which are not known —he retired to Sunderland, in the north of England, and seems there to have applied himself enthusiastically to the study of poetry—commencing, at the same time, a course of theological reading, with a view to the Church. He remained in Sunderland till the year 1753, when he came back to London to take possession of a small fortune which accrued to him through his wife. He had now reached the age of twenty-two, and had been three years married.

During the residence in the metropolis which succeeded, he frequented the theatres, and came thus in contact with a field where he was to gather his earliest and most untarnished laurels. In "The Rosciad," we find the results of several years' keen and close observation of the actors of the period, collected into one focus, and pointed and irradiated by the power of genius. As Scott, while carelessly galloping in his youth through Liddesdale, and listening to ballads and old-world stories, was "making himself" into the mighty minstrel of the border—so this big, clumsy, overgrown student, seated in the pit of Drury Lane, or exalted to the one-shilling gallery of Covent Garden, was silently growing into the greatest poet of the stage that, perhaps, ever lived.

Soon after, he was ordained deacon by the Bishop of Bath and Wells, on the curacy of Cadbury, in Somersetshire, where he immediately removed, and entered on a career of active ministerial work. Such were the golden opinions he gained in Cadbury, that, in 1756, although he had taken no degree, nor could be said to have studied at either of the universities, he was ordained priest by Dr Sherlock, the Bishop of London (celebrated for his Sermons and his "Trial of the Witnesses"), on his father's curacy of Rainham, Essex. Here he continued diligent in his pastoral duties—blameless in his conduct, and attentive to his theological studies. He seemed to have entirely escaped from the suction of the stage—to have forsworn the Muses, and to have turned the eye of his ambition away from the peaks of Parnassus to the summit of the Bishops' Bench.

But for Churchill's poor circumstances, it is likely that he would have reached this elevation, as surely as did his great contemporary, and the object of his implacable hatred and abuse, William Warburton. But his early marriage, and his increasing responsibilities, produced pecuniary embarrassments, and these must have tended gradually to sour him against his profession, and to prepare his mind for that rupture with it which ultimately ensued. To support himself and his family, he opened a school, and met with considerable encouragement—although we suspect that his scholars felt something of the spirit of the future satirist stirring in the motions of his rod, and that he who afterwards lashed his century did not spare his school. In the year 1758, his amiable and excellent father died, and (a striking testimony both to his own and his son's early worth) Charles was unanimously chosen to be his father's successor in the curacy and lectureship of St John's. There he laboured for a time, according to some statements, with much punctuality, energy, and acceptance. After "The Rosciad" had established his name, he sold ten of the sermons he had preached in St John's to a bookseller for £250. We have not read them; but Dr Kippis has pronounced them utterly unworthy of their author's fame—without a single gleam of his poetic fire—so poor, indeed, that he supposes that they were borrowed from some dull elderly divine, if not from Churchill's own father. This reminds us of a story which was lately communicated to us about the famous William Godwin. He, too, succeeded his father in his pastoral charge. Tinged, however, already with heterodox views, he was by no means so popular as his father had been. His own sermons were exceedingly cold and dry, but he possessed a chestful of his father's, and used to read them frequently, by way of grateful change to his hearers. The sermons of the elder Godwin were recognised by the orthodoxy of their sentiment, and the dinginess of their colour, and were much relished; and so long as the stock lasted, the future author of "Caleb Williams" commanded a tolerable audience; but so soon as he had read them all, and resumed his own lucubrations, his hearers melted away, and he moved off to become a literateur in London. Perhaps Churchill, in like manner, may have found that general audiences like plain sense better than poetry. That he had ever much real piety or zeal has been gravely doubted, and we share in the doubts. But although he himself speaks slightingly, in one of his latter poems, of his ministerial labours, he at least played his part with outward decorum. His great objection to the office was still his small salary, which amounted to scarcely £100 per annum. This compelled him to resume the occupation of a tutor, first to the young ladies attending a boarding-school in Queen Square, Bloomsbury, and then to several young gentlemen who were prosecuting the study of the classics.

When about twenty-seven years of age, he renewed his acquaintance with Robert Lloyd, the son of Dr Lloyd, one of the masters of Westminster School, and who had been an early chum of Churchill's. This young man had discovered very promising abilities, alike at Westminster and at Cambridge, and had been appointed usher in his father's seminary; but, sick of the drudgery, and infected with a fierce thirst both for fame and pleasure, had flung himself upon the literary arena. Although far inferior to Churchill in genius, and indeed little better than a clever copyist of his manner, he exerted a very pernicious influence on his friend's conduct. He borrowed in-

spiration from Churchill, and gave him infamy in exchange.
The poet could do nothing by halves.   Along with Lloyd, he
rushed into a wild career of dissipation.   He became a nightly
frequenter of the theatres, taverns, and worse haunts.   His
wife, with whom, after the first year, he never seems to have
been happy, instead of checking, outran her husband in ex-
travagance and imprudence.   He got deeply involved in debt,
and was repeatedly in danger of imprisonment, till Dr Lloyd,
his friend's father, nobly stept forward to his relief, persuaded
his creditors to accept five shillings in the pound, and himself
lent what was required to complete the sum.   It is said that,
when afterwards Churchill had made money by the sale of his
poems, he voluntarily paid the whole of the original debt.

Along with the new love of indulgence, there had arisen in
his bosom the old love of verse.   Stimulated by intercourse
with Lloyd, Colman, B. Thornton, and other wits of the
period, he had written a poem, in Hudibrastic rhyme, entitled
"The Bard."   This he offered to one Waller, a bookseller in
Fleet Street, who rejected it with scorn.   In this feeling
Churchill seems afterwards to have shared, as he never would
consent to its publication.   Not at all discouraged, he sat
down and wrote a satire entitled "The Conclave," directed
against the Dean and Chapter of Westminster,—Dr Zachary
Pearce, a favourite of Churchill's ire, being then Dean.
This would have been published but for the fear of legal pro-
ceedings.   It was extremely personal and severe.   His third
effort was destined to be more successful.   This was "The
Rosciad," written, it is said, after two months' close attend-
ance on the theatres.   This excessively clever satire he
offered to various booksellers, some say for twenty pounds,
others for five guineas.   It was refused, and he had to print
it at his own expense.   It appeared, without his name, in
March 1761.   Churchill now, like Byron, "awoke one morning and found himself famous."   A few days convinced him
and all men that a decided hit had been made, and that a
strong new satirist had burst, like a comet, into the sky—

"With fear of change perplexing" players.

The effect was prodigious. The critics admired—the victims of his satire writhed and raved—the public greedily bought, and all cried out, " Who can this be ? " The *Critical Review*, then conducted by Smollett, alone opposed the general opinion. It accused Colman and Lloyd of having concocted " The Rosciad," for the purpose of puffing themselves. This compelled Churchill to quit his mask. He announced his name as the author of the poem, and as preparing another—his " Apology "—addressed to the *Critical Reviewers*, which accordingly appeared ere the close of April. It proved a second bombshell, cast into the astonished town. Smollett was keenly assailed in it, and had to write to Churchill, through Garrick, that he was not the writer of the obnoxious critique. Garrick, himself the hero of " The Rosciad," was here rather broadly reminded that heroes are mortal, and that kings may be dethroned, and had to make humiliating concessions to the fearless satirist. Fearless, indeed, and strong he required to be, for many of his victims had vowed loud and deep to avenge their quarrel by inflicting corporal chastisement on their foe. He armed himself with a huge bludgeon, however, and stalked abroad and returned home unharmed and unattempted. None cared to meddle with such a brawny Hercules.

In another way his enemies soon had their revenge. He had gained one thousand pounds by his two poems, and this supplied him with the materials of unlimited indulgence, which he did not fail to use. He threw off every restraint. He donned, instead of his clerical costume, a blue coat and gold-laced waistcoat. He separated from his wife, giving her, indeed, a handsome allowance. His midnight potations became deeper and more habitual. Dean Zachary Pearce, afterwards Bishop of Rochester, in vain remonstrated. At last, on his parishioners taking the matter up, and raising an outcry as to his neglect of duty, and the unbecoming character of his dress, he resigned his curacy and lectureship, and became for the rest of his life a literary and dissipated " man about town."

In October 1761 he published a poem entitled " Night," addressed to Lloyd, in which, while seeking to vindicate himself from the charges against his *morale,* he in reality glories in his shame. His sudden celebrity had perhaps acted as a glare of light, revealing faults that might have been overlooked in an obscure person. With his dissipation, too, there mingled some elements of generosity and compassion, as in the story told of him by Charles Johnson in his "Chrysal" of the poet succouring a poor starving girl of the town, whom he met in the midnight streets,—an incident reminding one of 'the similar stories told of Dr Johnson, and Burke, and realising the parable of the good Samaritan. Yet his conduct on the whole could not be defended.

His next poem was "The Ghost," which he published in parts, and continued at intervals. It was a kind of rhymed diary or waste-book, in which he deposited his every-day thoughts and feelings, without any order or plan,—reminding us of "Tristram Shandy" or of "Don Juan," although not so whimsically delightful as the former, nor so brilliant and poignant as the latter.

But now, in 1762, the Poet was to degrade or to sublimate into the Politician, at the bidding of that gay magician, Jack Wilkes. That this man was much better than a clever and pre-eminently lucky scoundrel, is now denied by few. He had, indeed, immense *pluck* and convivial pleasantry, with considerable learning and talent. But he had no principle, no character, little power of writing, and did not even possess a particle of that mob eloquence which seduces multitudes. His depravities and vices were far too gross even for that gross age. In the very height of his reputation for patriotism, he was intriguing with the ministry for a place for himself. And he became in his latter days, as Burke had predicted (for we strongly suspect that Burke wrote the words in "Junius"), "a silent senator," sate down "infamous and contented," —proving that it had only been "the tempest which had lifted him from his place."

Wilkes introduced himself to Churchill, and they became speedily intimate. Soon after, indignant at the supremacy of Lord Bute, who, as a royal favourite, had obtained a power in the country which had not been equalled since Buckingham

fell before the assassin Felton's knife, and was employing all
his influence to patronise the Scotch, Wilkes commenced the
North Briton. In this, from the first, he was assisted by
Churchill, who, however, did not write prose so vigorously as
verse. He had sent to the *North Briton* a biting paper
against the Scotch. On reflection, he recalled and recast it in
rhyme. It was " The Prophecy of Famine ; " and became so
popular as to make a whole nation his enemies, and all *their*
enemies his friends. This completely filled up the measure
of Churchill's triumph. He actually dressed his youngest son
in the Highland garb, took him everywhere along with him,
and instructed him to say, when asked why he was thus
dressed, " Sir, my father hates the Scotch ; and does it to
plague them."

Lord Bute resigned early in 1763, and was succeeded by a
ministry comprising such men as Sir Francis Dashwood, and
Lord Sandwich, who had been intimates of Wilkes, and had
shared with him in certain disgusting orgies at Medmenham
Abbey. They now, however, changed their tactics, and became vehement upholders of morality and religion ; and began
to watch their opportunity for pouncing on their quondam
associate. This he himself furnished by the famous *North-
Briton*, No. 45. That paper may now seem, to those who
read it, a not very powerful, and not very daring diatribe.
But the times were inflammable—the nation was frantic with
rage at the peace—the ministry were young, and willing to
flesh their new-got power in some victim or other ; and Wilkes,
in this paper, had now exposed himself to their fury. Warrants were instantly issued to arrest him and Churchill, as
well as the publishers and printers. Wilkes was newly arrested when Churchill walked into his room. Knowing that
his friend's name was also in the warrant, he adroitly said to
Churchill, " Good morrow, Mr Thomson ; how is Mrs Thomson to-day ; does *she dine in the country ?* " The poet took the
hint—said that she was waiting on him—took his leave, and
retired to the country accordingly.

Immediately after occurred the controversy between Hogarth and our poet. While Wilkes's case was being tried, and

Chief-Justice Pratt, afterwards Lord Camden, was about to give the memorable decision in favour of the accused; and in condemnation of general warrants, Hogarth was sitting in the court, and immortalising Wilkes's villanous squint upon the canvas. In July 1763, Churchill avenged his friend's quarrel by the savage personalities of his "Epistle to William Hogarth." Here, while lauding highly the painter's genius, he denounces his vanity, his envy, and makes an unmanly and brutal attack on his supposed dotage. Hogarth, within a month, replied by caricaturing Churchill as a bear with torn clerical bands, paws in ruffles, a pot of porter in his right hand, and a knot of LIES and *North Britons* in his left. Churchill threatened him with a renewed and severer assault in the shape of an elegy, but was dissuaded from it by his mistress.

This was Miss Carr, daughter of a respectable sculptor in Westminster, whom Churchill had seduced. After a fortnight they were both struck with remorse, agreed to separate, and, through the intercession of a friend, the young lady was restored to her parents. Rendered miserable, however, by the taunts of an elder sister, she, in absolute despair, cast herself again on Churchill's protection, and they remained together till his death. In his letters we find him, during one of his sober intervals, living quietly with her in Richmond. In "The Conference," he makes some allusions to this unhappy affair, and discovers the spirit, if not of true penitence, certainly of keen remorse, and strong self-crimination. In the autumn of 1763 he became the comforter of his friend, Lloyd, in the Fleet, supported him in confinement, and opened a subscription for the discharge of his heavy debts, which, owing to the backwardness of others, proved of little service.

Toward the close of this year, the *North Briton* was ordered to be burnt by the common hangman; and, on the motion of Lord Sandwich, Wilkes was handed over for prosecution, for his infamous "Essay on Woman," a parody on Pope's "Essay on Man"—(one Kidgell, a clergyman, had stolen a copy, and informed the Government.) Lord Sandwich was backed by Warburton; and the result was, Wilkes's expulsion from the House of Commons, and his flight to France. He had previously fought a duel with one Martin, an M.P., by whom he was severely wounded. All this furnished Churchill with matter for his "Duellist," which even Horace Walpole pronounced "glorious." In this vigorous production, he mercilessly lashes Martin, Kidgell, Warburton, and especially Sandwich. At this time he, too, purposed a retreat to France —a country where his name was already so well known, that when the Honourable Mr Churchill, the son of a general of the name, was asked, in Paris, if he were Churchill, the famous poet, and replied that he was not, the answer of the Frenchman was, "*So much the worse for you.*" His time, however, to visit that coast, destined to be so fatal to him, was not yet quite come.

From Richmond he removed to Acton-Common, where he had a house furnished with great elegance—"kept a post-chaise, saddle-horses, and pointers—and fished, fowled, hunted, coursed, and lived in an easy independent manner." There he continued his irregular but rapid and energetic course of composition, pouring out poem after poem as if he felt his time to be short, or as if he were spurred on by the secret stings of misery and remorse. To "The Duellist" succeeded "The Author,"—a poem more general and less poisoned with personalities than any of his former. "Gotham," by far the most poetical of his works, came next. When Lord Sandwich stood for the High-Stewardship of Cambridge, Churchill's ancient grudge, as well as his itch for satire, revived, and he improvised "The Candidate," a piece of hasty but terrible sarcasm. With breathless and portentous rapidity followed "The Farewell," "The Times," and "Independence," which was his last published production. Two fragments were found among his MSS., one "A Dedication to Warburton," and another, "The Journey," his latest effort, and in which the *last* line now seems prophetic—

"*I on my journey all alone proceed.*"

A far and final journey was before this great and ill-fated poet. He was seized with one of those sudden longings to see a friend, which are not uncommon with the impulsive. He determined to visit Wilkes at Boulogne, and conveyed his purpose to his brother John in the following note:—" Dear Jack, adieu, C. C." On the 22d of October 1764, he started for France, met Wilkes; but on the 29th was seized with miliary fever, under which, while imprudently removed from his bed to be conveyed at his own desire to England, his constitution sunk, and he expired on the 4th of November, in the thirty-third year of his age. He is said to have died calmly and firmly, rebuking the excessive grief of his friends, and repeating some manly but not very Christian lines from his own poetry. By a will made during his sickness, he left an annuity of sixty pounds to his wife (in addition, we suppose, to her former allowance), fifty pounds a-year to Miss Carr, besides providing for his two boys, and leaving mourning rings to his more intimate friends. Wilkes got the charge of all his works. His body was brought to Dover, where he now sleeps in an old churchyard, which once belonged to the church of St Martin, with a stone over him, bearing his age, the date of his death, and this line from one of his own poems—

" Life to the last enjoy'd, here Churchill lies."

The words which he is reported to have used on his deathbed, *should* have been inscribed on the stone—

" What a fool I have been ! "

Hogarth had expired on the 25th of October, ten days before his opponent. Lloyd was finishing his dinner, when the news of his friend's death arrived. He was seized with sudden sickness, and crying out, " I shall soon follow poor Charles," was carried to a bed, whence he was never to rise. Churchill's favourite sister, Patty, who had been engaged to Lloyd, soon afterwards sank under the double blow. The premature death of this most popular of the poets of the time, excited a great sensation. His furniture and books sold excessively high; a steel pen, for instance, for five pounds, and a pair of plated spurs for sixteen guineas. Wilkes talked much about his " dear Churchill," but, with the exception of burning a MS. fragmentary satire, which Churchill had begun against Colman and Thornton, *two of his intimate friends*, and erecting an urn to him near his cottage in the Isle of Wight, with a flaming Latin inscription, he did nothing for his memory. The poet's brother, John, an apothecary, survived him only one year; and his two sons, Charles and John, inherited the vices without the genius of their father. There was, as late as 1825, a grand-daughter of his, a Mary Church-ill, who had been a governess, surviving as a patient in St George's Hospital,—a characteristic close to such a wayward, unfortunate race.

For the errors of Churchill, as a man, there does not seem to exist any plea of palliation, except what may be found in the poverty of his early circumstances, and in the strength of his later passions. The worst is, that he never seems to have been seduced into sin through the bewildering and be-witching mists of imagination. It was naked sensuality that he appeared to worship, and he always sinned with his eyes open. Yet his moral sense, though blunted, was never obli-terated; and many traits of generosity and good feeling mingled with his excesses. Choosing satire as the field of his Muse, was partly the cause and partly the effect of an imperfect *morale*. We are far from averring that no satirist can be a good man, but certainly most satirists have either been very good or very bad men. To the former class have belonged Cowper, Crabbe, &c.; to the latter, such names as Swift, Dryden, Byron, and, we must add, Churchill. Robust man-hood, honesty, and hatred of pretence, we admit him to have possessed; but of genuine love to humanity he seems to have been as destitute as of fear of God, or regard for the ordinary moralities.

We have to deal with him, however, principally as a poet; and there can, we think, now be but one opinion as to his peculiar merits. He possessed, beyond all doubt, a strong un-derstanding, a lively imagination, a keen perception of charac-ter—especially in its defects and weaknesses—considerable wit without any humour, fierce passions and hatreds, and a boundless command of a loose, careless, but bold and energetic diction; add to this, a constant tone of self-assertion, and rugged independence. He was emphatically a John Bull,

b

sublimated. He rushed into the poetic arena more like a pugilist than a poet, laying about him on all sides, giving and taking strong blows, and approving himself, in the phrase of "the fancy," game to the backbone. His faults, besides those incident to most satirists,—such as undue severity, intrusion into private life, anger darkening into malignity, and spleen fermenting into venom,—were carelessness of style, inequality, and want of condensation. Compared to the satires of Pope, Churchill's are far less polished, and less pointed. Pope stabs with a silver bodkin—Churchill hews down his opponent with a broadsword. Pope whispers a word in his enemy's ear which withers the heart within him, and he sinks lifeless to the ground; Churchill pours out a torrent of blasting invective which at once kills and buries his foe. Dryden was his favourite model; and although he has written no such condensed masterpieces of satire as the characters of Shaftesbury and Buckingham, yet his works as a whole are not much inferior, and justify the idea that had his life been spared, he might have risen to the level of "Glorious John." His versification, too, is decidedly of the Drydenic type. It is a free, fierce, rushing, sometimes staggering, race across meadow, moor, and mountain, dreading nothing except repose and languor, the lines chasing, and sometimes tumbling over each other in their haste, like impatient hounds at a fox-hunt. But more than Dryden, we think, has Churchill displayed the genuine poetic faculty, as well as often a loftier tone of moral indignation. This latter feeling is the inspiration of "The Candidate," and of "The Times," which, although coarse in subject, and coarse in style, burns with a fire of righteous indignation, reminding you of Juvenal. The finest display of his imaginative power is in "Gotham," which is throughout a glorious rhapsody, resembling some of the best prose effusions of Christopher North, and abounding in such lines as these:—

> "The cedar, whose top mates the highest cloud,
> Whilst his old father Lebanon grows proud
> Of such a child, and *his vast body laid*
> *Out many a mile, enjoys the filial shade.*"

It is of "Gotham" that Cowper says that few writers have

equalled it for its " bold and daring strokes of fancy; its numbers so hazardously ventured upon, and so happily finished;
its matter so compressed, and yet so clear; its colouring so
sparingly laid on, and yet with such a beautiful effect."

One great objection to Churchill's poetry lies in the tem-
porary interest of the subjects to which most of it is devoted.
The same objection, however, applies to the letters of Junius,
and to the speeches and papers of Burke; and the same answer
to it will avail for all.   Junius, by the charm of his style, by
his classic severities, and purged, poignant venom, contrives
to interest us in the paltry political feuds of the past.   Burke's
does the same, by the general principles he extracts from, and
by the poetry with which he gilds, the rubbish.   And so does
Churchill, by the weighty sense, the vigorous versification, the
inextinguishable spirit, and the trenchant satire and invective
of his song.   The wretched intrigues of Newcastle and Bute,
the squabbles of the aldermen and councillors of the day, the
petty quarrels of petty patriots among themselves, and the poverty, spites, and frailties of forgotten players, are all shown
as in a magnifying-glass, and shine upon us transfigured in the
light of the poet's genius.

We have not room for lengthened criticism on all his separate productions.   " The Rosciad " is the most finished, pointed, and Pope-like of his satires; it has more memorable and
quotable lines than any of the rest.   " The Prophecy of Famine" is full of trash; but contains, too, many lines in which
political hatred, through its intense fervour, sparkles into
poetry: such as—

> " No birds except as birds of passage flew ;"

the account of the creatures which, when admitted into the
ark,

> "Their saviour shunn'd, and rankled in the dark ;"

and the famous line—

> " Where half-starved spiders prey on half-starved flies."

" The Ghost " is the least felicitous of all his poems, although its picture of Pomposo (Dr Johnson) is exceedingly clever. The "Dedication to Warburton" is a strain of terrible irony, but fails to damage the Atlantean Bishop. "The Journey" is not only interesting as his last production, but contains some affecting personal allusions, intermingled with its stinging scorn—like pale passion-flowers blended with nettles and nightshade. The most of the others have been already characterised.

Churchill has had two very formidable enemies to his fame and detractors from his genius—Samuel Johnson and Christopher North. The first pronounced him "a prolific blockhead," "a huge and fertile crab-tree;" the second has wielded the knout against his back with peculiar gusto and emphasis, in a paper on satire and satirists, published in *Blackwood* for 1828. Had Churchill been alive, he could have easily "retorted scorn"—set a "Christophero" over against the portrait of "Pomposo:" the result had been, as always in such cases, a drawn battle; and damage would have accrued, not to the special literateurs, but to the general literary character. Prejudice or private pique always lurks at the bottom of such reckless assaults, and all men in the long run feel so. In Johnson's case, the *causa belli* was unquestionably political difference; and in Christopher North's it was the love of Scotland which so warmly glowed in his bosom, and which created a glow of hatred no less warm against Scotland's ablest, fiercest, and most inveterate poetical foe.

Churchill's poetry only requires to be better known to be highly appreciated for its masculine and thoroughly English qualities. In taking our leave of him, we are again haunted by the signal resemblance he bears, both in mental characteristics and in history, to Byron. Both were powerful in satire, and still more so in purely poetic composition. Both were irregular in life, and unfortunate in marriage. Both were distinguished by fitful generosity, and careless tenderness. Both obtained at once, and during all their career maintained, a pre-eminence in popularity over all their contemporaries. Both were severely handled by reviewers, and underrated by rivals. Both assumed an attitude of defiance to the world, and stood ostentatiously at bay.   Both mingled largely in the politics of their day, and both took the liberal side.   Both felt and expressed keen remorse for their errors, and purposed and in part began reformation.   Both died at an untimely age by fever, and in a foreign land.   The dust of both, not admitted into Westminster Abbey, nevertheless reposes in their native soil, and attracts daily visitors, who lean, and weep, and wonder over it—partly in sympathy with their fate—partly in pity for their errors—and partly in admiration of their genius.

Note.—We have not alluded to various anecdotes told about Churchill's journey to Wales, about his setting up as a cider merchant, &c., because some of them appear extremely apocryphal.   The author of an article on him in the *Edinburgh Review* for January 1845 asserts that he was rejected from Oxford because he had already been married.   But, if so, why was he admitted to Cambridge?   Besides, the writer adduces no proof of his assertion.   The paper, otherwise, is worthy of its author and of the poet.

CONTENTS.

CHURCHILL'S POEMS.

THE ROSCIAD.[1]

> Unknowing and unknown, the hardy Muse
> Boldly defies all mean and partial views ;
> With honest freedom plays the critic's part,
> And praises, as she censures, from the heart.

Roscius[2] deceased, each high aspiring player
Push'd all his interest for the vacant chair.
The buskin'd heroes of the mimic stage
No longer whine in love, and rant in rage ;
The monarch quits his throne, and condescends
Humbly to court the favour of his friends ;
For pity's sake tells undeserved mishaps,
And, their applause to gain, recounts his claps.
Thus the victorious chiefs of ancient Rome,
To win the mob, a suppliant's form assume;   10
In pompous strain fight o'er th' extinguish'd war,
And show where honour bled in every scar.
    But though bare merit might in Rome appear
The strongest plea for favour, 'tis not here ;
We form our judgment in another way ;
And they will best succeed, who best can pay :

[1] 'The Rosciad :' for occasion, &c., see Life.—[2] 'Roscius :' Quintus Roscius, a native of Gaul, and the most celebrated comedian of antiquity.

A

Those who would gain the votes of British tribes,   17
Must add to force of merit, force of bribes.
  What can an actor give ? In every age
Cash hath been rudely banish'd from the stage ;
Monarchs themselves, to grief of every player,
Appear as often as their image there :
They can't, like candidate for other seat,
Pour seas of wine, and mountains raise of meat.
Wine ! they could bribe you with the world as soon,
And of ' Roast Beef,' they only know the tune :
But what they have they give ; could Clive[1] do
    more,
Though for each million he had brought home four ?
  Shuter[2] keeps open house at Southwark fair,
And hopes the friends of humour will be there ;   30
In Smithfield, Yates[3] prepares the rival treat
For those who laughter love, instead of meat ;
Foote,[4] at Old House,—for even Foote will be,
In self-conceit, an actor,—bribes with tea ;
Which Wilkinson[5] at second-hand receives,
And at the New, pours water on the leaves.
  The town divided, each runs several ways,
As passion, humour, interest, party sways.
Things of no moment, colour of the hair,
Shape of a leg, complexion brown or fair,   40
A dress well chosen, or a patch misplaced,
Conciliate favour, or create distaste.

---

[1] ' Clive :' Robert Lord Clive. See Macaulay's paper on him.—[2] ' Shuter :'
Edward Shuter, a comic actor, who, after various theatrical vicissitudes, died
a zealous methodist and disciple of George Whitefield, in 1776.—[3] ' Yates :'
Richard Yates, another low actor of the period.—[4] ' Foote :' Samuel Foote,
the once well-known farcical writer, (now chiefly remembered from Boswell's
Life of Johnson), opened the Old House in the Haymarket, and, in order to
overrule the opposition of the magistrates, announced his entertainments as
' Mr Foote's giving tea to his friends.'— [5] ' Wilkinson :' Wilkinson, the
shadow of Foote, was the proprietor of Sadler's Wells Theatre.

From galleries loud peals of laughter roll,   43
And thunder Shuter's praises ; he 's so droll.
Embox'd, the ladies must have something smart,
Palmer ! oh ! Palmer[1] tops the jaunty part.
Seated in pit, the dwarf with aching eyes,
Looks up, and vows that Barry's[2] out of size ;
Whilst to six feet the vigorous stripling grown,
Declares that Garrick is another Coan.[3]   50

When place of judgment is by whim supplied,
And our opinions have their rise in pride ;
When, in discoursing on each mimic elf,
We praise and censure with an eye to self ;
All must meet friends, and Ackman[4] bids as fair,
In such a court, as Garrick, for the chair.

At length agreed, all squabbles to decide,
By some one judge the cause was to be tried ;
But this their squabbles did afresh renew,
Who should be judge in such a trial :—who ?   60

For Johnson some ; but Johnson, it was fear'd,
Would be too grave ; and Sterne[5] too gay appear'd ;
Others for Franklin[6] voted ; but 'twas known,
He sicken'd at all triumphs but his own :
For Colman[7] many, but the peevish tongue
Of prudent Age found out that he was young :

[1] 'Palmer:' John Palmer, a favourite actor in genteel comedy, who married Miss Pritchard, daughter of the celebrated actress of that name.—
[2] 'Barry:' Spranger Barry, an actor of first-rate eminence and tall of size. Barry was a competitor of Garrick. Every one remembers the lines in a poem comparing the two—

> 'To Barry we give loud applause ;
> To Garrick only tears.'

[3] 'Coan:' John Coan, a dwarf, showed himself, like another Tom Thumb, for sixpence a-head.—[4] 'Ackman:' Ackman ranked as one of the lowest comic actors of his time. — [5] 'Sterne:' the celebrated Laurence Sterne.—[6] 'Franklin:' Dr Thomas Franklin, the translator of Sophocles, Phalaris, and Lucian, and the author of a volume of sermons ; all forgotten.—[7] 'Colman:' Colman, the elder, translator of Terence, and author of many clever comedies.

For Murphy[1] some few pilfering wits declared,   67
Whilst Folly clapp'd her hands, and Wisdom stared.
   To mischief train'd, e'en from his mother's womb,
Grown old in fraud, though yet in manhood's bloom,
Adopting arts by which gay villains rise,
And reach the heights which honest men despise ;
Mute at the bar, and in the senate loud,
Dull 'mongst the dullest, proudest of the proud ;
A pert, prim, prater of the northern race,[2]
Guilt in his heart, and famine in his face,
Stood forth,—and thrice he waved his lily hand,
And thrice he twirl'd his tye, thrice stroked his
      band :—
   At Friendship's call (thus oft, with traitorous
      aim,
Men void of faith usurp Faith's sacred name)   80
At Friendship's call I come, by Murphy sent,
Who thus by me develops his intent :
But lest, transfused, the spirit should be lost,
That spirit which, in storms of rhetoric toss'd,
Bounces about, and flies like bottled beer,
In his own words his own intentions hear.
   Thanks to my friends ; but to vile fortunes born,
No robes of fur these shoulders must adorn.
Vain your applause, no aid from thence I draw ;
Vain all my wit, for what is wit in law ?   90
Twice, (cursed remembrance !) twice I strove to gain
Admittance 'mongst the law-instructed train,
Who, in the Temple and Gray's Inn, prepare
For clients' wretched feet the legal snare ;

---

[1] 'Murphy :' Arthur Murphy, Esq., a native of Ireland.   See Boswell's
Life of Johnson.   Churchill hated Murphy on account of his politics.   He
was in the pay of the Court. — [2] 'Northern race :' Wedderburn, afterwards
Lord Loughborough, and Earl Rosslyn, a patron of Murphy, and a bitter
enemy of Wilkes.

Dead to those arts which polish and refine, 95
Deaf to all worth, because that worth was mine,
Twice did those blockheads startle at my name,
And foul rejection gave me up to shame.
To laws and lawyers then I bade adieu,
And plans of far more liberal note pursue. 100
Who will may be a judge—my kindling breast
Burns for that chair which Roscius once possess'd.
Here give your votes, your interest here exert,
And let success for once attend desert.

With sleek appearance, and with ambling pace,
And, type of vacant head, with vacant face,
The Proteus Hill[1] put in his modest plea,—
Let Favour speak for others, Worth for me.—
For who, like him, his various powers could call
Into so many shapes, and shine in all? 110
Who could so nobly grace the motley list,
Actor, Inspector, Doctor, Botanist?
Knows any one so well—sure no one knows—
At once to play, prescribe, compound, compose?
Who can—but Woodward[2] came,—Hill slipp'd away,
Melting, like ghosts, before the rising day.
With that low cunning, which in fools[3] supplies,
And amply too, the place of being wise,
Which Nature, kind, indulgent parent, gave
To qualify the blockhead for a knave; 120
With that smooth falsehood, whose appearance charms,
And Reason of each wholesome doubt disarms,

---

[1] 'Proteus Hill:' Sir John Hill, a celebrated character of that day, of incredible industry and versatility, a botanist, apothecary, translator, actor, dramatic author, natural historian, multitudinous compiler, libeller, and, *intus et in cute*, a quack and coxcomb. See Boswell's account of the interview between the King and Dr Johnson, for a somewhat modified estimate of Hill.
—[2] 'Woodward:' Woodward the comedian had a paper war with Hill.—
[3] 'Fools:' the person here meant was a Mr Fitzpatrick, a bitter enemy of Garrick's, and who originated riots in the theatre on the subject of half-price.

Which to the lowest depths of guile descends,   123
By vilest means pursues the vilest ends ;
Wears Friendship's mask for purposes of spite,
Fawns in the day, and butchers in the night ;
With that malignant envy which turns pale,
And sickens, even if a friend prevail,
Which merit and success pursues with hate,
And damns the worth it cannot imitate ;   130
With the cold caution of a coward's spleen,
Which fears not guilt, but always seeks a screen,
Which keeps this maxim ever in her view—
What 's basely done, should be done safely too ;
With that dull, rooted, callous impudence,
Which, dead to shame and every nicer sense,
Ne'er blush'd, unless, in spreading Vice's snares,
She blunder'd on some virtue unawares ;
With all these blessings, which we seldom find
Lavish'd by Nature on one happy mind,   140
A motley figure, of the Fribble tribe,
Which heart can scarce conceive, or pen describe,
Came simpering on—to ascertain whose sex
Twelve sage impannell'd matrons would perplex.
Nor male, nor female ; neither, and yet both ;
Of neuter gender, though of Irish growth ;
A six-foot suckling, mincing in Its gait ;
Affected, peevish, prim, and delicate ;
Fearful It seem'd, though of athletic make,
Lest brutal breezes should too roughly shake   150
Its tender form, and savage motion spread,
O'er Its pale cheeks, the horrid manly red.
    Much did It talk, in Its own pretty phrase,
Of genius and of taste, of players and of plays ;
Much too of writings, which Itself had wrote,
Of special merit, though of little note ;

For Fate, in a strange humour, had decreed 157
That what It wrote, none but Itself should read ;
Much, too, It chatter'd of dramatic laws,
Misjudging critics, and misplaced applause ;
Then, with a self-complacent, jutting air,
It smiled, It smirk'd, It wriggled to the chair ;
And, with an awkward briskness not Its own,
Looking around, and perking on the throne,
Triumphant seem'd ; when that strange savage dame,
Known but to few, or only known by name,
Plain Common-Sense appear'd, by Nature there
Appointed, with plain Truth, to guard the chair,
The pageant saw, and, blasted with her-frown,
To Its first state of nothing melted down. 170
    Nor shall the Muse, (for even there the pride
Of this vain nothing shall be mortified)
Nor shall the Muse (should Fate ordain her rhymes,
Fond, pleasing thought ! to live in after-times)
With such a trifler's name her pages blot ; *(a trace.)*
Known be the character, the thing forgot :
Let It, to disappoint each future aim,
Live without sex, and die without a name !
    Cold-blooded critics, by enervate sires
Scarce hammer'd out, when Nature's feeble fires 180
Glimmer'd their last ; whose sluggish blood, half froze,
Creeps labouring through the veins ; whose heart ne'er glows
With fancy-kindled heat ;—a servile race,
Who, in mere want of fault, all merit place ;
Who blind obedience pay to ancient schools,
Bigots to Greece, and slaves to musty rules ;
With solemn consequence declared that none
Could judge that cause but Sophocles alone.
Dupes to their fancied excellence, the crowd,
Obsequious to the sacred dictate, bow'd. 190

When, from amidst the throng, a youth stood forth,[1]
Unknown his person, not unknown his worth ;   192
His look bespoke applause ; alone he stood,
Alone he stemm'd the mighty critic flood.
He talk'd of ancients, as the man became
Who prized our own, but envied not their fame ;
With noble reverence spoke of Greece and Rome,
And scorn'd to tear the laurel from the tomb.
  But, more than just to other countries grown,
Must we turn base apostates to our own ?   200
Where do these words of Greece and Rome excel,
That England may not please the ear as well ?
What mighty magic's in the place or air,
That all perfection needs must centre there?
In states, let strangers blindly be preferr'd ;
In state of letters, merit should be heard.
Genius is of no country ; her pure ray
Spreads all abroad, as general as the day ;
Foe to restraint, from place to place she flies,
And may hereafter e'en in Holland rise.   210
May not, (to give a pleasing fancy scope,
And cheer a patriot heart with patriot hope)
May not some great extensive genius raise
The name of Britain 'bove Athenian praise;
And, whilst brave thirst of fame his bosom warms,
Make England great in letters as in arms ?
There may—there hath,—and Shakspeare's Muse aspires
Beyond the reach of Greece ; with native fires
Mounting aloft, he wings his daring flight,
Whilst Sophocles below stands trembling at his height.
  Why should we then abroad for judges roam,   221
When abler judges we may find at home ?

---

[1] 'A youth:' Robert Lloyd, the friend and imitator of Churchill—an ingenious but improvident person, who died of grief at his friend's death, in 1764.

Happy in tragic and in comic powers,   223
Have we not Shakspeare ?—Is not Jonson ours ?
For them, your natural judges, Britons, vote ;
They 'll judge like Britons, who like Britons wrote.
 He said, and conquer'd—Sense resumed her sway,
And disappointed pedants stalk'd away.
Shakspeare and Jonson, with deserved applause,
Joint-judges were ordain'd to try the cause. 230
Meantime the stranger every voice employ'd,
To ask or tell his name. Who is it ? Lloyd.
 Thus, when the aged friends of Job stood mute,
And, tamely prudent, gave up the dispute,
Elihu, with the decent warmth of youth,
Boldly stood forth the advocate of Truth ;
Confuted Falsehood, and disabled Pride,
Whilst baffled Age stood snarling at his side.
 The day of trial 's fix'd, nor any fear
Lest day of trial should be put off here.   240
Causes but seldom for delay can call
In courts where forms are few, fees none at all.
 The morning came, nor find I that the Sun,
As he on other great events hath done,
Put on a brighter robe than what he wore
To go his journey in, the day before.
 Full in the centre of a spacious plain,
On plan entirely new, where nothing vain,
Nothing magnificent appear'd, but Art
With decent modesty perform'd her part, 250
Rose a tribunal : from no other court
It borrow'd ornament, or sought support :
No juries here were pack'd to kill or clear,
No bribes were taken, nor oaths broken here ;
No gownsmen, partial to a client's cause,
To their own purpose turn'd the pliant laws ;

Each judge was true and steady to his trust,   257
As Mansfield wise, and as old Foster [1] just.
In the first seat, in robe of various dyes,
A noble wildness flashing from his eyes,
Sat Shakspeare : in one hand a wand he bore,
For mighty wonders famed in days of yore ;
The other held a globe, which to his will
Obedient turn'd, and own'd the master's skill :
Things of the noblest kind his genius drew,
And look'd through Nature at a single view :
A loose he gave to his unbounded soul,
And taught new lands to rise, new seas to roll ;
Call'd into being scenes unknown before,
And passing Nature's bounds, was something more.   270
    Next Jonson sat, in ancient learning train'd,
His rigid judgment Fancy's flights restrain'd ;
Correctly pruned each wild luxuriant thought,
Mark'd out her course, nor spared a glorious fault.
The book of man he read with nicest art,
And ransack'd all the secrets of the heart ;
Exerted penetration's utmost force,
And traced each passion to its proper source ;
Then, strongly mark'd, in liveliest colours drew,
And brought each foible forth to public view :   280
The coxcomb felt a lash in every word,
And fools, hung out, their brother fools deterr'd.
His comic humour kept the world in awe,
And Laughter frighten'd Folly more than Law.
    But, hark ! the trumpet sounds, the crowd gives way,
And the procession comes in just array.
    Now should I, in some sweet poetic line,
Offer up incense at Apollo's shrine,

---

[1] 'Foster :' Sir Michael Foster, one of the puisne judges of the Court of King's Bench.

Invoke the Muse to quit her calm abode, 289
And waken Memory with a sleeping Ode :[1]
For how shall mortal man, in mortal verse,
Their titles, merits, or their names rehearse ?
But give, kind Dulness ! memory and rhyme,
We'll put off Genius till another time.

   First, Order came,—with solemn step, and slow,
In measured time his feet were taught to go.
Behind, from time to time, he cast his eye,
Lest this should quit his place, that step awry.
Appearances to save his only care ;
So things seem right, no matter what they are. 300
In him his parents saw themselves renew'd,
Begotten by Sir Critic on Saint Prude.

   Then came drum, trumpet, hautboy, fiddle, flute ;
Next snuffer, sweeper, shifter, soldier, mute :
Legions of angels all in white advance ;
Furies, all fire, come forward in a dance ;
Pantomime figures then are brought to view,
Fools, hand in hand with fools, go two by two.
Next came the treasurer of either house ;
One with full purse, t'other with not a sous. 310
Behind, a group of figures awe create,
Set off with all the impertinence of state ;
By lace and feather consecrate to fame,
Expletive kings, and queens without a name.

   Here Havard,[2] all serene, in the same strains,
Loves, hates, and rages, triumphs and complains ;
His easy vacant face proclaim'd a heart
Which could not feel emotions, nor impart.
With him came mighty Davies :[3]—on my life,
That Davies hath a very pretty wife !— 320

[1] 'Ode:' alluding to Mason's Ode to Memory.—[2] 'Havard:' William
Havard, an amiable man, but mediocre actor, of the period.—[3] 'Davies:'
Thomas Davies, a bookseller, actor, and author. See Boswell.

Statesman all over, in plots famous grown,   321
He mouths a sentence, as curs mouth a bone.
   Next Holland[1] came : with truly tragic stalk,
He creeps, he flies,—a hero should not walk.
As if with Heaven he warr'd, his eager eyes
Planted their batteries against the skies ;
Attitude, action, air, pause, start, sigh, groan,
He borrow'd, and made use of as his own.
By fortune thrown on any other stage,
He might, perhaps, have pleased an easy age ;   330
But now appears a copy, and no more,
Of something better we have seen before.
The actor who would build a solid fame,
Must Imitation's servile arts disclaim ;
Act from himself, on his own bottom stand ;
I hate e'en Garrick thus at second-hand.
   Behind came King.[2]—Bred up in modest lore,
Bashful and young, he sought Hibernia's shore ;
Hibernia, famed, 'bove every other grace,
For matchless intrepidity of face.   340
From her his features caught the generous flame,
And bid defiance to all sense of shame.
Tutor'd by her all rivals to surpass,
'Mongst Drury's sons he comes, and shines in Brass.
   Lo, Yates![3]   Without the least finesse of art
He gets applause—I wish he 'd get his part.
When hot Impatience is in full career,
How vilely ' Hark ye ! hark ye !' grates the
     ear ;
When active fancy from the brain is sent,
And stands on tip-toe for some wish'd event,   350

---

[1] 'Holland :' Holland, a pupil and imitator of Mr Garrick.—[2] 'King :' Thomas King, a voluble and pert but clever actor.—[3] 'Yates :' Yates had a habit of repeating his words twice or thrice over, such as ' Hark you, hark you.'

I hate those careless blunders, which recall   851
Suspended sense, and prove it fiction all.
  In characters of low and vulgar mould,
Where Nature's coarsest features we behold ;
Where, destitute of every decent grace,
Unmanner'd jests are blurted in your face,
There Yates with justice strict attention draws,
Acts truly from himself, and gains applause.
But when, to please himself or charm his wife,
He aims at something in politer life,   860
When, blindly thwarting Nature's stubborn plan,
He treads the stage by way of gentleman,
The clown, who no one touch of breeding knows,
Looks like Tom Errand[1] dress'd in Clincher's
    clothes.
Fond of his dress, fond of his person grown,
Laugh'd at by all, and to himself unknown,
From side to side he struts, he smiles, he prates,
And seems to wonder what's become of Yates.
  Woodward,[2] endow'd with various tricks of face,
Great master in the science of grimace,   870
From Ireland ventures, favourite of the town,
Lured by the pleasing prospect of renown ;
A speaking harlequin, made up of whim,
He twists, he twines, he tortures every limb ;
Plays to the eye with a mere monkey's art,
And leaves to sense the conquest of the heart.
We laugh indeed, but, on reflection's birth,
We wonder at ourselves, and curse our mirth.
His walk of parts he fatally misplaced,
And inclination fondly took for taste ;   880

[1] 'Tom Errand :' Tom Errand and Clincher, two well-known dramatic characters—a clown and a coxcomb.—[2] 'Woodward :' Henry Woodward, a comic actor of much power of face.

Hence hath the town so often seen display'd   881
Beau in burlesque, high life in masquerade.
  But when bold wits,—not such as patch up plays,
Cold and correct, in these insipid days,—
Some comic character, strong featured, urge
To probability's extremest verge ;
Where modest Judgment her decree suspends,
And, for a time, nor censures, nor commends ;
Where critics can't determine on the spot
Whether it is in nature found or not,   390
There Woodward safely shall his powers exert,
Nor fail of favour where he shows desert ;
Hence he in Bobadil such praises bore,
Such worthy praises, Kitely [1] scarce had more.
  By turns transform'd into all kind of shapes,
Constant to none, Foote laughs, cries, struts, and scrapes :
Now in the centre, now in van or rear,
The Proteus shifts, bawd, parson, auctioneer.
His strokes of humour, and his bursts of sport,
Are all contain'd in this one word—distort.   400
  Doth a man stutter, look a-squint, or halt ?
Mimics draw humour out of Nature's fault,
With personal defects their mirth adorn,
And hang misfortunes out to public scorn.
E'en I, whom Nature cast in hideous mould,
Whom, having made, she trembled to behold,
Beneath the load of mimicry may groan,
And find that Nature's errors are my own.
  Shadows behind of Foote and Woodward came ;
Wilkinson this, Obrien [2] was that name.   410
Strange to relate, but wonderfully true,
That even shadows have their shadows too !

---

[1] ' Kitely :' Kitely, in Johnson's ' Every Man in his Humour,' was a favourite
character of Garrick's.—[2] ' Obrien :' a small actor ; originally a fencing-master.

With not a single comic power endued,   413
The first a mere, mere mimic's mimic stood ;
The last, by Nature form'd to please, who shows,
In Johnson's Stephen, which way genius grows,
Self quite put off, affects with too much art
To put on Woodward in each mangled part ;
Adopts his shrug, his wink, his stare ; nay, more,
His voice, and croaks; for Woodward croak'd
        before.   420
When a dull copier simple grace neglects,
And rests his imitation in defects,
We readily forgive ; but such vile arts
Are double guilt in men of real parts.

By Nature form'd in her perversest mood,
With no one requisite of art endued,
Next Jackson came.[1]—Observe that settled glare,
Which better speaks a puppet than a player ;
List to that voice—did ever Discord hear
Sounds so well fitted to her untuned ear ?   430
When to enforce some very tender part,
The right hand slips by instinct on the heart,
His soul, of every other thought bereft,
Is anxious only where to place the left ;
He sobs and pants to soothe his weeping spouse ;
To soothe his weeping mother, turns and bows :
Awkward, embarrass'd, stiff, without the skill
Of moving gracefully, or standing still,
One leg, as if suspicious of his brother,
Desirous seems to run away from t' other.   440

Some errors, handed down from age to age,
Plead custom's force, and still possess the stage.
That's vile : should we a parent's faults adore,
And err, because our fathers err'd before ?

[1] 'Jackson :' afterwards manager of the Royal Theatre, Edinburgh.

If, inattentive to the author's mind,   445
Some actors made the jest they could not find;
If by low tricks they marr'd fair Nature's mien,
And blurr'd the graces of the simple scene,
Shall we, if reason rightly is employ'd,
Not see their faults, or seeing, not avoid?   450
When Falstaff stands detected in a lie,
Why, without meaning, rolls Love's[1] glassy eye?
Why? There's no cause—at least no cause we know—
It was the fashion twenty years ago.
Fashion!—a word which knaves and fools may use,
Their knavery and folly to excuse.
To copy beauties, forfeits all pretence
To fame—to copy faults, is want of sense.
Yet (though in some particulars he fails,
Some few particulars, where mode prevails)   460
If in these hallow'd times, when, sober, sad,
All gentlemen are melancholy mad;
When 'tis not deem'd so great a crime by half
To violate a vestal as to laugh,
Rude mirth may hope, presumptuous, to engage
An act of toleration for the stage;
And courtiers will, like reasonable creatures,
Suspend vain fashion, and unscrew their features;
Old Falstaff, play'd by Love, shall please once more,
And humour set the audience in a roar.   470
    Actors I've seen, and of no vulgar name,
Who, being from one part possess'd of fame,
Whether they are to laugh, cry, whine, or bawl,
Still introduce that favourite part in all.
Here, Love, be cautious—ne'er be thou betray'd
To call in that wag Falstaff's dangerous aid;

---

[1] 'Love:' James Love, an actor and dramatic writer, who could play nothing well but Falstaff.

Like Goths of old, howe'er he seems a friend,   477
He 'll seize that throne you wish him to defend.
In a peculiar mould by Humour cast,
For Falstaff framed—himself the first and last—
He stands aloof from all—maintains his state,
And scorns, like Scotsmen, to assimilate.
Vain all disguise—too plain we see the trick,
Though the knight wears the weeds of Dominic ;[1]
And Boniface[2] disgraced, betrays the smack,
In *anno Domini*, of Falstaff's sack.

  Arms cross'd, brows bent, eyes fix'd, feet marching slow,
A band of malcontents with spleen o'erflow;
Wrapt in Conceit's impenetrable fog,
Which Pride, like Phœbus, draws from every bog,   490
They curse the managers, and curse the town
Whose partial favour keeps such merit down.

  But if some man, more hardy than the rest,
Should dare attack these gnatlings in their nest,
At once they rise with impotence of rage,
Whet their small stings, and buzz about the stage :
'Tis breach of privilege ! Shall any dare
To arm satiric truth against a player ?
Prescriptive rights we plead, time out of mind ;
Actors, unlash'd themselves, may lash mankind.   500

  What ! shall Opinion then, of nature free,
And liberal as the vagrant air, agree
To rust in chains like these, imposed by things,
Which, less than nothing, ape the pride of kings ?
No—though half-poets with half-players join
To curse the freedom of each honest line ;
Though rage and malice dim their faded cheek,
What the Muse freely thinks, she 'll freely speak ;

---

[1] 'Dominic :' Dryden's 'Spanish Friar.'—[2] 'Boniface :' The jovial landlord
in Farquhar's 'Beaux Stratagem.'

B

With just disdain of every paltry sneer,   509
Stranger alike to flattery and fear,
In purpose fix'd, and to herself a rule,
Public contempt shall wait the public fool.
    Austin [1] would always glisten in French silks ;
Ackman would Norris be, and Packer, Wilkes :
For who, like Ackman, can with humour please ;
Who can, like Packer, charm with sprightly ease ?
Higher than all the rest, see Bransby strut :
A mighty Gulliver in Lilliput !
Ludicrous Nature ! which at once could show
A man so very high, so very low !   520
    If I forget thee, Blakes, or if I say
Aught hurtful, may I never see thee play.
Let critics, with a supercilious air,
Decry thy various merit, and declare
Frenchman is still at top ; but scorn that rage
Which, in attacking thee, attacks the age.
French follies, universally embraced, ·
At once provoke our mirth, and form our taste.
    Long, from a nation ever hardly used,
At random censured, wantonly abused,   530
Have Britons drawn their sport ; with partial view
Form'd general notions from the rascal few ;
Condemn'd a people, as for vices known,
Which from their country banish'd, seek our own.
At length, howe'er, the slavish chain is broke,
And Sense, awaken'd, scorns her ancient yoke :
Taught by thee, Moody,[2] we now learn to raise
Mirth from their foibles ; from their virtues, praise.
    Next came the legion which our summer Bayes,[3]
From alleys, here and there, contrived to raise,   540

---

[1] 'Austin,' &c. : all small and forgotten actors.—[2] 'Moody :' Moody excelled in Irish characters.—[3] 'Bayes :' alluding to the summer theatre in the

Flush'd with vast hopes, and certain to succeed,   541
With wits who cannot write, and scarce can read.
Veterans no more support the rotten cause,
No more from Elliot's [1] worth they reap applause ;
Each on himself determines to rely ;
Be Yates disbanded, and let Elliot fly.
Never did players so well an author fit,
To Nature dead, and foes declared to wit.
So loud each tongue, so empty was each head,
So much they talk'd, so very little said,   550
So wondrous dull, and yet so wondrous vain,
At once so willing, and unfit to reign,
That Reason swore, nor would the oath recall,
Their mighty master's soul inform'd them all.

 As one with various disappointments sad,
Whom dulness only kept from being mad,
Apart from all the rest great Murphy came—
Common to fools and wits, the rage of fame.
What though the sons of Nonsense hail him Sire,
Auditor, Author, Manager, and Squire,   560
His restless soul's ambition stops not there ;
To make his triumphs perfect, dub him Player.

 In person tall, a figure form'd to please,
If symmetry could charm deprived of ease ;
When motionless he stands, we all approve ;
What pity 'tis the thing was made to move.

 His voice, in one dull, deep, unvaried sound,
Seems to break forth from caverns under ground ;
From hollow chest the low sepulchral note
Unwilling heaves, and struggles in his throat.   570

 Could authors butcher'd give an actor grace,
All must to him resign the foremost place.

Haymarket, where Murphy's plays were got up and acted under the joint man-
agement of himself and Mr Foote.—[1] ' Elliot :' a female actress of great merit.

When he attempts, in some one favourite part,   573
To ape the feelings of a manly heart,
His honest features the disguise defy,
And his face loudly gives his tongue the lie.
    Still in extremes, he knows no happy mean,
Or raving mad, or stupidly serene.
In cold-wrought scenes, the lifeless actor flags ;
In passion, tears the passion into rags.   580
Can none remember ?   Yes—I know all must—
When in the Moor he ground his teeth to dust,
When o'er the stage he Folly's standard bore,
Whilst Common-Sense stood trembling at the door.
    How few are found with real talents blest !
Fewer with Nature's gifts contented rest.
Man from his sphere eccentric starts astray :
All hunt for fame, but most mistake the way.
Bred at St Omer's to the shuffling trade,
The hopeful youth a Jesuit might have made ;   590
With various readings stored his empty skull,
Learn'd without sense, and venerably dull ;
Or, at some banker's desk, like many more,
Content to tell that two and two make four ;
His name had stood in City annals fair,
And prudent Dulness mark'd him for a mayor.
    What, then, could tempt thee, in a critic age,
Such blooming hopes to forfeit on a stage ?
Could it be worth thy wondrous waste of pains
To publish to the world thy lack of brains ?   600
Or might not Reason e'en to thee have shown,
Thy greatest praise had been to live unknown ?
Yet let not vanity like thine despair :
Fortune makes Folly her peculiar care.
    A vacant throne, high-placed in Smithfield, view,
To sacred Dulness and her first-born due,

Thither with haste in happy hour repair,   607
Thy birthright claim, nor fear a rival there.
Shuter himself shall own thy juster claim,
And venal Ledgers[1] puff their Murphy's name ;
Whilst Vaughan,[2] or Dapper, call him which you
    will,
Shall blow the trumpet, and give out the bill.
    There rule, secure from critics and from sense,
Nor once shall Genius rise to give offence ;
Eternal peace shall bless the happy shore,
And little factions[3] break thy rest no more.
    From Covent Garden crowds promiscuous go,
Whom the Muse knows not, nor desires to know,
Veterans they seem'd, but knew of arms no more
Than if, till that time, arms they never bore :   620
Like Westminster militia[4] train'd to fight,
They scarcely knew the left hand from the right.
Ashamed among such troops to show the head,
Their chiefs were scatter'd, and their heroes fled.
    Sparks[5] at his glass sat comfortably down
To separate frown from smile, and smile from
    frown.
Smith,[6] the genteel, the airy, and the smart,
Smith was just gone to school to say his part.
Ross[7] (a misfortune which we often meet)
Was fast asleep at dear Statira's[8] feet ;
Statira, with her hero to agree,
Stood on her feet as fast asleep as he.

---

[1] 'Ledgers:' the Public Ledger, a newspaper. — [2] 'Vaughan :' Thomas Vaughan, a friend of Murphy.—[3] 'Little factions:' Murphy had called Churchill and his friends ' The Little Faction.'—[4] ' Militia :' the Westminster militia and the city of London trained bands and lumber troopers, afforded much amusement.—[5] 'Sparks :' Luke Sparks, an actor of the time, rather hard in his manner.—[6] ' Smith :' called ' Gentleman Smith,' an actor in genteel comedy, corpulent in person.—[7] ' Ross :' a Scotchman, dissipated in his habits — [8] ' Statira :' Ross's Statira was Mrs Palmer, the daughter of Mrs Pritchard.

Macklin,[1] who largely deals in half-form'd sounds,   633
Who wantonly transgresses Nature's bounds,
Whose acting 's hard, affected, and constrain'd,
Whose features, as each other they disdain'd,
At variance set, inflexible and coarse,
Ne'er know the workings of united force,
Ne'er kindly soften to each other's aid,
Nor show the mingled powers of light and shade ;   640
No longer for a thankless stage concern'd,
To worthier thoughts his mighty genius turn'd,
Harangued, gave lectures, made each simple elf
Almost as good a speaker as himself ;
Whilst the whole town, mad with mistaken zeal,
An awkward rage for elocution feel ;
Dull cits and grave divines his praise proclaim,
And join with Sheridan's[2] their Macklin's name.
Shuter, who never cared a single pin
Whether he left out nonsense, or put in,   650
Who aim'd at wit, though, levell'd in the dark,
The random arrow seldom hit the mark,
At Islington,[3] all by the placid stream
Where city swains in lap of Dulness dream,
Where quiet as her strains their strains do flow,
That all the patron by the bards may know,
Secret as night, with Rolt's[4] experienced aid,
The plan of future operations laid,
Projected schemes the summer months to cheer,
And spin out happy folly through the year.   660
 But think not, though these dastard chiefs are fled,
That Covent Garden troops shall want a head :

---

[1] 'Macklin:' Charles Macklin, *alias* M'Laughlin, good in such characters as Shylock, &c. ; no tragedian ; a lecturer on elocution ; coarse in features. —[2] 'Sheridan:' father of Richard Brinsley. See Boswell and Moore.— [3] 'Islington:' the new river.—[4] 'Rolt:' a drudge to the booksellers, who plagiarised Akenside's 'Pleasures of Imagination,' and was a coadjutor with Christopher Smart in the 'Universal Visitor.' See Boswell.

Harlequin comes their chief!   See from afar   663
The hero seated in fantastic car !
Wedded to Novelty, his only arms
Are wooden swords, wands, talismans, and charms ;
On one side Folly sits, by some call'd Fun,
And on the other his arch-patron, Lun ;[1]
Behind, for liberty athirst in vain,
Sense, helpless captive, drags the galling chain :   670
Six rude misshapen beasts the chariot draw,
Whom Reason loathes, and Nature never saw,
Monsters with tails of ice, and heads of fire ;
' Gorgons, and Hydras, and Chimeras dire.'
Each was bestrode by full as monstrous wight,
Giant, dwarf, genius, elf, hermaphrodite.
The Town, as usual, met him in full cry ;
The Town, as usual, knew no reason why :
But Fashion so directs, and Moderns raise
On Fashion's mouldering base their transient praise. 680
    Next, to the field a band of females draw
Their force, for Britain owns no Salique law :
Just to their worth, we female rights admit,
Nor bar their claim to empire or to wit.
    First giggling, plotting chambermaids arrive,
Hoydens and romps, led on by General Clive.[2]
In spite of outward blemishes, she shone,
For humour famed, and humour all her own :
Easy, as if at home, the stage she trod,
Nor sought the critic's praise, nor fear'd his rod :   690
Original in spirit and in ease,
She pleased by hiding all attempts to please :

[1] ' Lun :' Mr John Rich, the manager of Covent Garden and Lincoln's Inn
Fields Theatre, called Lun for his performance of Harlequin ; famous for panto-
mimes.—[2] ' Clive :' Catherine Clive, a celebrated comic actress, of very diver-
sified powers ; ' a better romp ' than Jonson ' ever saw in nature.'

No comic actress ever yet could raise,   693
On Humour's base, more merit or more praise.
 With all the native vigour of sixteen,
Among the merry troop conspicuous seen,
See lively Pope[1] advance, in jig, and trip
Corinna, Cherry, Honeycomb, and Snip :
Not without art, but yet to nature true,
She charms the town with humour just, yet new : 700
Cheer'd by her promise, we the less deplore
The fatal time when Clive shall be no more.
 Lo! Vincent[2] comes! With simple grace array'd,
She laughs at paltry arts, and scorns parade :
Nature through her is by reflection shown,
Whilst Gay once more knows Polly for his own.
 Talk not to me of diffidence and fear—
I see it all, but must forgive it here ;
Defects like these, which modest terrors cause,
From Impudence itself extort applause. 710
Candour and Reason still take Virtue's part ;
We love e'en foibles in so good a heart.
 Let Tommy Arne,[3]—with usual pomp of style,
Whose chief, whose only merit 's to compile ;
Who, meanly pilfering here and there a bit,
Deals music out as Murphy deals out wit,—
Publish proposals, laws for taste prescribe,
And chaunt the praise of an Italian tribe ;
Let him reverse kind Nature's first decrees,
And teach e'en Brent[4] a method not to please ; 720
But never shall a truly British age
Bear a vile race of eunuchs on the stage ;

---

[1] 'Pope:' a pleasing protégé of Mrs Clive.—[2] 'Vincent:' Mrs Vincent, a tolerable actress and a fine singer. —[3] 'Arne:' a fine musician, but no writer.—[4] 'Brent:' a female scholar of Arne's, very popular as Polly in the 'Beggars Opera.'

The boasted work's call'd national in vain,   723
If one Italian voice pollutes the strain.
Where tyrants rule, and slaves with joy obey,
Let slavish minstrels pour th' enervate lay ;
To Britons far more noble pleasures spring,
In native notes whilst Beard and Vincent[1] sing.
   Might figure give a title unto fame,
What rival should with Yates[2] dispute her claim ?   730
But justice may not partial trophies raise,
Nor sink the actress' in the woman's praise.
Still hand in hand her words and actions go,
And the heart feels more than the features show ;
For, through the regions of that beauteous face
We no variety of passions trace ;
Dead to the soft emotions of the heart,
No kindred softness can those eyes impart :
The brow, still fix'd in sorrow's sullen frame,
Void of distinction, marks all parts the same.   740
   What's a fine person, or a beauteous face,
Unless deportment gives them decent grace ?
Bless'd with all other requisites to please,
Some want the striking elegance of ease ;
The curious eye their awkward movement tires ;
They seem like puppets led about by wires.
Others, like statues, in one posture still,
Give great ideas of the workman's skill ;
Wond'ring, his art we praise the more we view,
And only grieve he gave not motion too.   750
Weak of themselves are what we beauties call,
It is the manner which gives strength to all ;
This teaches every beauty to unite,
And brings them forward in the noblest light ;

---

1 ' Beard and Vincent :' famous singers. — 2 ' Yates :' Anna Maria Yates,
the wife of Richard Yates, mentioned in a preceding note.

Happy in this, behold, amidst the throng,   755
With transient gleam of grace, Hart[1] sweeps along.
    If all the wonders of external grace,
A person finely turn'd, a mould of face,
Where—union rare—expression's lively force
With beauty's softest magic holds discourse,   760
Attract the eye; if feelings, void of art,
Rouse the quick passions, and inflame the heart;
If music, sweetly breathing from the tongue,
Captives the ear, Bride[2] must not pass unsung.
    When fear, which rank ill-nature terms conceit,
By time and custom conquer'd, shall retreat;
When judgment, tutor'd by experience sage,
Shall shoot abroad, and gather strength from age;
When Heaven, in mercy, shall the stage release
From the dull slumbers of a still-life piece;   770
When some stale flower,[3] disgraceful to the walk,
Which long hath hung, though wither'd, on the stalk,
Shall kindly drop, then Bride shall make her way,
And merit find a passage to the day;
Brought into action, she at once shall raise
Her own renown, and justify our praise.
    Form'd for the tragic scene, to grace the stage
With rival excellence of love and rage;
Mistress of each soft art, with matchless skill
To turn and wind the passions as she will;   780
To melt the heart with sympathetic woe,
Awake the sigh, and teach the tear to flow;
To put on frenzy's wild, distracted glare,
And freeze the soul with horror and despair;

---

[1] 'Hart:' Mrs Hart, a demirep, married to one Reddish, who, after her death, wedded Mrs Canning, mother of the great statesman. — [2] 'Bride:' another beautiful, but disreputable actress. — [3] 'Stale flower,' &c.: an unmanly allusion to Mrs Palmer, the daughter of Mrs Pritchard, who was greatly inferior to her mother.

With just desert enroll'd in endless fame,   785
Conscious of worth superior, Cibber[1] came.
When poor Alicia's madd'ning brains are rack'd,
And strongly imaged griefs her mind distract,
Struck with her grief, I catch the madness too,
My brain turns round, the headless trunk I view !   790
The roof cracks, shakes, and falls—new horrors rise,
And Reason buried in the ruin lies !
Nobly disdainful of each slavish art,
She makes her first attack upon the heart ;
Pleased with the summons, it receives her laws,
And all is silence, sympathy, applause.
But when, by fond ambition drawn aside,
Giddy with praise, and puff'd with female pride,
She quits the tragic scene, and, in pretence
To comic merit, breaks down nature's fence,   800
I scarcely can believe my ears or eyes,
Or find out Cibber through the dark disguise.
Pritchard,[2] by Nature for the stage design'd,
In person graceful, and in sense refined ;
Her art as much as Nature's friend became,
Her voice as free from blemish as her fame,
Who knows so well in majesty to please,
Attemper'd with the graceful charms of ease ?
When, Congreve's favoured pantomime[3] to grace,
She comes a captive queen, of Moorish race ;   810
When love, hate, jealousy, despair, and rage
With wildest tumults in her breast engage,

---

[1] 'Cibber:' sister to Arne, and wife to the once notorious Theophilus
Cibber, the son of the hero of the 'Dunciad.' She was no better in character
than many actresses of that day ; but sang so plaintively, that a bishop who
heard her once cried out, ' Woman, thy sins be forgiven thee !'—[2] ' Pritchard : '
according to Johnson, ' in private a vulgar idiot, but who, on the stage, seemed
to become inspired with gentility and understanding.'—[3] ' Pantomime :' the
' Mourning Bride.'

Still equal to herself is Zara seen ;   813
Her passions are the passions of a queen.
    When she to murder whets the timorous Thane,[1]
I feel ambition rush through every vein ;
Persuasion hangs upon her daring tongue,
My heart grows flint, and every nerve's new strung.
    In comedy—Nay, there, cries Critic, hold ;
Pritchard's for comedy too fat and old :   820
Who can, with patience, bear the gray coquette,
Or force a laugh with over-grown Julett ?[2]
Her speech, look, action, humour, all are just,
But then, her age and figure give disgust.
    Are foibles, then, and graces of the mind,
In real life, to size or age confined ?
Do spirits flow, and is good-breeding placed
In any set circumference of waist ?
As we grow old, doth affectation cease,
Or gives not age new vigour to caprice ?   830
If in originals these things appear,
Why should we bar them in the copy here ?
The nice punctilio-mongers of this age,
The grand minute reformers of the stage,
Slaves to propriety of every kind,
Some standard measure for each part should find,
Which, when the best of actors shall exceed,
Let it devolve to one of smaller breed.
All actors, too, upon the back should bear
Certificate of birth ; time, when ; place, where ;   840
For how can critics rightly fix their worth,
Unless they know the minute of their birth ?
An audience, too, deceived, may find, too late,
That they have clapp'd an actor out of date.

---

[1] 'Thane:' Macbeth.—[2] 'Juletta:' a witty maid-servant in the play of
'The Pilgrim.'

Figure, I own, at first may give offence,   845
And harshly strike the eye's too curious sense ;
But when perfections of the mind break forth,
Humour's chaste sallies, judgment's solid worth ;
When the pure genuine flame by Nature taught,
Springs into sense and every action 's thought ;   850
Before such merit all objections fly—
Pritchard's genteel, and Garrick's six feet high.
    Oft have I, Pritchard, seen thy wondrous skill,
Confess'd thee great, but find thee greater still ;
That worth, which shone in scatter'd rays
        before,
Collected now, breaks forth with double power.
The 'Jealous Wife!'[1] on that thy trophies raise,
Inferior only to the author's praise.
    From Dublin, famed in legends of romance
For mighty magic of enchanted lance,   860
With which her heroes arm'd, victorious prove,
And, like a flood, rush o'er the land of Love,
Mossop and Barry came—names ne'er design'd
By Fate in the same sentence to be join'd.
Raised by the breath of popular acclaim,
They mounted to the pinnacle of fame ;
There the weak brain, made giddy with the
        height,
Spurr'd on the rival chiefs to mortal fight.
Thus sportive boys, around some basin's brim,
Behold the pipe-drawn bladders circling swim ;   870
But if, from lungs more potent, there arise
Two bubbles of a more than common size,
Eager for honour, they for fight prepare,
Bubble meets bubble, and both sink to air.

[1] The 'Jealous Wife:' the 'Jealous Wife,' by Colman, was taken from the
story of Lady Bellaston, in 'Tom Jones.'

Mossop,[1] attach'd to military plan,   875
Still kept his eye fix'd on his right-hand [2] man ;
Whilst the mouth measures words with seeming
      skill,
The right hand labours, and the left lies still ;
For he, resolved on Scripture grounds to go,
What the right doth, the left-hand shall not know.   880
With studied impropriety of speech,
He soars beyond the hackney critic's reach ;
To epithets allots emphatic state,
Whilst principals, ungraced, like lackeys wait ;
In ways first trodden by himself excels,
And stands alone in indeclinables ;
Conjunction, preposition, adverb join
To stamp new vigour on the nervous line ;
In monosyllables his thunders roll,
He, she, it, and we, ye, they, fright the soul.   890
    In person taller than the common size,
Behold where Barry [3] draws admiring eyes !
When labouring passions, in his bosom pent,
Convulsive rage, and struggling heave for vent ;
Spectators, with imagined terrors warm,
Anxious expect the bursting of the storm :
But, all unfit in such a pile to dwell,
His voice comes forth, like Echo from her cell,
To swell the tempest needful aid denies,
And all adown the stage in feeble murmurs dies.   900
    What man, like Barry, with such pains, can err
In elocution, action, character ?
What man could give, if Barry was not here,
Such well applauded tenderness to Lear ?

---

[1] 'Mossop :' Henry Mossop, a powerful, fiery, but irregular actor, very unfortunate in life.—[2] 'Right-hand :' Mossop practised the 'tea-pot attitude.'
—[3] 'Barry :' Spranger Barry, mentioned above as Garrick's great rival. He acted in Covent Garden.

Who else can speak so very, very fine,   905
That sense may kindly end with every line?
  Some dozen lines before the ghost is there,
Behold him for the solemn scene prepare:
See how he frames his eyes, poises each limb,
Puts the whole body into proper trim:—   . 910
From whence we learn, with no great stretch of art,
Five lines hence comes a ghost, and, ha! a start.
  When he appears most perfect, still we find
Something which jars upon and hurts the mind:
Whatever lights upon a part are thrown,
We see too plainly they are not his own:
No flame from Nature ever yet he caught,
Nor knew a feeling which he was not taught:
He raised his trophies on the base of art,
And conn'd his passions, as he conn'd his part.   920
  Quin,[1] from afar, lured by the scent of fame,
A stage leviathan, put in his claim,
Pupil of Betterton[2] and Booth.   Alone,
Sullen he walk'd, and deem'd the chair his own:
For how should moderns, mushrooms of the day,
Who ne'er those masters knew, know how to play?
Gray-bearded veterans, who, with partial tongue,
Extol the times when they themselves were young,
Who, having lost all relish for the stage,
See not their own defects, but lash the age,   930
Received, with joyful murmurs of applause,
Their darling chief, and lined[3] his favourite cause.
  Far be it from the candid Muse to tread
Insulting o'er the ashes of the dead:

---

1 'Quin:' the friend of Thomson, (see 'Castle of Indolence'), instructor
in reading of George III., famous for indolence, wit, good nature, and corpu-
lence.—² 'Betterton:' the great actor of the seventeenth century, whose
funeral and character are described in the 'Tatler.' Booth was his successor
and copy.—³ 'Lined:' supported.

But, just to living merit, she maintains,   935
And dares the test, whilst Garrick's genius reigns,
Ancients in vain endeavour to excel,
Happily praised, if they could act as well.
But, though prescription's force we disallow,
Nor to antiquity submissive bow ;   940
Though we deny imaginary grace,
Founded on accidents of time and place,
Yet real worth of every growth shall bear
Due praise ; nor must we, Quin, forget thee there.
His words bore sterling weight ; nervous and
        strong,
In manly tides of sense they roll'd along:
Happy in art, he chiefly had pretence
To keep up numbers, yet not forfeit sense ;
No actor ever greater heights could reach
In all the labour'd artifice of speech.   950
    Speech ! is that all ?   And shall an actor found
An universal fame on partial ground ?
Parrots themselves speak properly by rote,
And, in six months, my dog shall howl by note.
I laugh at those who, when the stage they tread,
Neglect the heart, to compliment the head ;
With strict propriety their cares confined
To weigh out words, while passion halts behind:
To syllable-dissectors they appeal,
Allow them accent, cadence,—fools may feel ;   960
But, spite of all the criticising elves,
Those who would make us feel, must feel them-
        selves.
    His eyes, in gloomy socket taught to roll,
Proclaim'd the sullen ' habit of his soul :'
Heavy and phlégmatic he trod the stage,
Too proud for tenderness, too dull for rage.

When Hector's lovely widow shines in tears,   967
Or Rowe's[1] gay rake dependent virtue jeers,
With the same cast of features he is seen
To chide the libertine, and court the queen.
From the tame scene, which without passion flows,
With just desert his reputation rose ;
Nor less he pleased, when, on some surly plan,
He was, at once, the actor and the man.

    In Brute[2] he shone unequall'd : all agree
Garrick's not half so great a Brute as he.
When Cato's labour'd scenes are brought to view,
With equal praise the actor labour'd too ;
For still you'll find, trace passions to their root,
Small difference 'twixt the Stoic and the Brute.   980
In fancied scenes, as in life's real plan,
He could not, for a moment, sink the man.
In whate'er cast his character was laid,
Self still, like oil, upon the surface play'd.
Nature, in spite of all his skill, crept in :
Horatio, Dorax,[3] Falstaff,—still 'twas Quin.

    Next follows Sheridan.[4]   A doubtful name,
As yet unsettled in the rank of fame :
This, fondly lavish in his praises grown,
Gives him all merit ; that allows him none ;   990
Between them both, we'll steer the middle course,
Nor, loving praise, rob Judgment of her force.

    Just his conceptions, natural and great,
His feelings strong, his words enforced with weight.
Was speech-famed Quin himself to hear him speak,
Envy would drive the colour from his cheek ;

---

[1] 'Rowe.' Andromache, in the tragedy of the 'Distressed Mother,' by
Ambrose Philips, and Lothario, in the 'Fair Penitent,' by Rowe.—[2] 'Brute:'
Sir John Brute, in Vanbrugh's 'Provoked Wife.'—[3] 'Dorax:' a soldier in
Dryden's 'Don Sebastian.'—[4] 'Sheridan:' see a previous note.

But step-dame Nature, niggard of her grace,   907
Denied the social powers of voice and face.
Fix'd in one frame of features, glare of eye,
Passions, like chaos, in confusion lie ;
In vain the wonders of his skill are tried
To form distinctions Nature hath denied.
His voice no touch of harmony admits,
Irregularly deep, and shrill by fits.
The two extremes appear like man and wife,
Coupled together for the sake of strife.

    His action's always strong, but sometimes such,
That candour must declare he acts too much.
Why must impatience fall three paces back ?
Why paces three return to the attack ?   1010
Why is the right leg, too, forbid to stir,
Unless in motion semicircular ?
Why must the hero with the Nailor [1] vie,
And hurl the close-clench'd fist at nose or eye ?
In Royal John, with Philip angry grown,
I thought he would have knock'd poor Davies down.
Inhuman tyrant ! was it not a shame
To fright a king so harmless and so tame ?
But, spite of all defects, his glories rise,
And art, by judgment form'd, with nature vies.   1020
Behold him sound the depth of Hubert's [2] soul,
Whilst in his own contending passions roll ;
View the whole scene, with critic judgment scan,
And then deny him merit, if you can.
Where he falls short, 'tis Nature's fault alone ;
Where he succeeds, the merit's all his own.

    Last Garrick [3] came. Behind him throng a train
Of snarling critics, ignorant as vain.

---

[1] 'Nailor:' pugilist.—[2] 'Hubert:' in King John.—[3] 'Garrick:' see Boswell and Murphy's life of that great actor.

One finds out—He's of stature somewhat low— 1029
Your hero always should be tall, you know ;
True natural greatness all consists in height.
Produce your voucher, Critic.—Serjeant Kite.[1]
    Another can't forgive the paltry arts
By which he makes his way to shallow hearts ;
Mere pieces of finesse, traps for applause—
'Avaunt! unnatural start, affected pause !'
    For me, by Nature form'd to judge with phlegm,
I can't acquit by wholesale, nor condemn.
The best things carried to excess are wrong ;
The start may be too frequent, pause too long : 1040
But, only used in proper time and place,
Severest judgment must allow them grace.
    If bunglers, form'd on Imitation's plan,
Just in the way that monkeys mimic man,
Their copied scene with mangled arts disgrace,
And pause and start with the same vacant face,
We join the critic laugh ; those tricks we scorn
Which spoil the scenes they mean them to adorn.
But when, from Nature's pure and genuine
    source,
These strokes of acting flow with generous force, 1050
When in the features all the soul's portray'd,
And passions, such as Garrick's, are display'd,
To me they seem from quickest feelings caught—
Each start is nature, and each pause is thought.
    When reason yields to passion's wild alarms,
And the whole state of man is up in arms,
What but a critic could condemn the player
For pausing here, when cool sense pauses there ?
Whilst, working from the heart, the fire I trace,
And mark it strongly flaming to the face ; 1060

---

[1] ' Serjeant Kite :' the recruiting serjeant in Farquhar's ' Recruiting Officer.'

Whilst in each sound I hear the very man, 1061
I can't catch words, and pity those who can.
   Let wits, like spiders, from the tortured brain
Fine-draw the critic-web with curious pain ;
The gods,—a kindness I with thanks must pay,—
Have form'd me of a coarser kind of clay ;
Not stung with envy, nor with spleen diseased,
A poor dull creature, still with Nature pleased :
Hence to thy praises, Garrick, I agree,
And, pleased with Nature, must be pleased with thee.
   Now might I tell how silence reign'd throughout, 1071
And deep attention hush'd the rabble rout;
How every claimant, tortured with desire,
Was pale as ashes, or as red as fire ;
But loose to fame, the Muse more simply acts,
Rejects all flourish, and relates mere facts.
   The judges, as the several parties came,
With temper heard, with judgment weigh'd each claim ;
And, in their sentence happily agreed,
In name of both, great Shakspeare thus decreed :— 1080
   If manly sense, if Nature link'd with Art ;
If thorough knowledge of the human heart ;
If powers of acting vast and unconfined ;
If fewest faults with greatest beauties join'd ;
If strong expression, and strange powers which lie
Within the magic circle of the eye ;
If feelings which few hearts like his can know,
And which no face so well as his can show,
Deserve the preference—Garrick ! take the chair ;
Nor quit it—till thou place an equal there. 1090

THE APOLOGY.

ADDRESSED TO THE CRITICAL REVIEWERS.[1]

Tristitiam et Metus.—HORACE.

LAUGHS not the heart when giants, big with pride,
Assume the pompous port, the martial stride ;
O'er arm Herculean heave th' enormous shield,
Vast as a weaver's beam the javelin wield ;
With the loud voice of thund'ring Jove defy,
And dare to single combat—what ?—A fly !
    And laugh we less when giant names, which shine
Establish'd, as it were, by right divine ;
Critics, whom every captive art adores,
To whom glad Science pours forth all her stores ;   10
Who high in letter'd reputation sit,
And hold, Astræa-like, the scales of wit,
With partial rage rush forth—oh ! shame to tell !—
To crush a bard just bursting from the shell ?
   Great are his perils in this stormy time
Who rashly ventures on a sea of rhyme :
Around vast surges roll, winds envious blow,
And jealous rocks and quicksands lurk below :
Greatly his foes he dreads, but more his friends ;
He hurts me most who lavishly commends.   20
    Look through the world—in every other trade
The same employment 's cause of kindness made,
At least appearance of good will creates,
And every fool puffs off the fool he hates :

---

[1] For occasion, &c. of this, see Life.

Cobblers with cobblers smoke away the night,   25
And in the common cause e'en players unite ;
Authors alone, with more than savage rage,
Unnatural war with brother authors wage.
The pride of Nature would as soon admit
Competitors in empire as in wit ;   30
Onward they rush, at Fame's imperious call,
And, less than greatest, would not be at all.
    Smit with the love of honour,—or the pence,—
O'errun with wit, and destitute of sense,
Should any novice in the rhyming trade
With lawless pen the realms of verse invade,
Forth from the court, where sceptred sages sit,
Abused with praise, and flatter'd into wit,
Where in lethargic majesty they reign,
And what they won by dulness, still maintain,   40
Legions of factious authors throng at once,
Fool beckons fool, and dunce awakens dunce.
To Hamilton's [1] the ready lies repair—
Ne'er was lie made which was not welcome
        there—
Thence, on maturer judgment's anvil wrought,
The polish'd falsehood's into public brought.
Quick-circulating slanders mirth afford ;
And reputation bleeds in every word.
    A critic was of old a glorious name,
Whose sanction handed merit up to fame ;   50
Beauties as well as faults he brought to view ;
His judgment great, and great his candour too ;
No servile rules drew sickly taste aside ;
Secure he walk'd, for Nature was his guide.
But now—oh ! strange reverse !—our critics bawl
In praise of candour with a heart of gall ;

[1] 'Hamilton :' Archibald Hamilton, printer of the ' Critical Review.'

Conscious of guilt, and fearful of the light, 57
They lurk enshrouded in the vale of night ;
Safe from detection, seize th' unwary prey,
And stab, like bravoes, all who come that way.
  When first my Muse, perhaps more bold than wise,
Bade the rude trifle into light arise,
Little she thought such tempests would ensue ;
Less, that those tempests would be raised by you.
The thunder's fury rends the towering oak,
Rosciads, like shrubs, might 'scape the fatal stroke.
Vain thought ! a critic's fury knows no bound ;
Drawcansir-like, he deals destruction round ;
Nor can we hope he will a stranger spare,
Who gives no quarter to his friend Voltaire.[1] 70
  Unhappy Genius ! placed by partial Fate
With a free spirit in a slavish state ;
Where the reluctant Muse, oppress'd by kings,
Or droops in silence, or in fetters sings !
In vain thy dauntless fortitude hath borne
The bigot's furious zeal, and tyrant's scorn.
Why didst thou safe from home-bred dangers steer,
Reserved to perish more ignobly here ?
Thus, when, the Julian tyrant's pride to swell,
Rome with her Pompey at Pharsalia fell, 80
The vanquish'd chief escaped from Caesar's hand,
To die by ruffians in a foreign land.
  How could these self-elected monarchs raise
So large an empire on so small a base ?
In what retreat, inglorious and unknown,
Did Genius sleep when Dulness seized the throne ?
Whence, absolute now grown, and free from awe,
She to the subject world dispenses law.

---

[1] 'Voltaire:' Smollett had changed his opinion of Voltaire, and from
praising, had begun to abuse him.

Without her licence not a letter stirs,   . 89
And all the captive criss-cross-row is hers.
The Stagyrite, who rules from Nature drew,
Opinious gave, but gave his reasons too.
Our great Dictators take a shorter way—
Who shall dispute what the Reviewers say ?
Their word 's sufficient; and to ask a reason,
In such a state as theirs, is downright treason.
True judgment now with them alone can dwell ;
Like Church of Rome, they 're grown infallible.
Dull superstitious readers they deceive,
Who pin their easy faith on critic's sleeve,   100
And knowing nothing, everything believe !
But why repine we that these puny elves
Shoot into giants ?—we may thank ourselves :
Fools that we are, like Israel's fools of yore,
The calf ourselves have fashion'd we adore.
But let true Reason once resume her reign,
This god shall dwindle to a calf again.
    Founded on arts which shun the face of day,
By the same arts they still maintain their sway.
Wrapp'd in mysterious secrecy they rise,   110
And, as they are unknown, are safe and wise.
At whomsoever aim'd, howe'er severe,
Th' envenom'd slander flies, no names appear :
Prudence forbids that step ;—then all might
        know,
And on more equal terms engage the foe.
But now, what Quixote of the age would care
To wage a war with dirt, and fight with air ?
By interest join'd, th' expert confederates stand,
And play the game into each other's hand :
The vile abuse, in turn by all denied,   120
Is bandied up and down, from side to side :

It flies—hey!—presto!—like a juggler's ball,   122
Till it belongs to nobody at all.
    All men and things they know, themselves unknown,
And publish every name—except their own.
Nor think this strange,—secure from vulgar eyes,
The nameless author passes in disguise;
But veteran critics are not so deceived,
If veteran critics are to be believed.
Once seen, they know an author evermore,   130
Nay, swear to hands they never saw before.
Thus in 'The Rosciad,' beyond chance or doubt,
They by the writing found the writers out:
That's Lloyd's—his manner there you plainly trace,
And all the Actor stares you in the face.
By Colman that was written—on my life,
The strongest symptoms of the 'Jealous Wife.'
That little disingenuous piece of spite,
Churchill—a wretch unknown!—perhaps might
    write.
    How doth it make judicious readers smile,   140
When authors are detected by their style;
Though every one who knows this author, knows
He shifts his style much oftener than his clothes!
    Whence could arise this mighty critic spleen,
The Muse a trifler, and her theme so mean?
What had I done, that angry Heaven should send
The bitterest foe where most I wish'd a friend?
Oft hath my tongue been wanton at thy name,[1]
And hail'd the honours of thy matchless fame.
For me let hoary Fielding bite the ground,   150
So nobler Pickle stands superbly bound;

---

[1] 'Thy name:' Dr Tobias Smollett, the well-known author of 'Roderick Random,' 'The Regicide,' an unfortunate tragedy, and one of the editors of the 'Critical Review,' is here satirised.

From Livy's temples tear th' historic crown,   152
Which with more justice blooms upon thine own.
Compared with thee, be all life-writers dumb,
But he who wrote the Life of Tommy Thumb.
Who ever read 'The Regicide,' but swore
The author wrote as man ne'er wrote before ?
Others for plots and under-plots may call,
Here's the right method—have no plot at all.
Who can so often in his cause engage   160
The tiny pathos of the Grecian stage,
Whilst horrors rise, and tears spontaneous flow
At tragic Ha! and no less tragic Oh!
To praise his nervous weakness all agree ;
And then for sweetness, who so sweet as he!
Too big for utterance when sorrows swell,
The too big sorrows flowing tears must tell ;
But when those flowing tears shall cease to flow,
Why—then the voice must speak again, you
     know.

Rude and unskilful in the poet's trade,   170
I kept no Naïads by me ready made ;
Ne'er did I colours high in air advance,
Torn from the bleeding fopperies of France ; [1]
No flimsy linsey-woolsey scenes I wrote,
With patches here and there, like Joseph's coat.
Me humbler themes befit : secure, for me,
Let play-wrights smuggle nonsense duty free ;
Secure, for me, ye lambs, ye lambkins! bound,
And frisk and frolic o'er the fairy ground .
Secure, for me, thou pretty little fawn !   180
Lick Sylvia's hand, and crop the flowery lawn ;

---

[1] 'Fopperies of France,' &c. · in these lines the poet refers to Murphy's
practice of vamping up French plays, and to his ' Desert Island,' a ridiculous
pastoral drama.

Uncensured let the gentle breezes rove 182
Through the green umbrage of th' enchanted grove :
Secure, for me, let foppish Nature smile,
And play the coxcomb in the ' Desert Isle.'
  The stage I chose—a subject fair and free—
'Tis yours—'tis mine—'tis public property.
All common exhibitions open lie,
For praise or censure, to the common eye.
Hence are a thousand hackney writers fed ; 190
Hence Monthly Critics earn their daily bread.
This is a general tax which all must pay,
From those who scribble, down to those who play.
Actors, a venal crew, receive support
From public bounty for the public sport.
To clap or hiss all have an equal claim,
The cobbler's and his lordship's right 's the same.
All join for their subsistence ; all expect
Free leave to praise their worth, their faults correct.
When active Pickle Smithfield stage ascends, 200
The three days' wonder of his laughing friends,
Each, or as judgment or as fancy guides,
The lively witling praises or derides.
And where 's the mighty difference, tell me where,
Betwixt a Merry Andrew and a player ?
  The strolling tribe—a despicable race !—
Like wand'ring Arabs, shift from place to place.
Vagrants by law, to justice open laid,
They tremble, of the beadle's lash afraid,
And, fawning, cringe for wretched means of life 210
To Madam Mayoress, or his Worship's wife.
  The mighty monarch, in theatric sack,
Carries his whole regalia at his back ;
His royal consort heads the female band,
And leads the heir apparent in her hand ;

The pannier'd ass creeps on with conscious pride,   216
Bearing a future prince on either side.
No choice musicians in this troop are found,
To varnish nonsense with the charms of sound ;
No swords, no daggers, not one poison'd bowl ;   220
No lightning flashes here, no thunders roll ;
No guards to swell the monarch's train are shown ;
The monarch here must be a host alone :
No solemn pomp, no slow processions here ;
No Ammon's entry, and no Juliet's bier.
   By need compell'd to prostitute his art,
The varied actor flies from part to part ;
And—strange disgrace to all theatric pride !—
His character is shifted with his side.
Question and answer he by turns must be,   230
Like that small wit in modern tragedy,[1]
Who, to patch up his fame—or fill his purse—
Still pilfers wretched plans, and makes them
    worse ;
Like gypsies, lest the stolen brat be known,
Defacing first, then claiming for his own.
In shabby state they strut, and tatter'd robe,
The scene a blanket, and a barn the globe :
No high conceits their moderate wishes raise,
Content with humble profit, humble praise.
Let dowdies simper, and let bumpkins stare,   240
The strolling pageant hero treads in air :
Pleased, for his hour he to mankind gives law,
And snores the next out on a truss of straw.
   But if kind Fortune, who sometimes, we know,
Can take a hero from a puppet-show,
In mood propitious should her favourite call,
On royal stage in royal pomp to bawl,

      [1] ' Modern tragedy : ' Mr Murphy again.

Forgetful of himself, he rears the head,   248
And scorns the dunghill where he first was bred ;
Conversing now with well dress'd kings and
    queens,
With gods and goddesses behind the scenes,
He sweats beneath the terror-nodding plume,
Taught by mock honours real pride t' assume.
On this great stage, the world, no monarch e'er
Was half so haughty as a monarch player.

    Doth it more move our anger or our mirth
To see these things, the lowest sons of earth,
Presume, with self-sufficient knowledge graced,
To rule in letters, and preside in taste ?
The town's decisions they no more admit,   260
Themselves alone the arbiters of wit ;
And scorn the jurisdiction of that court
To which they owe their being and support.
Actors, like monks of old, now sacred grown,
Must be attack'd by no fools but their own.

    Let the vain tyrant [1] sit amidst his guards,
His puny green-room wits and venal bards,
Who meanly tremble at the puppet's frown,
And for a playhouse-freedom lose their own ;
In spite of new-made laws, and new-made kings,   270
The free-born Muse with liberal spirit sings.
Bow down, ye slaves ! before these idols fall ;
Let Genius stoop to them who 've none at all :
Ne'er will I flatter, cringe, or bend the knee
To those who, slaves to all, are slaves to me

    Actors, as actors, are a lawful game,
The poet's right, and who shall bar his claim ?

---

[1] 'Vain tyrant,' &c. : Garrick is here meant ; he had displeased Churchill
by pretending that he had written ' The Rosciad ' to gain the freedom of the
playhouse. He apologised very humbly to Churchill, and a reconciliation
took place

And if, o'erweening of their little skill,   278
When they have left the stage, they 're actors still ;
If to the subject world they still give laws,
With paper crowns, and sceptres made of straws ;
If they in cellar or in garret roar,
And, kings one night, are kings for evermore ;
Shall not bold Truth, e'en there, pursue her theme,
And wake the coxcomb from his golden dream ?
Or if, well worthy of a better fate,
They rise superior to their present state ;
If, with each social virtue graced, they blend
The gay companion and the faithful friend ; .
If they, like Pritchard, join in private life   290
The tender parent and the virtuous wife ;
Shall not our verse their praise with pleasure speak,
Though Mimics bark, and Envy split her cheek ?
No honest worth 's beneath the Muse's praise ;
No greatness can above her censure raise ;
Station and wealth to her are trifling things ;
She stoops to actors, and she soars to kings.
   Is there a man,[1] in vice and folly bred,
To sense of honour as to virtue dead,
Whom ties, nor human, nor divine can bind,   300
Alien from God, and foe to all mankind ;
Who spares no character ; whose every word,
Bitter as gall, and sharper than the sword,
Cuts to the quick ; whose thoughts with rancour
       swell ;
Whose tongue, on earth, performs the work of hell ?
If there be such a monster, the Reviews
Shall find him holding forth against abuse :
Attack profession !—'tis a deadly breach !
The Christian laws another lesson teach :—

---

[1] 'A man:' Dr Smollett again.

Unto the end shall Charity endure, 310
And Candour hide those faults it cannot cure.
　Thus Candour's maxims flow from Rancour's throat,
As devils, to serve their purpose, Scripture quote.
　The Muse's office was by Heaven design'd
To please, improve, instruct, reform mankind ;
To make dejected Virtue nobly rise
Above the towering pitch of splendid Vice ;
To make pale Vice, abash'd, her head hang down,
And, trembling, crouch at Virtue's awful frown.
Now arm'd with wrath, she bids eternal shame, 320
With strictest justice, brand the villain's name ;
Now in the milder garb of ridicule
She sports, and pleases while she wounds the fool.
Her shape is often varied ; but her aim,
To prop the cause of Virtue, still the same.
In praise of Mercy let the guilty bawl ;
When Vice and Folly for correction call,
Silence the mark of weakness justly bears,
And is partaker of the crimes it spares.
But if the Muse, too cruel in her mirth, 330
With harsh reflections wounds the man of worth ;
If wantonly she deviates from her plan,
And quits the actor to expose the man ; [1]
Ashamed, she marks that passage with a blot,
And hates the line where candour was forgot.
　But what is candour, what is humour's vein,
Though judgment join to consecrate the strain,
If curious numbers will not aid afford,
Nor choicest music play in every word ?
Verses must run, to charm a modern ear, 340
From all harsh, rugged interruptions clear.

---

[1] 'Expose the man :' referring to some personal lines on one Mr John
Palmer, which occurred in the first edition, but which he expunged.

Soft let them breathe, as Zephyr's balmy breeze,   342
Smooth let their current flow, as summer seas ;
Perfect then only deem'd when they dispense
A happy tuneful vacancy of sense.
Italian fathers thus, with barb' rous rage,
Fit helpless infants for the squeaking stage ;
Deaf to the calls of pity, Nature wound,
And mangle vigour for the sake of sound.
Henceforth farewell, then, feverish thirst of fame ;   350
Farewell the longings for a poet's name ;
Perish my Muse—a wish 'bove all severe
To him who ever held the Muses dear—
If e'er her labours weaken to refine
The generous roughness of a nervous line.
     Others affect the stiff and swelling phrase ;
Their Muse must walk in stilts, and strut in stays ;
The sense they murder, and the words transpose,
Lest poetry approach too near to prose.
See tortured Reason how they pare and trim,   360
And, like Procrustes, stretch, or lop the limb.
     Waller ! whose praise succeeding bards rehearse,
Parent of harmony in English verse,
Whose tuneful Muse in sweetest accents flows,
In couplets first taught straggling sense to close.
     In polish'd numbers and majestic sound,
Where shall thy rival, Pope ! be ever found ?
But whilst each line with equal beauty flows,
E'en excellence, unvaried, tedious grows.
Nature, through all her works, in great degree,   370
Borrows a blessing from variety.
Music itself her needful aid requires
To rouse the soul, and wake our dying fires.
Still in one key, the nightingale would tease ;
Still in one key, not Brent would always please.

Here let me bend, great Dryden! at thy shrine, 376
Thou dearest name to all the Tuneful Nine!
What if some dull lines in cold order creep,
And with his theme the poet seems to sleep?
Still, when his subject rises proud to view, 380
With equal strength the poet rises too:
With strong invention, noblest vigour fraught,
Thought still springs up and rises out of thought;
Numbers ennobling numbers in their course,
In varied sweetness flow, in varied force;
The powers of genius and of judgment join,
And the whole Art of Poetry is thine.
But what are numbers, what are bards to me,
Forbid to tread the paths of poesy?
A sacred Muse should consecrate her pen— 390
Priests must not hear nor see like other men—
Far higher themes should her ambition claim:
Behold where Sternhold points the way to fame!
Whilst with mistaken zeal dull bigots burn,
Let Reason for a moment take her turn.
When coffee-sages hold discourse with kings,
And blindly walk in paper leading-strings,
What if a man delight to pass his time
In spinning reason into harmless rhyme,
Or sometimes boldly venture to the play? 400
Say, where's the crime, great man of prudence, say?
No two on earth in all things can agree;
All have some darling singularity:
Women and men, as well as girls and boys,
In gew-gaws take delight, and sigh for toys.
Your sceptres and your crowns, and such like things,
Are but a better kind of toys for kings.
In things indifferent Reason bids us choose,
Whether the whim's a monkey or a Muse.

D

.What the grave triflers on this busy scene,   410
When they make use of this word Reason, mean,
I know not; but according to my plan,
'Tis Lord Chief-Justice in the court of man;
Equally form'd to rule in age or youth,
The friend of virtue and the guide to truth;
To her I bow, whose sacred power I feel;
To her decision make my last appeal;
Condemn'd by her, applauding worlds in vain
Should tempt me to take up the pen again;
By her absolved, my course I'll still pursue: 420
If Reason's for me, God is for me too.

NIGHT.[1]

AN EPISTLE TO ROBERT LLOYD.

Contrarius evehor orbi.—OVID, Met. lib. ii.

WHEN foes insult, and prudent friends dispense,
In pity's strains, the worst of insolence,
Oft with thee, Lloyd, I steal an hour from grief,
And in thy social converse find relief.
The mind, of solitude impatient grown,
Loves any sorrows rather than her own.
    Let slaves to business, bodies without soul,
Important blanks in Nature's mighty roll,
Solemnise nonsense in the day's broad glare,
'We Night prefer, which heals or hides our care.   10

[1] 'Night:' this poem was written to defend the irregularities imputed to
the poet.

Rogues justified, and by success made bold,   11
Dull fools and coxcombs sanctified by gold,
Freely may bask in fortune's partial ray,
And spread their feathers opening to the day ;
But threadbare Merit dares not show the head
Till vain Prosperity retires to bed.
Misfortunes, like the owl, avoid the light ;
The sons of Care are always sons of Night.
   The wretch, bred up in Method's drowsy school,
Whose only merit is to err by rule,   20
Who ne'er through heat of blood was tripping caught,
Nor guilty deem'd of one eccentric thought ;
Whose soul directed to no use is seen,
Unless to move the body's dull machine,
Which, clock-work like, with the same equal pace
Still travels on through life's insipid space,
Turns up his eyes to think that there should be,
Among God's creatures, two such things as we ;
Then for his nightcap calls, and thanks the powers
Which kindly gave him grace to keep good hours.   30
   Good hours !—fine words—but was it ever seen
That all men could agree in what they mean ?
Florio, who many years a course hath run
In downright opposition to the sun,
Expatiates on good hours, their cause defends
With as much vigour as our prudent friends.
Th' uncertain term no settled notion brings,
But still in different mouths means different things ;
Each takes the phrase in his own private view ;
With Prudence it is ten, with Florio two.   40
   Go on, ye fools ! who talk for talking sake,
Without distinguishing, distinctions make ;
Shine forth in native folly, native pride,
Make yourselves rules to all the world beside ;

Reason, collected in herself, disdains 45
The slavish yoke of arbitrary chains;
Steady and true, each circumstance she weighs,
Nor to bare words inglorious tribute pays.
Men of sense live exempt from vulgar awe,
And Reason to herself alone is law: 50
That freedom she enjoys with liberal mind,
Which she as freely grants to all mankind.
No idol-titled name her reverence stirs,
No hour she blindly to the rest prefers;
All are alike, if they 're alike employ'd,
And all are good if virtuously enjoy'd.
　　Let the sage Doctor (think him one we know)
With scraps of ancient learning overflow,
In all the dignity of wig declare
The fatal consequence of midnight air, 60
How damps and vapours, as it were by stealth,
Undermine life, and sap the walls of health:
For me let Galen moulder on the shelf,
I 'll live, and be physician to myself.
Whilst soul is join'd to body, whether fate
Allot a longer or a shorter date,
I 'll make them live, as brother should with brother,
And keep them in good humour with each other.
　　The surest road to health, say what they will,
Is never to suppose we shall be ill. 70
Most of those evils we poor mortals know,
From doctors and imagination flow.
Hence to old women with your boasted rules,
Stale traps, and only sacred now to fools;
As well may sons of physic hope to find
One medicine, as one hour, for all mankind!
　　If Rupert after ten is out of bed,
The fool next morning can't hold up his head;

What reason this which me to bed must call,   79
Whose head, thank Heaven, never aches at all?
In different courses different tempers run;
He hates the moon, I sicken at the sun.
Wound up at twelve at noon, his clock goes right;
Mine better goes, wound up at twelve at night.
    Then in oblivion's grateful cup I drown
The galling sneer, the supercilious frown,
The strange reserve, the proud, affected state
Of upstart knaves grown rich, and fools grown great.
No more that abject wretch [1] disturbs my rest,
Who meanly overlooks a friend distress'd.   90
Purblind to poverty, the worldling goes,
And scarce sees rags an inch beyond his nose;
But from a crowd can single out his Grace,
And cringe and creep to fools who strut in lace.
    Whether those classic regions are survey'd
Where we in earliest youth together stray'd,
Where hand in hand we trod the flowery shore,
Though now thy happier genius runs before;
When we conspired a thankless wretch [2] to raise,
And taught a stump to shoot with pilfer'd praise,   100
Who once, for reverend merit famous grown,
Gratefully strove to kick his maker down;
Or if more general arguments engage,—
The court or camp, the pulpit, bar, or stage;
If half-bred surgeons, whom men doctors call,
And lawyers, who were never bred at all,
Those mighty letter'd monsters of the earth,
Our pity move, or exercise our mirth;

---

[1] 'Abject wretch:' Thornton, who abandoned Lloyd in his distress. —
[2] 'Thankless wretch:' one Sellon, a popular clergyman, aided at first by
Churchill and his set, but who betrayed and blackened them afterwards. We
meet with him again in 'The Ghost' as Plausible.

Or if in tittle-tattle, toothpick way,   109
Our rambling thoughts with easy freedom stray,—
A gainer still thy friend himself must find,
His grief suspended, and improved his mind.
    Whilst peaceful slumbers bless the homely bed
Where virtue, self-approved, reclines her head ;
Whilst vice beneath imagined horrors mourns,
And conscience plants the villain's couch with thorns ;
Impatient of restraint, the active mind,
No more by servile prejudice confined,
Leaps from her seat, as waken'd from a trance
And darts through Nature at a single glance   120
Then we our friends, our foes, ourselves, survey,
And see by Night what fools we are by day.
    Stripp'd of her gaudy plumes, and vain disguise,
See where ambition, mean and loathsome, lies ;
Reflection with relentless hand pulls down
The tyrant's bloody wreath and ravish'd crown.
In vain he tells of battles bravely won,
Of nations conquer'd, and of worlds undone ;
Triumphs like these but ill with manhood suit,
And sink the conqueror beneath the brute.   130
But if, in searching round the world, we find
Some generous youth, the friend of all mankind,
Whose anger, like the bolt of Jove, is sped
In terrors only at the guilty head,
Whose mercies, like heaven's dew, refreshing fall
In general love and charity to all,
Pleased we behold such worth on any throne,
And doubly pleased we find it on our own.
    Through a false medium things are shown by day ;
Pomp, wealth, and titles, judgment lead astray.   140
How many from appearance borrow state,
Whom Night disdains to number with the great !

Must not we laugh to see yon lordling proud   148
Snuff up vile incense from a fawning crowd ?
Whilst in his beam surrounding clients play,
Like insects in the sun's enlivening ray,
Whilst, Jehu-like, he drives at furious rate,
And seems the only charioteer of state,
Talking himself into a little god,
And ruling empires with a single nod ;   150
Who would not think, to hear him law dispense,
That he had interest, and that they had sense ?
Injurious thought ! beneath Night's honest shade,
When pomp is buried, and false colours fade,
Plainly we see at that impartial hour,
Them dupes to pride, and him the tool of power.
    God help the man, condemn'd by cruel fate
To court the seeming, or the real great !
Much sorrow shall he feel, and suffer more
Than any slave who labours at the oar !   160
By slavish methods must he learn to please,
By smooth-tongued flattery, that cursed court-disease;
Supple, to every wayward mood strike sail,
And shift with shifting humour's peevish gale.
To nature dead, he must adopt vile art,
And wear a smile, with anguish in his heart.
A sense of honour would destroy his schemes,
And conscience ne'er must speak unless in dreams.
When he hath tamely borne, for many years,
Cold looks, forbidding frowns, contemptuous sneers,   170
When he at last expects, good easy man !
To reap the profits of his labour'd plan,
Some cringing lackey, or rapacious whore,
To favours of the great the surest door,
Some catamite, or pimp, in credit grown,
Who tempts another's wife, or sells his own,

Steps 'cross his hopes, the promised boon denies,   177
And for some minion's minion claims the prize.
   Foe to restraint, unpractised in deceit,
Too resolute, from nature's active heat,
To brook affronts, and tamely pass them by,
Too proud to flatter, too sincere to lie,
Too plain to please, too honest to be great,
Give me, kind Heaven, an humbler, happier state :
Far from the place where men with pride deceive,
Where rascals promise, and where fools believe ;
Far from the walk of folly, vice, and strife,
Calm, independent, let me steal through life ;
Nor one vain wish my steady thoughts beguile
To fear his Lordship's frown, or court his smile.   190
Unfit for greatness, I her snares defy,
And look on riches with untainted eye :
To others let the glittering baubles fall,
Content shall place us far above them all.
   Spectators only on this bustling stage,
We see what vain designs mankind engage :
Vice after vice with ardour they pursue,
And one old folly brings forth twenty new.
Perplex'd with trifles through the vale of life,
Man strives 'gainst man, without a cause for strife :   200
Armies embattled meet, and thousands bleed
For some vile spot, where fifty cannot feed.
Squirrels for nuts contend, and, wrong or right,
For the world's empire kings, ambitious, fight.
What odds ?—to us 'tis all the self-same thing,
A nut, a world, a squirrel, and a king.
   Britons, like Roman spirits famed of old,
Are cast by nature in a patriot mould ;
No private joy, no private grief, they know,
Their souls engross'd by public weal or woe ;   210

Inglorious ease, like ours, they greatly scorn ;   211
Let care with nobler wreaths their brows adorn :
Gladly they toil beneath the statesman's pains,
Give them but credit for a statesman's brains.
All would be deem'd, e'en from the cradle, fit
To rule in politics as well as wit.
The grave, the gay, the fopling, and the dunce,
Start up (God bless us !) statesman all at once.
   His mighty charge of souls the priest forgets,
The court-bred lord his promises and debts ;   220
Soldiers their fame, misers forget their pelf,
The rake his mistress, and the fop himself ;
Whilst thoughts of higher moment claim their care,
And their wise heads the weight of kingdoms bear.
   Females themselves the glorious ardour feel,
And boast an equal or a greater zeal ;
From nymph to nymph the state-infection flies,
Swells in her breast, and sparkles in her eyes.
O'erwhelm'd by politics lie malice, pride,
Envy, and twenty other faults beside.   230
No more their little fluttering hearts confess
A passion for applause, or rage for dress ;
No more they pant for public raree-shows,
Or lose one thought on monkeys or on beaux :
Coquettes no more pursue the jilting plan,
And lustful prudes forget to rail at man :
The darling theme Cecilia's self will choose,
Nor thinks of scandal whilst she talks of news.
   The cit, a common-councilman by place,
Ten thousand mighty nothings in his face,   240
By situation as by nature great,
With nice precision parcels out the state ;
Proves and disproves, affirms and then denies,
Objects himself, and to himself replies ;

Wielding aloft the politician rod,   245
Makes Pitt by turns a devil and a god;
Maintains, e'en to the very teeth of Power,
The same thing right and wrong in half an
    hour:
Now all is well, now he suspects a plot,
And plainly proves, whatever is, is not: 250
Fearfully wise, he shakes his empty head,
And deals out empires as he deals out thread;
His useless scales are in a corner flung,
And Europe's balance hangs upon his tongue.
    Peace to such triflers! be our happier plan
To pass through life as easy as we can.
Who's in or out, who moves this grand machine,
Nor stirs my curiosity, nor spleen.
Secrets of state no more I wish to know
Than secret movements of a puppet-show: 260
Let but the puppets move, I've my desire,
Unseen the hand which guides the master-
    wire.
    What is't to us if taxes rise or fall?
Thanks to our fortune, we pay none at all.
Let muckworms, who in dirty acres deal,
Lament those hardships which we cannot feel.
His Grace, who smarts, may bellow if he please,
But must I bellow too, who sit at ease?
By custom safe, the poet's numbers flow
Free as the light and air some years ago.   270
No statesman e'er will find it worth his pains
To tax our labours, and excise our brains.
Burthens like these, vile earthly buildings bear;
No tribute's laid on castles in the air.
    Let, then, the flames of war destructive reign,
And England's terrors awe imperious Spain;

Let every venal clan[1] and neutral tribe   277
Learn to receive conditions, not prescribe ;
Let each new year call loud for new supplies,
And tax on tax with double burthen rise ;
Exempt we sit, by no rude cares oppress'd,
And, having little, are with little bless'd.
All real ills in dark oblivion lie,
And joys, by fancy form'd, their place supply ;
Night's laughing hours unheeded slip away,
Nor one dull thought foretells approach of day.
     Thus have we lived, and whilst the Fates afford
Plain plenty to supply the frugal board ;
Whilst Mirth with Decency, his lovely bride,
And wine's gay god, with Temperance by his side,   290
Their welcome visit pay ; whilst Health attends
The narrow circle of our chosen friends ;
Whilst frank Good-humour consecrates the treat,
And woman makes society complete,
Thus will we live, though in our teeth are hurl'd
Those hackney strumpets, Prudence and the World.
     Prudence, of old a sacred term, implied
Virtue, with godlike wisdom for her guide ;
But now in general use is known to mean
The stalking-horse of vice, and folly's screen.   300
The sense perverted, we retain the name ;
Hypocrisy and Prudence are the same.
     A tutor once, more read in men than books,
A kind of crafty knowledge in his looks,
Demurely sly, with high preferment bless'd,
His favourite pupil in these words address'd :—
Wouldst thou, my son, be wise and virtuous deem'd ;
By all mankind a prodigy esteem'd ?

---

[1] 'Venal Clan : ' alluding to Mr Pitt's employing the Highland clans in the American war.

Be this thy rule ; be what men prudent call ;   309
Prudence, almighty Prudence, gives thee all.
Keep up appearances ; there lies the test ;
The world will give thee credit for the rest.
Outward be fair, however foul within ;
Sin if thou wilt, but then in secret sin.
This maxim 's into common favour grown,
Vice is no longer vice, unless 'tis known.
Virtue, indeed, may barefaced take the field ;
But vice is virtue when 'tis well conceal'd.
Should raging passion drive thee to a whore,
Let Prudence lead thee to a postern door ;   320
Stay out all night, but take especial care
That Prudence bring thee back to early prayer.
As one with watching and with study faint,
Reel in a drunkard, and reel out a saint.
    With joy the youth this useful lesson heard,
And in his memory stored each precious word ;
Successfully pursued the plan, and now,
Room for my Lord—Virtue, stand by and bow.
    And is this all—is this the worldling's art,
To mask, but not amend a vicious heart ?   330
Shall lukewarm caution, and demeanour grave,
For wise and good stamp every supple knave ?
Shall wretches, whom no real virtue warms,
Gild fair their names and states with empty forms ;
While Virtue seeks in vain the wish'd-for prize,
Because, disdaining ill, she hates disguise ;
Because she frankly pours fourth all her store,
Seems what she is, and scorns to pass for more ?
Well—be it so—let vile dissemblers hold
Unenvied power, and boast their dear-bought gold ;   340
Me neither power shall tempt, nor thirst of pelf,
To flatter others, or deny myself ;

Might the whole world be placed within my span,   343
I would not be that thing, that prudent man.
  What! cries Sir Pliant, would you then oppose
Yourself, alone, against a host of foes?
Let not conceit, and peevish lust to rail,
Above all sense of interest prevail.
Throw off, for shame! this petulance of wit;
Be wise, be modest, and for once submit: 350
Too hard the task 'gainst multitudes to fight;
You must be wrong; the World is in the right.
  What is this World?—A term which men have got
To signify, not one in ten knows what;
A term, which with no more precision passes
To point out herds of men than herds of asses;
In common use no more it means, we find,
Than many fools in same opinions join'd.
  Can numbers, then, change Nature's stated laws?
Can numbers make the worse the better cause?   360
Vice must be vice, virtue be virtue still,
Though thousands rail at good, and practise ill.
Wouldst thou defend the Gaul's destructive rage,
Because vast nations on his part engage?
Though, to support the rebel Cæsar's cause,
Tumultuous legions arm against the laws;
Though scandal would our patriot's name impeach,
And rails at virtues which she cannot reach,
What honest man but would with joy submit
To bleed with Cato, and retire with Pitt?[1]   370
  Steadfast and true to virtue's sacred laws,
Unmoved by vulgar censure, or applause,
Let the World talk, my friend; that World, we know,
Which calls us guilty, cannot make us so.

---

[1] 'Pitt:' who retired in 1761, because the cabinet would not go to war
with Spain.

Unawed by numbers, follow Nature's plan ;   375
Assert the rights, or quit the name of man.
Consider well, weigh strictly right and wrong ;
Resolve not quick, but once resolved, be strong.
In spite of Dulness, and in spite of Wit,
If to thyself thou canst thyself acquit,   380
Rather stand up, assured with conscious pride,
Alone, than err with millions on thy side.

THE PROPHECY OF FAMINE.

A SCOTS PASTORAL INSCRIBED TO JOHN WILKES, ESQ.

Nos patriam fugimus.—VIRGIL.

WHEN Cupid first instructs his darts to fly
From the sly corner of some cook-maid's eye,
The stripling raw, just enter'd in his teens,
Receives the wound, and wonders what it means ;
His heart, like dripping, melts, and new desire
Within him stirs, each time she stirs the fire ;
Trembling and blushing, he the fair one views,
And fain would speak, but can't—without a Muse.
　　So to the sacred mount he takes his way,
Prunes his young wings, and tunes his infant lay,   10
His oaten reed to rural ditties frames,
To flocks and rocks, to hills and rills, proclaims,
In simplest notes, and all unpolish'd strains,
The loves of nymphs, and eke the loves of swains.
　　Clad, as your nymphs were always clad of yore,
In rustic weeds—a cook-maid now no more—
Beneath an aged oak Lardella lies—
Green moss her couch, her canopy the skies.

From aromatic shrubs the roguish gale 19
Steals young perfumes and wafts them through the vale.
The youth, turn'd swain, and skill'd in rustic lays,
Fast by her side his amorous descant plays.
Herds low, flocks bleat, pies chatter, ravens scream,
And the full chorus dies a-down the stream :
The streams, with music freighted, as they pass
Present the fair Lardella with a glass ;
And Zephyr, to complete the love-sick plan,
Waves his light wings, and serves her for a fan
    But when maturer Judgment takes the lead,
These childish toys on Reason's altar bleed ; 30
Form'd after some great man, whose name breeds awe,
Whose every sentence Fashion makes a law ;
Who on mere credit his vain trophies rears,
And founds his merit on our servile fears ;
Then we discard the workings of the heart,
And nature's banish'd by mechanic art ;
Then, deeply read, our reading must be shown ;
Vain is that knowledge which remains unknown :
Then Ostentation marches to our aid,
And letter'd Pride stalks forth in full parade ; 40
Beneath their care behold the work refine,
Pointed each sentence, polish'd every line ;
Trifles are dignified, and taught to wear
The robes of ancients with a modern air ;
Nonsense with classic ornaments is graced,
And passes current with the stamp of taste.
    Then the rude Theocrite is ransack'd o'er,
And courtly Maro call'd from Mincio's shore ;
Sicilian Muses on our mountains roam,
Easy and free as if they were at home ; 50
Nymphs, naïads, nereïds, dryads, satyrs, fauns,
Sport in our floods, and trip it o'er our lawns ;

Flowers which once flourish'd fair in Greece and Rome,
More fair revive in England's meads to bloom ;   54
Skies without cloud, exotic suns adorn,
And roses blush, but blush without a thorn ;
Landscapes, unknown to dowdy Nature, rise,
And new creations strike our wondering eyes.
 For bards like these, who neither sing nor say,   ¹
Grave without thought, and without feeling gay,   60
Whose numbers in one even tenor flow,
Attuned to pleasure, and attuned to woe ;
Who, if plain Common-Sense her visit pays,
And mars one couplet in their happy lays,
As at some ghost affrighted, start and stare,
And ask the meaning of her coming there :
For bards like these a wreath shall Mason[1] bring,
Lined with the softest down of Folly's wing ;
In Love's pagoda shall they ever doze,
And Gisbal[2] kindly rock them to repose ;   70
My Lord ——, to letters as to faith most true—
At once their patron and example too—
Shall quaintly fashion his love-labour'd dreams,
Sigh with sad winds, and weep with weeping streams ;[3]
Curious in grief (for real grief, we know,
Is curious to dress up the tale of woe),
From the green umbrage of some Druid's seat
Shall his own works, in his own way, repeat.
 Me, whom no Muse of heavenly birth inspires,
No judgment tempers when rash genius fires ;   80
Who boast no merit but mere knack of rhyme,
Short gleams of sense, and satire out of time ;-

---

[1] 'Mason:' William Mason, author of 'Elfrida,' 'Caractacus,' and an
'Elegy on the Death of the Countess of Coventry,' the intimate friend, executor,
and biographer of Gray. — [2] 'Gisbal:' a stupid and scurrilous attack on
Scotland. — [3] 'Weeping streams:' referring to Lord Lyttelton's Monody on
his wife's death, and his Essay on the conversion of Paul.

Who cannot follow where trim fancy leads,   83
By prattling streams, o'er flower-empurpled meads;
Who often, but without success, have pray'd
For apt Alliteration's artful aid ;
Who would, but cannot, with a master's skill,
Coin fine new epithets, which mean no ill :
Me, thus uncouth, thus every way unfit
For pacing poesy, and ambling wit,   90
Taste with contempt beholds, nor deigns to place
Amongst the lowest of her favour'd race.
   Thou, Nature, art my goddess—to thy law
Myself I dedicate ! Hence, slavish awe !
Which bends to fashion, and obeys the rules
Imposed at first, and since observed by fools ;
Hence those vile tricks which mar fair Nature's hue,
And bring the sober matron forth to view,
With all that artificial tawdry glare
Which virtue scorns, and none but strumpets wear ! 100
Sick of those pomps, those vanities, that waste
Of toil, which critics now mistake for taste ;
Of false refinements sick, and labour'd ease,
Which art, too thinly veil'd, forbids to please ;
By Nature's charms (inglorious truth !) subdued,
However plain her dress, and 'haviour rude,
To northern climes my happier course I steer,
Climes where the goddess reigns throughout the
     year ;
Where, undisturb'd by Art's rebellious plan,
She rules the loyal laird, and faithful clan.   110
   To that rare soil, where virtues clust'ring grow,
What mighty blessings doth not England owe !
What waggon-loads of courage, wealth, and sense,
Doth each revolving day import from thence ?

E

To us she gives, disinterested friend!   115
Faith without fraud, and Stuarts[1] without end.
When we prosperity's rich trappings wear,
Come not her generous sons and take a share?
And if, by some disastrous turn of fate,
Change should ensue, and ruin seize the state,   120
Shall we not find, safe in that hallow'd ground,
Such refuge as the holy martyr[2] found?
    Nor less our debt in science, though denied
By the weak slaves of prejudice and pride.
Thence came the Ramsays,[3] names of worthy note,
Of whom one paints, as well as t'other wrote;
Thence, Home,[4] disbanded from the sons of prayer
For loving plays, though no dull Dean[5] was there;
Thence issued forth, at great Macpherson's[6] call,
That old, new, epic pastoral, Fingal;   130
Thence Malloch,[7] friend alike to Church and State,
Of Christ and Liberty, by grateful Fate
Raised to rewards, which, in a pious reign,
All daring infidels should seek in vain;
Thence simple bards, by simple prudence taught,
To this wise town by simple patrons brought,
In simple manner utter simple lays,
And take, with simple pensions, simple praise.
    Waft me, some Muse, to Tweed's inspiring stream,
Where all the little Loves and Graces dream;   140

[1] 'Stuarts:' the family name of Lord Bute.—[2] 'Holy martyr:' Charles I.
— [3] 'Ramsays:' Allan Ramsay, author of the 'Gentle Shepherd,' and his son
(Allan), a fine painter, intimate with Reynolds and Johnson. — [4] 'Home:'
John Home, the well known author of 'Douglas.' See Mackenzie's Life. —
[5] 'Dull Dean:' Dr Zachary Pearce, Bishop of Rochester and Dean of Westminster, who rebuked Churchill for writing on players and dressing like a
layman.—[6] 'Great Macpherson:' James Macpherson, translator or author of
'Ossian.'—[7] 'Malloch:' David Mallett, son of an innkeeper in Crieff, friend of
Thomson's, author of a poor life of Bacon, and of one good ballad, 'William
and Margaret,' editor of Bolingbroke's posthumous infidel works, under-
secretary to the Prince of Wales, and a pensioner.

Where, slowly winding, the dull waters creep,   141
And seem themselves to own the power of sleep ;
Where on the surface lead, like feathers, swims ;
There let me bathe my yet unhallow'd limbs,
As once a Syrian bathed in Jordan's flood—
Wash off my native stains, correct that blood
Which mutinies at call of English pride,
And, deaf to prudence, rolls a patriot tide.
    From solemn thought which overhangs the brow
Of patriot care, when things are—God knows how ;   150
From nice trim points, where Honour, slave to Rule,
In compliment to Folly, plays the fool ;
From those gay scenes, where Mirth exalts his power,
And easy Humour wings the laughing hour ;
From those soft better moments, when desire
Beats high, and all the world of man's on fire ;
When mutual ardours of the melting fair
More than repay us for whole years of care,
At Friendship's summons will my Wilkes retreat,
And see, once seen before, that ancient seat,   160
That ancient seat, where majesty display'd
Her ensigns, long before the world was made !
    Mean narrow maxims, which enslave mankind,
Ne'er from its bias warp thy settled mind :
Not duped by party, nor opinion's slave,
Those faculties which bounteous nature gave,
Thy honest spirit into practice brings,
Nor courts the smile, nor dreads the frown of kings.
Let rude licentious Englishmen comply
With tumult's voice, and curse—they know not why ; 170
Unwilling to condemn, thy soul disdains
To wear vile faction's arbitrary chains,
And strictly weighs, in apprehension clear,
Things as they are, and not as they appear.

With thee good humour tempers lively wit ;   175
Enthroned with Judgment, Candour loves to sit ;
And nature gave thee, open to distress,
A heart to pity, and a hand to bless.
    Oft have I heard thee mourn the wretched lot
Of the poor, mean, despised, insulted Scot,   180
Who, might calm reason credit idle tales,
By rancour forged where prejudice prevails,
Or starves at home, or practises, through fear
Of starving, arts which damn all conscience here.
When scribblers, to the charge by interest led,
The fierce North Briton [1] foaming at their head,
Pour forth invectives, deaf to Candour's call,
And, injured by one alien, rail at all ;
On northern Pisgah when they take their stand,
To mark the weakness of that Holy Land,   190
With needless truths their libels to adorn,
And hang a nation up to public scorn,
Thy generous soul condemns the frantic rage,
And hates the faithful, but ill-natured page.
    The Scots are poor, cries surly English pride ;
True is the charge, nor by themselves denied.
Are they not, then, in strictest reason clear,
Who wisely come to mend their fortunes here ?
If, by low supple arts successful grown,
They sapp'd our vigour to increase their own ;   200
If, mean in want, and insolent in power,
They only fawn'd more surely to devour,
Roused by such wrongs, should Reason take alarm,
And e'en the Muse for public safety arm ?
But if they own ingenuous virtue's sway,
And follow where true honour points the way,

---

[1] ' North Briton : ' the famous paper conducted by Wilkes.

If they revere the hand by which they 're fed,   207
And bless the donors for their daily bread,
Or, by vast debts of higher import bound,
Are always humble, always grateful found :
If they, directed by Paul's holy pen,
Become discreetly all things to all men,
That all men may become all things to them,
Envy may hate, but Justice can't condemn.
Into our places, states, and beds they creep ;
They 've sense to get, what we want sense to keep.
    Once—be the hour accursed, accursed the place !—
I ventured to blaspheme the chosen race.
Into those traps, which men call'd patriots laid,
By specious arts unwarily betray'd,   220
Madly I leagued against that sacred earth,
Vile parricide! which gave a parent birth :
But shall I meanly error's path pursue,
When heavenly truth presents her friendly clue ?
Once plunged in ill, shall I go farther in ?
To make the oath, was rash: to keep it, sin.
Backward I tread the paths I trod before,
And calm reflection hates what passion swore.
Converted, (blessèd are the souls which know
Those pleasures which from true conversion flow,   230
Whether to reason, who now rules my breast,
Or to pure faith, like Lyttelton and West),[1]
Past crimes to expiate, be my present aim
To raise new trophies to the Scottish name ;
To make (what can the proudest Muse do more ?)
E'en faction's sons her brighter worth adore ;

---

[1] 'Lyttelton and West:' George Lord Lyttelton, author of the history of
Henry II. and Gilbert West, the translator of Pindar, both originally sceptical,
but both converted,—the one, the author of a Dissertation on Paul's conversion ; the other, of a book on the resurrection of Christ.

To make her glories, stamp'd with honest rhymes,   237
In fullest tide roll down to latest times.
    Presumptuous wretch! and shall a Muse like
      thine,
An English Muse, the meanest of the Nine,
Attempt a theme like this?   Can her weak strain
Expect indulgence from the mighty Thane ?
Should he from toils of government retire,
And for a moment fan the poet's fire ;
Should he, of sciences the moral friend,
Each curious, each important search suspend,
Leave unassisted Hill [1] of herbs to tell,
And all the wonders of a cockleshell ;
Having the Lord's good grace before his eyes,
Would not the Home [2] step forth and gain the prize ?
Or if this wreath of honour might adorn   251
The humble brows of one in England born,
Presumptuous still thy daring must appear ;
Vain all thy towering hopes whilst I am here.
    Thus spake a form, by silken smile and tone,
Dull and unvaried, for the Laureate [3] known,
Folly's chief friend, Decorum's eldest son,
In every party found, and yet of none.
This airy substance, this substantial shade,
Abash'd I heard, and with respect obey'd.   260
    From themes too lofty for a bard so mean,
Discretion beckons to an humbler scene ;
The restless fever of ambition laid,
Calm I retire, and seek the sylvan shade.
Now be the Muse disrobed of all her pride,
Be all the glare of verse by truth supplied.

---

    [1] 'Hill,' a protégé of Lord Bute's.   See a note upon 'The Rosciad.'—
[2] 'Home:' John Home, another of Lord Bute's protégés.—[3] 'Laureate:' William
Whitehead, Laureate after C. Cibber, who had somehow provoked Churchill.

And if plain nature pours a simple strain,   267
Which Bute may praise, and Ossian not disdain,—
Ossian, sublimest, simplest bard of all,
Whom English infidels Macpherson call,—
Then round my head shall Honour's ensigns wave,
And pensions mark me for a willing slave.

   Two boys, whose birth, beyond all question, springs
From great and glorious, though forgotten, kings—
Shepherds, of Scottish lineage, born and bred
On the same bleak and barren mountain's head ;
By niggard nature doom'd on the same rocks
To spin out life, and starve themselves and flocks ;
Fresh as the morning, which, enrobed in mist,
The mountain's top with usual dulness kiss'd,   280
Jockey and Sawney to their labours rose ;
Soon clad, I ween, where nature needs no clothes ;
Where, from their youth inured to winter-skies,
Dress and her vain refinements they despise.

   Jockey, whose manly high-boned cheeks to crown,
With freckles spotted, flamed the golden down,
With meikle art could on the bagpipes play,
E'en from the rising to the setting day ;
Sawney as long without remorse could bawl
Home's madrigals, and ditties from Fingal :   290
Oft at his strains, all natural though rude,
The Highland lass forgot her want of food ;
And, whilst she scratch'd her lover into rest,
Sunk pleased, though hungry, on her Sawney's breast.

   Far as the eye could reach, no tree was seen ;
Earth, clad in russet, scorn'd the lively green :
The plague of locusts they secure defy,
For in three hours a grasshopper must die :
No living thing, whate'er its food, feasts there,
But the cameleon, who can feast on air.   300

No birds, except as birds of passage, flew ;   301
No bee was known to hum, no dove to coo :
No streams, as amber smooth, as amber clear,
Were seen to glide, or heard to warble here :
Rebellion's spring, which through the country ran,
Furnish'd, with bitter draughts, the steady clan :
No flowers embalm'd the air, but one white rose,[1]
Which on the tenth of June by instinct blows ;
By instinct blows at morn, and when the shades
Of drizzly eve prevail, by instinct fades.   310
    One, and but one poor solitary cave,
Too sparing of her favours, nature gave ;
That one alone (hard tax on Scottish pride !)
Shelter at once for man and beast supplied.
There snares without, entangling briars spread,
And thistles, arm'd against th' invader's head,
Stood in close ranks, all entrance to oppose ;
Thistles now held more precious than the rose.
All creatures which, on nature's earliest plan,
Were formed to loathe and to be loathed by man,   320
Which owed their birth to nastiness and spite,
Deadly to touch, and hateful to the sight ;
Creatures which, when admitted in the ark,
Their saviour shunn'd, and rankled in the dark,
Found place within : marking her noisome road
With poison's trail, here crawl'd the bloated toad ;
There webs were spread of more than common size,
And half-starved spiders prey'd on half-starved flies ;
In quest of food, efts strove in vain to crawl ;
Slugs, pinch'd with hunger, smear'd the slimy wall :   330
The cave around with hissing serpents rung ;
On the damp roof unhealthy vapour hung ;

---

[1] 'White rose :' The emblem of the Jacobites, a white rose, was worn by
them, in honour of the young Pretender's birthday, on the 10th of June.

And Famine, by her children always known,   333
As proud as poor, here fix'd her native throne.
  Here, for the sullen sky was overcast,
And summer shrunk beneath a wintry blast—
A native blast, which, arm'd with hail and rain,
Beat unrelenting on the naked swain,
The boys for shelter made ; behind, the sheep,
Of which those shepherds every day *take keep*,   340
Sickly crept on, and, with complainings rude,
On nature seem'd to call, and bleat for food.

JOCKEY.

  Sith to this cave by tempest we 're confined,
And within *ken* our flocks, under the wind,
Safe from the pelting of this per'lous storm,
Are laid *emong* yon thistles, dry and warm,
What, Sawney, if by shepherds' art we try
To mock the rigour of this cruel sky ?
What if we tune some merry roundelay ?
Well dost thou sing, nor ill doth Jockey play.   350

SAWNEY.

  Ah ! Jockey, ill advisest thou, *I wis*,
To think of songs at such a time as this :
Sooner shall herbage crown these barren rocks,
Sooner shall fleeces clothe these ragged flocks,
Sooner shall want seize shepherds of the south,
And we forget to live from hand to mouth,
Than Sawney, out of season, shall impart
The songs of gladness with an aching heart.

JOCKEY.

  Still have I known thee for a silly swain ;
Of things past help, what boots it to complain ?   360

Nothing but mirth can conquer fortune's spite ;   361
No sky is heavy, if the heart be light :
Patience is sorrow's salve : what can't be cured,
So Donald right areads, must be endured.

SAWNEY.

Full silly swain, *I wot*, is Jockey now. '.
How didst thou bear thy Maggy's falsehood ? How,
When with a foreign loon she stole away,
Didst thou forswear thy pipe and shepherd's lay ?
Where was thy boasted wisdom then, when I
Applied those proverbs which you now apply ?   370

JOCKEY.

Oh, she was *bonny!* All the Highlands round
Was there a rival to my Maggy found ?
More precious (though that precious is to all)
Than the rare medicine which we Brimstone call,
Or that choice plant,[1] so grateful to the nose,
Which, in I know not what far country, grows,
Was Maggy unto me : dear do I rue
A lass so fair should ever prove untrue.

SAWNEY.

Whether with pipe or song to charm the ear,
Through all the land did Jamie find a peer ?   380
Cursed be that year[2] by every honest Scot,
And in the shepherd's calendar forgot,
That fatal year when Jamie, hapless swain !
In evil hour forsook the peaceful plain :
Jamie, when our young laird discreetly fled,
Was seized, and hang'd till he was dead, dead, dead.

[1] 'Choice plant :' Tobacco. — [2] 'That year :' the year 1745.

JOCKEY.

Full sorely may we all lament that day,   387
For all were losers in the deadly fray.
Five brothers had I on the Scottish plains,
Well dost thou know were none more hopeful swains ;
Five brothers there I lost, in manhood's pride ;
Two in the field, and three on gibbets died.
Ah, silly swains ! to follow war's alarms ;
Ah ! what hath shepherds' life to do with arms ?

SAWNEY.

Mention it not—there saw I strangers clad
In all the honours of our ravish'd plaid ;
Saw the Ferrara, too, our nation's pride,
Unwilling grace the awkward victor's side.
There fell our choicest youth, and from that day
Mote never Sawney tune the merry lay ;   400
Bless'd those which fell ! cursed those which still
     survive,
To mourn Fifteen renew'd in Forty-five !

Thus plain'd the boys, when, from her throne of turf,
With boils emboss'd, and overgrown with scurf,
Vile humours which, in life's corrupted well
Mix'd at the birth, not abstinence could quell,
Pale Famine rear'd the head ; her eager eyes,
Where hunger e'en to madness seem'd to rise,
Speaking aloud her throes and pangs of heart,
Strain'd to get loose, and from their orbs to start :   410
Her hollow cheeks were each a deep-sunk cell,
Where wretchedness and horror loved to dwell ;
With double rows of useless teeth supplied,
Her mouth, from ear to ear, extended wide,

Which, when for want of food her entrails pined,   415
She oped, and, cursing, swallow'd naught but wind :
All shrivell'd was her skin ; and here and there,
Making their way by force, her bones lay bare :
Such filthy sight to hide from human view,
O'er her foul limbs a tatter'd plaid she threw.   420
    Cease, cried the goddess, cease, despairing swains !)
And from a parent hear what Jove ordains.
    Pent in this barren corner of the isle,
Where partial fortune never deign'd to smile ;
Like nature's bastards, reaping for our share
What was rejected by the lawful heir ;
Unknown amongst the nations of the earth,
Or only known to raise contempt and mirth ;
Long free, because the race of Roman braves
Thought it not worth their while to make us slaves ; 430
Then into bondage by that nation brought,
Whose ruin we for ages vainly sought ;
Whom still with unslaked hate we view, and still,
The power of mischief lost, retain the will ;
Consider'd as the refuse of mankind,
A mass till the last moment left behind,
Which frugal nature doubted, as it lay,
Whether to stamp with life or throw away ;
Which, form'd in haste, was planted in this nook,
But never enter'd in Creation's book ;   440
Branded as traitors who, for love of gold,
Would sell their God, as once their king they sold,—
Long have we borne this mighty weight of ill,
These vile injurious taunts, and bear them still.
But times of happier note are now at hand,
And the full promise of a better land :
There, like the sons of Israel, having trod,
For the fix'd term of years ordain'd by God,

A barren desert, we shall seize rich plains,   449
Where milk with honey flows, and plenty reigns :
With some few natives join'd, some pliant few,
Who worship Interest and our track pursue ;
There shall we, though the wretched people grieve,
Ravage at large, nor ask the owners' leave.
    For us, the earth shall bring forth her increase ;
For us, the flocks shall wear a golden fleece ;
Fat beeves shall yield us dainties not our own,
And the grape bleed a nectar yet unknown :
For our advantage shall their harvests grow,
And Scotsmen reap what they disdain'd to sow :   460
For us, the sun shall climb the eastern hill ;
For us, the rain shall fall, the dew distil.
When to our wishes Nature cannot rise,
Art shall be task'd to grant us fresh supplies ;
His brawny arm shall drudging Labour strain,
And for our pleasure suffer daily pain :
Trade shall for us exert her utmost powers,
Hers all the toil, and all the profit ours :
For us, the oak shall from his native steep
Descend, and fearless travel through the deep :   470
The sail of commerce, for our use unfurl'd,
Shall waft the treasures of each distant world :
For us, sublimer heights shall science reach ;
For us, their statesman plot, their churchmen preach :
Their noblest limbs of council we 'll disjoint,
And, mocking, new ones of our own appoint.
Devouring War, imprison'd in the North,
Shall, at our call, in horrid pomp break forth,
And when, his chariot-wheels with thunder hung,
Fell Discord braying with her brazen tongue,   480
Death in the van, with Anger, Hate, and Fear,
And Desolation stalking in the rear,

Revenge, by Justice guided, in his train,   483
He drives impetuous o'er the trembling plain,
Shall, at our bidding, quit his lawful prey,
And to meek, gentle, generous Peace give way.
　　Think not, my sons, that this so bless'd estate
Stands at a distance on the roll of fate ;
Already big with hopes of future sway,
E'en from this cave I scent my destined prey.   490
Think not that this dominion o'er a race,
Whose former deeds shall time's last annals grace,
In the rough face of peril must be sought,
And with the lives of thousands dearly bought :
No—fool'd by cunning, by that happy art
Which laughs to scorn the blundering hero's heart,
Into the snare shall our kind neighbours fall
With open eyes, and fondly give us all.
　　When Rome, to prop her sinking empire, bore
Their choicest levies to a foreign shore,   500
What if we seized, like a destroying flood,
Their widow'd plains, and fill'd the realm with blood ;
Gave an unbounded loose to manly rage,
And, scorning mercy, spared nor sex, nor age ?
When, for our interest too mighty grown,
Monarchs of warlike bent possessed the throne,
What if we strove divisions to foment,
And spread the flames of civil discontent,
Assisted those who 'gainst their king made head,
And gave the traitors refuge when they fled ?   510
When restless Glory bade her sons advance,
And pitch'd her standard in the fields of France,
What if, disdaining oaths,—an empty sound,
By which our nation never shall be bound,—
Bravely we taught unmuzzled War to roam,
Through the weak land, and brought cheap laurels home ?

When the bold traitors, leagued for the defence   517
Of law, religion, liberty, and sense,
When they against their lawful monarch rose,
And dared the Lord's anointed to oppose,
What if we still revered the banish'd race,
And strove the royal vagrants to replace;
With fierce rebellions shook th' unsettled state,
And greatly dared, though cross'd by partial fate?
These facts, which might, where wisdom held the sway,
Awake the very stones to bar our way,
There shall be nothing, nor one trace remain
In the dull region of an English brain;
Bless'd with that faith which mountains can remove,
First they shall dupes, next saints, last martyrs, prove.

    Already is this game of Fate begun   531
Under the sanction of my darling son;[1]
That son, of nature royal as his name,
Is destined to redeem our race from shame:
His boundless power, beyond example great,
Shall make the rough way smooth, the crooked straight;
Shall for our ease the raging floods restrain,
And sink the mountain level to the plain.
Discord, whom in a cavern under ground
With massy fetters their late patriot bound;   540
Where her own flesh the furious hag might tear,
And vent her curses to the vacant air;
Where, that she never might be heard of more,
He planted Loyalty to guard the door,
For better purpose shall our chief release,
Disguise her for a time, and call her Peace.[2]

    Lured by that name—fine engine of deceit!—
Shall the weak English help themselves to cheat;

---

1 'Darling son:' Bute. —2 'Peace:' that of 1763, abused by all the Opposition.

To gain our love, with honours shall they grace   549
The old adherents of the Stuart race,
Who, pointed out no matter by what name,
Tories or Jacobites, are still the same ;
To soothe our rage the temporising brood
Shall break the ties of truth and gratitude,
Against their saviour venom'd falsehoods frame,
And brand with calumny their William's name :
To win our grace, (rare argument of wit!)
To our untainted faith shall they commit
(Our faith, which, in extremest perils tried,
Disdain'd, and still disdains, to change her side)   560
That sacred Majesty they all approve,
Who most enjoys, and best deserves their love.

AN EPISTLE TO WILLIAM HOGARTH.[1]

AMONGST the sons of men how few are known
Who dare be just to merit not their own !
Superior virtue and superior sense,
To knaves and fools, will always give offence ;
Nay, men of real worth can scarcely bear,
So nice is jealousy, a rival there.
    Be wicked as thou wilt ; do all that's base ;
Proclaim thyself the monster of thy race :
Let vice and folly thy black soul divide ;
Be proud with meanness, and be mean with pride.   10
Deaf to the voice of Faith and Honour, fall
From side to side, yet be of none at all :

---

[1] For occasion of this poem, see Life.

Spurn all those charities, those sacred ties,   13
Which Nature, in her bounty, good as wise,
To work our safety, and ensure her plan,
Contrived to bind and rivet man to man :
Lift against Virtue, Power's oppressive rod ;
Betray thy country, and deny thy God ;.
And, in one general comprehensive line,
To group, which volumes scarcely could define,   20
Whate'er of sin and dulness can be said,
Join to a Fox's[1] heart a Dashwood's[2] head ;
Yet may'st thou pass unnoticed in the throng,
And, free from envy, safely sneak along :
The rigid saint, by whom no mercy's shown
To saints whose lives are better than his own,
Shall spare thy crimes ; and Wit, who never once
Forgave a brother, shall forgive a dunce.
    But should thy soul, form'd in some luckless hour,
Vile interest scorn, nor madly grasp at power ;   30
Should love of fame, in every noble mind
A brave disease, with love of virtue join'd,
Spur thee to deeds of pith, where courage, tried
In Reason's court, is amply justified :
Or, fond of knowledge, and averse to strife,
Shouldst thou prefer the calmer walk of life ;
Shouldst thou, by pale and sickly study led,
Pursue coy Science to the fountain-head ;
Virtue thy guide, and public good thy end,
Should every thought to our improvement tend,   40
To curb the passions, to enlarge the mind,
Purge the sick Weal, and humanise mankind ;
Rage in her eye, and malice in her breast,
Redoubled Horror grining on her crest,

[1] 'Fox:' Henry Fox, afterwards Lord Holland, supposed not to be over-honest. — [2] 'Dashwood:' Sir Francis Dashwood, generally thought a bigoted and stupid Tory.

Fiercer each snake, and sharper every dart,   45
Quick from her cell shall maddening Envy start.
Then shalt thou find, but find, alas! too late,
How vain is worth! how short is glory's date!
Then shalt thou find, whilst friends with foes conspire,
To give more proof than virtue would desire,   50
Thy danger chiefly lies in acting well;
No crime's so great as daring to excel.

    Whilst Satire thus, disdaining mean control,
Urged the free dictates of an honest soul,
Candour, who, with the charity of Paul,
Still thinks the best, whene'er she thinks at all,
With the sweet milk of human kindness bless'd,
The furious ardour of my zeal repress'd.

    Canst thou, with more than usual warmth she cried,
Thy malice to indulge, and feed thy pride;   60
Canst thou, severe by nature as thou art,
With all that wondrous rancour in thy heart,
Delight to torture truth ten thousand ways,
To spin detraction forth from themes of praise,
To make Vice sit, for purposes of strife,
And draw the hag much larger than the life,
To make the good seem bad, the bad seem worse,
And represent our nature as our curse?

    Doth not humanity condemn that zeal
Which tends to aggravate and not to heal?   70
Doth not discretion warn thee of disgrace,
And danger, grinning, stare thee in the face,
Loud as the drum, which, spreading terror round,
From emptiness acquires the power of sound?
Doth not the voice of Norton[1] strike thy ear,
And the pale Mansfield[2] chill thy soul with fear?

    [1] 'Norton:' Sir Fletcher Norton, Attorney-General from 1763 to 1765,
created a peer in 1782 by the title of Lord Grantley. — [2] 'Mansfield:' the
celebrated Murray, Lord Mansfield. See Junius.

Dost thou, fond man, believe thyself secure   77
Because thou 'rt honest, and because thou 'rt poor ?
Dost thou on law and liberty depend ?
Turn, turn thy eyes, and view thy injured friend.
Art thou beyond the ruffian gripe of Power,
When Wilkes, prejudged, is sentenced to the Tower ?
Dost thou by privilege exemption claim,
When privilege is little more than name ?
Or to prerogative (that glorious ground
On which state scoundrels oft have safety found)
Dost thou pretend, and there a sanction find,
Unpunish'd, thus to libel human-kind ?
    When poverty, the poet's constant crime,
Compell'd thee, all unfit, to trade in rhyme,   90
Had not romantic notions turn'd thy head,
Hadst thou not valued honour more than bread ;
Had Interest, pliant Interest, been thy guide,
And had not Prudence been debauch'd by Pride,
In Flattery's stream thou wouldst have dipp'd thy pen,
Applied to great and not to honest men ;
Nor should conviction have seduced thy heart
To take the weaker, though the better part.
    What but rank folly, for thy curse decreed,
Could into Satire's barren path mislead,   100
When, open to thy view, before thee lay
Soul-soothing Panegyric's flowery way ?
There might the Muse have saunter'd at her ease,
And, pleasing others, learn'd herself to please ;
Lords should have listen'd to the sugar'd treat,
And ladies, simp'ring, own'd it vastly sweet ;
Rogues, in thy prudent verse with virtue graced,
Fools mark'd by thee as prodigies of taste,
Must have forbid, pouring preferments down,
Such wit, such truth as thine to quit the gown.   110

Thy sacred brethren, too, (for they, no less   111
Than laymen, bring their offerings to success)
Had hail'd thee good if great, and paid the vow
Sincere as that they pay to God, whilst thou
In lawn hadst whisper'd to a sleeping crowd,
As dull as Rochester,[1] and half as proud.
    Peace, Candour—wisely hadst thou said, and
        well,
Could Interest in this breast one moment dwell ;
Could she, with prospect of success, oppose
The firm resolves which from conviction rose.   120
I cannot truckle to a fool of state,
Nor take a favour from the man I hate :
Free leave have others by such means to shine ;
I scorn their practice ; they may laugh at mine.
   But in this charge, forgetful of thyself,
Thou hast assumed the maxims of that elf,
Whom God in wrath, for man's dishonour framed,
Cunning in heaven, amongst us Prudence named,
That servile prudence, which I leave to those
Who dare not be my friends, can't be my foes.   130
    Had I, with cruel and oppressive rhymes,
Pursued and turn'd misfortunes into crimes ;
Had I, when Virtue gasping lay and low,
Join'd tyrant Vice, and added woe to woe ;
Had I made Modesty in blushes speak,
And drawn the tear down Beauty's sacred cheek ;
Had I (damn'd then) in thought debased my lays,
To wound that sex which honour bids me praise ;
Had I, from vengeance, by base views betray'd,
In endless night sunk injured Ayliffe's [2] shade ;   140

    [1] 'Rochester :' Pearce, Bishop of Rochester, mentioned above as a foe to
Churchill.—[2] 'Ayliffe :' a forger of the period, said to have been ill-used
by Lord Holland. Churchill intended to write a poem, entitled, ' Ayliffe's
Ghost,' but did not live to accomplish his intention.

Had I (which satirists of mighty name,[1]   141
Renown'd in rhyme, revered for moral fame,
Have done before, whom Justice shall pursue
In future verse) brought forth to public view
A noble friend, and made his foibles known,
Because his worth was greater than my own ;
Had I spared those (so Prudence had decreed)
Whom, God so help me at my greatest need !
I ne'er will spare, those vipers to their king
Who smooth their looks, and flatter whilst they   150
    sting ;
Or had I not taught patriot zeal to boast
Of those who flatter least, but love him most ;
Had I thus sinn'd, my stubborn soul should bend
At Candour's voice, and take, as from a friend
The deep rebuke ; myself should be the first
To hate myself, and stamp my Muse accursed.
    But shall my arm—forbid it, manly pride !
Forbid it, reason ! warring on my side—
For vengeance lifted high, the stroke forbear,
And hang suspended in the desert air,   160
Or to my trembling side unnerved sink down,
Palsied, forsooth, by Candour's half-made frown ?
When Justice bids me on, shall I delay
Because insipid Candour bars my way ?
When she, of all alike the puling friend,
Would disappoint my satire's noblest end ;
When she to villains would a sanction give,
And shelter those who are not fit to live ;
When she would screen the guilty from a blush,
And bids me spare whom Reason bids me crush,   170
All leagues with Candour proudly I resign ;
She cannot be for Honour's turn, nor mine.

[1] ' Mighty name : ' Pope, referring to his famous attack on Addison.

Yet come, cold Monitor! half foe, half friend,   178
Whom Vice can't fear, whom Virtue can't commend;
Come, Candour, by thy dull indifference known,
Thou equal-blooded judge, thou lukewarm drone,
Who, fashion'd without feelings, dost expect
We call that virtue which we know defect;
Come, and observe the nature of our crimes,
The gross and rank complexion of the times;   180
Observe it well, and then review my plan,
Praise if you will, or censure if you can.

    Whilst Vice presumptuous lords it as in sport,
And Piety is only known at court;
Whilst wretched Liberty expiring lies,
Beneath the fatal burthen of Excise;
Whilst nobles act, without one touch of shame,
What men of humble rank would blush to name;
Whilst Honour's placed in highest point of view,
Worshipp'd by those who Justice never knew;   190
Whilst bubbles of distinction waste in play
The hours of rest, and blunder through the day;
With dice and cards opprobrious vigils keep,
Then turn to ruin empires in their sleep;
Whilst fathers,[1] by relentless passion led,
Doom worthy injured sons to beg their bread,
Merely with ill-got, ill-saved, wealth to grace,
An alien, abject, poor, proud, upstart race!
Whilst Martin[2] flatters only to betray,
And Webb[3] gives up his dirty soul for pay,   200
Whilst titles serve to hush a villain's fears;
Whilst peers are agents made, and agents peers;

---

[1] 'Fathers:' Thomas Potter, Esq., a man of splendid abilities, was disinherited by his father, the Archbishop of Canterbury, on account of his dissolute life. — [2] 'Martin:' Samuel Martin, Esq., F.R.S., M.P. for Camelford; the hero of 'The Duellist.' — [3] 'Webb:' Philip Carteret Webb, Esq., Solicitor to the Treasury.

Whilst base betrayers are themselves betray'd,   203
And makers ruin'd by the thing they made ;
Whilst C——,[1] false to God and man, for gold,
Like the old traitor who a Saviour sold,
To shame his master, friend, and father gives ;
Whilst Bute remains in power, whilst Holland lives ;—
Can Satire want a subject, where Disdain,
By Virtue fired, may point her sharpest strain,   210
Where, clothed with thunder, Truth may roll along,
And Candour justify the rage of song ?
    Such things ! such men before thee ! such an
      age !
Where Rancour, great as thine, may glut her rage,
And sicken e'en to surfeit ; where the pride
Of Satire, pouring down in fullest tide,
May spread wide vengeance round, yet all the while
Justice behold the ruin with a smile ;
Whilst I, thy foe misdeem'd, cannot condemn,
Nor disapprove that rage I wish to stem,   220
Wilt thou, degenerate and corrupted, choose
To soil the credit of thy haughty Muse ?
With fallacy, most infamous, to stain
Her truth, and render all her anger vain ?
When I beheld thee, incorrect, but bold,
A various comment on the stage unfold ;
When players on players before thy satire fell,
And poor Reviews conspired thy wrath to swell ;
When states and statesmen next became thy care,
And only kings were safe if thou wast there,   230
Thy every word I weigh'd in judgment's scale,
And in thy every word found truth prevail ;
Why dost thou now to falsehood meanly fly ?
Not even Candour can forgive a lie.

    [1] ' C—— : ' name not known.

Bad as men are, why should thy frantic rhymes   235
Traffic in slander, and invent new crimes?—
Crimes which, existing only in thy mind,
Weak spleen brings forth to blacken all mankind.
By pleasing hopes we lure the human heart
To practise virtue and improve in art;   240
To thwart these ends (which, proud of honest fame,
A noble Muse would cherish and inflame)
Thy drudge contrives,—and in our full career
Sicklies our hopes with the pale hue of fear;
Tells us that all our labours are in vain;
That what we seek, we never can obtain;
That, dead to virtue, lost to Nature's plan,
Envy possesses the whole race of man;
That worth is criminal, and danger lies,
Danger extreme, in being good and wise.   250
 'Tis a rank falsehood; search the world around,
There cannot be so vile a monster found,
Not one so vile, on whom suspicions fall
Of that gross guilt which you impute to all.
Approved by those who disobey her laws,
Virtue from Vice itself extorts applause:
Her very foes bear witness to her state;
They will not love her, but they cannot hate.
Hate Virtue for herself! with spite pursue
Merit for Merit's sake! might this be true,
I would renounce my nature with disdain,   260
And with the beasts that perish graze the plain;
Might this be true,—had we so far fill'd up
The measure of our crimes, and from the cup
Of guilt so deeply drank, as not to find,
Thirsting for sin, one drop, one dreg behind;
Quick ruin must involve this flaming ball,
And Providence in justice crush us all.

None but the damn'd, and amongst them the worst, 269
Those who for double guilt are doubly cursed,
Can be so lost; nor can the worst of all
At once into such deep damnation fall;
By painful slow degrees they reach this crime,
Which e'en in hell must be a work of time.
Cease, then, thy guilty rage, thou wayward son,
With the foul gall of Discontent o'errun;
List to my voice,—be honest, if you can,
Nor slander Nature in her favourite, man.
But if thy spirit, resolute in ill,
Once having err'd, persists in error still,   280
Go on at large, no longer worth my care,
And freely vent those blasphemies in air,
Which I would stamp as false, though on the tongue
Of angels the injurious slander hung.
    Duped by thy vanity (that cunning elf
Who snares the coxcomb to deceive himself),
Or blinded by thy rage, didst thou believe
That we too, coolly, would ourselves deceive?
That we, as sterling, falsehood would admit,
Because 'twas season'd with some little wit?   290
When fiction rises pleasing to the eye,
Men will believe, because they love the lie;
But Truth herself, if clouded with a frown,
Must have some solemn proof to pass her down.
Hast thou, maintaining that which must disgrace
And bring into contempt the human race,
Hast thou, or canst thou, in Truth's sacred court,
To save thy credit, and thy cause support,
Produce one proof, make out one real ground,
On which so great, so gross a charge to found?   300
Nay, dost thou know one man (let that appear,
From wilful falsehood I'll proclaim thee clear),

One man so lost, to nature so untrue,   303
From whom this general charge thy rashness drew ?
On this foundation shalt thou stand or' fall—
Prove that in one which you have charged on all.
Reason determines, and it must be done ;
'Mongst men, or past, or present, name me one.
    Hogarth,—I take thee, Candour, at thy word,
Accept thy proffer'd terms, and will be heard ;   310
Thee have I heard with virulence declaim,
Nothing retain'd of Candour but the name ;
By thee have I been charged in angry strains
With that mean falsehood which my soul disdains—
Hogarth, stand forth ;—Nay, hang not thus aloof—
Now, Candour, now thou shalt receive such proof,
Such damning proof, that henceforth thou shalt fear
To tax my wrath, and own my conduct clear ;—
Hogarth, stand forth—I dare thee to be tried
In that great court where Conscience must preside ; 320
At that most solemn bar hold up thy hand ;
Think before whom, on what account, you stand ;
Speak, but consider well ;—from first to last
Review thy life, weigh every action past ;
Nay, you shall have no reason to complain—
Take longer time, and view them o'er again.
Canst thou remember from thy earliest youth,
And as thy God must judge thee, speak the truth,
A single instance where, self laid aside,
And Justice taking place of Fear and Pride,   330
Thou with an equal eye didst Genius view,
And give to Merit what was Merit's due ?
Genius and Merit are a sure offence,
And thy soul sickens at the name of sense.
Is any one so foolish to succeed ?
On Envy's altar he is doom'd to bleed.

Hogarth, a guilty pleasure in his eyes,   337
The place of executioner supplies :
See how he gloats, enjoys the sacred feast,
And proves himself by cruelty a priest !
  Whilst the weak artist, to thy whims a slave,
Would bury all those powers which Nature gave ;
Would suffer blank concealment to obscure
Those rays thy jealousy could not endure ;
To feed thy vanity would rust unknown,
And to secure thy credit, blast his own,
In Hogarth he was sure to find a friend ;
He could not fear, and therefore might commend.
But when his spirit, roused by honest shame,
Shook off that lethargy, and soar'd to fame ;   350
When, with the pride of man, resolved and strong,
He scorn'd those fears which did his honour wrong,
And, on himself determined to rely,
Brought forth his labours to the public eye,
No friend in thee could such a rebel know ;
He had desert, and Hogarth was his foe.
  Souls of a timorous cast, of petty name
In Envy's court, not yet quite dead to shame,
May some remorse, some qualms of conscience feel,
And suffer honour to abate their zeal ;   360
But the man truly and completely great,
Allows no rule of action but his hate ;
Through every bar he bravely breaks his way,
Passion his principle, and parts his prey.
Mediums in vice and virtue speak a mind
Within the pale of temperance confined ;
The daring spirit scorns her narrow schemes,
And, good or bad, is always in extremes.
  Man's practice duly weigh'd, through every age
On the same plan hath Envy form'd her rage,   370

'Gainst those whom fortune hath our rivals made,   371
In way of science, and in way of trade :
Stung with mean jealousy she arms her spite,
First works, then views their ruin with delight.
Our Hogarth here a grand improver shines,
And nobly on the general plan refines ;
He like himself o'erleaps the servile bound ;
Worth is his mark, wherever worth is found.
Should painters only his vast wrath suffice ?
Genius in every walk is lawful prize :   380
'Tis a gross insult to his o'ergrown state ;
His love to merit is to feel his hate.
    When Wilkes, our countryman, our common friend,
Arose, his king, his country to defend ;
When tools of power he bared to public view,
And from their holes the sneaking cowards drew ;
When Rancour found it far beyond her reach
To soil his honour, and his truth impeach ;
What could induce thee, at a time and place
Where manly foes had blush'd to show their face,   390
To make that effort which must damn thy name,
And sink thee deep, deep in thy grave with shame ?
Did virtue move thee ?   No ; 'twas pride, rank pride,
And if thou hadst not done it, thou hadst died.
Malice (who, disappointed of her end,
Whether to work the bane of foe or friend,
Preys on herself, and, driven to the stake,
Gives Virtue that revenge she scorns to take)
Had kill'd thee, tottering on life's utmost verge,
Had Wilkes and Liberty escaped thy scourge.   400
    When that Great Charter, which our fathers bought
With their best blood, was into question brought ;
When, big with ruin, o'er each English head
Vile Slavery hung suspended by a thread ;

When Liberty, all trembling and aghast,   405
Fear'd for the future, knowing what was past ;
When every breast was chill'd with deep despair,
Till Reason pointed out that Pratt[1] was there ;—
Lurking, most ruffian-like, behind the screen,
So placed all things to see, himself unseen,   410
Virtue, with due contempt, saw Hogarth stand,
The murderous pencil in his palsied hand.
What was the cause of Liberty to him,
Or what was Honour ? let them sink or swim,
So he may gratify, without control,
The mean resentments of his selfish soul ;
Let Freedom perish, if, to Freedom true,
In the same ruin Wilkes may perish too.
    With all the symptoms of assured decay,
With age and sickness pinch'd and worn away,   420
Pale quivering lips, lank cheeks, and faltering tongue,
The spirits out of tune, the nerves unstrung,
Thy body shrivell'd up, thy dim eyes sunk
Within their sockets deep, thy weak hams shrunk,
The body's weight unable to sustain,
The stream of life scarce trembling through the vein,
More than half kill'd by honest truths which fell,
Through thy own fault, from men who wish'd thee well—
Canst thou, e'en thus, thy thoughts to vengeance give,
And, dead to all things else, to malice live ?   430
Hence, dotard, to thy closet ; shut thee in ;
By deep repentance wash away thy sin ;
From haunts of men to shame and sorrow fly,
And, on the verge of death, learn how to die !
    Vain exhortation ! wash the Ethiop white,
Discharge the leopard's spots, turn day to night,

[1] 'Pratt:' Charles Pratt, Earl Camden, Chief-Justice of the Common Pleas, friendly to Wilkes. See Junius.

Control the course of Nature, bid the deep   437
Hush at thy pigmy voice her waves to sleep—
Perform things passing strange, yet own thy art
Too weak to work a change in such a heart;
That Envy, which was woven in the frame
At first, will to the last remain the same.
Reason may droop, may die; but Envy's rage
Improves by time, and gathers strength from age.
Some, and not few, vain triflers with the pen,
Unread, unpractised in the ways of men,
Tell us that Envy, who, with giant stride,
Stalks through the vale of life by Virtue's side,
Retreats when she hath drawn her latest breath,
And calmly hears her praises after death.   450
To such observers Hogarth gives the lie;
Worth may be hearsed, but Envy cannot die;
Within the mansion of his gloomy breast,
A mansion suited well to such a guest,
Immortal, unimpair'd, she rears her head,
And damns alike the living and the dead.
    Oft have I known thee, Hogarth, weak and vain,
Thyself the idol of thy awkward strain,
Through the dull measure of a summer's day,
In phrase most vile, prate long, long hours away,   460
Whilst friends with friends, all gaping sit, and gaze,
To hear a Hogarth babble Hogarth's praise.
But if athwart thee Interruption came,
And mention'd with respect some ancient's name,
Some ancient's name who, in the days of yore,
The crown of Art with greatest honour wore,
How have I seen thy coward cheek turn pale,
And blank confusion seize thy mangled tale!
How hath thy jealousy to madness grown,
And deem'd his praise injurious to thy own!   470

Then without mercy did thy wrath make way,   471
And arts and artists all became thy prey ;
Then didst thou trample on establish'd rules,
And proudly levell'd all the ancient schools ;
Condemn'd those works, with praise through ages graced,
Which you had never seen, or could not taste ;
But would mankind have true perfection shown,
It must be found in labours of my own :
I dare to challenge, in one single piece,
Th' united force of Italy and Greece.   480
Thy eager hand the curtain then undrew,
And brought the boasted masterpiece to view.
Spare thy remarks—say not a single word—
The picture seen, why is the painter heard ?
Call not up shame and anger in our cheeks ;
Without a comment Sigismunda[1] speaks.

    Poor Sigismunda ! what a fate is thine !
Dryden, the great high-priest of all the Nine,
Revived thy name, gave what a Muse could give,
And in his numbers bade thy memory live ;   490
Gave thee those soft sensations which might move
And warm the coldest anchorite to love ;
Gave thee that virtue, which could curb desire,
Refine and consecrate love's headstrong fire ;
Gave thee those griefs, which made the Stoic feel,
And call'd compassion forth from hearts of steel ;
Gave thee that firmness, which our sex may shame,
And make man bow to woman's juster claim ;
So that our tears, which from compassion flow,
Seem to debase thy dignity of woe.   500
But, oh, how much unlike ! how fall'n ! how changed !
How much from Nature and herself estranged !

---

[1] ' Sigismunda : ' a detestable miscreation of Hogarth's pencil, admired by none but himself.

How totally deprived of all the powers   503
To show her feelings, and awaken ours,
Doth Sigismunda now devoted stand,
The helpless victim of a dauber's hand!
     But why, my Hogarth, such a progress made,
So rare a pattern for the sign-post trade,
In the full force and whirlwind of thy pride,
Why was heroic painting laid aside?   510
Why is it not resumed? thy friends at court,
Men all in place and power, crave thy support;
Be grateful then for once, and through the field
Of politics thy epic pencil wield;
Maintain the cause, which they, good lack! avow,
And would maintain too, but they know not how.
Through every pannel let thy virtue tell
How Bute prevail'd, how Pitt and Temple fell;
How England's sons (whom they conspired to bless,
Against our will, with insolent success)   520
Approve their fall, and with addresses run—
How got, God knows—to hail the Scottish sun; [1]
Point out our fame in war, when vengeance, hurl'd
From the strong arm of Justice, shook the world;
Thine, and thy country's honour to increase,
Point out the honours of succeeding peace;
Our moderation, Christian-like, display,
Show what we got, and what we gave away;
In colours, dull and heavy as the tale,
Let a state-chaos through the whole prevail.   530
     But, of events regardless, whilst the Muse,
Perhaps with too much heat, her theme pursues;
Whilst her quick spirits rouse at Freedom's call,
And every drop of blood is turn'd to gall;

[1] 'The Scottish sun:' The addresses to the King which followed the parliamentary approbation of the preliminary articles of peace in 1763, were obtained by means equally dishonourable and corrupt.

Whilst a dear country, and an injured friend,　　535
Urge my strong anger to the bitterest end ;
Whilst honest trophies to Revenge are raised,
Let not one real virtue pass unpraised ;
Justice with equal course bids Satire flow,
And loves the virtue of her greatest foe.　　540
　　Oh! that I here could that rare virtue mean,
Which scorns the rule of envy, pride, and spleen,
Which springs not from the labour'd works of art,
But hath its rise from Nature in the heart ;
Which in itself with happiness is crown'd,
And spreads with joy the blessing all around!
But truth forbids, and in these simple lays,
Contented with a different kind of praise,
Must Hogarth stand; that praise which Genius gives,
In which to latest time the artist lives,　　550
But not the man ; which, rightly understood,
May make us great, but cannot make us good :
That praise be Hogarth's ; freely let him wear
The wreath which Genius wove, and planted there :
Foe as I am, should Envy tear it down,
Myself would labour to replace the crown.
　　In walks of humour, in that cast of style,
Which, probing to the quick, yet makes us smile ;
In comedy, his natural road to fame,—
Nor let me call it by a meaner name,　　560
Where a beginning, middle, and an end,
Are aptly join'd ; where parts on parts depend,
Each made for each, as bodies for their soul,
So as to form one true and perfect whole ;
Where a plain story to the eye is told,
Which we conceive the moment we behold,—
Hogarth unrivall'd stands, and shall engage
Unrivall'd praise to the most distant age.

G

How couldst thou, then, to shame perversely run,   569
And tread that path which Nature bade thee shun ?
Why did ambition overleap her rules,
And thy vast parts become the sport of fools ?
By different methods different men excel ;
But where is he who can do all things well ?
Humour thy province, for some monstrous crime
Pride struck thee with the frenzy of sublime ;
But, when the work was finish'd, could thy mind
So partial be, and to herself so blind,
What with contempt all view'd, to view with awe,
Nor see those faults which every blockhead saw ?   580
Blush, thou vain man ! and if desire of fame,
Founded on real art, thy thoughts inflame,
To quick destruction Sigismunda give,
And let her memory die, that thine may live.
But should fond Candour, for her mercy sake,
With pity view, and pardon this mistake ;
Or should Oblivion, to thy wish most kind,
Wipe off that stain, nor leave one trace behind ;
Of arts despised, of artists, by thy frown
Awed from just hopes, of rising worth kept down,   590
Of all thy meanness through this mortal race,
Canst thou the living memory erase ?
Or shall not vengeance follow to the grave,
And give back just that measure which you gave ?
With so much merit, and so much success,
With so much power to curse, so much to bless,
Would he have been man's friend, instead of foe,
Hogarth had been a little god below.
Why, then, like savage giants, famed of old,
Of whom in Scripture story we are told,   600
Dost thou in cruelty that strength employ,
Which Nature meant to save, not to destroy ?

Why dost thou, all in horrid pomp array'd,   603
Sit grinning o'er the ruins thou hast made?
Most rank ill-nature must applaud thy art,
But even Candour must condemn thy heart.
    For me, who, warm and zealous for my friend,
In spite of railing thousands, will commend;
And no less warm and zealous 'gainst my foes,
Spite of commending thousands, will oppose,   610
I dare thy worst, with scorn behold thy rage,
But with an eye of pity view thy age;
Thy feeble age, in which, as in a glass,
We see how men to dissolution pass.
Thou wretched being, whom, on Reason's plan,
So changed, so lost, I cannot call a man,
What could persuade thee, at this time of life,
To launch afresh into the sea of strife?
Better for thee, scarce crawling on the earth,
Almost as much a child as at thy birth,   620
To have resign'd in peace thy parting breath,
And sunk unnoticed in the arms of Death.
Why would thy gray, gray hairs resentment brave,
Thus to go down with sorrow to the grave?
Now, by my soul! it makes me blush to know,
My spirit could descend to such a foe:
Whatever cause the vengeance might provoke,
It seems rank cowardice to give the stroke.
    Sure 'tis a curse which angry fates impose,
To mortify man's arrogance, that those   630
Who're fashion'd of some better sort of clay,
Much sooner than the common herd decay.
What bitter pangs must humbled Genius feel,
In their last hours to view a Swift and Steele!
How must ill-boding horrors fill her breast,
When she beholds men mark'd above the rest

For qualities most dear, plunged from that height,   637
And sunk, deep sunk, in second childhood's night!
Are men, indeed, such things? and are the best
More subject to this evil than the rest,
To drivel out whole years of idiot breath,
And sit the monuments of living death?
Oh, galling circumstance to human pride!
Abasing thought, but not to be denied!
With curious art the brain, too finely wrought,
Preys on herself, and is destroy'd by thought.
Constant attention wears the active mind,
Blots out her powers, and leaves a blank behind.
But let not youth, to insolence allied,
In heat of blood, in full career of pride,   . 650
Possess'd of genius, with unhallow'd rage
Mock the infirmities of rev'rend age:
The greatest genius to this fate may bow;
Reynolds, in time, may be like Hogarth now.

THE DUELLIST.[1]

IN THREE BOOKS.

BOOK I.

THE clock struck twelve; o'er half the globe
Darkness had spread her pitchy robe:
Morpheus, his feet with velvet shod,
Treading as if in fear he trod,

---

[1] 'The Duellist:' the *North Briton* had fiercely assailed Mr Martin, M.P. for Camelford, who, on the first day of the next session of Parliament, complained of it; Mr Wilkes owned himself the author, and the result was a duel in Hyde Park, in which Wilkes was severely wounded. He always owned that Martin acted honourably in the rencontre, but not so thought Churchill.

Gentle as dews at even-tide,   5
Distill'd his poppies far and wide.
  Ambition, who, when waking, dreams
Of mighty, but fantastic schemes,
Who, when asleep, ne'er knows that rest
With which the humbler soul is blest,   10
Was building castles in the air,
Goodly to look upon, and fair,
But on a bad foundation laid,
Doom'd at return of morn to fade.
  Pale Study, by the taper's light,
Wearing away the watch of night,
Sat reading ; but, with o'ercharged head,
Remember'd nothing that he read.
  Starving 'midst plenty, with a face
Which might the court of Famine grace,   20
Ragged, and filthy to behold,
Gray Avarice nodded o'er his gold.
  Jealousy, his quick eye half-closed,
With watchings worn, reluctant dozed ;
And, mean Distrust not quite forgot,
Slumber'd as if he slumber'd not.
  Stretch'd at his length on the bare ground,
His hardy offspring sleeping round,
Snored restless Labour ; by his side
Lay Health, a coarse but comely bride.   30
  Virtue, without the doctor's aid,
In the soft arms of Sleep was laid ;
Whilst Vice, within the guilty breast,
Could not be physic'd into rest.
  Thou bloody man ! whose ruffian knife
Is drawn against thy neighbour's life,
And never scruples to descend
Into the bosom of a friend ;

A firm, fast friend, by vice allied,   59
And to thy secret service tied,
In whom ten murders breed no awe,
If properly secured from law :
Thou man of lust! whom passion fires
To foulest deeds, whose hot desires
O'er honest bars with ease make way,
Whilst idiot beauty falls a prey,
And to indulge thy brutal flame
A Lucrece must be brought to shame ;
Who dost, a brave, bold sinner, bear
Rank incest to the open air,   50
And rapes, full blown upon thy crown,
Enough to weigh a nation down :
Thou simular of lust! vain man,
Whose restless thoughts still form the plan
Of guilt, which, wither'd to the root,
Thy lifeless nerves can't execute,
Whilst in thy marrowless, dry bones
Desire without enjoyment groans :
Thou perjured wretch! whom falsehood clothes
E'en like a garment ; who with oaths   60
Dost trifle, as with brokers, meant
To serve thy every vile intent,
In the day's broad and searching eye,
Making God witness to a lie,
Blaspheming heaven and earth for pelf,
And hanging friends[1] to save thyself :
Thou son of Chance ! whose glorious soul
On the four aces doom'd to roll,
Was never yet with Honour caught,
Nor on poor Virtue lost one thought ;   70
Who dost thy wife, thy children set,
Thy all, upon a single bet,

---

[1] ' Hanging friends :' See note on v. 140 of the Epistle to William Hogarth.

Risking, the desperate stake to try,   73
Here and hereafter on a die ;
Who, thy own private fortune lost,
Dost game on at thy country's cost,
And, grown expert in sharping rules,
First fool'd thyself, now prey'st on fools :
Thou noble gamester ! whose high place
Gives too much credit to disgrace ;   80
Who, with the motion of a die,
Dost make a mighty island fly—
The sums, I mean, of good French gold
For which a mighty island sold ;
Who dost betray intelligence,
Abuse the dearest confidence,
And, private fortune to create,
Most falsely play the game of state ;
Who dost within the Alley sport
Sums which might beggar a whole court,   90
And make us bankrupts all, if Care,
With good Earl Talbot,[1] was not there :
Thou daring infidel ! whom pride
And sin have drawn from Reason's side ;
Who, fearing his avengeful rod,
Dost wish not to believe a God ;
Whose hope is founded on a plan
Which should distract the soul of man,
And make him curse his abject birth ;
Whose hope is, once return'd to earth,   100
There to lie down, for worms a feast,
To rot and perish like a beast ;
Who dost, of punishment afraid,
And by thy crimes a coward made,

[1] ' Earl Talbot : ' Lord Steward of the King's Household from 1761 to 1782, an economical Reformer.

To every generous soul a curse   105
Than Hell and all her torments worse,
When crawling to thy latter end,
Call on Destruction as a friend,
Choosing to crumble into dust
Rather than rise, though rise you must: 110
Thou hypocrite! who dost profane,
And take the patriot's name in vain;
Then most thy country's foe, when most
Of love and loyalty you boast;
Who, for the love of filthy gold,
Thy friend, thy king, thy God hast sold,
And, mocking the just claim of Hell,
Were bidders found, thyself wouldst sell:
Ye villains! of whatever name,
Whatever rank, to whom the claim   120
Of Hell is certain, on whose lids
That worm, which never dies, forbids
Sweet sleep to fall, come, and behold,
Whilst envy makes your blood run cold,
Behold, by pitiless Conscience led,
So Justice wills, that holy bed
Where Peace her full dominion keeps,
And Innocence with Holland sleeps.
    Bid Terror, posting on the wind,
Affray the spirits of mankind;   130
Bid Earthquakes, heaving for a vent,
Rive their concealing continent,
And, forcing an untimely birth
Through the vast bowels of the earth,
Endeavour, in her monstrous womb,
At once all Nature to entomb;
Bid all that's horrible and dire,
All that man hates and fears, conspire

To make night hideous as they can,　　　　130
Still is thy sleep, thou virtuous man!
Pure as the thoughts which in thy breast
Inhabit, and insure thy rest;
Still shall thy Ayliffe, taught, though late,
Thy friendly justice in his fate,
Turn'd to a guardian angel, spread
Sweet dreams of comfort round thy head.
　　Dark was the night, by Fate decreed
For the contrivance of a deed
More black than common, which might make
This land from her foundations shake,　　　　150
Might tear up Freedom by the root,
Destroy a Wilkes, and fix a Bute.
Deep Horror held her wide domain;
The sky in sullen drops of rain
Forewept the morn, and through the air,
Which, opening, laid its bosom bare,
Loud thunders roll'd, and lightning stream'd;
The owl at Freedom's window scream'd,
The screech-owl, prophet dire, whose breath
Brings sickness, and whose note is death:　　　　160
The churchyard teem'd, and from the tomb,
All sad and silent, through the gloom
The ghosts of men, in former times,
Whose public virtues were their crimes,
Indignant stalk'd; sorrow and rage
Blank'd their pale cheeks; in his own age
The prop of Freedom, Hampden there
Felt after death the generous care;
Sidney by grief from heaven was kept,
And for his brother patriot wept:　　　　170
All friends of Liberty, when Fate
Prepared to shorten Wilkes's date,

Heaved, deeply hurt, the heartfelt groan,   178
And knew that wound to be their own.
   Hail, Liberty ! a glorious word,
In other countries scarcely heard,
Or heard but as a thing of course,
Without, or energy, or force :
Here felt, enjoy'd, adored, she springs,
Far, far beyond the reach of kings,   180
Fresh blooming from our mother Earth :
With pride and joy she owns her birth
Derived from us, and in return
Bids in our breasts her genius burn ;
Bids us with all those blessings live
Which Liberty alone can give,
Or nobly with that spirit die
Which makes death more than victory.
   Hail, those old patriots ! on whose tongue
Persuasion in the senate hung,   190
Whilst they the sacred cause maintain'd.
Hail, those old chiefs ! to honour train'd,
Who spread, when other methods fail'd,
War's bloody banner, and prevail'd.
Shall men like these unmention'd sleep
Promiscuous with the common heap,
And (Gratitude forbid the crime !)
Be carried down the stream of time
In shoals, unnoticed and forgot,
On Lethe's stream, like flags, to rot ?   200
No—they shall live, and each fair name,
Recorded in the book of Fame,
Founded on Honour's basis, fast
As the round earth to ages last.
Some virtues vanish with our breath ;
Virtue like this lives after death.

Old Time himself, his scythe thrown by,   207
Himself lost in eternity,
An everlasting crown shall twine
To make a Wilkes and Sidney join.
   But should some slave-got villain dare
Chains for his country to prepare,
And, by his birth to slavery broke,
Make her, too, feel the galling yoke,
May he be evermore accursed,
Amongst bad men be rank'd the worst;
May he be still himself, and still
Go on in vice, and perfect ill;
May his broad crimes each day increase,
Till he can't live, nor die in peace;   220
May he be plunged so deep in shame,
That Satan mayn't endure his name,
And hear, scarce crawling on the earth,
His children curse him for their birth;
May Liberty, beyond the grave,
Ordain him to be still a slave,
Grant him what here he most requires,
And damn him with his own desires!
   But should some villain, in support
And zeal for a despairing court,   230
Placing in craft his confidence,
And making honour a pretence
To do a deed of deepest shame,
Whilst filthy lucre is his aim;
Should such a wretch, with sword or knife,
Contrive to practise 'gainst the life
Of one who, honour'd through the land,
For Freedom made a glorious stand;
Whose chief, perhaps his only crime,
Is (if plain Truth at such a time   240

May dare her sentiments to tell)   241
That he his country loves too well:
May he—but words are all too weak
The feelings of my heart to speak—
May he—oh for a noble curse,
Which might his very marrow pierce !—
The general contempt engage,
And be the Martin of his age !

Book II.

Deep in the bosom of a wood,
Out of the road, a Temple [1] stood :
Ancient, and much the worse for wear,
It call'd aloud for quick repair,
And, tottering from side to side,
Menaced destruction far and wide ;
Nor able seem'd, unless made stronger,
To hold out four or five years longer.
Four hundred pillars, from the ground
Rising in order, most unsound,   10
Some rotten to the heart, aloof
Seem'd to support the tottering roof,
But, to inspection nearer laid,
Instead of giving, wanted aid.
    The structure, rare and curious, made
By men most famous in their trade,
A work of years, admired by all,
Was suffer'd into dust to fall ;
Or, just to make it hang together,
And keep off the effects of weather,   20
Was patch'd and patch'd from time to time
By wretches, whom it were a crime,

---

[1] ' Temple : ' the British Constitution.

A crime, which Art would treason hold   23
To mention with those names of old.
　Builders, who had the pile survey'd,
And those not Flitcrofts[1] in their trade,
Doubted (the wise hand in a doubt
Merely, sometimes, to hand her out)
Whether (like churches in a brief,[2]
Taught wisely to obtain relief   30
Through Chancery, who gives her fees
To this and other charities)
It must not, in all parts unsound,
Be ripp'd, and pull'd down to the ground ;
Whether (though after ages ne'er
Shall raise a building to compare)
Art, if they should their art employ,
Meant to preserve, might not destroy ;
As human bodies, worn away,
Batter'd and hasting to decay,   40
Bidding the power of Art despair,
Cannot those very medicines bear,
Which, and which only, can restore,
And make them healthy as before.
　To Liberty, whose gracious smile
Shed peace and plenty o'er the isle,
Our grateful ancestors, her plain
But faithful children, raised this fane.
　Full in the front, stretch'd out in length,
Where Nature put forth all her strength   50
In spring eternal, lay a plain
Where our brave fathers used to train
Their sons to arms, to teach the art
Of war, and steel the infant heart.

[1] ' Flitcrofts : ' Henry Flitcroft, an architect of some eminence. — [2] ' Brief : '
alluding to the practice of obtaining contributions for the repair of churches,
&c., by reading briefs in church.

Labour, their hardy nurse, when young,   55
Their joints had knit, their nerves had strung ;
Abstinence, foe declared to Death,
Had, from the time they first drew breath,
The best of doctors, with plain food,
Kept pure the channel of their blood ;   60
Health in their cheeks bade colour rise,
And Glory sparkled in their eyes.
 The instruments of husbandry,
As in contempt, were all thrown by,
And, flattering a manly pride,
War's keener tools their place supplied.
Their arrows to the head they drew ;
Swift to the points their javelins flew ;
They grasp'd the sword, they shook the spear ;
Their fathers felt a pleasing fear ;   70
And even Courage, standing by,
Scarcely beheld with steady eye.
Each stripling, lesson'd by his sire,
Knew when to close, when to retire,
When near at hand, when from afar
To fight, and was himself a war.
 Their wives, their mothers, all around,
Careless of order, on the ground
Breathed forth to Heaven the pious vow,
And for a son's or husband's brow,   80
With eager fingers, laurel wove ;
Laurel, which in the sacred grove,
Planted by Liberty, they find,
The brows of conquerors to bind,
To give them pride and spirit, fit
To make a world in arms submit.
 What raptures did the bosom fire
Of the young, rugged, peasant sire,

When, from the toil of mimic fight,   89
Returning with return of night,
He saw his babe resign the breast,
And, smiling, stroke those arms in jest,
With which hereafter he shall make
The proudest heart in Gallia quake !
   Gods ! with what joy, what honest pride,
Did each fond, wishing rustic bride
Behold her manly swain return !
How did her love-sick bosom burn,
Though on parades he was not bred,
Nor wore the livery of red,   100
When, Pleasure heightening all her charms,
She strain'd her warrior in her arms,
And begg'd, whilst love and glory fire,
A son, a son just like his sire !
   Such were the men in former times,
Ere luxury had made our crimes
Our bitter punishment, who bore
Their terrors to a foreign shore :
Such were the men, who, free from dread,
By Edwards and by Henries led,   110
Spread, like a torrent swell'd with rains,
O'er haughty Gallia's trembling plains :
Such were the men, when lust of power,
To work him woe, in evil hour
Debauch'd the tyrant from those ways
On which a king should found his praise ;
When stern Oppression, hand in hand
With Pride, stalk'd proudly through the land ;
When weeping Justice was misled
From her fair course, and Mercy dead :   120
Such were the men, in virtue strong,
Who dared not see their country's wrong,

Who left the mattock and the spade,   123
And, in the robes of War array'd,
In their rough arms, departing, took
Their helpless babes, and with a look
Stern and determined, swore to see
Those babes no more, or see them free :
Such were the men whom tyrant Pride
Could never fasten to his side   130
By threats or bribes ; who, freemen born,
Chains, though of gold, beheld with scorn ;
Who, free from every servile awe,
Could never be divorced from Law,
From that broad general law, which Sense
Made for the general defence ;
Could never yield to partial ties
Which from dependant stations rise ;
Could never be to slavery led,
For Property was at their head :   140
Such were the men, in days of yore,
Who, call'd by Liberty, before
Her temple on the sacred green,
In martial pastimes oft were seen—
Now seen no longer—in their stead,
To laziness and vermin bred,
A race who, strangers to the cause
Of Freedom, live by other laws,
On other motives fight, a prey
To interest, and slaves for pay.   150
Valour—how glorious, on a plan
Of honour founded !—leads their van ;
Discretion, free from taint of fear,
Cool, but resolved, brings up their rear—
Discretion, Valour's better half ;
Dependence holds the general's staff.

In plain and home-spun garb array'd,   157
Not for vain show, but service made,
In a green flourishing old age,
Not damn'd yet with an equipage,
In rules of Porterage untaught,
Simplicity, not worth a groat,
For years had kept the Temple-door ;
Full on his breast a glass he wore,
Through which his bosom open lay
To every one who pass'd that way :
Now turn'd adrift, with humbler face,
But prouder heart, his vacant place
Corruption fills, and bears the key ;
No entrance now without a fee.   170

   With belly round, and full fat face,
Which on the house reflected grace,
Full of good fare, and honest glee,
The steward Hospitality,
Old Welcome smiling by his side,
A good old servant, often tried,
And faithful found, who kept in view
His lady's fame and interest too,
Who made each heart with joy rebound,
Yet never ran her state aground,   180
Was turn'd off, or (which word I find
Is more in modern use) resign'd.[1]

   Half-starved, half-starving others, bred
In beggary, with carrion fed,
Detested, and detesting all,
Made up of avarice and gall,

---

[1] 'Resign'd : ' the Dukes of Newcastle and Devonshire, Lord Temple, &c.
who resigned their offices in 1762. Their successors pretended to economy,
but it was a mere pretence.

H

Boasting great thrift, yet wasting more   187
Than ever steward did before,
Succeeded one, who, to engage
The praise of an exhausted age,
Assumed a name of high degree,
And call'd himself Economy.
    Within the Temple, full in sight,
Where, without ceasing, day and night
The workmen toil'd ; where Labour bared
His brawny arm ; where Art prepared,
In regular and even rows,
Her types, a printing-press arose ;
Each workman knew his task, and each
Was honest and expert as Leach.[1]   200
    Hence Learning struck a deeper root,
And Science brought forth riper fruit ;
Hence Loyalty received support,
Even when banish'd from the court ;
Hence Government gain'd strength, and hence
Religion sought and found defence ;
Hence England's fairest fame arose,
And Liberty subdued her foes.
    On a low, simple, turf-made throne,
Raised by Allegiance, scarcely known   210
From her attendants, glad to be
Pattern of that equality
She wish'd to all, so far as could
Safely consist with social good,
The goddess sat ; around her head
A cheerful radiance Glory spread :

---

[1] ' Leach : ' Dryden Leach, an expert and tasteful printer in Crane Court, Fleet Street, was unjustly imprisoned on account of Wilkes.

Courage, a youth of royal race,   217
Lovelily stern, possess'd a place
On her left hand, and on her right
Sat Honour, clothed with robes of light;
Before her Magna Charta lay,
Which some great lawyer, of his day
The Pratt,[1] was officed to explain,
And make the basis of her reign:
Peace, crown'd with olive, to her breast
Two smiling twin-born infants press'd;
At her feet, couching, War was laid,
And with a brindled lion play'd:
Justice and Mercy, hand in hand,
Joint guardians of the happy land,   230
Together held their mighty charge,
And Truth walk'd all about at large;
Health for the royal troop the feast
Prepared, and Virtue was high-priest.
  Such was the fame our Goddess bore
Her Temple such, in days of yore.
What changes ruthless Time presents!
Behold her ruin'd battlements,
Her walls decay'd, her nodding spires,
Her altars broke, her dying fires,   240
Her name despised, her priests destroy'd,
Her friends disgraced, her foes employ'd,
Herself (by ministerial arts
Deprived e'en of the people's hearts,
Whilst they, to work her surer woe,
Feign her to Monarchy a foe)
Exiled by grief, self-doom'd to dwell
With some poor hermit in a cell;

[1] 'Pratt:' Lord Camden.

Or, that retirement tedious grown,   249
If she walks forth, she walks unknown,
Hooted, and pointed at with scorn,
As one in some strange country born.
   Behold a rude and ruffian race,
A band of spoilers, seize her place ;
With looks which might the heart disseat,
And make life sound a quick retreat !
To rapine from the cradle bred,
A staunch old blood-hound at their head,
Who, free from virtue and from awe,
Knew none but the bad part of law,   260
They roved at large ; each on his breast
Mark'd with a greyhound stood confess'd :
Controlment waited on their nod,
High-wielding Persecution's rod ;
Confusion follow'd at their heels,
And a cast statesman held the seals ;[1]
Those seals, for which he dear shall pay,
When awful Justice takes her day.
   The printers saw—they saw and fled—
Science, declining, hung her head.   270
Property in despair appear'd,
And for herself destruction fear'd ;
Whilst underfoot the rude slaves trod
The works of men, and word of God ;
Whilst, close behind, on many a book,
In which he never deigns to look,
Which he did not, nay, could not read,
A bold, bad man (by power decreed

---

[1] 'Seals :' The general warrant for the apprehension of Wilkes was signed
by the Earls of Egremont and Halifax, joint secretaries of state for the home
department.

For that bad end, who in the dark   279
Scorn'd to do mischief) set his mark
In the full day, the mark of Hell,
And on the Gospel stamp'd an L.
   Liberty fled, her friends withdrew—
Her friends, a faithful, chosen few ;
Honour in grief threw up ; and Shame,
Clothing herself with Honour's name,
Usurp'd his station ; on the throne
Which Liberty once call'd her own,
(Gods ! that such mighty ills should spring
Under so great, so good a king,   290
So loved, so loving, through the arts
Of statesmen, cursed with wicked hearts !)
For every darker purpose fit,
Behold in triumph State-craft sit !

Book III.

Ah me ! what mighty perils wait
The man who meddles with a state,
Whether to strengthen, or oppose !
False are his friends, and firm his foes :
How must his soul, once ventured in,
Plunge blindly on from sin to sin !
What toils he suffers, what disgrace,
To get, and then to keep, a place !
How often, whether wrong or right,
Must he in jest or earnest fight,   10
Risking for those both life and limb
Who would not risk one groat for him !
   Under the Temple lay a Cave,
Made by some guilty, coward slave,

Whose actions fear'd rebuke : a maze   15
Of intricate and winding ways,
Not to be found without a clue ;
One passage only, known to few,
In paths direct led to a cell,
Where Fraud in secret loved to dwell,   20
With all her tools and slaves about her,
Nor fear'd lest Honesty should rout her.
   In a dark corner, shunning sight
Of man, and shrinking from the light,
One dull, dim taper through the cell
Glimm'ring, to make more horrible
The face of darkness, she prepares,
Working unseen, all kinds of snares,
With curious, but destructive art :
Here, through the eye to catch the heart,   30
Gay stars their tinsel beams afford,
Neat artifice to trap a lord ;
There, fit for all whom Folly bred,
Wave plumes of feathers for the head ;
Garters the hag contrives to make,
Which, as it seems, a babe might break,
But which ambitious madmen feel
More firm and sure than chains of steel ;
Which, slipp'd just underneath the knee,
Forbid a freeman to be free.   40
Purses she knew, (did ever curse
Travel more sure than in a purse ?)
Which, by some strange and magic bands,
Enslave the soul, and tie the hands.
   Here Flattery, eldest-born of Guile,
Weaves with rare skill the silken smile,
The courtly cringe, the supple bow,
The private squeeze, the levee vow,

With which—no strange or recent case— 49
Fools in, deceive fools out of place.
Corruption, (who, in former times,
Through fear or shame conceal'd her crimes,
And what she did, contrived to do it
So that the public might not view it)
Presumptuous grown, unfit was held
For their dark councils, and expell'd,
Since in the day her business might
Be done as safe as in the night.
Her eye down-bending to the ground,
Planning some dark and deadly wound, 60
Holding a dagger, on which stood,
All fresh and reeking, drops of blood,
Bearing a lantern, which of yore,
By Treason borrow'd, Guy Fawkes bore,
By which, since they improved in trade,
Excisemen have their lanterns made,
Assassination, her whole mind
Blood-thirsting, on her arm reclined;
Death, grinning, at her elbow stood,
And held forth instruments of blood,— 70
Vile instruments, which cowards choose,
But men of honour dare not use;
Around, his Lordship and his Grace,
Both qualified for such a place,
With many a Forbes, and many a Dun,[1]
Each a resolved, and pious son,
Wait her high bidding; each prepared,
As she around her orders shared,
Proof 'gainst remorse, to run, to fly,
And bid the destined victim die, 80

---

[1] 'Forbes and Dun:' two Scotchmen, one of whom challenged Wilkes, and the other tried to assassinate him. Dun was insane.

Posting on Villany's black wing,   81
Whether he patriot is, or king.
　Oppression, willing to appear
An object of our love, not fear,
Or, at the most, a reverend awe
To breed, usurp'd the garb of Law.
A book she held, on which her eyes
Were deeply fix'd, whence seem'd to rise
Joy in her breast ; a book, of might
Most wonderful, which black to white   90
Could turn, and without help of laws,
Could make the worse the better cause.
She read, by flattering hopes deceived ;
She wish'd, and what she wish'd, believed,
To make that book for ever stand
The rule of wrong through all the land ;
On the back, fair and worthy note,
At large was Magna Charta wrote ;
But turn your eye within, and read,
A bitter lesson, Norton's Creed.   100
Ready, e'en with a look, to run,
Fast as the coursers of the sun,
To worry Virtue, at her hand
Two half-starved greyhounds took their stand.
A curious model, cut in wood,
Of a most ancient castle stood
Full in her view ; the gates were barr'd,
And soldiers on the watch kept guard ;
In the front, openly, in black
Was wrote, The Tower ; but on the back,   110
Mark'd with a secretary's seal,
In bloody letters, The Bastile.[1]

---

[1] ' The Bastile : ' Wilkes was six days in the Tower.

Around a table, fully bent   113
On mischief of most black intent,
Deeply determined that their reign
Might longer last, to work the bane
Of one firm patriot, whose heart, tied
To Honour, all their power defied,
And brought those actions into light
They wish'd to have conceal'd in night,   120
Begot, born, bred to infamy,
A privy-council sat of three :
Great were their names, of high repute
And favour through the land of Bute.

The first [1] (entitled to the place
Of Honour both by gown and grace,
Who never let occasion slip
To take right-hand of fellowship,
And was so proud, that should he meet
The twelve apostles in the street,   130
He'd turn his nose up at them all,
And shove his Saviour from the wall !
Who was so mean (Meanness and Pride
Still go together side by side)
That he would cringe, and creep, be civil,
And hold a stirrup for the Devil ;
If in a journey to his mind,
He'd let him mount and ride behind ;
Who basely fawn'd through all his life,
For patrons first, then for a wife :   140
Wrote Dedications which must make
The heart of every Christian quake ;
Made one man equal to, or more
Than God, then left him, as before

---

[1] ' First : ' the great William Warburton, who rose partly through his marriage with the niece of the rich Ralph Allen.

His God he left, and, drawn by pride,   145
Shifted about to t' other side)
Was by his sire a parson made,
Merely to give the boy a trade;
But he himself was thereto drawn
By some faint omens of the lawn,   150
And on the truly Christian plan
To make himself a gentleman,—
A title in which Form array'd him,
Though Fate ne'er thought on 't when she made him.

   The oaths he took, 'tis very true,
But took them as all wise men do,
With an intent, if things should turn,
Rather to temporise, than burn;
Gospel and loyalty were made
To serve the purposes of trade;   160
Religions are but paper ties,
Which bind the fool, but which the wise,
Such idle notions far above,
Draw on and off, just like a glove;
All gods, all kings (let his great aim
Be answer'd) were to him the same.

   A curate first, he read and read,
And laid in, whilst he should have fed
The souls of his neglected flock,
Of reading such a mighty stock,   170
That he o'ercharged the weary brain
With more than she could well contain;
More than she was with spirits fraught
To turn and methodise to thought,
And which, like ill-digested food,
To humours turn'd, and not to blood.
Brought up to London, from the plough
And pulpit, how to make a bow

He tried to learn ; he grew polite, 179
And was the poet's parasite.
With wits conversing, (and wits then
Were to be found 'mongst noblemen)
He caught, or would have caught, the flame,
And would be nothing, or the same.
He drank with drunkards, lived with sinners,
Herded with infidels for dinners ;
With such an emphasis and grace
Blasphemed, that Potter[1] kept not pace :
He, in the highest reign of noon,
Bawled bawdy songs to a psalm tune ; 190
Lived with men infamous and vile,
Truck'd his salvation for a smile ;
To catch their humour caught their plan,
And laugh'd at God to laugh with man ;
Praised them, when living, in each breath,
And damn'd their memories after death.
    To prove his faith, which all admit
Is at least equal to his wit,
And make himself a man of note,
He in defence of Scripture wrote : 200
So long he wrote, and long about it,
That e'en believers 'gan to doubt it :
He wrote, too, of the inward light,
Though no one knew how he came by 't,
And of that influencing grace
Which in his life ne'er found a place :
He wrote, too, of the Holy Ghost,
Of whom no more than doth a post
He knew ; nor, should an angel show him,
Would he, or know, or choose to know him. 210

[1] ' Potter : ' mentioned above. He was suspected by Warburton of being
the author of the infamous notes to Wilkes's infamous ' Essay on Woman.'

Next (for he knew 'twixt every science   211
There was a natural alliance)
He wrote, to advance his Maker's praise,
Comments[1] on rhymes, and notes on plays,
And with an all-sufficient air
Placed himself in the critic's chair ;
Usurp'd o'er Reason full dominion,
And govern'd merely by Opinion.
At length dethroned, and kept in awe
By one plain simple man of law,[2]   220
He arm'd dead friends, to vengeance true,
To abuse the man they never knew.

   Examine strictly all mankind,
Most characters are mix'd, we find ;
And Vice and Virtue take their turn
In the same breast to beat and burn.
Our priest was an exception here,
Nor did one spark of grace appear,
Not one dull, dim spark in his soul ;
Vice, glorious Vice, possess'd the whole,   230
And, in her service truly warm,
He was in sin most uniform.

   Injurious Satire ! own at least
One sniv'lling virtue in the priest,
One sniv'lling virtue, which is placed,
They say, in or about the waist,
Call'd Chastity ; the prudish dame
Knows it at large by Virtue's name.
To this his wife (and in these days
Wives seldom without reason praise)   240

1 'Comments :' referring to the notes to 'The Dunciad,' and on Shakspeare.
—2 'Man of law :' Mr Thomas Edwards, a barrister, wrote a clever book
against Warburton's criticism. Warburton alluded to him contemptuously
afterwards, in a note to a new edition of ' The Dunciad.'

Bears evidence—then calls her child,   241
And swears that Tom [1] was vastly wild.
  Ripen'd by a long course of years,
He great and perfect now appears.
In shape scarce of the human kind,
A man, without a manly mind ;
No husband, though he 's truly wed ;
Though on his knees a child is bred,
No father ; injured, without end
A foe ; and though obliged, no friend ;   250
A heart, which virtue ne'er disgraced ;
A head, where learning runs to waste ;
A gentleman well-bred, if breeding
Rests in the article of reading ;
A man of this world, for the next
Was ne'er included in his text ;
A judge of genius, though confess'd
With not one spark of genius bless'd ;
Amongst the first of critics placed,
Though free from every taint of taste ;   260
A Christian without faith or works,
As he would be a Turk 'mongst Turks ;
A great divine, as lords agree,
Without the least divinity ;
To crown all, in declining age,
Inflamed with church and party rage,
Behold him, full and perfect quite,
A false saint, and true hypocrite.
  Next sat a lawyer,[2] often tried
In perilous extremes ; when Pride   270
And Power, all wild and trembling, stood,
Nor dared to tempt the raging flood ;

[1] 'Tom :' this son was Warburton's only child, and died before his father.
—[2] 'A lawyer :' Sir Fletcher Norton, who as well as Warburton is caricatured.

This bold, bad man arose to view,
And gave his hand to help them through :
Steel'd 'gainst compassion, as they pass'd
He saw poor Freedom breathe her last ;
He saw her struggle, heard her groan ;
He saw her helpless and alone,
Whelm'd in that storm, which, fear'd and praised
By slaves less bold, himself had raised.
    Bred to the law, he from the first
Of all bad lawyers was the worst.
Perfection (for bad men maintain
In ill we may perfection gain)
In others is a work of time,
And they creep on from crime to crime ;
He, for a prodigy design'd,
To spread amazement o'er mankind,
Started full ripen'd all at once
A perfect knave, and perfect dunce.
    Who will, for him, may boast of sense,
His better guard is impudence ;
His front, with tenfold plates of brass
Secured, Shame never yet could pass,
Nor on the surface of his skin
Blush for that guilt which dwelt within.
How often, in contempt of laws,
To sound the bottom of a cause,
To search out every rotten part,
And worm into its very heart,
Hath he ta'en briefs on false pretence,
And undertaken the defence
Of trusting fools, whom in the end
He meant to ruin, not defend !
How often, e'en in open court,
Hath the wretch made his shame his sport,

And laugh'd off, with a villain's ease,   307
Throwing up briefs, and keeping fees!
Such things as, though to roguery bred,
Had struck a little villain dead!
   Causes, whatever their import,
He undertakes, to serve a court;
For he by art this rule had got,
Power can effect what Law cannot.
   Fools he forgives, but rogues he fears;
If Genius, yoked with Worth, appears,
His weak soul sickens at the sight,
And strives to plunge them down in night.
   So loud he talks, so very loud,
He is an angel with the crowd;   320
Whilst he makes Justice hang her head,
And judges turn from pale to red.
   Bid all that Nature, on a plan
Most intimate, makes dear to man,
All that with grand and general ties
Binds good and bad, the fool and wise,
Knock at his heart; they knock in vain;
No entrance there such suitors gain;
Bid kneeling kings forsake the throne,
Bid at his feet his country groan;   330
Bid Liberty stretch out her hands,
Religion plead her stronger bands;
Bid parents, children, wife, and friends,
If they come 'thwart his private ends—
Unmoved he hears the general call,
And bravely tramples on them all.
   Who will, for him, may cant and whine,
And let weak Conscience with her line
Chalk out their ways; such starving rules
Are only fit for coward fools;   340

Fellows who credit what priests tell,   341
And tremble at the thoughts of Hell;
His spirit dares contend with Grace,
And meets Damnation face to face.

   Such was our lawyer; by his side,
In all bad qualities allied,
In all bad counsels, sat a third,
By birth a lord.[1]   Oh, sacred word!
Oh, word most sacred! whence men get
A privilege to run in debt;   350
Whence they at large exemption claim
From Satire, and her servant Shame;
Whence they, deprived of all her force,
Forbid bold Truth to hold her course.

   Consult his person, dress, and air,
He seems, which strangers well might swear,
The master, or, by courtesy,
The captain of a colliery.
Look at his visage, and agree
Half-hang'd he seems, just from the tree   360
Escaped; a rope may sometimes break,
Or men be cut down by mistake.

   He hath not virtue (in the school
Of Vice bred up) to live by rule,
Nor hath he sense (which none can doubt
Who know the man) to live without.
His life is a continued scene
Of all that's infamous and mean;
He knows not change, unless, grown nice
And delicate, from vice to vice;   370
Nature design'd him, in a rage,
To be the Wharton[2] of his age;

---

[1] 'A lord:' Sandwich. — [2] 'Wharton:' Philip Duke of Wharton, whose character is found in Pope's 'Moral Essays,' was noted for the greatness of his talents, and for his dissolute life.

But, having given all the sin,   373
Forgot to put the virtues in.
To run a horse, to make a match,
To revel deep, to roar a catch,
To knock a tott'ring watchman down,
To sweat a woman of the town ;
By fits to keep the peace, or break it,
In turn to give a pox, or take it ;   380
He is, in faith, most excellent,
And, in the word's most full intent,
A true choice spirit, we admit ;
With wits a fool, with fools a wit :
Hear him but talk, and you would swear
Obscenity herself was there,
And that Profaneness had made choice,
By way of trump, to use his voice ;
That, in all mean and low things great,
He had been bred at Billingsgate ;   390
And that, ascending to the earth
Before the season of his birth,
Blasphemy, making way and room,
Had mark'd him in his mother's womb.
Too honest (for the worst of men
In forms are honest, now and then)
Not to have, in the usual way,
His bills sent in ; too great to pay :
Too proud to speak to, if he meets
The honest tradesman whom he cheats :   400
Too infamous to have a friend ;
Too bad for bad men to commend,
Or good to name ; beneath whose weight
Earth groans ; who hath been spared by Fate
Only to show, on Mercy's plan,
How far and long God bears with man.

I

Such were the three, who, mocking sleep,   407
At midnight sat, in counsel deep,
Plotting destruction 'gainst a head
Whose wisdom could not be misled ;
Plotting destruction 'gainst a heart
Which ne'er from honour would depart.
  ' Is he not rank'd amongst our foes ?
Hath not his spirit dared oppose
Our dearest measures, made our name
Stand forward on the roll of Shame ?
Hath he not won the vulgar tribes,
By scorning menaces and bribes,
And proving that his darling cause
Is, of their liberties and laws   420
To stand the champion ? In a word,
Nor need one argument be heard
Beyond this to awake our zeal,
To quicken our resolves, and steel
Our steady souls to bloody bent,
(Sure ruin to each dear intent,
Each flattering hope) he, without fear,
Hath dared to make the truth appear.'
  They said, and, by resentment taught,
Each on revenge employ'd his thought ;   430
Each, bent on mischief, rack'd his brain
To her full stretch, but rack'd in vain ;
Scheme after scheme they brought to view ;
All were examined ; none would do :
When Fraud, with pleasure in her face,
Forth issued from her hiding-place,
And at the table where they meet,
First having bless'd them, took her seat.
  ' No trifling cause, my darling boys,
Your present thoughts and cares employs ;   440

No common snare, no random blow,   441
Can work the bane of such a foe :
By nature cautious as he 's brave,
To Honour only he 's a slave ;
In that weak part without defence,
We must to honour make pretence ;
That lure shall to his ruin draw
The wretch, who stands secure in law.
Nor think that I have idly plann'd
This full-ripe scheme ; behold at hand,   450
With three months' training on his head,
An instrument, whom I have bred,
Born of these bowels, far from sight
Of Virtue's false but glaring light,
My youngest-born, my dearest joy,
Most like myself, my darling boy !
He, never touch'd with vile remorse,
Resolved and crafty in his course,
Shall work our ends, complete our schemes,
Most mine, when most he Honour's seems ;   460
Nor can be found, at home, abroad,
So firm and full a slave of Fraud.'
    She said, and from each envious son
A discontented murmur run
Around the table ; all in place
Thought his full praise their own disgrace,
Wond'ring what stranger she had got,
Who had one vice that they had not ;
When straight the portals open flew,
And, clad in armour, to their view   470
Martin, the Duellist, came forth.
All knew, and all confess'd his worth ;
All justified, with smiles array'd,
The happy choice their dam had made.

GOTHAM.[1]

IN THREE BOOKS.

Book I.

FAR off (no matter whether east or west,
A real country, or one made in jest,
Nor yet by modern Mandevilles[2] disgraced,
Nor by map-jobbers wretchedly misplaced)
There lies an island, neither great nor small,
Which, for distinction sake, I Gotham call.
    The man who finds an unknown country out,
By giving it a name, acquires, no doubt,
A Gospel title, though the people there
The pious Christian thinks not worth his care   10
Bar this pretence, and into air is hurl'd
The claim of Europe to the Western world.
    Cast by a tempest on the savage coast,
Some roving buccaneer set up a post;
A beam, in proper form transversely laid,
Of his Redeemer's cross the figure made—
Of that Redeemer, with whose laws his life,
From first to last, had been one scene of strife;
His royal master's name thereon engraved,
Without more process the whole race enslaved,   20
Cut off that charter they from Nature drew,
And made them slaves to men they never knew.
    Search ancient histories, consult records,
Under this title the most Christian lords
Hold (thanks to conscience) more than half the ball;
O'erthrow this title, they have none at all;

---

[1] 'Gotham:' is designed as a satire on England and its kings, and as a
picture of what a king of England should be. The first book is a wild and
fanciful bravura. — [2] 'Mandeville:' the famous lying traveller.

For never yet might any monarch dare,   27
Who lived to Truth, and breathed a Christian air,
Pretend that Christ, (who came, we all agree,
To bless his people, and to set them free)
To make a convert, ever one law gave
By which converters made him first a slave.

Spite of the glosses of a canting priest,
Who talks of charity, but means a feast ;
Who recommends it (whilst he seems to feel
The holy glowings of a real zeal)
To all his hearers as a deed of worth,
To give them heaven whom they have robb'd of earth ;
Never shall one, one truly honest man,
Who, bless'd with Liberty, reveres her plan,   40
Allow one moment that a savage sire
Could from his wretched race, for childish hire,
By a wild grant, their all, their freedom pass,
And sell his country for a bit of glass.

Or grant this barb'rous right, let Spain and France,
In slavery bred, as purchasers advance ;
Let them, whilst Conscience is at distance hurl'd,
With some gay bauble buy a golden world :
An Englishman, in charter'd freedom born,
Shall spurn the slavish merchandise, shall scorn   50
To take from others, through base private views,
What he himself would rather die, than lose.

Happy the savage of those early times,
Ere Europe's sons were known, and Europe's crimes !
Gold, cursèd gold ! slept in the womb of earth,
Unfelt its mischiefs, as unknown its worth ;
In full content he found the truest wealth,
In toil he found diversion, food, and health ;
Stranger to ease and luxury of courts,
His sports were labours, and his labours sports ;   60

His youth was hardy, and his old age green ;   61
Life's morn was vigorous, and her eve serene ;
No rules he held, but what were made for use,
No arts he learn'd, nor ills which arts produce ;
False lights he follow'd, but believed them true ;
He knew not much, but lived to what he knew.

　　Happy, thrice happy now the savage race,
Since Europe took their gold, and gave them grace !
Pastors she sends to help them in their need,
Some who can't write ; with others who can't read ;   70
And on sure grounds the gospel pile to rear,
Sends missionary felons every year ;
Our vices, with more zeal than holy prayers,
She teaches them, and in return takes theirs.
Her rank oppressions give them cause to rise,
Her want of prudence, means and arms supplies,
Whilst her brave rage, not satisfied with life,
Rising in blood, adopts the scalping-knife.
Knowledge she gives, enough to make them know
How abject is their state, how deep their woe ;   80
The worth of freedom strongly she explains,
Whilst she bows down, and loads their necks with chains.
Faith, too, she plants, for her own ends impress'd,
To make them bear the worst, and hope the best ;
And whilst she teaches, on vile Interest's plan,
As laws of God, the wild decrees of man,
Like Pharisees, of whom the Scriptures tell,
She makes them ten times more the sons of Hell.

　　But whither do these grave reflections tend ?
Are they design'd for any, or no end ?   90
Briefly but this—to prove, that by no act
Which Nature made, that by no equal pact
'Twixt man and man, which might, if Justice heard,
Stand good ; that by no benefits conferr'd,

Or purchase made, Europe in chains can hold   95
The sons of India, and her mines of gold.
Chance led her there in an accursed hour ;
She saw, and made the country hers by power ;
Nor, drawn by virtue's love from love of fame,
Shall my rash folly controvert the claim,   100
Or wish in thought that title overthrown
Which coincides with and involves my own.
     Europe discover'd India first ; I found
My right to Gotham on the self-same ground ;
I first discover'd it, nor shall that plea
To her be granted, and denied to me ;
I plead possession, and, till one more bold
Shall drive me out, will that possession hold.
With Europe's rights my kindred rights I twine ;
Hers be the Western world, be Gotham mine.   110
     Rejoice, ye happy Gothamites ! rejoice ;
Lift up your voice on high, a mighty voice,
The voice of gladness ; and on every tongue,
In strains of gratitude, be praises hung,
The praises of so great and good a king :
Shall Churchill reign, and shall not Gotham sing ?
     As on a day, a high and holy day,
Let every instrument of music play,
Ancient and modern ; those which drew their birth
(Punctilios laid aside) from Pagan earth,   120
As well as those by Christian made and Jew ;
Those known to many, and those known to few ;
Those which in whim and frolic lightly float,
And those which swell the slow and solemn note ;
Those which (whilst Reason stands in wonder by)
Make some complexions laugh, and others cry;
Those which, by some strange faculty of sound,
Can build walls up, and raze them to the ground ;

Those which can tear up forests by the roots,   129
And make brutes dance like men, and men like brutes ;
Those which, whilst Ridicule leads up the dance,
Make·clowns of Monmouth [1] ape the fops of France ;
Those which, where Lady Dulness with Lord Mayors
Presides, disdaining light and trifling airs,
Hallow the feast with psalmody ; and those
Which, planted in our churches to dispose
And lift the mind to Heaven, are disgraced
With what a foppish organist calls Taste :
All, from the fiddle (on which every fool,
The pert son of dull sire, discharged from school,   140
Serves an apprenticeship in college ease,
And rises through the gamut to degrees)
To those which (though less common, not less sweet)
From famed Saint Giles's, and more famed Vine Street,
(Where Heaven, the utmost wish of man to grant,
Gave me an old house, and an older aunt)
Thornton,[2] whilst Humour pointed out the road
To her arch cub, hath hitch'd into an ode ;—
All instruments (attend, ye listening spheres !
Attend, ye sons of men ! and hear with ears),   150
All instruments (nor shall they seek one hand
Impress'd from modern Music's coxcomb band),
All instruments, self-acted, at my name
Shall pour forth harmony, and loud proclaim,
Loud but yet sweet, to the according globe,
My praises ; whilst gay Nature, in a robe,
A coxcomb doctor's robe, to the full sound
Keeps time, like Boyce,[3] and the world dances round.
    Rejoice, ye happy Gothamites ! rejoice ;
Lift up your voice on high, a mighty voice,   160

---

[1] 'Monmouth :' in Wales, once visited, and ever afterwards hated by the
poet. — [2] 'Bonnell Thornton :' author of a humorous burlesque, 'Ode on St
Cecilia's Day.' See Boswell. — [3] 'William Boyce :' a celebrated musician.

The voice of gladness; and on every tongue,   161
In strains of gratitude, be praises hung,
The praises of so great and good a king:
Shall Churchill reign, and shall not Gotham sing?

Infancy, straining backward from the breast,
Tetchy and wayward, what he loveth best
Refusing in his fits, whilst all the while
The mother eyes the wrangler with a smile,
And the fond father sits on t' other side,
Laughs at his moods, and views his spleen with pride,
Shall murmur forth my name, whilst at his hand   171
Nurse stands interpreter, through Gotham's land.

Childhood, who like an April morn appears,
Sunshine and rain, hopes clouded o'er with fears,
Pleased and displeased by starts, in passion warm,
In reason weak; who, wrought into a storm,
Like to the fretful billows of the deep,
Soon spends his rage, and cries himself asleep;
Who, with a feverish appetite oppress'd,
For trifles sighs, but hates them when possess'd;   180
His trembling lash suspended in the air,
Half-bent, and stroking back his long lank hair,
Shall to his mates look up with eager glee,
And let his top go down to prate of me.

Youth, who, fierce, fickle, insolent, and vain,
Impatient urges on to Manhood's reign,
Impatient urges on, yet with a cast
Of dear regard looks back on Childhood past,
In the mid-chase, when the hot blood runs high,
And the quick spirits mount into his eye;   190
When pleasure, which he deems his greatest wealth,
Beats in his heart, and paints his cheeks with health;
When the chafed steed tugs proudly at the rein,
And, ere he starts, hath run o'er half the plain;

When, wing'd with fear, the stag flies full in view,   195
And in full cry the eager hounds pursue,
Shall shout my praise to hills which shout again,
And e'en the huntsman stop to cry, Amen.

Manhood, of form erect, who would not bow
Though worlds should crack around him ; on his brow
Wisdom serene, to passion giving law,   201
Bespeaking love, and yet commanding awe ;
Dignity into grace by mildness wrought ;
Courage attemper'd and refined by thought ;
Virtue supreme enthroned ; within his breast
The image of his Maker deep impress'd ;
Lord of this earth, which trembles at his nod,
With reason bless'd, and only less than God ;
Manhood, though weeping Beauty kneels for aid,
Though Honour calls, in Danger's form array'd,   210
Though clothed with sackloth, Justice in the gates,
By wicked elders chain'd, Redemption waits,
Manhood shall steal an hour, a little hour,
(Is't not a little one ?) to hail my power.

Old Age, a second child, by Nature cursed
With more and greater evils than the first ;
Weak, sickly, full of pains, in every breath
Railing at life, and yet afraid of death ;
Putting things off, with sage and solemn air,
From day to day, without one day to spare ;   220
Without enjoyment, covetous of pelf,
Tiresome to friends, and tiresome to himself ;
His faculties impair'd, his temper sour'd,
His memory of recent things devour'd
E'en with the acting, on his shatter'd brain
Though the false registers of youth remain ;
From morn to evening babbling forth vain praise
Of those rare men, who lived in those rare days,

When he, the hero of his tale, was young ;   229
Dull repetitions falt'ring on his tongue ;
Praising gray hairs, sure mark of Wisdom's sway,
E'en whilst he curses Time, which made him gray ;
Scoffing at youth, e'en whilst he would afford
All but his gold to have his youth restored,
Shall for a moment, from himself set free,
Lean on his crutch, and pipe forth praise to me.

   Rejoice, ye happy Gothamites ! rejoice ;
Lift up your voice on high, a mighty voice,
The voice of gladness ; and on every tongue,
In strains of gratitude, be praises hung,   240
The praises of so great and good a king :
Shall Churchill reign, and shall not Gotham sing ?

   Things without life shall in this chorus join,
And, dumb to others' praise, be loud in mine.

   The snowdrop, who, in habit white and plain,
Comes on, the herald of fair Flora's train ;
The coxcomb crocus, flower of simple note,
Who by her side struts in a herald's coat ;
The tulip, idly glaring to the view,
Who, though no clown, his birth from Holland drew ;
Who, once full dress'd, fears from his place to stir, 251
The fop of flowers, the More of a parterre ;
The woodbine, who her elm in marriage meets,
And brings her dowry in surrounding sweets ;
The lily, silver mistress of the vale ;
The rose of Sharon, which perfumes the gale ;
The jessamine, with which the queen of flowers,
To charm her god, adorns his favourite bowers,
Which brides, by the plain hand of Neatness dress'd,
Unenvied rival, wear upon their breast,   260
Sweet as the incense of the morn, and chaste
As the pure zone which circles Dian's waist ;

All flowers, of various names, and various forms,   263
Which the sun into strength and beauty warms,
From the dwarf daisy, which, like infants, clings,
And fears to leave the earth from whence it springs,
To the proud giant of the garden race,
Who, madly rushing to the sun's embrace,
O'ertops her fellows with aspiring aim,
Demands his wedded love, and bears his name;   270
All, one and all, shall in this chorus join,
And, dumb to others' praise, be loud in mine.

　　Rejoice, ye happy Gothamites! rejoice;
Lift up your voice on high, a mighty voice,
The voice of gladness; and on every tongue,
In strains of gratitude, be praises hung,
The praises of so great and good a king:
Shall Churchill reign, and shall not Gotham sing?

　　Forming a gloom, through which, to spleen-struck minds,
Religion, horror-stamp'd, a passage finds,   280
The ivy crawling o'er the hallow'd cell
Where some old hermit's wont his beads to tell
By day, by night; the myrtle ever green,
Beneath whose shade Love holds his rites unseen;
The willow, weeping o'er the fatal wave
Where many a lover finds a watery grave;
The cypress, sacred held, when lovers mourn
Their true love snatch'd away; the laurel worn
By poets in old time, but destined now,
In grief, to wither on a Whitehead's brow;   290
The fig, which, large as what in India grows,
Itself a grove, gave our first parents clothes;
The vine, which, like a blushing new-made bride,
Clustering, empurples all the mountain's side;
The yew, which, in the place of sculptured stone,
Marks out the resting-place of men unknown;

The hedge-row elm ; the pine, of mountain race ;   297
The fir, the Scotch fir, never out of place ;
The cedar, whose top mates the highest cloud,
Whilst his old father Lebanon grows proud
Of such a child, and his vast body laid
Out many a mile, enjoys the filial shade ;
The oak, when living, monarch of the wood ;
The English oak, which, dead, commands the flood ;
All, one and all, shall in this chorus join,
And, dumb to others' praise, be loud in mine.
   Rejoice, ye happy Gothamites ! rejoice ;
Lift up your voice on high, a mighty voice,
The voice of gladness ; and on every tongue,
In strains of gratitude, be praises hung,   310
The praises of so great and good a king :
Shall Churchill reign, and shall not Gotham sing ?
   The showers, which make the young hills, like young lambs,
Bound and rebound ; the old hills, like old rams,
Unwieldy, jump for joy ; the streams which glide,
Whilst Plenty marches smiling by their side,
And from their bosom rising Commerce springs ;
The winds, which rise with healing on their wings,
Before whose cleansing breath Contagion flies ;
The sun, who, travelling in eastern skies,   320
Fresh, full of strength, just risen from his bed,
Though in Jove's pastures they were born and bred,
With voice and whip can scarce make his steeds stir,
Step by step, up the perpendicular ;
Who, at the hour of eve, panting for rest,
Rolls on amain, and gallops down the west
As fast as Jehu, oil'd for Ahab's sin,
Drove for a crown, or postboys for an inn ;
The moon, who holds o'er night her silver reign,
Regent of tides, and mistress of the brain,   330

Who to her sons, those sons who own her power,   331
And do her homage at the midnight hour,
Gives madness as a blessing, but dispenses
Wisdom to fools, and damns them with their senses ;
The stars, who, by I know not what strange right,
Preside o'er mortals in their own despite,
Who, without reason, govern those who most
(How truly, judge from thence !) of reason boast,
And, by some mighty magic yet unknown,
Our actions guide, yet cannot guide their own ;   340
All, one and all, shall in this chorus join,
And, dumb to others' praise, be loud in mine.
    Rejoice, ye happy Gothamites ! rejoice ;
Lift up your voice on high, a mighty voice,
The voice of gladness ; and on every tongue,
In strains of gratitude, be praises hung,
The praises of so great and good a king :
Shall Churchill reign, and shall not Gotham sing ?
    The moment, minute, hour, day, week, month, year,
Morning and eve, as they in turn appear ;   350
Moments and minutes, which, without a crime,
Can't be omitted in accounts of time,
Or, if omitted, (proof we might afford)
Worthy by parliaments to be restored ;
The hours, which, dress'd by turns in black and white,
Ordain'd as handmaids, wait on Day and Night ;
The day, those hours, I mean, when light presides,
And Business in a cart with Prudence rides ;
The night, those hours, I mean, with darkness hung,
When Sense speaks free, and Folly holds her tongue ;
The morn, when Nature, rousing from her strife   361
With death-like sleep, awakes to second life ;
The eve, when, as unequal to the task,
She mercy from her foe descends to ask ;

The week, in which six days are kindly given   365
To think of earth, and one to think of heaven ;
The months, twelve sisters, all of different hue,
Though there appears in all a likeness too ;
Not such a likeness as, through Hayman's[1] works,
Dull mannerist ! in Christians, Jews, and Turks,   370
Cloys with a sameness in each female face,
But a strange something, born of Art and Grace,
Which speaks them all, to vary and adorn,
At different times of the same parents born ;
All, one and all, shall in this chorus join,
And, dumb to others' praise, be loud in mine.

   Rejoice, ye happy Gothamites ! rejoice ;
Lift up your voice on high, a mighty voice,
The voice of gladness ; and on every tongue,
In strains of gratitude, be praises hung,   380
The praises of so great and good a king :
Shall Churchill reign, and shall not Gotham sing ?

   Frore January, leader of the year,
Minced-pies in van, and calves' heads in the rear ;
Dull February, in whose leaden reign
My mother bore a bard without a brain ;
March, various, fierce, and wild, with wind-crack'd cheeks,
By wilder Welshmen led, and crown'd with leeks ;
April, with fools, and May, with bastards bless'd ;
June, with White Roses on her rebel breast ;   390
July, to whom, the Dog-star in her train,
Saint James[2] gives oysters, and Saint Swithin rain ;
August,[3] who, banish'd from her Smithfield stand,
To Chelsea flies, with Doggett in her hand ;

---

[1] 'Hayman :' Francis Hayman, the painter, was monotonous in his style.—
[2] 'Saint James :' The 25th of July, St James's day, or the first day of oysters.
—[3] 'August :' alluding to a rowing match, held on 1st August, in honour of George the First's accession ; instituted by one Doggett, an actor, &c.

September, when by custom (right divine)   395
Geese are ordain'd to bleed at Michael's shrine,
Whilst the priest, not so full of grace as wit,
Falls to, unbless'd, nor gives the saint a bit ;
October, who the cause of Freedom join'd,
And gave a second George[1] to bless mankind ;   400
November, who, at once to grace our earth,
Saint Andrew boasts, and our Augusta's[2] birth ;
December, last of months, but best, who gave
A Christ to man, a Saviour to the slave,
Whilst, falsely grateful, man, at the full feast,
To do God honour makes himself a beast ;
All, one and all, shall in this chorus join,
And, dumb to others' praise, be loud in mine.
   Rejoice, ye happy Gothamites! rejoice ;
Lift up your voice on high, a mighty voice,   410
The voice of gladness ; and on every tongue,
In strains of gratitude, be praises hung,
The praises of so great and good a king :
Shall Churchill reign, and shall not Gotham sing ?
   The seasons as they roll ; Spring, by her side
Lechery and Lent, lay-folly and church-pride,
By a rank monk to copulation led,
A tub of sainted salt-fish on her head ;
Summer, in light transparent gauze array'd,
Like maids of honour at a masquerade,   420
In bawdry gauze, for which our daughters leave
The fig, more modest, first brought up by Eve,
Panting for breath, inflamed with lustful fires,
Yet wanting strength to perfect her desires,
Leaning on Sloth, who, fainting with the heat,
Stops at each step, and slumbers on his feet ;

[1] 'George:' George the Second was born on the 30th of October 1683. —
[2] 'Augusta:' wife of Frederic, Prince of Wales, a great friend of Lord Bute's.

Autumn, when Nature, who with sorrow feels   427
Her dread foe Winter treading on her heels,
Makes up in value what she wants in length,
Exerts her powers, and puts forth all her strength,
Bids corn and fruits in full perfection rise,
Corn fairly tax'd, and fruits without excise;
Winter, benumb'd with cold, no longer known
By robes of fur, since furs became our own ;
A hag, who, loathing all, by all is loathed,
With weekly, daily, hourly, libels clothed,
Vile Faction at her heels, who, mighty grown,
Would rule the ruler, and foreclose the throne,
Would turn all state affairs into a trade,
Make laws one day, the next to be unmade,   440
Beggar at home, a people fear'd abroad,
And, force defeated, make them slaves by fraud ;
All, one and all, shall in this chorus join,
And, dumb to others' praise, be loud in mine.
   Rejoice, ye happy Gothamites ! rejoice ;
Lift up your voice on high, a mighty voice,
The voice of gladness ; and on every tongue,
In strains of gratitude, be praises hung,
The praises of so great and good a king :
Shall Churchill reign, and shall not Gotham sing ?   450
   The year, grand circle ! in whose ample round
The seasons regular and fix'd are bound,
(Who, in his course repeated o'er and o'er,
Sees the same things which he had seen before ;
The same stars keep their watch, and the same sun
Runs in the track where he from first hath run ;
The same moon rules the night ; tides ebb and flow ;
Man is a puppet, and this world a show ;
Their old dull follies, old dull fools pursue,
And vice in nothing, but in mode, is new ;   460
   K

He —— a lord (now fair befall that pride,   461
He lived a villain, but a lord he died)
Dashwood is pious, Berkeley[1] fix'd as Fate,
Sandwich (thank Heaven!) first minister of state;
And, though by fools despised, by saints unbless'd,
By friends neglected, and by foes oppress'd,
Scorning the servile arts of each court elf,
Founded on honour, Wilkes is still himself)
The year, encircled with the various train
Which waits, and fills the glories of his reign,   470
Shall, taking up this theme, in chorus join,
And, dumb to others' praise, be loud in mine.

   Rejoice, ye happy Gothamites! rejoice;
Lift up your voice on high, a mighty voice,
The voice of gladness; and on every tongue,
In strains of gratitude, be praises hung,
The praises of so great and good a king:
Shall Churchill reign, and shall not Gotham sing?

   Thus far in sport—nor let our critics hence,
Who sell out monthly trash, and call it sense,   480
Too lightly of our present labours deem,
Or judge at random of so high a theme:
High is our theme, and worthy are the men
To feel the sharpest stroke of Satire's pen;
But when kind Time a proper season brings,
In serious mood to treat of serious things,
Then shall they find, disdaining idle play,
That I can be as grave and dull as they.

   Thus far in sport—nor let half patriots, those
Who shrink from every blast of Power which blows,   490
Who, with tame cowardice familiar grown,
Would hear my thoughts, but fear to speak their own;

---

[1] 'Colonel Norborne Berkeley:' second to Lord Talbot in his duel with Wilkes.

Who (lest bold truths, to do sage Prudence spite, 493
Should burst the portals of their lips by night,
Tremble to trust themselves one hour in sleep)
Condemn our course, and hold our caution cheap ;
When brave Occasion bids, for some great end,
When Honour calls the poet as a friend,
Then shall they find that, e'en on Danger's brink,
He dares to speak what they scarce dare to think. 500

Book II.

How much mistaken are the men who think
That all who will, without restraint may drink,
May largely drink, e'en till their bowels burst,
Pleading no right but merely that of thirst,
At the pure waters of the living well,
Beside whose streams the Muses love to dwell !
Verse is with them a knack, an idle toy,
A rattle gilded o'er, on which a boy
May play untaught, whilst, without art or force,
Make it but jingle, music comes of course. 10
   Little do such men know the toil, the pains,
The daily, nightly racking of the brains,
To range the thoughts, the matter to digest,
To cull fit phrases, and reject the rest ;
To know the times when Humour on the cheek
Of Mirth may hold her sports ; when Wit should speak,
And when be silent ; when to use the powers
Of ornament, and how to place the flowers,
So that they neither give a tawdry glare,
' Nor waste their sweetness in the desert air ;' 20
To form, (which few can do, and scarcely one,
One critic in an age, can find when done)

To form a plan, to strike a grand outline,   23
To fill it up, and make the picture shine
A full and perfect piece ; to make coy Rhyme
Renounce her follies, and with Sense keep time ;
To make proud Sense against her nature bend,
And wear the chains of Rhyme, yet call her friend.
   Some fops there are, amongst the scribbling tribe,
Who make it all their business to describe,   30
No matter whether in or out of place ;
Studious of finery, and fond of lace,
Alike they trim, as coxcomb Fancy brings,
The rags of beggars, and the robes of kings.
Let dull Propriety in state preside
O'er her dull children, Nature is their guide ;
Wild Nature, who at random breaks the fence
Of those tame drudges, Judgment, Taste, and Sense,
Nor would forgive herself the mighty crime
Of keeping terms with Person, Place, and Time.   40
   Let liquid gold emblaze the sun at noon,
With borrow'd beams let silver pale the moon ;
Let surges hoarse lash the resounding shore,
Let streams meander, and let torrents roar ;
Let them breed up the melancholy breeze,
To sigh with sighing, sob with sobbing trees ;
Let vales embroidery wear ; let flowers be tinged
With various tints ; let clouds be laced or fringed,
They have their wish ; like idle monarch boys,
Neglecting things of weight, they sigh for toys ;   50
Give them the crown, the sceptre, and the robe,
Who will may take the power, and rule the globe.
   Others there are, who, in one solemn pace,
With as much zeal as Quakers rail at lace,
Railing at needful ornament, depend
On Sense to bring them to their journey's end :

They would not (Heaven forbid!) their course delay, 57
Nor for a moment step out of the way,
To make the barren road those graces wear
Which Nature would, if pleased, have planted there.
    Vain men! who, blindly thwarting Nature's plan,
Ne'er find a passage to the heart of man;
Who, bred 'mongst fogs in academic land,
Scorn every thing they do not understand;
Who, destitute of humour, wit, and taste,
Let all their little knowledge run to waste,
And frustrate each good purpose, whilst they wear
The robes of Learning with a sloven's air.
Though solid reasoning arms each sterling line,
Though Truth declares aloud, ' This work is mine,'
Vice, whilst from page to page dull morals creep,   70
Throws by the book, and Virtue falls asleep.
    Sense, mere dull, formal Sense, in this gay town,
Must have some vehicle to pass her down;
Nor can she for an hour insure her reign,
Unless she brings fair Pleasure in her train.
Let her from day to day, from year to year,
In all her grave solemnities appear,
And with the voice of trumpets, through the streets,
Deal lectures out to every one she meets;   80
Half who pass by are deaf, and t' other half
Can hear indeed, but only hear to laugh.
    Quit then, ye graver sons of letter'd Pride!
Taking for once Experience as a guide,
Quit this grand error, this dull college mode;
Be your pursuits the same, but change the road;
Write, or at least appear to write, with ease,
' And if you mean to profit, learn to please.'
    In vain for such mistakes they pardon claim,
Because they wield the pen in Virtue's name: 90

Thrice sacred is that name, thrice bless'd the man   91
Who thinks, speaks, writes, and lives on such a plan!
This, in himself, himself of course must bless,
But cannot with the world promote success.
He may be strong, but, with effect to speak,
Should recollect his readers may be weak;
Plain, rigid truths, which saints with comfort bear,
Will make the sinner tremble and despair.
True Virtue acts from love, and the great end
At which she nobly aims is to amend.   100
How then do those mistake who arm her laws
With rigour not their own, and hurt the cause
They mean to help, whilst with a zealot rage
They make that goddess, whom they'd have engage
Our dearest love, in hideous terror rise!
Such may be honest, but they can't be wise.
    In her own full and perfect blaze of light,
Virtue breaks forth too strong for human sight;
The dazzled eye, that nice but weaker sense,
Shuts herself up in darkness for defence: 110
But to make strong conviction deeper sink,
To make the callous feel, the thoughtless think,
Like God, made man, she lays her glory by,
And beams mild comfort on the ravish'd eye:
In earnest most, when most she seems in jest,
She worms into, and winds around, the breast,
To conquer Vice, of Vice appears the friend,
And seems unlike herself to gain her end.
The sons of Sin, to while away the time
Which lingers on their hands, of each black crime   120
To hush the painful memory, and keep
The tyrant Conscience in delusive sleep,
Read on at random, nor suspect the dart
Until they find it rooted in their heart.

'Gainst vice they give their vote, nor know at first   125
That, cursing that, themselves too they have cursed ;
They see not, till they fall into the snares,
Deluded into virtue unawares.
Thus the shrewd doctor, in the spleen-struck mind,
When pregnant horror sits, and broods o'er wind,   130
Discarding drugs, and striving how to please,
Lures on insensibly, by slow degrees,
The patient to those manly sports which bind
The slacken'd sinews, and relieve the mind ;
The patient feels a change as wrought by stealth,
And wonders on demand to find it health.

    Some few, whom Fate ordain'd to deal in rhymes
In other lands, and here, in other times,
Whom, waiting at their birth, the midwife Muse
Sprinkled all over with Castalian dews,   140
To whom true Genius gave his magic pen,
Whom Art by just degrees led up to men ;
Some few, extremes well shunn'd, have steer'd between
These dangerous rocks, and held the golden mean ;
Sense in their works maintains her proper state,
But never sleeps, or labours with her weight ;
Grace makes the whole look elegant and gay,
But never dares from Sense to run astray:
So nice the master's touch, so great his care,
The colours boldly glow, not idly glare ;   150
Mutually giving and receiving aid,
They set each other off, like light and shade,
And, as by stealth, with so much softness blend,
'Tis hard to say where they begin or end :
Both give us charms, and neither gives offence ;
Sense perfects Grace, and Grace enlivens Sense.

    Peace to the men who these high honours claim,
Health to their souls, and to their memories fame !

Be it my task, and no mean task, to teach   159
A reverence for that worth I cannot reach :
Let me at distance, with a steady eye,
Observe and mark their passage to the sky ;
From envy free, applaud such rising worth,
And praise their heaven, though pinion'd down to earth!
    Had I the power, I could not have the time,
Whilst spirits flow, and life is in her prime,
Without a sin 'gainst Pleasure, to design
A plan, to methodise each thought, each line
Highly to finish, and make every grace,
In itself charming, take new charms from place.   170
Nothing of books, and little known of men,
When the mad fit comes on, I seize the pen,
Rough as they run, the rapid thoughts set down,
Rough as they run, discharge them on the town.
Hence rude, unfinish'd brats, before their time,
Are born into this idle world of Rhyme,
And the poor slattern Muse is brought to bed
'With all her imperfections on her head.'
Some, as no life appears, no pulses play
Through the dull dubious mass, no breath makes way,   180
Doubt, greatly doubt, till for a glass they call,
Whether the child can be baptized at all ;
Others, on other grounds, objections frame,
And, granting that the child may have a name,
Doubt, as the sex might well a midwife pose,
Whether they should baptize it Verse or Prose.
    E'en what my masters please ; bards, mild, meek men,
In love to critics, stumble now and then.
Something I do myself, and something too,
If they can do it, leave for them to do.   190
In the small compass of my careless page
Critics may find employment for an age :

Without my blunders, they were all undone ; 193
I twenty feed, where Mason can feed one.
  When Satire stoops, unmindful of her state,
To praise the man I love, curse him I hate ;
When Sense, in tides of passion borne along,
Sinking to prose, degrades the name of song,
The censor smiles, and, whilst my credit bleeds,
With as high relish on the carrion feeds 200
As the proud earl fed at a turtle feast,
Who, turn'd by gluttony to worse than beast,
Ate till his bowels gush'd upon the floor,
Yet still ate on, and dying call'd for more.
  When loose Digression, like a colt unbroke,
Spurning Connexion and her formal yoke,
Bounds through the forest, wanders far astray
From the known path, and loves to lose her way,
'Tis a full feast to all the mongrel pack
To run the rambler down, and bring her back. 210
  When gay Description, Fancy's fairy child,
Wild without art, and yet with pleasure wild,
Waking with Nature at the morning hour
To the lark's call, walks o'er the opening flower
Which largely drank all night of heaven's fresh dew,
And, like a mountain nymph of Dian's crew,
So lightly walks, she not one mark imprints,
Nor brushes off the dews, nor soils the tints ;
When thus Description sports, even at the time
That drums should beat, and cannons roar in rhyme, 220
Critics can live on such a fault as that
From one month to the other, and grow fat.
  Ye mighty Monthly Judges ! in a dearth
Of letter'd blockheads, conscious of the worth
Of my materials, which against your will
Oft you've confess'd, and shall confess it still ;

Materials rich, though rude, inflamed with thought,   227
Though more by Fancy than by Judgment wrought;
Take, use them as your own, a work begin
Which suits your genius well, and weave them in,
Framed for the critic loom, with critic art,
Till, thread on thread depending, part on part,
Colour with colour mingling, light with shade,
To your dull taste a formal work is made,
And, having wrought them into one grand piece,
Swear it surpasses Rome, and rivals Greece.

Nor think this much, for at one single word,
Soon as the mighty critic fiat's heard,
Science attends their call; their power is own'd;
Order takes place, and Genius is dethroned :   240
Letters dance into books, defiance hurl'd
At means, as atoms danced into a world.

Me higher business calls, a greater plan,
Worthy man's whole employ, the good of man,
The good of man committed to my charge :
If idle Fancy rambles forth at large,
Careless of such a trust, these harmless lays
May Friendship envy, and may Folly praise.
The crown of Gotham may some Scot assume,
And vagrant Stuarts reign in Churchill's room!   250

O my poor People! O thou wretched Earth!
To whose dear love, though not engaged by birth,
My heart is fix'd, my service deeply sworn,
How, (by thy father can that thought be borne?—
For monarchs, would they all but think like me,
Are only fathers in the best degree)
How must thy glories fade, in every land
Thy name be laugh'd to scorn, thy mighty hand
Be shorten'd, and thy zeal, by foes confess'd,
Bless'd in thyself, to make thy neighbours bless'd,   260

Be robb'd of vigour ; how must Freedom's pile,　　261
The boast of ages, which adorns the isle
And makes it great and glorious, fear'd abroad,
Happy at home, secure from force and fraud ;
How must that pile, by ancient Wisdom raised
On a firm rock, by friends admired and praised,
Envied by foes, and wonder'd at by all,
In one short moment into ruins fall,
Should any slip of Stuart's tyrant race,
Or bastard or legitimate, disgrace　　　　270
Thy royal seat of empire ! But what care,
What sorrow must be mine, what deep despair
And self-reproaches, should that hated line
Admittance gain through any fault of mine !
Cursed be the cause whence Gotham's evils spring,
Though that cursed cause be found in Gotham's king.
　　Let War, with all his needy ruffian band,
In pomp of horror stalk through Gotham's land
Knee-deep in blood ; let all her stately towers
Sink in the dust ; that court which now is ours　　280
Become a den, where beasts may, if they can,
A lodging find, nor fear rebuke from man ;
Where yellow harvests rise, be brambles found ;
Where vines now creep, let thistles curse the ground ;
Dry in her thousand valleys be the rills ;
Barren the cattle on her thousand hills ;
Where Power is placed, let tigers prowl for prey ;
Where Justice lodges, let wild asses bray ;
Let cormorants in churches make their nest,
And on the sails of Commerce bitterns rest ;　　290
Be all, though princes in the earth before,
Her merchants bankrupts, and her marts no moré ;
Much rather would I, might the will of Fate
Give me to choose, see Gotham's ruin'd state

By ills on ills thus to the earth weigh'd down,   295
Than live to see a Stuart wear a crown.
    Let Heaven in vengeance arm all Nature's host,
Those servants who their Maker know, who boast
Obedience as their glory, and fulfil,
Unquestion'd, their great Master's sacred will ;   300
Let raging winds root up the boiling deep,
And, with Destruction big, o'er Gotham sweep ;
Let rains rush down, till Faith, with doubtful eye,
Looks for the sign of mercy in the sky ;
Let Pestilence in all her horrors rise ;
Where'er I turn, let Famine blast my eyes ;
Let the earth yawn, and, ere they 've time to think,
In the deep gulf let all my subjects sink
Before my eyes, whilst on the verge I reel ;
Feeling, but as a monarch ought to feel,   310
Not for myself, but them, I'll kiss the rod,
And, having own'd the justice of my God,
Myself with firmness to the ruin give,
And die with those for whom I wish to live.
    This, (but may Heaven's more merciful decrees
Ne'er tempt his servant with such ills as these !)
This, or my soul deceives me, I could bear ;
But that the Stuart race my crown should wear,
That crown, where, highly cherish'd, Freedom shone
Bright as the glories of the midday sun ;   320
Born and bred slaves, that they, with proud misrule,
Should make brave freeborn men, like boys at school,
To the whip crouch and tremble—Oh, that thought !
The labouring brain is e'en to madness brought
By the dread vision ; at the mere surmise
The thronging spirits, as in tumult, rise ;
My heart, as for a passage, loudly beats,
And, turn me where I will, distraction meets.

O my brave fellows ! great in arts and arms,   329
The wonder of the earth, whom glory warms
To high achievements ; can your spirits bend,
Through base control (ye never can descend
So low by choice) to wear a tyrant's chain,
Or let, in Freedom's seat, a Stuart reign ?
If Fame, who hath for ages, far and wide,
Spread in all realms the cowardice, the pride,
The tyranny and falsehood of those lords,
Contents you not, search England's fair records ;
England, where first the breath of life I drew,
Where, next to Gotham, my best love is due ;   340
There once they ruled, though crush'd by William's hand,
They rule no more, to curse that happy land.

    The first,[1] who, from his native soil removed,
Held England's sceptre, a tame tyrant proved :
Virtue he lack'd, cursed with those thoughts which spring
In souls of vulgar stamp, to be a king ;
Spirit he had not, though he laugh'd at laws,
To play the bold-faced tyrant with applause ;
On practices most mean he raised his pride,
And Craft oft gave what Wisdom oft denied.   350

    Ne'er could he feel how truly man is blest
In blessing those around him ; in his breast,
Crowded with follies, Honour found no room ;
Mark'd for a coward in his mother's womb,
He was too proud without affronts to live,
Too timorous to punish or forgive.

    To gain a crown which had, in course of time,
By fair descent, been his without a crime,
He bore a mother's exile ; to secure
A greater crown, he basely could endure   360

---

[1] ' First : ' James the First.

The spilling of her blood by foreign knife,　　　361
Nor dared revenge her death who gave him life :
Nay, by fond Fear, and fond Ambition led,
Struck hands with those by whom her blood was shed.[1]

Call'd up to power, scarce warm on England's throne,
He fill'd her court with beggars from his own :
Turn where you would, the eye with Scots was caught,
Or English knaves, who would be Scotsmen thought.
To vain expense unbounded loose he gave,
The dupe of minions, and of slaves the slave ;　　　370
On false pretences mighty sums he raised,
And damn'd those senates rich, whom poor he praised ;
From empire thrown, and doom'd to beg her bread,
On foreign bounty whilst a daughter fed,
He lavish'd sums, for her received, on men
Whose names would fix dishonour on my pen.

Lies were his playthings, parliaments his sport ;
Book-worms and catamites engross'd the court :
Vain of the scholar, like all Scotsmen since,
The pedant scholar, he forgot the prince ;　　　380
And having with some trifles stored his brain,
Ne'er learn'd, nor wish'd to learn, the art to reign.
Enough he knew, to make him vain and proud,
Mock'd by the wise, the wonder of the crowd ;
False friend, false son, false father,[2] and false king,
False wit, false statesman, and false everything,
When he should act, he idly chose to prate,
And pamphlets wrote, when he should save the state.

Religious, if religion holds in whim ;
To talk with all, he let all talk with him ;　　　390

---

[1] 'Blood was shed:' Secretary Cecil, who had been a bitter foe of Queen
Mary, and became a favourite of James.—[2] 'False father:' alluding to the
death of the very promising Prince Henry, popularly supposed to have been
hated and removed by his father.

Not on God's honour, but his own intent,   391
Not for religion's sake, but argument;
More vain if some sly, artful High-Dutch slave,
Or, from the Jesuit school, some precious knave
Conviction feign'd, than if, to peace restored
By his full soldiership, worlds hail'd him lord.
   Power was his wish, unbounded as his will,
The power, without control, of doing ill;
But what he wish'd, what he made bishops preach,
And statesmen warrant, hung within his reach   400
He dared not seize; Fear gave, to gall his pride,
That freedom to the realm his will denied.
   Of treaties fond, o'erweening of his parts,
In every treaty of his own mean arts
He fell the dupe; peace was his coward care,
E'en at a time when Justice call'd for war:
His pen he'd draw to prove his lack of wit,
But rather than unsheath the sword, submit.
Truth fairly must record; and, pleased to live
In league with Mercy, Justice may forgive   410
Kingdoms betray'd, and worlds resign'd to Spain,
But never can forgive a Raleigh slain.
   At length, (with white let Freedom mark that year)
Not fear'd by those whom most he wish'd to fear,
Not loved by those whom most he wish'd to love,
He went to answer for his faults above;
To answer to that God, from whom alone
He claim'd to hold, and to abuse the throne;
Leaving behind, a curse to all his line,
The bloody legacy of Right Divine.[1]   420
   With many virtues which a radiance fling
Round private men; with few which grace a king,

---

[1] 'Right Divine:' see, as a *per contra* to this fierce invective against poor 'King Jamie,' Scott's 'Fortunes of Nigel.'

And speak the monarch; at that time of life   423
When Passion holds with Reason doubtful strife,
Succeeded Charles, by a mean sire undone,
Who envied virtue even in a son.

   His youth was froward, turbulent, and wild;
He took the Man up ere he left the Child;
His soul was eager for imperial sway,
Ere he had learn'd the lesson to obey.   430
Surrounded by a fawning, flattering throng,
Judgment each day grew weak, and humour strong;
Wisdom was treated as a noisome weed,
And all his follies left to run to seed.

   What ills from such beginnings needs must spring!
What ills to such a land from such a king!
What could she hope! what had she not to fear!
Base Buckingham[1] possess'd his youthful ear;
Strafford and Laud, when mounted on the throne,
Engross'd his love, and made him all their own;   440
Strafford and Laud, who boldly dared avow
The trait'rous doctrine taught by Tories now;
Each strove t' undo him in his turn and hour,
The first with pleasure, and the last with power.
Thinking (vain thought, disgraceful to the throne!)
That all mankind were made for kings alone;
That subjects were but slaves; and what was whim,
Or worse, in common men, was law in him;
Drunk with Prerogative, which Fate decreed
To guard good kings, and tyrants to mislead;   450
Which in a fair proportion to deny
Allegiance dares not; which to hold too high,
No good can wish, no coward king can dare,
And, held too high, no English subject bear;

---

[1] 'Buckingham:' George Villiers, Duke of Buckingham.

Besieged by men of deep and subtle arts, 455
Men void of principle, and damn'd with parts,
Who saw his weakness, made their king their tool,
Then most a slave, when most he seem'd to rule ;
Taking all public steps for private ends,
Deceived by favourites, whom he called friends, 460
He had not strength enough of soul to find
That monarchs, meant as blessings to mankind,
Sink their great state, and stamp their fame undone,
When what was meant for all, they give to one.
Listening uxorious whilst a woman's prate [1]
Modell'd the church, and parcell'd out the state,
Whilst (in the state not more than women read)
High-churchmen preach'd, and turn'd his pious head ;
Tutor'd to see with ministerial eyes ;
Forbid to hear a loyal nation's cries ; 470
Made to believe (what can't a favourite do ?)
He heard a nation, hearing one or two ;
Taught by state-quacks himself secure to think,
And out of danger e'en on danger's brink ;
Whilst power was daily crumbling from his hand,
Whilst murmurs ran through an insulted land,
As if to sanction tyrants Heaven was bound,
He proudly sought the ruin which he found.

Twelve years, twelve tedious and inglorious years,[2]
Did England, crush'd by power, and awed by fears. 480
Whilst proud Oppression struck at Freedom's root,
Lament her senates lost, her Hampden mute.
Illegal taxes and oppressive loans,
In spite of all her pride, call'd forth her groans ;
Patience was heard her griefs aloud to tell,
And Loyalty was tempted to rebel.

---

[1] ' Woman's prate : ' Henrietta, the intriguing Queen of Charles the First.
—[2] ' Inglorious years : ' no parliament was summoned from 1628 to 1640.

Each day new acts of outrage shook the state,   487
New courts were raised to give new doctrines weight ;
State inquisitions kept the realm in awe,
And cursed Star-Chambers made or ruled the law ;
Juries were ·pack'd, and judges were unsound ;
Through the whole kingdom not one Pratt was found.
    From the first moments of his giddy youth
He hated senates, for they told him truth.
At length, against his will compell'd to treat,
Those whom he could not fright, he strove to cheat ;
With base dissembling every grievance heard,
And, often giving, often broke his word.
Oh, where shall hapless Truth for refuge fly,
If kings, who should protect her, dare to lie ?   500
    Those who, the general good their real aim,
Sought in their country's good their monarch's fame ;
Those who were anxious for his safety ; those
Who were induced by duty to oppose,
Their truth suspected, and their worth unknown,
He held as foes and traitors to his throne ;
Nor found his fatal error till the hour
Of saving him was gone and past ; till power
Had shifted hands, to blast his hapless reign,
Making their faith and his repentance vain.   510
    Hence (be that curse confined to Gotham's foes !)
War, dread to mention, Civil War arose ;
All acts of outrage, and all acts of shame,
Stalk'd forth at large, disguised with Honour's name ;
Rebellion, raising high her bloody hand,
Spread universal havoc through the land ;
With zeal for party, and with passion drunk,
In public rage all private love was sunk ;
Friend against friend, brother 'gainst brother stood,
And the son's weapon drank the father's blood ;   520

Nature, aghast, and fearful lest her reign   521
Should last no longer, bled in every vein.
   Unhappy Stuart! harshly though that name
Grates on my ear, I should have died with shame
To see my king before his subjects stand,
And at their bar hold up his royal hand ;
At their commands to hear the monarch plead,
By their decrees to see that monarch bleed.
What though thy faults were many and were great ?
What though they shook the basis of the state ?   530
In royalty secure thy person stood,
And sacred was the fountain of thy blood.
Vile ministers, who dared abuse their trust,
Who dared seduce a king to be unjust,
Vengeance, with Justice leagued, with Power made strong,
Had nobly crush'd—' The king could do no wrong.'
   .Yet grieve not, Charles ! nor thy hard fortunes blame ;
They took thy life, but they secured thy fame.
Their greatest crimes made thine like specks appear,
From which the sun in glory is not clear.   540
Hadst thou in peace and years resign'd thy breath
At Nature's call ; hadst thou laid down in death
As in a sleep, thy name, by Justice borne
On the four winds, had been in pieces torn.
Pity, the virtue of a generous soul,
Sometimes the vice, hath made thy memory whole.
Misfortunes gave what Virtue could not give,
And bade, the tyrant slain, the martyr live.
   Ye Princes of the earth ! ye mighty few !
Who, worlds subduing, can't yourselves subdue ;   550
Who, goodness scorn'd, wish only to be great ;
Whose breath is blasting, and whose voice is fate ;
Who own no law, no reason, but your will,
And scorn restraint, though 'tis from doing ill ;

Who of all passions groan beneath the worst,   555
Then only bless'd when they make others cursed ;
Think not, for wrongs like these, unscourged to live ;
Long may ye sin, and long may Heaven forgive ;
But when ye least expect, in sorrow's day,
Vengeance shall fall more heavy for delay ;   560
Nor think that vengeance heap'd on you alone
Shall (poor amends !) for injured worlds atone ;
No, like some base distemper, which remains,
Transmitted from the tainted father's veins,
In the son's blood, such broad and general crimes
Shall call down vengeance e'en to latest times,
Call vengeance down on all who bear your name,
And make their portion bitterness and shame.
        From land to land for years compell'd to roam,
Whilst Usurpation lorded it at home,   570
Of majesty unmindful, forced to fly,
Not daring, like a king, to reign or die,
Recall'd to repossess his lawful throne,
More at his people's seeking than his own,
Another Charles succeeded.   In the school
Of Travel he had learn'd to play the fool ;
And, like pert pupils with dull tutors sent
To shame their country on the Continent,
From love of England by long absence wean'd,
From every court he every folly glean'd,   580
And was—so close do evil habits cling—
Till crown'd, a beggar ; and when crown'd, no king.
        Those grand and general powers, which Heaven design'd,
An instance of his mercy to mankind,
Were lost, in storms of dissipation hurl'd,
Nor would he give one hour to bless a world ;
Lighter than levity which strides the blast,
And, of the present fond, forgets the past,

He changed and changed, but, every hope to curse,   589
Changed only from one folly to a worse :
State he resign'd to those whom state could please ;
Careless of majesty, his wish was ease ;
Pleasure, and pleasure only, was his aim ;
Kings of less wit might hunt the bubble Fame ;
Dignity through his reign was made a sport,
Nor dared Decorum show her face at court ;
Morality was held a standing jest,
And Faith a necessary fraud at best.
Courtiers, their monarch ever in their view,
Possess'd great talents, and abused them too ;   600
Whate'er was light, impertinent, and vain,
Whate'er was loose, indecent, and profane,
(So ripe was Folly, Folly to acquit)
Stood all absolved in that poor bauble, Wit.

   In gratitude, alas ! but little read,
He let his father's servants beg their bread—
His father's faithful servants, and his own,
To place the foes of both around his throne.

   Bad counsels he embraced through indolence,
Through love of ease, and not through want of sense ;
He saw them wrong, but rather let them go   611
As right, than take the pains to make them so.
Women ruled all, and ministers of state
Were for commands at toilets forced to wait :
Women, who have, as monarchs, graced the land,
But never govern'd well at second-hand.

   To make all other errors slight appear,
In memory fix'd, stand Dunkirk [1] and Tangier ; [2]
In memory fix'd so deep, that Time in vain
Shall strive to wipe those records from the brain,   620

---

[1] ' Dunkirk : ' Dunkirk was, in 1662, sold by Charles the Second to the French for £400,000.— [2] ' Tangier : ' Tangier, in Africa, was also shamefully sacrificed by Charles the Second.

Amboyna [1] stands—Gods! that a king could hold   621
In such high estimate vile paltry gold,
And of his duty be so careless found,
That when the blood of subjects from the ground
For vengeance call'd, he should reject their cry,
And, bribed from honour, lay his thunders by,
Give Holland peace, whilst English victims groan'd,
And butcher'd subjects wander'd unatoned!
Oh, dear, deep injury to England's fame,
To them, to us, to all! to him deep shame!   630
Of all the passions which from frailty spring,
Avarice is that which least becomes a king.

To crown the whole, scorning the public good,
Which through his reign he little understood,
Or little heeded, with too narrow aim
He reassumed a bigot brother's claim,
And having made time-serving senates bow,
Suddenly died—that brother best knew how.

No matter how—he slept amongst the dead,
And James his brother reignèd in his stead: 640
But such a reign—so glaring an offence
In every step 'gainst freedom, law, and sense,
'Gainst all the rights of Nature's general plan,
'Gainst all which constitutes an Englishman,
That the relation would mere fiction seem,
The mock creation of a poet's dream;
And the poor bards would, in this sceptic age,
Appear as false as *their* historian's page.

Ambitious Folly seized the seat of Wit,
Christians were forced by bigots to submit;   650
Pride without sense, without religion Zeal,
Made daring inroads on the Commonweal;

---

[1] 'Amboyna:' where the Dutch inflicted dreadful and unavenged cruelties on the English. This happened, however, in 1622, under James the First, not Charles the Second.

Stern Persecution raised her iron rod,   653
And call'd the pride of kings, the power of God ;
Conscience and Fame were sacrificed to'Rome,
And England wept at Freedom's sacred tomb.
    Her laws despised, her constitution wrench'd
From its due natural frame, her rights retrench'd
Beyond a coward's suff'rance, conscience forced,
And healing Justice from the Crown divorced,   660
Each moment pregnant with vile acts of power,
Her patriot Bishops sentenced to the Tower,
Her Oxford (who yet loves the Stuart name)
Branded with arbitrary marks of shame,
She wept—but wept not long : to arms she flew,
At Honour's call th' avenging sword she drew,
Turn'd all her terrors on the tyrant's head,
And sent him in despair to beg his bread ;
Whilst she, (may every State in such distress
Dare with such zeal, and meet with such success!)   670
Whilst she, (may Gotham, should my abject mind
Choose to enslave rather than free mankind,
Pursue her steps, tear the proud tyrant down,
Nor let me wear if I abuse the crown !)
Whilst she, (through every age, in every land
Written in gold, let Revolution stand!)
Whilst she, secured in liberty and law,
Found what she sought, a saviour in Nassau.

Book III.

Can the fond mother from herself depart ?[1]
Can she forget the darling of her heart,
The little darling whom she bore and bred,
Nursed on her knees, and at her bosom fed ;

[1] Isa. xlix. 15.

To whom she seem'd her every thought to give, 5
And in whose life alone she seem'd to live ?
Yes, from herself the mother may depart,
She may forget the darling of her heart,
The little darling whom she bore and bred,
Nursed on her knees, and at her bosom fed, 10
To whom she seem'd her every thought to give,
And in whose life alone she seem'd to live ;
But I cannot forget, whilst life remains,
And pours her current through these swelling veins,
Whilst Memory offers up at Reason's shrine ;
But I cannot forget that Gotham 's mine.
  Can the stern mother, than the brutes more wild,
From her disnatured breast tear her young child,
Flesh of her flesh, and of her bone the bone,
And dash the smiling babe against a stone ? 20
Yes, the stern mother, than the brutes more wild,
From her disnatured breast may tear her child,
Flesh of her flesh, and of her bone the bone,
And dash the smiling babe against a stone ;
But I, (forbid it, Heaven !) but I can ne'er
The love of Gotham from this bosom tear ;
Can ne'er so far true royalty pervert
From its fair course, to do my people hurt.
  With how much ease, with how much confidence—
As if, superior to each grosser sense, 30
Reason had only, in full power array'd,
To manifest her will, and be obey'd—
Men make resolves, and pass into decrees
The motions of the mind ! with how much ease,
In such resolves, doth passion make a flaw,
And bring to nothing what was raised to law !
  In empire young, scarce warm on Gotham's throne,
The dangers and the sweets of power unknown,

Pleased, though I scarce know why, like some young child,
Whose little senses each new toy turns wild,   40
How do I hold sweet dalliance with my crown,
And wanton with dominion, how lay down,
Without the sanction of a precedent,
Rules of most large and absolute extent ;
Rules, which from sense of public virtue spring,
And all at once commence a Patriot King !   .
    But, for the day of trial is at hand,
And the whole fortunes of a mighty land
Are staked on me, and all their weal or woe
Must from my good or evil conduct flow,   50
Will I, or can I, on a fair review,
As I assume that name, deserve it too ?
Have I well weigh'd the great, the noble part
I 'm now to play ? have I explored my heart,
That labyrinth of fraud, that deep dark cell,
Where, unsuspected e'en by me, may dwell
Ten thousand follies ? have I found out there
What I am fit to do, and what to bear ?
Have I traced every passion to its rise,
Nor spared one lurking seed of treacherous vice ?   60
Have I familiar with my nature grown ?
And am I fairly to myself made known ?
A Patriot King !—why, 'tis a name which bears
The more immediate stamp of Heaven ; which wears
The nearest, best resemblance we can show
Of God above, through all his works below.
    To still the voice of Discord in the land ;
To make weak Faction's discontented band,
Detected, weak, and crumbling to decay,
With hunger pinch'd, on their own vitals prey ;   70
Like brethren, in the self-same interests warm'd,
Like different bodies, with one soul inform'd ;

To make a nation, nobly raised above   73
All meaner thought, grow up in common love ;
To give the laws due vigour, and to hold
That secret balance, temperate, yet bold,
With such an equal hand, that those who fear
May yet approve, and own my justice clear ;
To be a common father, to secure
The weak from violence, from pride the poor ;   80
Vice and her sons to banish in disgrace,
To make Corruption dread to show her face ;
To bid afflicted Virtue take new state,
And be at last acquainted with the great ;
Of all religions to elect the best,
Nor let her priests be made a standing jest ;
Rewards for worth with liberal hand to carve,
To love the arts, nor let the artists starve ;
To make fair Plenty through the realm increase,
Give fame in war, and happiness in peace ;   90
To see my people virtuous, great, and free,
And know that all those blessings flow from me ;
Oh ! 'tis a joy too exquisite, a thought
Which flatters Nature more than flattery ought ;
'Tis a great, glorious task, for man too hard ;
But no less great, less glorious the reward,
The best reward which here to man is given,
'Tis more than earth, and little short of heaven ;
A task (if such comparison may be)
The same in Nature, diff'ring in degree,   100
Like that which God, on whom for aid I call,
Performs with ease, and yet performs to all.
    How much do they mistake, how little know
Of kings, of kingdoms, and the pains which flow
From royalty, who fancy that a crown,
Because it glistens, must be lined with down !

With outside show, and vain appearance caught,   107
They look no farther, and, by Folly taught,
Prize high the toys of thrones, but never find
One of the many cares which lurk behind.
The gem they worship which a crown adorns,
Nor once suspect that crown is lined with thorns.
Oh, might Reflection Folly's place supply,
Would we one moment use her piercing eye,
Then should we find what woe from grandeur springs,
And learn to pity, not to envy kings !
  The villager, born humbly and bred hard,
Content his wealth, and Poverty his guard,
In action simply just, in conscience clear,
By guilt untainted, undisturb'd by fear,   120
His means but scanty, and his wants but few,
Labour his business, and his pleasure too,
Enjoys more comforts in a single hour
Than ages give the wretch condemn'd to power.
  Call'd up by health, he rises with the day,
And goes to work, as if he went to play,
Whistling off toils, one half of which might make
The stoutest Atlas of a palace quake ;
'Gainst heat and cold, which make us cowards faint,
Harden'd by constant use, without complaint   130
He bears what we should think it death to bear ;
Short are his meals, and homely is his fare ;
His thirst he slakes at some pure neighbouring brook,
Nor asks for sauce where appetite stands cook.
When the dews fall, and when the sun retires
Behind the mountains, when the village fires,
Which, waken'd all at once, speak supper nigh,
At distance catch, and fix his longing eye,
Homeward he hies, and with his manly brood
Of raw-boned cubs enjoys that clean, coarse food,   140

Which, season'd with good-humour, his fond bride   141
'Gainst his return is happy to provide ;
Then, free from care, and free from thought, he creeps
Into his straw, and till the morning sleeps.
    Not so the king—with anxious cares oppress'd
His bosom labours, and admits not rest :
A glorious wretch, he sweats beneath the weight
Of majesty, and gives up ease for state.
E'en when his smiles, which, by the fools of pride,
Are treasured and preserved from side to side,   150
Fly round the court, e'en when, compell'd by form,
He seems most calm, his soul is in a storm.
Care, like a spectre, seen by him alone,
With all her nest of vipers, round his throne
By day crawls full in view ; when Night bids sleep,
Sweet nurse of Nature ! o'er the senses creep ;
When Misery herself no more complains,
And slaves, if possible, forget their chains ;
Though his sense weakens, though his eyes grow dim,
That rest which comes to all, comes not to him.   160
E'en at that hour, Care, tyrant Care, forbids
The dew of sleep to fall upon his lids ;
From night to night she watches at his bed ;
Now, as one moped, sits brooding o'er his head ;
Anon she starts, and, borne on raven's wings,
Croaks forth aloud—'Sleep was not made for kings !'
    Thrice hath the moon, who governs this vast ball,
Who rules most absolute o'er me and all ;
To whom, by full conviction taught to bow,
At new, at full, I pay the duteous vow ;   170
Thrice hath the moon her wonted course pursued,
Thrice hath she lost her form, and thrice renew'd,
Since, (bless'd be that season, for before
I was a mere, mere mortal, and no more,

One of the herd, a lump of common clay,   175
Inform'd with life, to die and pass away)
Since I became a king, and Gotham's throne,
With full and ample power, became my own ;
Thrice hath the moon her wonted course pursued,
Thrice hath she lost her form, and thrice renew'd,   180
Since sleep, kind sleep ! who. like a friend supplies
New vigour for new toil, hath closed these eyes.
Nor, if my toils are answer'd with success,
And I am made an instrument to bless
The people whom I love, shall I repine ;
Theirs be the benefit, the labour mine.

    Mindful of that high rank in which I stand,
Of millions lord, sole ruler in the. land,
Let me,—and Reason shall her aid afford,—
Rule my own spirit, of myself be lord.   190
With an ill grace that monarch wears his crown,
Who, stern and hard of nature, wears a frown
'Gainst faults in other men, yet all the while
Meets his own vices with a partial smile.
How can a king (yet on record we find
Such kings have been, such curses of mankind)
Enforce that law 'gainst some poor subject elf
Which conscience tells him he hath broke himself ?
Can he some petty rogue to justice call
For robbing one, when he himself robs all ?   200
Must not, unless extinguish'd, Conscience fly
Into his cheek, and blast his fading eye,
To scourge th' oppressor, when the State, distress'd
And sunk to ruin, is by him oppress'd ?
Against himself doth he not sentence give ;
If one must die, t' other's not fit to live.

    Weak is that throne, and in itself unsound,
Which takes not solid virtue for its ground.

All envy power in others, and complain   209
Of that which they would perish to obtain.
Nor can those spirits, turbulent and bold,
Not to be awed by threats, nor bought with gold,
Be hush'd to peace, but when fair legal sway
Makes it their real interest to obey ;
When kings, and none but fools can then rebel,
Not less in virtue, than in power, excel.
    Be that my object, that my constant care,
And may my soul's best wishes centre there ;
Be it my task to seek, nor seek in vain,
Not only how to live, but how to reign ;   220
And to those virtues which from Reason spring,
And grace the man, join those which grace the king.
    First, (for strict duty bids my care extend
And reach to all who on that care depend,
Bids me with servants keep a steady hand,
And watch o'er all my proxies in the land)
First, (and that method Reason shall support)
Before I look into, and purge my court,
Before I cleanse the stable of the State,
Let me fix things which to myself relate.   230
That done, and all accounts well settled here,
In resolution firm, in honour clear,
Tremble, ye slaves ! who dare abuse your trust,
Who dare be villains, when your king is just.
    Are there, amongst those officers of state,
To whom our sacred power we delegate,
Who hold our place and office in the realm,
Who, in our name commission'd, guide the helm ;
Are there, who, trusting to our love of ease,
Oppress our subjects, wrest our just decrees,   240
And make the laws, warp'd from their fair intent,
To speak a language which they never meant ;

Are there such men, and can the fools depend   243
On holding out in safety to their end ?
Can they so much, from thoughts of danger free,
Deceive themselves. so much misdeem of me,
To think that I will prove a statesman's tool,
And live a stranger where I ought to rule ?
What ! to myself and to my state unjust,
Shall I from ministers take things on trust,   250
And, sinking low the credit of my throne,
Depend upon dependants of my own ?
Shall I,—most certain source of future cares,—
Not use my judgment, but depend on theirs ?
Shall I, true puppet-like, be mock'd with state,
Have nothing but the name of being great ;
Attend at councils which I must not weigh ;
Do what they bid, and what they dictate, say ;
Enrobed, and hoisted up into my chair,
Only to be a royal cipher there ?   260
Perish the thought—'tis treason to my throne—
And who but thinks it, could his thoughts be known
Insults me more than he, who, leagued with Hell,
Shall rise in arms, and 'gainst my crown rebel.
    The wicked statesman, whose false heart pursues
A train of guilt ; who acts with double views,
And wears a double face ; whose base designs
Strike at his monarch's throne ; who undermines
E'en whilst he seems his wishes to support ;
Who seizes all departments ; packs a court ;   270
Maintains an agent on the judgment-seat,
To screen his crimes, and make his frauds complete ;
New-models armies, and around the throne
Will suffer none but creatures of his own,
Conscious of such his baseness, well may try,
Against the light to shut his master's eye,

To keep him coop'd, and far removed from those   277
Who, brave and honest, dare his crimes disclose,
Nor ever let him in one place appear,
Where truth, unwelcome truth, may wound his ear.
    Attempts like these, well weigh'd, themselves proclaim,
And, whilst they publish, balk their author's aim.
Kings must be blind into such snares to run,
Or, worse, with open eyes must be undone.
The minister of honesty and worth
Demands the day to bring his actions forth ;
Calls on the sun to shine with fiercer rays,
And braves that trial which must end in praise.
None fly the day, and seek the shades of night,
But those whose actions cannot bear the light ;   290
None wish their king in ignorance to hold
But those who feel that knowledge must unfold
Their hidden guilt ; and, that dark mist dispell'd
By which their places and their lives are held,
Confusion wait them, and, by Justice led,
In vengeance fall on every traitor's head.
    Aware of this, and caution'd 'gainst the pit
Where kings have oft been lost, shall I submit,
And rust in chains like these ? shall I give way,
And whilst my helpless subjects fall a prey   300
To power abused, in ignorance sit down,
Nor dare assert the honour of my crown ?
When stern Rebellion, (if that odious name
Justly belongs to those whose only aim,
Is to preserve their country ; who oppose,
In honour leagued, none but their country's foes ;
Who only seek their own, and found their cause
In due regard for violated laws)
When stern Rebellion, who no longer feels
Nor fears rebuke, a nation at her heels,   310

A nation up in arms, though strong not proud,   311
Knocks at the palace gate, and, calling loud
For due redress, presents, from Truth's fair pen,
A list of wrongs, not to be borne by men :
How must that king be humbled, how disgrace
All that is royal in his name and place,
Who, thus call'd forth to answer, can advance
No other plea but that of ignorance !
A vile defence, which, was his all at stake,
The meanest subject well might blush to make ;   320
A filthy source, from whence shame ever springs ;
A stain to all, but most a stain to kings.
The soul with great and manly feelings warm'd,
Panting for knowledge, rests not till inform'd ;
And shall not I, fired with the glorious zeal,
Feel those brave passions which my subjects feel ?
Or can a just excuse from ignorance flow
To me, whose first great duty is—to know ?

   Hence, Ignorance !—thy settled, dull, blank eye
Would hurt me, though I knew no reason why.   330
Hence, Ignorance !—thy slavish shackles bind
The free-born soul, and lethargise the mind.
Of thee, begot by Pride, who look'd with scorn
On every meaner match, of thee was born
That grave inflexibility of soul,
Which Reason can't convince, nor Fear control ;
Which neither arguments nor prayers can reach,
And nothing less than utter ruin teach.
Hence, Ignorance !—hence to that depth of night
Where thou wast born, where not one gleam of light 340
May wound thine eye—hence to some dreary cell
Where monks with superstition love to dwell ;
Or in some college soothe thy lazy pride,
And with the heads of colleges reside ;

M

Fit mate for Royalty thou canst not be,   345
And if no mate for kings, no mate for me.
   Come, Study! like a torrent swell'd with rains,
Which, rushing down the mountains, o'er the plains
Spreads horror wide, and yet, in horror kind,
Leaves seeds of future fruitfulness behind ;   350
Come, Study !—painful though thy course, and slow,
Thy real worth by thy effects we know—
Parent of Knowledge, come !—Not thee I call,
Who, grave and dull, in college or in hall
Dost sit, all solemn sad, and moping weigh
Things which, when found, thy labours can't repay—
Nor, in one hand, fit emblem of thy trade,
A rod ; in t' other, gaudily array'd,
A hornbook gilt and letter'd, call I thee,
Who dost in form preside o'er A, B, C :   360
Nor (siren though thou art, and thy strange charms,
As 'twere by magic, lure men to thine arms)
Do I call thee, who, through a winding maze,
A labyrinth of puzzling, pleasing ways,
Dost lead us at the last to those rich plains,
Where, in full glory, real Science reigns ;
Fair though thou art, and lovely to mine eye,
Though full rewards in thy possession lie
To crown man's wish, and do thy favourites grace ;
Though (was I station'd in an humbler place)   370
I could be ever happy in thy sight,
Toil with thee all the day, and through the night,
Toil on from watch to watch, bidding my eye,
Fast rivetted on Science, sleep defy ;
Yet (such the hardships which from empire flow)
Must I thy sweet society forego,
And to some happy rival's arms resign
Those charms which can, alas ! no more be mine !

No more from hour to hour, from day to day,   379
Shall I pursue thy steps, and urge my way
Where eager love of science calls ; no more
Attempt those paths which man ne'er trod before ;
No more, the mountain scaled, the desert cross'd,
Losing myself, nor knowing I was lost,
Travel through woods, through wilds, from morn to night,
From night to morn, yet travel with delight,
And having found thee, lay me down content,
Own all my toil well paid, my time well spent.

Farewell, ye Muses too !—for such mean things
Must not presume to dwell with mighty kings—   390
Farewell, ye Muses ! though it cuts my heart
E'en to the quick, we must for ever part.

When the fresh morn bade lusty Nature wake ;
When the birds, sweetly twitt'ring through the brake,
Tune their soft pipes ; when, from the neighbouring bloom
Sipping the dew, each zephyr stole perfume ;
When all things with new vigour were inspired,
And seem'd to say they never could be tired ;
How often have we stray'd, whilst sportive rhyme
Deceived the way and clipp'd the wings of Time,   400
O'er hill, o'er dale ; how often laugh'd to see,
Yourselves made visible to none but me,
The clown, his works suspended, gape and stare,
And seem to think that I conversed with air !

When the sun, beating on the parchéd soil,
Seem'd to proclaim an interval of toil ;
When a faint langour crept through every breast,
And things most used to labour wish'd for rest,
How often, underneath a reverend oak,
Where safe, and fearless of the impious stroke,   410
Some sacred Dryad lived ; or in some grove,
Where, with capricious fingers, Fancy wove

Her fairy bower, whilst Nature all the while   413
Look'd on, and view'd her mock'ries with a smile,
Have we held converse sweet!   How often laid,
Fast by the Thames, in Ham's inspiring shade,
Amongst those poets which make up your train,
And, after death, pour forth the sacred strain,
Have I, at your command, in verse grown gray,
But not impair'd, heard Dryden tune that lay   420
Which might have drawn an angel from his sphere,
And kept him from his office listening here!
    When dreary Night, with Morpheus in her train,
Led on by Silence to resume her reign,
With darkness covering, as with a robe,
The scene of levity, blank'd half the globe;
How oft, enchanted with your heavenly strains,
Which stole me from myself; which in soft chains
Of music bound my soul; how oft have I,
Sounds more than human floating through the sky,   430
Attentive sat, whilst Night, against her will,
Transported with the harmony, stood still!
How oft in raptures, which man scarce could bear,
Have I, when gone, still thought the Muses there;
Still heard their music, and, as mute as death,
Sat all attention, drew in every breath,
Lest, breathing all too rudely, I should wound,
And mar that magic excellence of sound;
Then, Sense returning with return of day,
Have chid the Night, which fled so fast away!   440
    Such my pursuits, and such my joys of yore,
Such were my mates, but now my mates no more.
Placed out of Envy's walk, (for Envy, sure,
Would never haunt the cottage of the poor,
Would never stoop to wound my homespun lays)
With some few friends, and some small share of praise,

Beneath oppression, undisturb'd by strife, 447
In peace I trod the humble vale of life.
Farewell, these scenes of ease, this tranquil state ;
Welcome the troubles which on empire wait !
Light toys from this day forth I disavow ;
They pleased me once, but cannot suit me now :
To common men all common things are free,
What honours them, might fix disgrace on me.
Call'd to a throne, and o'er a mighty land
Ordain'd to rule, my head, my heart, my hand,
Are all engross'd ; each private view withstood,
And task'd to labour for the public good :
Be this my study ; to this one great end
May every thought, may every action tend ! 460
    Let me the page of History turn o'er,
Th' instructive page, and heedfully explore
What faithful pens of former times have wrote
Of former kings ; what they did worthy note,
What worthy blame ; and from the sacred tomb
Where righteous monarchs sleep, where laurels bloom,
Unhurt by Time, let me a garland twine,
Which, robbing not their fame, may add to mine.
    Nor let me with a vain and idle eye
Glance o'er those scenes, and in a hurry fly, 470
Quick as the post, which travels day and night ;
Nor let me dwell there, lured by false delight ;
And, into barren theory betray'd,
Forget that monarchs are for action made.
When amorous Spring, repairing all his charms,
Calls Nature forth from hoary Winter's arms,
Where, like a virgin to some lecher sold,
Three wretched months she lay benumb'd, and cold ;
When the weak flower, which, shrinking from the breath
Of the rude North, and timorous of death, 480

To its kind mother earth for shelter fled,   481
And on her bosom hid its tender head,
Peeps forth afresh, and, cheer'd by milder skies,
Bids in full splendour all her beauties rise ;
The hive is up in arms—expert to teach,
Nor, proudly, to be taught unwilling, each
Seems from her fellow a new zeal to catch ;
Strength in her limbs, and on her wings dispatch,
The bee goes forth ; from herb to herb she flies,   489
From flower to flower, and loads her labouring thighs
With treasured sweets, robbing those flowers, which, left,
Find not themselves made poorer by the theft,
Their scents as lively, and their looks as fair,
As if the pillager had not been there.
Ne'er doth she flit on Pleasure's silken wing ;
Ne'er doth she, loitering, let the bloom of Spring
Unrifled pass, and on the downy breast
Of some fair flower indulge untimely rest ;
Ne'er doth she, drinking deep of those rich dews
Which chemist Night prepared, that faith abuse   500
Due to the hive, and, selfish in her toils,
To her own private use convert the spoils.
Love of the stock first call'd her forth to roam,
And to the stock she brings her booty home.
     Be this my pattern—as becomes a king,
Let me fly all abroad on Reason's wing ;
Let mine eye, like the lightning, through the earth
Run to and fro, nor let one deed of worth,
In any place and time, nor let one man,
Whose actions may enrich dominion's plan,   510
Escape my note ; be all, from the first day
Of Nature to this hour, be all my prey.
From those whom Time, at the desire of Fame,
Hath spared, let Virtue catch an equal flame ;

From those who, not in mercy, but in rage,   515
Time hath reprieved, to damn from age to age,
Let me take warning, lesson'd to distil,
And, imitating Heaven, draw good from ill.
Nor let these great researches, in my breast
A monument of useless labour rest;   520
No—let them spread—th' effects let Gotham share,
And reap the harvest of their monarch's care :
Be other times, and other countries known,
Only to give fresh blessings to my own.
   Let me, (and may that God to whom I fly,
On whom for needful succour I rely
In this great hour, that glorious God of truth,
Through whom I reign, in mercy to my youth,
Assist my weakness, and direct me right ;
From every speck which hangs upon the sight   530
Purge my mind's eye, nor let one cloud remain
To spread the shades of Error o'er my brain !)
Let me, impartial, with unwearied thought,
Try men and things ; let me, as monarchs ought,
Examine well on what my power depends ;
What are the general principles and ends
Of government ; how empire first began ;
And wherefore man was raised to reign o'er man.
   Let me consider, as from one great source
We see a thousand rivers take their course,   540
Dispersed, and into different channels led,
Yet by their parent still supplied and fed,
That Government, (though branch'd out far and wide,
In various modes to various lands applied)
Howe'er it differs in its outward frame,
In the main groundwork 's every where the same ;
The same her view, though different her plan,
Her grand and general view—the good of man.

Let me find out, by Reason's sacred beams,   549
What system in itself most perfect seems,
Most worthy man, most likely to conduce
To all the purposes of general use ;
Let me find, too, where, by fair Reason tried,
It fails, when to particulars applied ;
Why in that mode all nations do not join,
And, chiefly, why it cannot suit with mine.
    Let me the gradual rise of empires trace,
Till they seem founded on Perfection's base ;
Then (for when human things have made their way
To excellence, they hasten to decay)   560
Let me, whilst Observation lends her clue
Step after step to their decline pursue,
Enabled by a chain of facts to tell
Not only how they rose, but why they fell.
    Let me not only the distempers know
Which in all states from common causes grow,
But likewise those, which, by the will of Fate,
On each peculiar mode of empire wait ;
Which in its very constitution lurk,
Too sure at last to do its destined work :   570
Let me, forewarn'd, each sign, each symptom learn,
That I my people's danger may discern,
Ere 'tis too late wish'd health to reassure,
And, if it can be found, find out a cure.
    Let me, (though great, grave brethren of the gown
Preach all Faith up, and preach all Reason down,
Making those jar whom Reason meant to join,
And vesting in themselves a right divine),
Let me, through Reason's glass, with searching eye,
Into the depth of that religion pry   580
Which law hath sanction'd ; let me find out there
What's form, what's essence ; what, like vagrant air,

We well may change ; and what, without a crime, 583
Cannot be changed to the last hour of time.
Nor let me suffer that outrageous zeal
Which, without knowledge, furious bigots feel,
Fair in pretence, though at the heart unsound,
These separate points at random to confound.
   The times have been when priests have dared to tread,
Proud and insulting, on their monarch's head ; 590
When, whilst they made religion a pretence,
Out of the world they banish'd common-sense ;
When some soft king, too open to deceit,
Easy and unsuspecting join'd the cheat,
Duped by mock piety, and gave his name
To serve the vilest purposes of shame.
Fear not, my people ! where no cause of fear
Can justly rise—your king secures you here ;
Your king, who scorns the haughty prelate's nod,
Nor deems the voice of priests the voice of God. 600
   Let me, (though lawyers may perhaps forbid
Their monarch to behold what they wish hid,
And for the purposes of knavish gain,
Would have their trade a mystery remain)
Let me, disdaining all such slavish awe,
Dive to the very bottom of the law ;
Let me (the weak, dead letter left behind)
Search out the principles, the spirit find,
Till, from the parts, made master of the whole,
I see the Constitution's very soul. 610
   Let me, (though statesmen will no doubt resist,
And to my eyes present a fearful list
Of men, whose wills are opposite to mine,
Of men, great men, determined to resign)
Let me, (with firmness, which becomes a king,
Conscious from what a source my actions spring,

Determined not by worlds to be withstood,   617
When my grand object is my country's good)
Unravel all low ministerial scenes,
Destroy their jobs, lay bare their ways and means,
And track them step by step ; let me well know
How places, pensions, and preferments go ;
Why Guilt's provided for when Worth is not,
And why one man of merit is forgot ;
Let me in peace, in war, supreme preside,
And dare to know my way without a guide.
 Let me, (though Dignity, by nature proud,
Retires from view, and swells behind a cloud,—
As if the sun shone with less powerful ray,
Less grace, less glory, shining every day,—   630
Though when she comes forth into public sight,
Unbending as a ghost, she stalks upright,
With such an air as we have often seen,
And often laugh'd at, in a tragic queen,
Nor, at her presence, though base myriads crook
The supple knee, vouchsafes a single look)
Let me, (all vain parade, all empty pride,
All terrors of dominion laid aside,
All ornament, and needless helps of art,
All those big looks, which speak a little heart)   640
Know (which few kings, alas ! have ever known)
How Affability becomes a throne,
Destroys all fear, bids Love with Reverence live,
And gives those graces Pride can never give.
Let the stern tyrant keep a distant state,
And, hating all men, fear return of hate,
Conscious of guilt, retreat behind his throne,
Secure from all upbraidings but his own :
Let all my subjects have access to me,
Be my ears open, as my heart is free ;   650

In full fair tide let information flow ;   651
That evil is half cured, whose cause we know.
    And thou, where'er thou art, thou wretched thing,
Who art afraid to look up to a king,
Lay by thy fears ; make but thy grievance plain,
And, if I not redress thee, may my reign
Close up that very moment.   To prevent
The course of Justice from her vain intent,
In vain my nearest, dearest friend shall plead,
In vain my mother kneel ; my soul may bleed,   660
But must not change.   When Justice draws the dart,
Though it is doom'd to pierce a favourite's heart,
'Tis mine to give it force, to give it aim—
I know it duty, and I feel it fame.

THE AUTHOR.[1]

ACCURSED the man, whom Fate ordains, in spite,
And cruel parents teach, to read and write !
What need of letters ? wherefore should we spell ?
Why write our names ?   A mark will do as well.
    Much are the precious hours of youth misspent,
In climbing Learning's rugged, steep ascent ;
When to the top the bold adventurer's got,
He reigns, vain monarch, o'er a barren spot ;
Whilst in the vale of Ignorance below,
Folly and Vice to rank luxuriance grow ;   10
Honours and wealth pour in on every side,
And proud Preferment rolls her golden tide.

[1] 'The Author:' published in 1763. For this poem and ' The Duellist,'
Churchill received £450.

O'er crabbed authors life's gay prime to waste,   13
To cramp wild genius in the chains of taste,
To bear the slavish drudgery of schools,
And tamely stoop to every pedant's rules ;
For seven long years debarr'd of liberal ease,
To plod in college trammels to degrees ;
Beneath the weight of solemn toys to groan,
Sleep over books, and leave mankind unknown ;   20
To praise each senior blockhead's threadbare tale,
And laugh till reason blush, and spirits fail ;
Manhood with vile submission to disgrace,
And cap the fool, whose merit is his place,
Vice-Chancellors, whose knowledge is but small,
And Chancellors, who nothing know at all :
Ill-brook'd the generous spirit in those days
When learning was the certain road to praise,
When nobles, with a love of science bless'd,
Approved in others what themselves possess'd.   30
    But now, when Dulness rears aloft her throne,
When lordly vassals her wide empire own ;
When Wit, seduced by Envy, starts aside,
And basely leagues with Ignorance and Pride ;
What, now, should tempt us, by false hopes misled,
Learning's unfashionable paths to tread ;
To bear those labours which our fathers bore,
That crown withheld, which they in triumph wore ?
    When with much pains this boasted learning's got,
'Tis an affront to those who have it not :   40
In some it causes hate, in others fear,
Instructs our foes to rail, our friends to sneer.
With prudent haste the worldly-minded fool
Forgets the little which he learn'd at school :
The elder brother, to vast fortunes born,
Looks on all science with an eye of scorn ;

Dependent brethren the same features wear,   47
And younger sons are stupid as the heir.
In senates, at the bar, in church and state,
Genius is vile, and learning out of date.
    Is this—oh, death to think!—is this the land
Where Merit and Reward went hand in hand ?
Where heroes, parent-like, the poet view'd,
By whom they saw their glorious deeds renew'd ?
Where poets, true to honour, tuned their lays,
And by their patrons sanctified their praise ?
Is this the land, where, on our Spenser's tongue,
Enamour'd of his voice, Description hung ?
Where Jonson rigid Gravity beguiled,
Whilst Reason through her critic fences smiled ?   60
Where Nature listening stood whilst Shakspeare play'd,
And wonder'd at the work herself had made ?
Is this the land, where, mindful of her charge
And office high, fair Freedom walk'd at large ?
Where, finding in our laws a sure defence,
She mock'd at all restraints, but those of sense ?
Where, Health and Honour trooping by her side,
She spread her sacred empire far and wide ;
Pointed the way, Affliction to beguile,
And bade the face of Sorrow wear a smile ;   70
Bade those, who dare obey the generous call,
Enjoy her blessings, which God meant for all ?
Is this the land, where, in some tyrant's reign,
When a weak, wicked, ministerial train,
The tools of power, the slaves of interest, plann'd
Their country's ruin, and with bribes unmann'd
Those wretches, who, ordain'd in Freedom's cause,
Gave up our liberties, and sold our laws ;
When Power was taught by Meanness where to go,
Nor dared to love the virtue of a foe ;   80

When, like a leprous plague, from the foul head   81
To the foul heart her sores Corruption spread ;
Her iron arm when stern Oppression rear'd ;
And Virtue, from her broad base shaken, fear'd
The scourge of Vice ; when, impotent and vain,
Poor Freedom bow'd the neck to Slavery's chain ?
Is this the land, where, in those worst of times,
The hardy poet raised his honest rhymes
To dread rebuke, and bade Controlment speak
In guilty blushes on the villain's cheek ;   90
Bade Power turn pale, kept mighty rogues in awe,
And made them fear the Muse, who fear'd not law ?
 How do I laugh, when men of narrow souls,
Whom Folly guides, and Prejudice controls ;
Who, one dull drowsy track of business trod,
Worship their Mammon, and neglect their God ;
Who, breathing by one musty set of rules,
Dote from their birth, and are by system fools ;
Who, form'd to dulness from their very youth,
Lies of the day prefer to gospel truth ;   100
Pick up their little knowledge from Reviews,
And lay out all their stock of faith in news ;
How do I laugh, when creatures, form'd like these,
Whom Reason scorns, and I should blush to please,
Rail at all liberal arts, deem verse a crime,
And hold not truth, as truth, if told in rhyme !
 How do I laugh, when Publius,[1] hoary grown
In zeal for Scotland's welfare, and his own,
By slow degrees, and course of office, drawn
In mood and figure at the helm to yawn,   110
Too mean (the worst of curses Heaven can send)
To have a foe, too proud to have a friend ;

[1] 'Publius :' Smollett.

Erring by form, which blockheads sacred hold,   113
Ne'er making new faults, and ne'er mending old,
Rebukes my spirit, bids the daring Muse
Subjects more equal to her weakness choose ;
Bids her frequent the haunts of humble swains,
Nor dare to traffic in ambitious strains ;
Bids her, indulging the poetic whim
In quaint-wrought ode, or sonnet pertly trim,   120
Along the church-way path complain with Gray,
Or dance with Mason on the first of May !
' All sacred is the name and power of kings ;
All states and statesmen are those mighty things
Which, howsoe'er they out of course may roll,
Were never made for poets to control.'
   Peace, peace, thou dotard ! nor thus vilely deem
Of sacred numbers, and their power blaspheme.
I tell thee, wretch, search all creation round,
In earth, in heaven, no subject can be found   130
(Our God alone except) above whose height
The poet cannot rise, and hold his state.
The blessèd saints above in numbers speak
The praise of God, though there all praise is weak ;
In numbers here below the bard shall teach
Virtue to soar beyond the villain's reach ;
Shall tear his labouring lungs, strain his hoarse throat,
And raise his voice beyond the trumpet's note,
Should an afflicted country, awed by men
Of slavish principles, demand his pen.   140
This is a great, a glorious point of view,
Fit for an English poet to pursue ;
Undaunted to pursue, though, in return,
IIis writings by the common hangman burn
   How do I laugh, when men, by fortune placed
Above their betters, and by rank disgraced,

Who found their pride on titles which they stain,   147
And, mean themselves, are of their fathers vain ;
Who would a bill of privilege prefer,
And treat a poet like a creditor ;
The generous ardour of the Muse condemn,
And curse the storm they know must break on them !
' What ! shall a reptile bard, a wretch unknown,
Without one badge of merit but his own,
Great nobles lash, and lords, like common men,
Smart from the vengeance of a scribbler's pen ?'
　　What's in this name of lord, that I should fear
To bring their vices to the public ear ?
Flows not the honest blood of humble swains
Quick as the tide which swells a monarch's veins ?   160
Monarchs, who wealth and titles can bestow,
Cannot make virtues in succession flow.
Wouldst thou, proud man ! be safely placed above
The censure of the Muse ?   Deserve her love :
Act as thy birth demands, as nobles ought ;
Look back, and, by thy worthy father taught,
Who earn'd those honours thou wert born to wear,
Follow his steps, and be his virtue's heir.
But if, regardless of the road to fame,
You start aside, and tread the paths of shame ;   170
If such thy life, that should thy sire arise,
The sight of such a son would blast his eyes,
Would make him curse the hour which gave thee birth,
Would drive him shuddering from the face of earth,
Once more, with shame and sorrow, 'mongst the dead
In endless night to hide his reverend head ;
If such thy life, though kings had made thee more
Than ever king a scoundrel made before ;
Nay, to allow thy pride a deeper spring,
Though God in vengeance had made thee a king,   180

Taking on Virtue's wing her daring flight,   181
The Muse should drag thee, trembling, to the light,
Probe thy foul wounds, and lay thy bosom bare
To the keen question of the searching air.
  Gods! with what pride I see the titled slave,
Who smarts beneath the stroke which Satire gave,
Aiming at ease, and with dishonest art
Striving to hide the feelings of his heart!
How do I laugh, when, with affected air,
(Scarce able through despite to keep his chair,   190
Whilst on his trembling lip pale Anger speaks,
And the chafed blood flies mounting to his cheeks)
He talks of Conscience, which good men secures
From all those evil moments Guilt endures,
And seems to laugh at those who pay regard
To the wild ravings of a frantic bard.
' Satire, whilst envy and ill-humour sway
The mind of man, must always make her way ;
Nor to a bosom, with discretion fraught,
Is all her malice worth a single thought.   200
The wise have not the will, nor fools the power,
To stop her headstrong course ; within the hour,
Left to herself, she dies ; opposing strife
Gives her fresh vigour, and prolongs her life.
All things her prey, and every man her aim,
I can no patent for exemption claim,
Nor would I wish to stop that harmless dart
Which plays around, but cannot wound my heart ;
Though pointed at myself, be Satire free ;
To her 'tis pleasure, and no pain to me.'   210
  Dissembling wretch ! hence to the Stoic school,
And there amongst thy brethren play the fool ;
There, unrebuked, these wild, vain doctrines preach.
Lives there a man whom Satire cannot reach ?

N

Lives there a man who calmly can stand by,   215
And see his conscience ripp'd with steady eye ?
When Satire flies abroad on Falsehood's wing,
Short is her life, and impotent her sting ;
But when to Truth allied, the wound she gives
Sinks deep, and to remotest ages lives.   220
When in the tomb thy pamper'd flesh shall rot,
And e'en by friends thy memory be forgot,
Still shalt thou live, recorded for thy crimes,
Live in her page, and stink to after-times.
    Hast thou no feeling yet ?   Come, throw off pride,
And own those passions which thou shalt not hide.
Sandwich, who, from the moment of his birth,
Made human nature a reproach on earth,
Who never dared, nor wish'd, behind to stay,
When Folly, Vice, and Meanness led the way,   230
Would blush, should he be told, by Truth and Wit,
Those actions which he blush'd not to commit.
Men the most infamous are fond of fame,
And those who fear not guilt, yet start at shame.
    But whither runs my zeal, whose rapid force,
Turning the brain, bears Reason from her course ;
Carries me back to times, when poets, bless'd
With courage, graced the science they profess'd ;
When they, in honour rooted, firmly stood,
The bad to punish, and reward the good ;   240
When, to a flame by public virtue wrought,
The foes of freedom they to justice brought,
And dared expose those slaves who dared support
A tyrant plan, and call'd themselves a Court ?
Ah ! what are poets now ? As slavish those
Who deal in verse, as those who deal in prose.
Is there an Author, search the kingdom round,
In whom true worth and real spirit's found ?

The slaves of booksellers, or (doom'd by Fate   249
To baser chains) vile pensioners of state ;
Some, dead to shame, and of those shackles proud
Which Honour scorns, for slavery roar aloud ;
Others, half-palsied only, mutes become,
And what makes Smollett write, makes Johnson dumb.
    Why turns yon villain pale ? Why bends his eye
Inward, abash'd, when Murphy passes by ?
Dost thou sage Murphy for a blockhead take,
Who wages war with Vice for Virtue's sake ?
No, no, like other worldlings, you will find
He shifts his sails and catches every wind.   260
His soul the shock of Interest can't endure :
Give him a pension then, and sin secure.
    With laurell'd wreaths the flatterer's brows adorn ;
Bid Virtue crouch, bid Vice exalt her horn ;
Bid cowards thrive, put Honesty to flight,
Murphy shall prove, or try to prove it right.
Try, thou state-juggler, every paltry art ;
Ransack the inmost closet of my heart ;
Swear thou'rt my friend ; by that base oath make way
Into my breast, and flatter to betray.   270
Or, if those tricks are vain ; if wholesome doubt
Detects the fraud, and points the villain out;
Bribe those who daily at my board are fed,
And make them take my life who eat my bread.
On Authors for defence, for praise depend ;
Pay him but well, and Murphy is thy friend :
He, he shall ready stand with venal rhymes,
To varnish guilt, and consecrate thy crimes;
To make Corruption in false colours shine,
And damn his own good name, to rescue thine.   280
    But, if thy niggard hands their gifts withhold,
And Vice no longer rains down showers of gold,

Expect no mercy ; facts, well-grounded, teach,   283
Murphy, if not rewarded, will impeach.
What though each man of nice and juster thought,
Shunning his steps, decrees, by Honour taught,
He ne'er can be a friend, who stoops so low
To be the base betrayer of a foe ?
What though, with thine together link'd, his name
Must be with thine transmitted down to shame ?   290
To every manly feeling callous grown,
Rather than not blast thine, he 'll blast his own.

 To ope the fountain whence sedition springs,
To slander government, and libel kings ;
With Freedom's name to serve a present hour,
Though born and bred to arbitrary power ;
To talk of William with insidious art,
Whilst a vile Stuart's lurking in his heart;
And, whilst mean Envy rears her loathsome head,
Flattering the living, to abuse the dead,   300
Where is Shebbeare ?[1] Oh, let not foul reproach,
Travelling thither in a city-coach,
The pillory dare to name : the whole intent
Of that parade was fame, not punishment ;
And that old staunch Whig, Beardmore,[2] standing by,
Can in full court give that report the lie.

 With rude unnatural jargon to support,
Half-Scotch, half-English, a declining court ;
To make most glaring contraries unite,
And prove beyond dispute that black is white ;   310
To make firm Honour tamely league with Shame,
Make Vice and Virtue differ but in name ;
To prove that chains and freedom are but one,
That to be saved must mean to be undone,

---

[1] 'Shebbeare:' Dr John Shebbeare, a physician and notorious jacobitical writer, who, after having been pilloried for a seditious production, was pensioned by George the Third.— [2] 'Beardmore:' under sheriff.

Is there not Guthrie ? [1]   Who, like him, can call   315
All opposites to proof, and conquer all ?
He calls forth living waters from the rock ;
He calls forth children from the barren stock ;
He, far beyond the springs of Nature led,
Makes women bring forth after they are dead ;   320
He, on a curious, new, and happy plan,
In wedlock's sacred bands joins man to man ;
And to complete the whole, most strange, but true,
By some rare magic, makes them fruitful too ;
Whilst from their loins, in the due course of years,
Flows the rich blood of 'Guthrie's ' English Peers.'

Dost thou contrive some blacker deed of shame,
Something which Nature shudders but to name,
Something which makes the soul of man retreat,
And the life-blood run backward to her seat ?   330
Dost thou contrive, for some base private end,
Some selfish view, to hang a trusting friend ;
To lure him on, e'en to his parting breath,
And promise life, to work him surer death ?
Grown old in villany, and dead to grace,
Hell in his heart, and Tyburn in his face,
Behold, a parson at thy elbow stands,
Lowering damnation, and with open hands,
Ripe to betray his Saviour for reward,
The Atheist chaplain of an Atheist lord ! [2]   340

Bred to the church, and for the gown decreed,
Ere it was known that I should learn to read ;
Though that was nothing, for my friends, who knew
What mighty Dulness of itself could do,
Never design'd me for a working priest,
But hoped I should have been a Dean at least :

[1] ' Guthrie:' William Guthrie, a literary hack. See Boswell. He wrote an absurd History of the Peerage.— [2] ' Atheist lord :' See note on ' Epistle to William Hogarth.'

Condemn'd, (like many more, and worthier men,   347
To whom I pledge the service of my pen) [1]
Condemn'd (whilst proud and pamper'd sons of lawn,
Cramm'd to the throat, in lazy plenty yawn)
In pomp of reverend beggary to appear,
To pray, and starve on forty pounds a-year:
My friends, who never felt the galling load,
Lament that I forsook the packhorse road,
Whilst Virtue to my conduct witness bears,
In throwing off that gown which Francis [2] wears.

    What creature's that, so very pert and prim,
So very full of foppery, and whim,
So gentle, yet so brisk ; so wondrous sweet,
So fit to prattle at a lady's feet ;   360
Who looks as he the Lord's rich vineyard trod,
And by his garb appears a man of God ?
Trust not to looks, nor credit outward show ;
The villain lurks beneath the cassock'd beau ;
That's an informer ; what avails the name ?
Suffice it that the wretch from Sodom came.
His tongue is deadly—from his presence run,
Unless thy rage would wish to be undone.
No ties can hold him, no affection bind,
And fear alone restrains his coward mind ;   370
Free him from that, no monster is so fell,
Nor is so sure a blood-hound found in Hell.
His silken smiles, his hypocritic air,
His meek demeanour, plausible and fair,
Are only worn to pave Fraud's easier way,
And make gull'd Virtue fall a surer prey.
Attend his church—his plan of doctrine view—
The preacher is a Christian, dull, but true ;

---

[1] ' Service of my pen : ' he designed, and partly executed, a poem entitled
' The Curate.'—[2] ' Francis : ' the Rev. Philip Francis, the translator of Horace,
and father of Sir Philip Francis.

But when the hallow'd hour of preaching's o'er,   379
That plan of doctrine's never thought of more ;
Christ is laid by neglected on the shelf,
And the vile priest is gospel to himself.
    By Cleland[1] tutor'd, and with Blacow[2] bred,
(Blacow, whom, by a brave resentment led,
Oxford, if Oxford had not sunk in fame,
Ere this, had damn'd to everlasting shame)
Their steps he follows, and their crimes partakes ;
To virtue lost, to vice alone he wakes,   ·
Most lusciously declaims 'gainst luscious themes,
And whilst he rails at blasphemy, blasphemes.   390
    Are these the arts which policy supplies ?
Are these the steps by which grave churchmen rise ?
Forbid it, Heaven ; or, should it turn out so,
Let me and mine continue mean and low.
Such be their arts whom interest controls ;
Kidgell[3] and ·I have free and modest souls :
We scorn preferment which is gain'd by sin,
And will, though poor without, have peace within.

THE CONFERENCE.[4]

GRACE said in form, which sceptics must agree,
When they are told that grace was said by me ;
The servants gone to break the scurvy jest
On the proud landlord, and his threadbare guest ;

---

[1] 'Cleland:' John Cleland, an infamous witling of the time.—[2] 'Blacow:' an Oxfordian, who informed against some riotous students, who were shouting out drunken Jacobitism. — [3] 'Kidgell:' Rector of Horne, the subject of the above sketch, and here ironically praised, had obtained surreptitiously a copy of Wilkes's 'Essay on Woman,' and betrayed it to the secretaries of state. —[4] 'The Conference:' this poem was published by our author in November 1763, soon after his elopement with Miss Carr.

'The King' gone round, my lady too withdrawn ;   5
My lord, in usual taste, began to yawn,
And, lolling backward in his elbow-chair,
With an insipid kind of stupid stare,
Picking his teeth, twirling his seals about—
Churchill, you have a poem coming out :   10
You 've my best wishes ; but I really fear
Your Muse, in general, is too severe ;
Her spirit seems her interest to oppose,
And where she makes one friend, makes twenty foes.

    C. Your lordship's fears are just ; I feel their force,
But only feel it as a thing of course.
The man whose hardy spirit shall engage
To lash the vices of a guilty age,
At his first setting forward ought to know
That every rogue he meets must be his foe ;   20
That the rude breath of satire will provoke
Many who feel, and more who fear the stroke.
But shall the partial rage of selfish men
From stubborn Justice wrench the righteous pen ?
Or shall I not my settled course pursue,
Because my foes are foes to Virtue too ?

    L. What is this boasted Virtue, taught in schools,
And idly drawn from antiquated rules ?
What is her use ?   Point out one wholesome end.
Will she hurt foes, or can she make a friend ?   30
When from long fasts fierce appetites arise,
Can this same Virtue stifle Nature's cries ?
Can she the pittance of a meal afford,
Or bid thee welcome to one great man's board ?
When northern winds the rough December arm
With frost and snow, can Virtue keep thee warm ?
Canst thou dismiss the hard unfeeling dun
Barely by saying, thou art Virtue's son ?

Or by base blundering statesmen sent to jail,   39
Will Mansfield take this Virtue for thy bail?
Believe it not, the name is in disgrace ;
Virtue and Temple now are out of place.
  Quit then this meteor, whose delusive ray
From wealth and honour leads thee far astray.
True virtue means—let Reason use her eyes—
Nothing with fools, and interest with the wise.
Wouldst thou be great, her patronage disclaim,
Nor madly triumph in so mean a name :
Let nobler wreaths thy happy brows adorn,
And leave to Virtue poverty and scorn.   50
Let Prudence be thy guide ; who doth not know
How seldom Prudence can with Virtue go ?
To be successful try thy utmost force,
And Virtue follows as a thing of course.
  Hirco—who knows not Hirco ?—stains the bed
Of that kind master who first gave him bread ;
Scatters the seeds of discord through the land,
Breaks every public, every private band ;
Beholds with joy a trusting friend undone ;
Betrays a brother, and would cheat a son :   60
What mortal in his senses can endure
The name of Hirco ? for the wretch is poor!
Let him hang, drown, starve, on a dunghill rot,
By all detested live, and die forgot ;
Let him—a poor return—in every breath
Feel all Death's pains, yet be whole years in death,
Is now the general cry we all pursue.
Let Fortune change, and Prudence changes too ;
Supple and pliant, a new system feels,
Throws up her cap, and spaniels at his heels :   70
Long live great Hirco, cries, by interest taught,
And let his foes, though I prove one, be naught.

C. Peace to such men, if such men can have peace ;　73
Let their possessions, let their state increase ;
Let their base services in courts strike root,
And in the season bring forth golden fruit.
I envy not ; let those who have the will,
And, with so little spirit, so much skill,
With such vile instruments their fortunes carve ;
Rogues may grow fat, an honest man dares starve.[1]　80

　　L. These stale conceits thrown off, let us advance
For once to real life, and quit romance.
Starve ! pretty talking ! but I fain would view
That man, that honest man, would do it too.
Hence to yon mountain which outbraves the sky,
And dart from pole to pole thy strengthen'd eye,
Through all that space you shall not view one man,
Not one, who dares to act on such a plan.
Cowards in calms will say, what in a storm
The brave will tremble at, and not perform.　90
Thine be the proof, and, spite of all you 've said,
You 'd give your honour for a crust of bread.

　　C. What proof might do, what hunger might effect,
What famish'd Nature, looking with neglect
On all she once held dear ; what fear, at strife
With fainting virtue for the means of life,
Might make this coward flesh, in love with breath,
Shuddering at pain, and shrinking back from death,
In treason to my soul, descend to bear,
Trusting to fate, I neither know nor care.　100
　　Once,—at this hour those wounds afresh I feel,
Which, nor prosperity, nor time, can heal ;
Those wounds which Fate severely hath decreed,
Mention'd or thought of, must for ever bleed ;

---

[1] 'Dares starve :' this will suggest Burns's noble line, 'We daur be poor, for a' that.'

Those wounds which humbled all that pride of man, 105
Which brings such mighty aid to Virtue's plan—
Once, awed by Fortune's most oppressive frown,
By legal rapine to the earth bow'd down,
My credit at last gasp, my state undone,
Trembling to meet the shock I could not shun, 110
Virtue gave ground, and blank despair prevail'd ;
Sinking beneath the storm, my spirits fail'd
Like Peter's faith, till one, a friend indeed—
May all distress find such in time of need !—
One kind good man, in act, in word, in thought,
By Virtue guided, and by Wisdom taught,
Image of Him whom Christians should adore,
Stretch'd forth his hand, and brought me safe to shore.[1]
  Since, by good fortune into notice raised,
And for some little merit largely praised, 120
Indulged in swerving from prudential rules,
Hated by rogues, and not beloved by fools ;
Placed above want, shall abject thirst of wealth,
So fiercely war 'gainst my soul's dearest health,
That, as a boon, I should base shackles crave,
And, born to freedom, make myself a slave ?
That I should in the train of those appear,
Whom Honour cannot love, nor Manhood fear ?
  That I no longer skulk from street to street,
Afraid lest duns assail, and bailiffs meet ; 130
That I from place to place this carcase bear ;
Walk forth at large, and wander free as air ;
That I no longer dread the awkward friend,
Whose very obligations must offend ;
Nor, all too froward, with impatience burn
At suffering favours which I can't return ;

[1] ' Shore: ' Churchill, sunk in deep debt, was delivered from the impending
horrors of a jail, by Dr Peirson Lloyd, second master of Westminster school.

That, from dependence and from pride secure,   137
I am not placed so high to scorn the poor,
Nor yet so low that I my lord should fear,
Or hesitate to give him sneer for sneer ;
That, whilst sage Prudence my pursuits confirms,
I can enjoy the world on equal terms ;
That, kind to others, to myself most true,
Feeling no want, I comfort those who do,
And, with the will, have power to aid distress :
These, and what other blessings I possess,
From the indulgence of the public rise,
All private patronage my soul defies.
By candour more inclined to save, than damn,
A generous Public made me what I am.   150
All that I have, they gave ; just Memory bears
The grateful stamp, and what I am is theirs.
    L. To feign a red-hot zeal for Freedom's cause,
To mouth aloud for liberties and laws,
For public good to bellow all abroad,
Serves well the purposes of private fraud.
Prudence, by public good intends her own ;
If you mean otherwise, you stand alone.
What do we mean by country and by court ?
What is it to oppose ? what to support ?   160
Mere words of course ; and what is more absurd
Than to pay homage to an empty word ?
Majors and minors differ but in name ;
Patriots and ministers are much the same ;
The only difference, after all their rout,
Is, that the one is in, the other out.
    Explore the dark recesses of the mind,
In the soul's honest volume read mankind,
And own, in wise and simple, great and small,
The same grand leading principle in all.   170

Whate'er we talk of wisdom to the wise,   171
Of goodness to the good, of public ties
Which to our country link, of private bands
Which claim most dear attention at our hands ;
For parent and for child, for wife and friend,
Our first great mover, and our last great end
Is one, and, by whatever name we call
The ruling tyrant, Self is all in all.
This, which unwilling Faction shall admit,
Guided in different ways a Bute and Pitt ;   180
Made tyrants break, made kings observe the law ;
And gave the world a Stuart and Nassau.

    Hath Nature (strange and wild conceit of pride !)
Distinguish'd thee from all her sons beside ?
Doth virtue in thy bosom brighter glow,
Or from a spring more pure doth action flow ?
Is not thy soul bound with those very chains
Which shackle us ? or is that Self, which reigns
O'er kings and beggars, which in all we see
Most strong and sovereign, only weak in thee ?   190
Fond man, believe it not ; experience tells
'Tis not thy virtue, but thy pride rebels.
Think, (and for once lay by thy lawless pen)
Think, and confess thyself like other men ;
Think but one hour, and, to thy conscience led
By Reason's hand, bow down and hang thy head :
Think on thy private life, recall thy youth,
View thyself now, and own, with strictest truth,
That Self hath drawn thee from fair Virtue's way
Farther than Folly would have dared to stray ;   200
And that the talents liberal Nature gave,
To make thee free, have made thee more a slave.

    Quit then, in prudence quit, that idle train
Of toys, which have so long abused thy brain,

And captive led thy powers ; with boundless will   205
Let Self maintain her state and empire still ;
But let her, with more worthy objects caught,
Strain all the faculties and force of thought
To things of higher daring ; let her range
Through better pastures, and learn how to change ; 210
Let her, no longer to weak Faction tied,
Wisely revolt, and join our stronger side.
    C. Ah ! what, my lord, hath private life to do
With things of public nature ? Why to view
Would you thus cruelly those scenes unfold
Which, without pain and horror to behold,
Must speak me something more or less than man,
Which friends may pardon, but I never can ?
Look back ! a thought which borders on despair,
Which human nature must, yet cannot bear.   220
'Tis not the babbling of a busy world,
Where praise and censure are at random hurl'd,
Which can the meanest of my thoughts control,
Or shake one settled purpose of my soul ;
Free and at large might their wild curses roam,
If all, if all, alas ! were well at home. ·
No—'tis the tale which angry Conscience tells,
When she with more than tragic horror swells
Each circumstance of guilt ; when, stern but true,
She brings bad actions forth into review ;   230
And like the dread handwriting on the wall,
Bids late Remorse awake at Reason's call ;
Arm'd at all points, bids scorpion Vengeance pass,
And to the mind holds up Reflection's glass,—
The mind which, starting, heaves the heartfelt groan,
And hates that form she knows to be her own.
    Enough of this,—let private sorrows rest,—
As to the public, I dare stand the test ;

Dare proudly boast, I feel no wish above 239
The good of England, and my country's love.
Stranger to party-rage, by Reason's voice,
Unerring guide! directed in my choice,
Not all the tyrant powers of earth combined,
No, nor of hell, shall make me change my mind.
What! herd with men my honest soul disdains,
Men who, with servile zeal, are forging chains
For Freedom's neck, and lend a helping hand
To spread destruction o'er my native land?
What! shall I not, e'en to my latest breath,
In the full face of danger and of death, 250
Exert that little strength which Nature gave,
And boldly stem, or perish in the wave?

    L. When I look backward for some fifty years,
And see protesting patriots turn'd to peers;
Hear men, most loose, for decency declaim,
And talk of character, without a name;
See infidels assert the cause of God,
And meek divines wield Persecution's rod;
See men transform'd to brutes, and brutes to men;
See Whitehead take a place, Ralph[1] change his pen;
I mock the zeal, and deem the men in sport, 261
Who rail at ministers, and curse a court.
Thee, haughty as thou art, and proud in rhyme,
Shall some preferment, offer'd at a time
When Virtue sleeps, some sacrifice to Pride,
Or some fair victim, move to change thy side.
Thee shall these eyes behold, to health restored,
Using, as Prudence bids, bold Satire's sword,
Galling thy present friends, and praising those
Whom now thy frenzy holds thy greatest foes. 270

---

[1] 'Ralph:' Mr James Ralph a hack author. See 'The Dunciad,' and Franklin's 'Autobiography.' He was hired by Pelham to abuse Sir R. Walpole, whom he had supported before.

    C. May I (can worse disgrace on manhood fall ?) 271
Be born a Whitehead,[1] and baptized a Paul ;
May I (though to his service deeply tied.
By sacred oaths, and now by will allied),
With false, feign'd zeal an injured God defend,
And use his name for some base private end ;
May I (that thought bids double horrors roll
O'er my sick spirits, and unmans my soul)
Ruin the virtue which I held most dear,
And still must hold ; may I, through abject fear, 280
Betray my friend ; may to succeeding times,
Engraved on plates of adamant, my crimes
Stand blazing forth, whilst, mark'd with envious blot,
Each little act of virtue is forgot ;
Of all those evils which, to stamp men cursed,
Hell keeps in store for vengeance, may the worst
Light on my head ; and in my day of woe,
To make the cup of bitterness o'erflow,
May I be scorn'd by every man of worth,
Wander, like Cain, a vagabond on earth ; 290
Bearing about a hell in my own mind,
Or be to Scotland for my life confined ;
If I am one among the many known
Whom Shelburne[2] fled, and Calcraft[3] blush'd to own.
    L. Do you reflect what men you make your foes ?
    C. I do, and that's the reason I oppose.
Friends I have made, whom Envy must commend,
But not one foe whom I would wish a friend.
What if ten thousand Butes and Hollands bawl ?
One Wilkes had made a large amends for all. 300
    'Tis not the title, whether handed down
From age to age, or flowing from the crown

---

  1 'Whitehead :' author of 'Manners, a Satire.'— 2 'Shelburne :' William
Petty, Earl of Shelburne, afterwards Marquis of Lansdowne.— 3 'Calcraft :'
John Calcraft, Esq., M.P., army agent and contractor.

In copious streams, on recent men, who came   303
From stems unknown, and sires without a name :
'Tis not the star which our great Edward gave
To mark the virtuous, and reward the brave,
Blazing without, whilst a base heart within
Is rotten to the core with filth and sin ;
'Tis not the tinsel grandeur, taught to wait,
At Custom's call, to mark a fool of state   310
From fools of lesser note, that soul can awe,
Whose pride is reason, whose defence is law.

   L. Suppose, (a thing scarce possible in art,
Were it thy cue to play a common part)
Suppose thy writings so well fenced in law,
That Norton cannot find nor make a flaw—
Hast thou not heard, that 'mongst our ancient tribes,
By party warp'd, or lull'd asleep by bribes,
Or trembling at the ruffian hand of Force,
Law hath suspended stood, or changed its course ?   320
Art thou assured, that, for destruction ripe,
Thou may'st not smart beneath the self-same gripe ?
What sanction hast thou, frantic in thy rhymes,
Thy life, thy freedom to secure ?

   C.   The Times.
'Tis not on law, a system great and good,
By wisdom penn'd, and bought by noblest blood,
My faith relies ; by wicked men and vain,
Law, once abused, may be abused again.
No; on our great Lawgiver I depend,
Who knows and guides her to her proper end ;   330
Whose royalty of nature blazes out
So fierce, 'twere sin to entertain a doubt.
Did tyrant Stuarts now the law dispense,
(Bless'd be the hour and hand which sent them hence !)

o

For something, or for nothing, for a word   335
Or thought, I might be doom'd to death, unheard.
Life we might all resign to lawless power,
Nor think it worth the purchase of an hour ;
But Envy ne'er shall fix so foul a stain
On the fair annals of a Brunswick's reign.   340
    If, slave to party, to revenge, or pride ;
If, by frail human error drawn aside,
I break the law, strict rigour let her wear ;
'Tis hers to punish, and 'tis mine to bear ;
Nor, by the voice of Justice doom'd to death
Would I ask mercy with my latest breath :
But, anxious only for my country's good,
In which my king's, of course, is understood ;
Form'd on a plan with some few patriot friends,
Whilst by just means I aim at noblest ends,   350
My spirits cannot sink ; though from the tomb
Stern Jeffries should be placed in Mansfield's room ;
Though he should bring, his base designs to aid,
Some black attorney, for his purpose made,
And shove, whilst Decency and Law retreat,
The modest Norton from his maiden seat ;
Though both, in ill confederates, should agree,
In damnèd league, to torture law and me,
Whilst George is king, I cannot fear endure ;
Not to be guilty, is to be secure.   360
    But when, in after-times, (be far removed
That day !) our monarch, glorious and beloved,
Sleeps with his fathers, should imperious Fate,
In vengeance, with fresh Stuarts curse our state ;
Should they, o'erleaping every fence of law,
Butcher the brave to keep tame fools in awe ;
Should they, by brutal and oppressive force,
Divert sweet Justice from her even course ;

Should they, of every other means bereft,   369
Make my right hand a witness 'gainst my left ;
Should they, abroad by inquisitions taught,
Search out my soul, and damn me for a thought ;
Still would I keep my course, still speak, still write,
Till Death had plunged me in the shades of night.

Thou God of truth, thou great, all-searching eye,
To whom our thoughts, our spirits, open lie !
Grant me thy strength, and in that needful hour,
(Should it e'er come) when Law submits to Power,
With firm resolve my steady bosom steel,
Bravely to suffer, though I deeply feel.   380

Let me, as hitherto, still draw my breath,
In love with life, but not in fear of death ;
And if Oppression brings me to the grave,
And marks me dead, she ne'er shall mark a slave.
Let no unworthy marks of grief be heard,
No wild laments, not one unseemly word ;
Let sober triumphs wait upon my bier ;
I won't forgive that friend who drops one tear.
Whether he 's ravish'd in life's early morn,
Or in old age drops like an ear of corn,   390
Full ripe he falls, on Nature's noblest plan,
Who lives to Reason, and who dies a Man.

THE GHOST.[1]

IN FOUR BOOKS.

Book I.

WITH eager search to dart the soul,
Curiously vain, from pole to pole,
And from the planets' wandering spheres
To extort the number of our years,
And whether all those years shall flow
Serenely smooth, and free from woe,
Or rude misfortune shall deform
Our life with one continual storm ;
Or if the scene shall motley be,
Alternate joy and misery,   10
Is a desire which, more or less,
All men must feel, though few confess.
Hence, every place and every age
Affords subsistence to the sage,
Who, free from this world and its cares,
Holds an acquaintance with the stars,
From whom he gains intelligence
Of things to come some ages hence,
Which unto friends, at easy rates,
He readily communicates.   20

---

[1] 'The Ghost:' the famous Cock-lane Ghost, a conspiracy of certain parties in London against one Kent, whose paramour had died, and whose ghost was said to have returned to accuse him of having murdered her. A little girl named Frazer, who appears to have had ventriloquial powers, was the principal cause of the noises, scratchings, &c., thought to be supernatural.

At its first rise, which all agree on,   21
This noble science was Chaldean ;
That ancient people, as they fed
Their flocks upon the mountain's head,
Gazed on the stars, observed their motions,
And suck'd in astrologic notions,
Which they so eagerly pursue,
As folks are apt whate'er is new,
That things below at random rove,
Whilst they 're consulting things above ;   30
And when they now so poor were grown,
That they 'd no houses of their own,
They made bold with their friends the stars,
And prudently made use of theirs.

To Egypt from Chaldee it travell'd,
And Fate at Memphis was unravell'd :
Th' exotic science soon struck root,
And flourish'd into high repute.
Each learned priest, oh strange to tell !
Could circles make, and cast a spell ;   40
Could read and write, and taught the nation
The holy art of divination.
Nobles themselves, for at that time
Knowledge in nobles was no crime,
Could talk as learned as the priest,
And prophesy as much, at least.
Hence all the fortune-telling crew,
Whose crafty skill mars Nature's hue,
Who, in vile tatters, with smirch'd face,
Run up and down from place to place,   50
To gratify their friends' desires,
From Bampfield Carew,[1] to Moll Squires,[2]

[1] Bampfield Carew:' Bampfylde Moore Carew, the famous king of the gypsies. His life used to be a favourite with schoolboys.—[2] ' Moll Squires: Mary Squires, a gypsy, and one of Carew's subjects.

Are rightly term'd Egyptians all ;   55
Whom we, mistaking, Gypsies call.
    The Grecian sages borrow'd this,
As they did other sciences,
From fertile Egypt, though the loan
They had not honesty to own.
Dodona's oaks, inspired by Jove,
A learned and prophetic grove,   60
Turn'd vegetable necromancers,
And to all comers gave their answers.
At Delphos, to Apollo dear,
All men the voice of Fate might hear ;
Each subtle priest on three-legg'd stool,
To take in wise men, play'd the fool.
A mystery, so made for gain,
E'en now in fashion must remain ;
Enthusiasts never will let drop
What brings such business to their shop ;   70
And that great saint we Whitefield call,
Keeps up the humbug spiritual.
    Among the Romans, not a bird
Without a prophecy was heard ;
Fortunes of empires often hung
On the magician magpie's tongue,
And every crow was to the state
A sure interpreter of Fate.
Prophets, embodied in a college [1]
(Time out of mind your seat of knowledge ;   80
For genius never fruit can bear
Unless it first is planted there,
And solid learning never falls
Without the verge of college walls)

[1] 'College:' that of the fifteen Augurs in Rome.

Infallible accounts would keep   85
When it was best to watch or sleep,
To eat or drink, to go or stay,
And when to fight or run away ;
When matters were for action ripe,
By looking at a double tripe ;   90
When emperors would live or die,
They in an ass's skull could spy ;
When generals would their station keep,
Or turn their backs, in hearts of sheep.
In matters, whether small or great, ·
In private families or state
As amongst us, the holy seer
Officiously would interfere ;
With pious arts and reverend skill
Would bend lay bigots to his will ;   100
Would help or injure foes or friends,
Just as it served his private ends.
Whether in honest way of trade
Traps for virginity were laid ;
Or if, to make their party great,
Designs were form'd against the state,
Regardless of the common weal,
By interest led, which they call zeal,
Into the scale was always thrown
The will of Heaven to back their own.   110
    England—a happy land we know,
Where follies naturally grow,
Where without culture they arise
And tower above the common size ;
England, a fortune-telling host,
As numerous as the stars, could boast,—
Matrons, who toss the cup, and see
The grounds of Fate in grounds of tea,

Who, versed in every modest lore,   119
Can a lost maidenhead restore,
Or, if their pupils rather choose it,
Can show the readiest way to lose it ;
Gypsies, who every ill can cure,
Except the ill of being poor,
Who charms 'gainst love and agues sell,
Who can in hen-roost set a spell,
Prepared by arts, to them best known,
To catch all feet except their own,
Who, as to fortune, can unlock it
As easily as pick a pocket ;   130
Scotchmen, who, in their country's right,
Possess the gift of second-sight,
Who (when their barren heaths they quit,
Sure argument of prudent wit,
Which reputation to maintain,
They never venture back again)
By lies prophetic heap up riches,
And boast the luxury of breeches.
    Amongst the rest, in former years,
Campbell [1] (illustrious name !) appears,   140
Great hero of futurity,
Who, blind, could every thing foresee,
Who, dumb, could every thing foretell,
Who, Fate with equity to sell,
Always dealt out the will of Heaven
According to what price was given.
    Of Scottish race, in Highlands born,
Possess'd with native pride and scorn,
He hither came, by custom led,
To curse the hands which gave him bread.   150

----

[1] 'Campbell :' a deaf and dumb fortune-teller.

With want of truth, and want of sense,   151
Amply made up by impudence
(A succedaneum, which we find
In common use with all mankind) ;
Caress'd and favour'd too by those
Whose heart with patriot feelings glows,
Who foolishly, where'er dispersed,
Still place their native country first;
(For Englishmen alone have sense
To give a stranger preference,   160
Whilst modest merit of their own
Is left in poverty to groan)
Campbell foretold just what he would,
And left the stars to make it good,
On whom he had impress'd such awe,
His dictates current pass'd for law ;
Submissive, all his empire own'd ;
No star durst smile, when Campbell frown'd.
    This sage deceased,—for all must die,
And Campbell's no more safe than I,   170
No more than I can guard the heart,
When Death shall hurl the fatal dart,—
Succeeded, ripe in art and years,
Another favourite of the spheres ;
Another and another came,
Of equal skill, and equal fame ;
As white each wand, as black each gown,
As long each beard, as wise each frown,
In every thing so like, you'd swear
Campbell himself was sitting there :   180
To all the happy art was known,
To tell our fortunes, make their own.
    Seated in garret,—for, you know,
The nearer to the stars we go

The greater we esteem his art,—   185
Fools, curious, flock'd from every part ;
The rich, the poor, the maid, the married,
And those who could not walk, were carried.
    The butler, hanging down his head,
By chambermaid, or cookmaid led,   190
Inquires, if from his friend the Moon
He has advice of pilfer'd spoon.
    The court-bred woman of condition,
(Who, to approve her disposition
As much superior as her birth
To those composed of common earth,
With double spirit must engage
In every folly of the age)
The honourable arts would buy,
To pack the cards, and cog a die.   200
    The hero—who, for brawn and face,
May claim right honourable place
Amongst the chiefs of Butcher-row : [1]
Who might, some thirty years ago,
If we may be allow'd to guess
At his employment by his dress,
Put medicines off from cart or stage,
The grand Toscano of the age ;
Or might about the country go
High-steward of a puppet-show,—   210
Steward and stewardship most meet,
For all know puppets never eat :
Who would be thought (though, save the mark!
That point is something in the dark)
The man of honour, one like those
Renown'd in story, who loved blows

───────────────

[1] 'Butcher-row :' an old street in London, now removed.

Better than victuals, and would fight,   217
Merely for sport, from morn to night :
Who treads like Mavors firm, whose tongue
Is with the triple thunder hung,
Who cries to Fear, 'Stand off—aloof,'
And talks as he were cannon-proof ;
Would be deem'd ready, when you list,
With sword and pistol, stick and fist,
Careless of points, balls, bruises, knocks,
At once to fence, fire, cudgel, box,
But at the same time bears about,
Within himself, some touch of doubt,
Of prudent doubt, which hints—that fame
Is nothing but an empty name ;   230
That life is rightly understood
By all to be a real good ;
That, even in a hero's heart,
Discretion is the better part ;
That this same honour may be won,
And yet no kind of danger run—
Like Drugger [1] comes, that magic powers
May ascertain his lucky hours ;
For at some hours the fickle dame,
Whom Fortune properly we name,   240
Who ne'er considers wrong or right,
When wanted most, plays least in sight,
And, like a modern court-bred jilt,
Leaves her chief favourites in a tilt.
Some hours there are, when from the heart
Courage into some other part,
No matter wherefore, makes retreat,
And Fear usurps the vacant seat ;

[1] 'Drugger :' Abel Drugger, in Jonson's ' Alchymist.

Whence, planet-struck, we often find   249
Stuarts[1] and Sackvilles [2] of mankind.
    Farther, he'd know (and by his art
A conjurer can that impart)
Whether politer it is reckon'd
To have, or not to have, a second ;
To drag the friends in, or alone
To make the danger all their own ;
Whether repletion is not bad,
And fighters with full stomachs mad ;
Whether, before he seeks the plain,
It were not well to breathe a vein ;   230
Whether a gentle salivation,
Consistently with reputation,
Might not of precious use be found,
Not to prevent, indeed, a wound,
But to prevent the consequence
Which oftentimes arises thence,
Those fevers, which the patient urge on
To gates of death, by help of surgeon ;
Whether a wind at east or west
Is for green wounds accounted best ;   270
Whether (was he to choose) his mouth
Should point towards the north or south ;
Whether more safely he might use,
On these occasions, pumps or shoes ;
Whether it better is to fight
By sunshine or by candlelight ;
Or, lest a candle should appear
Too mean to shine in such a sphere,

---

[1] 'Stuarts:' James the Second's dastardly conduct. at the battle of the
Boyne. — [2] 'Sackvilles:' Lord George Sackville, accused of cowardice at
the battle of Minden, afterwards degraded by a court martial, but ultimately
raised to promotion as a Peer and Secretary of State.

For who could of a candle tell 279
To light a hero into hell ;
And, lest the sun should partial rise
To dazzle one or t' other's eyes,
Or one or t' other's brains to scorch,
Might not Dame Luna hold a torch ?
 These points with dignity discuss'd,
And gravely fix'd,—a task which must
Require no little time and pains,
To make our hearts friends with our brains,—
The man of war would next engage
The kind assistance of the sage, 290
Some previous method to direct,
Which should make these of none effect.
 Could he not, from the mystic school
Of Art, produce some sacred rule,
By which a knowledge might be got
Whether men valiant were, or not ;
So he that challenges might write
Only to those who would not fight?
 Or could he not some way dispense
By help of which (without offence 300
To Honour, whose nice nature's such
She scarce endures the slightest touch)
When he, for want of t' other rule,
Mistakes his man, and, like a fool,
With some vain fighting blade gets in,
He fairly may get out again ?
 Or should some demon lay a scheme
To drive him to the last extreme,
So that he must confess his fears,
In mercy to his nose and ears, 310
And like a prudent recreant knight,
Rather do anything than fight,

Could he not some expedient buy   313
To keep his shame from public eye ?
For well he held,—and, men review,
Nine in ten hold the maxim too,—
That honour 's like a maidenhead,
Which, if in private brought to bed,
Is none the worse, but walks the town,
Ne'er lost, until the loss be known.   320
    The parson, too, (for now and then
Parsons are just like other men,
And here and there a grave divine
Has passions such as yours and mine)
Burning with holy lust to know
When Fate preferment will bestow,
'Fraid of detection, not of sin,
With circumspection sneaking in
To conjurer, as he does to whore,
Through some bye-alley or back-door,   330
With the same caution orthodox
Consults the stars, and gets a pox.
    The citizen, in fraud grown old,
Who knows no deity but gold,
Worn out, and gasping now for breath,
A medicine wants to keep off death ;
Would know, if that he cannot have,
What coins are current in the grave :
If, when the stocks (which, by his power,
Would rise or fall in half an hour ;   340
For, though unthought of and unseen,
He work'd the springs behind the screen)
By his directions came about,
And rose to par, he should sell out ;
Whether he safely might, or no,
Replace it in the funds below ?

By all address'd, believed, and paid,   347
Many pursued the thriving trade,
And, great in reputation grown,
Successive held the magic throne.
Favour'd by every darling passion,
The love of novelty and fashion,
Ambition, avarice, lust, and pride,
Riches pour'd in on every side.
But when the prudent laws thought fit
To curb this insolence of wit;
When senates wisely had provided,
Decreed, enacted, and decided,
That no such vile and upstart elves
Should have more knowledge than themselves; 360
When fines and penalties were laid
To stop the progress of the trade,
And stars no longer could dispense,
With honour, farther influence;
And wizards (which must be confess'd
Was of more force than all the rest)
No certain way to tell had got
Which were informers, and which not;
Affrighted sages were, perforce,
Obliged to steer some other course.   370
By various ways, these sons of Chance
Their fortunes labour'd to advance,
Well knowing, by unerring rules,
Knaves starve not in the land of fools.
    Some, with high titles and degrees,
Which wise men borrow when they please,
Without or trouble, or expense,
Physicians instantly commence,
And proudly boast an equal skill
With those who claim the right to kill.   380

Others about the country roam,   381
(For not one thought of going home)
With pistol and adopted leg,
Prepared at once to rob or beg.
 Some, the more subtle of their race,
(Who felt some touch of coward grace,
Who Tyburn to-avoid had wit,
But never fear'd deserving it)
Came to their brother Smollett's aid,
·And carried on the critic trade.   390
 Attach'd to letters and the Muse,
Some verses wrote, and some wrote news ;
Those each revolving month are seen,
The heroes of a magazine ;
These, every morning, great appear
In Ledger, or in Gazetteer,
Spreading the falsehoods of the day,
By turns for Faden and for Say.[1]
Like Swiss, their force is always laid
On that side where they best are paid :   400
Hence mighty prodigies arise,
And daily monsters strike our eyes ;
Wonders, to propagate the trade,
More strange than ever Baker [2] made,
Are hawk'd about from street to street,
And fools believe, whilst liars eat.
 Now armies in the air engage,
To fright a superstitious age ;
Now comets through the ether range,
In governments portending change ;   410
Now rivers to the ocean fly
So quick, they leave their channels dry ;

---

[1] 'Faden and Say :' two anti-Wilkite editors. — [2] 'Baker :' Sir Richard
Baker, the famous chronicler.

Now monstrous whales on Lambeth shore   413
Drink the Thames dry, and thirst for more ;
And every now and then appears
An Irish savage, numbering years
More than those happy sages could
Who drew their breath before the flood ;
Now, to the wonder of all people,
A church is left without a steeple ;   420
A steeple now is left in lurch,
And mourns departure of the church,
Which, borne on wings of mighty wind,
Removed a furlong off we find ;
Now, wrath on cattle to discharge,
Hailstones as deadly fall, and large,
As those which were on Egypt sent,
At once their crime and punishment ;
Or those which, as the prophet writes,
Fell on the necks of Amorites,   430
When, struck with wonder and amaze,
The sun, suspended, stay'd to gaze,
And, from her duty longer kept,
In Ajalon his sister slept.
    But if such things no more engage
The taste of a politer age,
To help them out in time of need
Another Tofts [1] must rabbits breed :
Each pregnant female trembling hears,
And, overcome with spleen and fears,   440
Consults her faithful glass no more,
But, madly bounding o'er the floor,
Feels hairs all o'er her body grow,
By Fancy turn'd into a doe.

---

[1] 'Tofts:' Mary Tofts of Godalming, who first dreamed of, and was at last brought to bed of, rabbits! She confessed afterwards that it was a fraud.

Now, to promote their private ends,   445
Nature her usual course suspends,
And varies from the stated plan
Observed e'er since the world began.
Bodies—which foolishly we thought,
By Custom's servile maxims taught,   450
Needed a regular supply,
And without nourishment must die—
With craving appetites, and sense
Of hunger easily dispense,
And, pliant to their wondrous skill,
Are taught, like watches, to stand still,
Uninjured, for a month or more,
Then go on as they did before.
The novel takes, the tale succeeds,
Amply supplies its author's needs,   460
And Betty Canning [1] is at least,
With Gascoyne's help, a six months' feast.
   Whilst, in contempt of all our pains,
The tyrant Superstition reigns
Imperious in the heart of man,
And warps his thoughts from Nature's plan ;
Whilst fond Credulity, who ne'er
The weight of wholesome doubts could bear,
To Reason and herself unjust,
Takes all things blindly upon trust ;   470
Whilst Curiosity, whose rage
No mercy shows to sex or age,
Must be indulged at. the expense
Of judgment, truth, and common sense,
Impostures cannot but prevail ;
And when old miracles grow stale,

---

[1] ' Betty Canning :' a woman who pretended, in 1753, that she had been confined in a garret by a gypsy woman, for twenty-seven days, with scarcely any food, but turned out to be an impostor.

Jugglers will still the art pursue,   477
And entertain the world with new.
  For them, obedient to their will,
And trembling at their mighty skill,
Sad spirits, summon'd from the tomb,
Glide, glaring ghastly, through the gloom ;
In all the usual pomp of storms,
In horrid customary forms,
A wolf, a bear, a horse, an ape,
As Fear and Fancy give them shape,
Tormented with despair and pain,
They roar, they yell, and clank the chain.
Folly and Guilt (for Guilt, howe'er
The face of Courage it may wear,   490
Is still a coward at the heart)
At fear-created phantoms start.
The priest—that very word implies
That he's both innocent and wise—
Yet fears to travel in the dark,
Unless escorted by his clerk.
  But let not every bungler deem
Too lightly of so deep a scheme ;
For reputation of the art,
Each ghost must act a proper part,   500
Observe Decorum's needful grace,
And keep the laws of Time and Place :
Must change, with happy variation,
His manners with his situation ;
What in the country might pass down,
Would be impertinent in town.
No spirit of discretion here
Can think of breeding awe and fear ;
'Twill serve the purpose more by half
To make the congregation laugh.   510

We want no ensigns of surprise,   511
Locks stiff with gore, and saucer eyes ;
Give us an entertaining sprite,
Gentle, familiar, and polite,
One who appears in such a form
As might an holy hermit warm,
Or who on former schemes refines,
And only talks by sounds and signs,
Who will not to the eye appear,
But pays her visits to the ear,   520
And knocks so gently, 't would not fright
A lady in the darkest night.
Such is our Fanny, whose good-will,
Which cannot in the grave lie still,
Brings her on earth to entertain
Her friends and lovers in Cock-lane.

Book II.

A sacred standard rule we find,
By poets held time out of mind,
To offer at Apollo's shrine,
And call on one, or all the Nine.
   This custom, through a bigot zeal,
Which moderns of fine taste must feel
For those who wrote in days of yore,
Adopted stands, like many more ;
Though every cause which then conspired
To make it practised and admired,   10
Yielding to Time's destructive course,
For ages past hath lost its force.
   With ancient bards, an invocation
Was a true act of adoration,

Of worship an essential part,   · 15
And not a formal piece of art,
Of paltry reading a parade,
A dull solemnity in trade,
A pious fever, taught to burn
An hour or two, to serve a turn.   20
　　They talk'd not of Castalian springs,
By way of saying pretty things,
As we dress out our flimsy rhymes;
'Twas the religion of the times;
And they believed that holy stream
With greater force made Fancy teem,
Reckon'd by all a true specific
To make the barren brain prolific:
Thus Romish Church, (a scheme which bears
Not half so much excuse as theirs)   30
Since Faith implicitly hath taught her,
Reveres the force of holy water.
　　The Pagan system, whether true
Or false, its strength, like buildings, drew
From many parts disposed to bear,
In one great whole, their proper share.
Each god of eminent degree
To some vast beam compared might be;
Each godling was a peg, or rather
A cramp, to keep the beams together: 40
And man as safely might pretend
From Jove the thunderbolt to rend,
As with an impious pride aspire
To rob Apollo of his lyre.
　　With settled faith and pious awe,
Establish'd by the voice of Law,
Then poets to the Muses came,
And from their altars caught the flame.

Genius, with Phœbus for his guide,   49
The Muse ascending by his side,
With towering pinions dared to soar,
Where eye could scarcely strain before.
But why should we, who cannot feel
These glowings of a Pagan zeal,
That wild enthusiastic force,
By which, above her common course,
Nature, in ecstasy upborne, .
Look'd down on earthly things with scorn ;
Who have no more regard, 'tis known,
For their religion than our own,   60
And feel not half so fierce a flame
At Clio's as at Fisher's[1] name ;
Who know these boasted sacred streams
Were mere romantic, idle dreams,
That Thames has waters clear as those
Which on the top of Pindus rose,
And that, the fancy to refine,
Water's not half so good as wine ;
Who know, if profit strikes our eye,
Should we drink Helicon quite dry,   70
The whole fountain would not thither lead
So soon as one poor jug from Tweed :
Who, if to raise poetic fire,
The power of beauty we require,
In any public place can view
More than the Grecians ever knew ;
If wit into the scale is thrown,
Can boast a Lennox[2] of our own ;

[1] 'Fisher's:' Catherine Fisher, better known by the name of Kitty Fisher, a courtezan of great beauty.—[2] 'Lennox:' Mrs Arabella Lennox, the author of some pleasing novels, and a friend of Dr Johnson's. See Boswell and Hawkins.

Why should we servile customs choose,   7&
And court an antiquated Muse ?
No matter why—to ask a reason,
In pedant bigotry is treason.
In the broad, beaten turnpike-road
Of hacknied panegyric ode,
No modern poet dares to ride
Without Apollo by his side,
Nor in a sonnet take the air,
Unless his lady Muse be there ;
She, from some amaranthine grove,
Where little Loves and Graces rove,   90
The laurel to my lord must bear,
Or garlands make for whores to wear ;
She, with soft elegiac verse,
Must grace some mighty villain's hearse,
Or for some infant, doom'd by Fate
To wallow in a large estate,
With rhymes the cradle must adorn,
To tell the world a fool is born.
    Since then our critic lords expect
No hardy poet should reject   100
Establish'd maxims, or presume
To place much better in their room,
By nature fearful, I submit,
And in this dearth of sense and wit—
With nothing done, and little said,
(By wild excursive Fancy led
Into a second Book thus far,
Like some unwary traveller,
Whom varied scenes of wood and lawn,
With treacherous delight, have drawn,   116
Deluded from his purposed way,
Whom every step leads more astray :

Who, gazing round, can no where spy,   113
Or house, or friendly cottage nigh,
And resolution seems to lack
To venture forward, or go back)
Invoke some goddess to descend,
And help me to my journey's end ;
Though conscious Arrow all the while
Hears the petition with a smile,   120
Before the glass her charms unfolds,
And in herself my Muse beholds.
    Truth, Goddess of celestial birth,
But little loved or known on earth,
Whose power but seldom rules the heart,
Whose name, with hypocritic art,
An arrant stalking-horse is made,
A snug pretence to drive a trade,
An instrument, convenient grown,
To plant more firmly Falsehood's throne,   130
As rebels varnish o'er their cause
With specious colouring of laws,
And pious traitors draw the knife
In the king's name against his life ;
Whether (from cities far away,
Where Fraud and Falsehood scorn thy sway)
The faithful nymph's and shepherd's pride,
With Love and Virtue by thy side,
Your hours in harmless joys are spent
Amongst the children of Content ;   140
Or, fond of gaiety and sport,
You tread the round of England's court,
Howe'er my lord may frowning go,
And treat the stranger as a foe,
Sure to be found a welcome guest
In George's and in Charlotte's breast ;

If, in the giddy hours of youth,   147
My constant soul adhered to truth ;
If, from the time I first wrote Man,
I still pursued thy sacred plan,
Tempted by Interest in vain
To wear mean Falsehood's golden chain ;
If, for a season drawn away,
Starting from Virtue's path astray,
All low disguise I scorn'd to try,
And dared to sin, but not to lie ;
Hither, oh ! hither condescend,
Eternal Truth ! thy steps to bend,
And favour him, who, every hour,
Confesses and obeys thy power.   160
    But come not with that easy mien
By which you won the lively Dean ;
Nor yet assume that strumpet air
Which Rabelais taught thee first to wear ;
Nor yet that arch ambiguous face
Which with Cervantes gave thee grace ;
But come in sacred vesture clad,
Solemnly dull, and truly sad !
    Far from thy seemly matron train
Be idiot Mirth, and Laughter vain !   170
For Wit and Humour, which pretend
At once to please us and amend,
They are not for my present turn ;
Let them remain in France with Sterne.
    Of noblest City parents born,
Whom wealth and dignities adorn,
Who still one constant tenor keep,
Not quite awake, nor quite asleep ;
With thee let formal Dulness come,
And deep Attention, ever dumb,   180

Who on her lips her finger lays,   181
Whilst every circumstance she weighs,
Whose downcast eye is often found
Bent without motion to the ground,
Or, to some outward thing confined,
Remits no image to the mind,
No pregnant mark of meaning bears,
But, stupid, without vision stares ;
Thy steps let Gravity attend,
Wisdom's and Truth's unerring friend ;   190
For one may see with half an eye,
That Gravity can never lie,
And his arch'd brow, pull'd o'er his eyes,
With solemn proof proclaims him wise.

 Free from all waggeries and sports,
The produce of luxurious courts,
Where sloth and lust enervate youth,
Come thou, a downright City-Truth :
The City, which we ever find
A sober pattern for mankind ;   200
Where man, in equilibrio hung,
Is seldom old, and never young,
And, from the cradle to the grave,
Not Virtue's friend nor Vice's slave ;
As dancers on the wire we spy,
Hanging between the earth and sky.

 She comes—I see her from afar
Bending her course to Temple-Bar ;
All sage and silent is her train,
Deportment grave, and garments plain,   210
Such as may suit a parson's wear,
And fit the headpiece of a mayor.

 By Truth inspired, our Bacon's force
Open'd the way to Learning's source ;

Boyle through the works of Nature ran ;   215
And Newton, something more than man,
Dived into Nature's hidden springs,
Laid bare the principles of things,
Above the earth our spirits bore,
And gave us worlds unknown before.   220
By Truth inspired, when Lauder's[1] spite
O'er Milton cast the veil of night,
Douglas arose, and through the maze
Of intricate and winding ways,
Came where the subtle traitor lay,
And dragg'd him, trembling, to the day ;
Whilst he, (oh, shame to noblest parts,
Dishonour to the liberal arts,
To traffic in so vile a scheme !)
Whilst he, our letter'd Polypheme,[2]   230
Who had confed'rate forces join'd,
Like a base coward skulk'd behind.
By Truth inspired, our critics go
To track Fingál in Highland snow,
To form their own and others' creed
From manuscripts they cannot read.
By Truth inspired, we numbers see
Of each profession and degree,
Gentle and simple, lord and cit,
Wit without wealth, wealth without wit,   240
When Punch and Sheridan have done,
To Fanny's[2] ghostly lectures run.
By Truth and Fanny now inspired,
I feel my glowing bosom fired ;

[1] 'Lauder's:' William Lauder, the notorious forger and interpolator of Milton, detected by Dr Douglas, Bishop of Salisbury. — [2] 'Polypheme:' Johnson, who at first took Lauder's side. See Boswell. — [3] 'Fanny:' the supposed ghost.

Desire beats high in every vein   245
To sing the spirit of Cock-lane ;
To tell (just as the measure flows
In halting rhyme, half verse, half prose)
With more than mortal arts endued,
How she united force withstood,   250
And proudly gave a brave defiance
To Wit and Dulness in alliance.
    This apparition (with relation
To ancient modes of derivation,
This we may properly so call,
Although it ne'er appears at all,
As by the way of inuendo,
Lucus is made *à non lucendo*)
Superior to the vulgar mode,
Nobly disdains that servile road   260
Which coward ghosts, as it appears,
Have walk'd in full five thousand years,
And, for restraint too mighty grown,
Strikes out a method of her own.
    Others may meanly start away,
Awed by the herald of the day ;
With faculties too weak to bear
The freshness of the morning air,
May vanish with the melting gloom,
And glide in silence to the tomb ;   270
She dares the sun's most piercing light,
And knocks by day as well as night.
Others, with mean and partial view,
Their visits pay to one or two ;
She, in great reputation grown,
Keeps the best company in town.
Our active enterprising ghost
As large and splendid routs can boast

As those which, raised by Pride's command,[1] 279
Block up the passage through the Strand.
   Great adepts in the fighting trade,
Who served their time on the parade ;
She-saints, who, true to Pleasure's plan,
Talk about God, and lust for man ;
Wits, who believe nor God, nor ghost,
And fools who worship every post ;
Cowards, whose lips with war are hung ;
Men truly brave, who hold their tongue ;
Courtiers, who laugh they know not why,
And cits, who for the same cause cry ; 290
The canting tabernacle-brother,
(For one rogue still suspects another) ;
Ladies, who to a spirit fly,
Rather than with their husbands lie ;
Lords, who as chastely pass their lives
With other women as their wives ;
Proud of their intellects and clothes,
Physicians, lawyers, parsons, beaux,
And, truant from their desks and shops,
Spruce Temple clerks and 'prentice fops, 300
To Fanny come, with the same view,
To find her false, or find her true.
   Hark ! something creeps about the house !
Is it a spirit, or a mouse ?
Hark ! something scratches round the room !
A cat, a rat, a stubb'd birch-broom.
Hark ! on the wainscot now it knocks !
' If thou 'rt a ghost,' cried Orthodox,
With that affected solemn air
Which hypocrites delight to wear, 310

[1] ' Pride's command : ' The Countess-Duchess of Northumberland was celebrated for the splendour of her parties.

And all those forms of consequence   311
Which fools adopt instead of sense ;
'If thou 'rt a ghost, who from the tomb
Stalk'st sadly silent through this gloom,
In breach of Nature's stated laws,
For good, or bad, or for no cause,
Give now nine knocks ;[1] like priests of old,
Nine we a sacred number hold.'

    ''Psha,' cried Profound, (a man of parts,
Deep read in all the curious arts,   320
Who to their hidden springs had traced
The force of numbers, rightly placed)
'As to the number, you are right ;
As to the form, mistaken quite.
What 's nine ? Your adepts all agree
The virtue lies in three times three.'

    He said ; no need to say it twice,
For thrice she knock'd, and thrice, and thrice.

    The crowd, confounded and amazed,
In silence at each other gazed.   330
From Cælia's hand the snuff-box fell ;
Tinsel, who ogled with the belle,
To pick it up attempts in vain,
He stoops, but cannot rise again.
Immane Pomposo[2] was not heard
T' import one crabbed foreign word.
Fear seizes heroes, fools, and wits,
And Plausible his prayers forgets.

    At length, as people just awake,
Into wild dissonance they break ;   340
All talk'd at once, but not a word
Was understood or plainly heard.

---

[1] 'Nine knocks:' a curious anticipation of modern spirit-rappings! —
[2] 'Immane Pomposo:' Dr Johnson; 'immane,' referring to Virgil's 'Monstrum horrendum immane;' and ridiculing Dr J.'s Latinisms.

Such is the noise of chattering geese,)   343
Slow sailing on the summer breeze ;
Such is the language Discord speaks
In Welsh women o'er beds of leeks ;
Such the confused and horrid sounds
Of Irish in potatoe-grounds.
    But tired, for even C——'s [1] tongue
Is not on iron hinges hung,   35
Fear and Confusion sound retreat,
Reason and Order take their seat.
The fact, confirm'd beyond all doubt,
They now would find the causes out.
For this a sacred rule we find
Among the nicest of mankind,
Which never might exception brook
From Hobbes even down to Bolingbroke,
To doubt of facts, however true,
Unless they know the causes too.   360
    Trifle, of whom 'twas hard to tell
When he intended ill or well ;
Who, to prevent all farther pother,
Probably meant nor one, nor t' other ;
Who to be silent always loth,
Would speak on either side, or both ;
Who, led away by love of fame,
If any new idea came,
Whate'er it made for, always said it,
Not with an eye to truth, but credit ;   370
For orators profess'd, 'tis known,
Talk not for our sake, but their own ;
Who always show'd his talents best
When serious things were turn'd to jest,

[1] ' C——'s :' not known.

And, under much impertinence,   375
Possess'd no common share of sense ;
Who could deceive the flying hours
With chat on butterflies and flowers ;
Could talk of powder, patches, paint,
With the same zeal as of a saint ;   380
Could prove a Sibyl brighter far
Than Venus or the Morning Star ;
Whilst something still so gay, so new,
The smile of approbation drew,
And females eyed the charming man,
Whilst their hearts flutter'd with their fan ;
Trifle, who would by no means miss
An opportunity like this,
Proceeding on his usual plan,
Smiled, stroked his chin, and thus began :   390
   ' With shears or scissors, sword or knife,
When the Fates cut the thread of life,
(For if we to the grave are sent,
No matter with what instrument)
The body in some lonely spot,
On dunghill vile, is laid to rot,
Or sleep among more holy dead
With prayers irreverently read ;
The soul is sent where Fate ordains,
To reap rewards, to suffer pains.   400
    The virtuous to those mansions go
Where pleasures unembitter'd flow,
Where, leading up a jocund band,
Vigour and Youth dance hand in hand,
Whilst Zephyr, with harmonious gales,
Pipes softest music through the vales,
And Spring and Flora, gaily crown'd,
With velvet carpet spread the ground ;

With livelier blush where roses bloom, 409
And every shrub expires perfume ;
Where crystal streams meandering glide,
Where warbling flows the amber tide ;
Where other suns dart brighter beams,
And light through purer ether streams.
 Far other seats, far different state,
The sons of Wickedness await.
Justice (not that old hag I mean
Who 's nightly in the Garden seen,[1]
Who lets no spark of mercy rise,
For crimes, by which men lose their eyes ; 420
Nor her who, with an equal hand,
Weighs tea and sugar in the Strand ;
Nor her who, by the world deem'd wise,
Deaf to the widow's piercing cries,
Steel'd 'gainst the starving orphan's tears,
On pawns her base tribunal rears ;
But her who after death presides,
Whom sacred Truth unerring guides ;
Who, free from partial influence,
Nor sinks nor raises evidence, 430
Before whom nothing's in the dark,
Who takes no bribe, and keeps no clerk)
Justice, with equal scale below,
In due proportion weighs out woe,
And always with such lucky aim
Knows punishments so fit to frame,
That she augments their grief and pain,
Leaving no reason to complain.
 Old maids and rakes are join'd together,
Coquettes and prudes, like April weather. 440

[1] ' Garden :' Covent, where a set of low and mercenary wretches, called *trading justices*, superintended the administration of police.

Q

Wit's forced to chum with Common-Sense,   441
And Lust is yoked to Impotence.
Professors (Justice so decreed)
Unpaid, must constant lectures read ;
On earth it often doth befall,
They're paid, and never read at all.
Parsons must practise what they teach,
And bishops are compell'd to preach.

   She who on earth was nice and prim,
Of delicacy full, and whim ;   450
Whose tender nature could not bear
The rudeness of the churlish air,
Is doom'd, to mortify her pride,
The change of weather to abide,
And sells, whilst tears with liquor mix,
Burnt brandy on the shore of Styx.

   Avaro,[1] by long use grown bold
In every ill which brings him gold,
Who his Reedemer would pull down,
And sell his God for half-a-crown ;   460
Who, if some blockhead should be willing
To lend him on his soul a shilling,
A well-made bargain would esteem it,
And have more sense than to redeem it,
Justice shall in those shades confine,
To drudge for Plutus in the mine,
All the day long to toil and roar,
And, cursing, work the stubborn ore,
For coxcombs here, who have no brains,
Without a sixpence for his pains :   470
Thence, with each due return of night,
Compell'd, the tall, thin, half-starved sprite

---

[1] 'Avaro:' Pearce, Bishop of Rochester, a favourite object of Churchill's
ire, as some of the previous poems prove.

Shall earth revisit, and survey   473
The place where once his treasure lay,
Shall view the stall where holy Pride,
With letter'd Ignorance allied,
Once hail'd him mighty and adored,
Descended to another lord :
Then shall he, screaming, pierce the air,
Hang his lank jaws, and scowl despair ;   480
Then shall he ban at Heaven's decrees,
And, howling, sink to Hell for ease.
   Those who on earth through life have pass'd
With equal pace from first to last,
Nor vex'd with passions nor with spleen,
Insipid, easy, and serene ;
Whose heads were made too weak to bear
The weight of business, or of care ;
Who, without merit, without crime,
Contrive to while away their time ;   490
Nor good nor bad, nor fools nor wits,
Mild Justice, with a smile, permits
Still to pursue their darling plan,
And find amusement how they can.
   The beau, in gaudiest plumage dress'd,
With lucky fancy o'er the rest
Of air a curious mantle throws,
And chats among his brother beaux ;
Or, if the weather 's fine and clear,
No sign of rain or tempest near,   500
Encouraged by the cloudless day,
Like gilded butterflies at play,
So lively all, so gay, so brisk,
In air they flutter, float, and frisk.
   The belle (what mortal doth not know
Belles after death admire a beau ?)

With happy grace renews her art 507
To trap the coxcomb's wandering heart ;
And, after death as whilst they live,
A heart is all which beaux can give.
    In some still, solemn, sacred shade,
Behold a group of authors laid,
Newspaper wits, and sonneteers,
Gentleman bards, and rhyming peers,
Biographers, whose wondrous worth
Is scarce remember'd now on earth,
Whom Fielding's humour led astray,
And plaintive fops, debauch'd by Gray,
All sit together in a ring,
And laugh and prattle, write and sing. 520
    On his own works, with laurel crown'd,
Neatly and elegantly bound,
(For this is one of many rules,
With writing lords, and laureate fools,
And which for ever must succeed
With other lords who cannot read,
However destitute of wit,
To make their works for bookcase fit)
Acknowledged master of those seats,
Cibber his Birth-day Odes repeats. 530
    With triumph now possess that seat,
With triumph now thy Odes repeat ;
Unrivall'd vigils proudly keep,
Whilst every hearer 's lull'd to sleep ;
But know, illustrious bard ! when Fate,
Which still pursues thy name with hate,
The regal laurel blasts, which now
Blooms on the placid Whitehead's brow,
Low must descend thy pride and fame,
And Cibber's be the second name.'— 540

Here Trifle cough'd, (for coughing still   541
Bears witness of the speaker's skill,
A necessary piece of art,
Of rhetoric an essential part,
And adepts in the speaking trade
Keep a cough by them ready made,
Which they successfully dispense
When at a loss for words or sense)
Here Trifle cough'd, here paused—but while
He strove to recollect his smile,   550
That happy engine of his art,
Which triumph'd o'er the female heart,
Credulity, the child of Folly,
Begot on cloister'd Melancholy,
Who heard, with grief, the florid fool
Turn sacred things to ridicule,
And saw him, led by Whim away,
Still farther from the subject stray,
Just in the happy nick, aloud,
In shape of Moore,[1] address'd the crowd :   560
    ' Were we with patience here to sit,
Dupes to th' impertinence of Wit,
Till Trifle his harangue should end,
A Greenland night we might attend,
Whilst he, with fluency of speech,
Would various mighty nothings teach'—
(Here Trifle, sternly looking down,
Gravely endeavour'd at a frown,
But Nature unawares stept in,
And, mocking, turn'd it to a grin)—   570
'And when, in Fancy's chariot hurl'd,
We had been carried round the world,

---

[1] 'Moore:' the Rev. Mr Moore, then curate of St Sepulchre's, who had a share in the Cock-lane conspiracy.

Involved in error still and doubt,   673
He 'd leave us where we first set out.
Thus soldiers (in whose exercise
Material use with grandeur vies)
/ Lift up their legs with mighty pain,
Only to set them down again.
   Believe ye not (yes, all, I see,
In sound belief concur with me)   580
That Providence, for worthy ends,
To us unknown, this spirit sends ?
Though speechless lay the trembling tongue,
Your faith was on your features hung ;
Your faith I in your eyes could see,
When all were pale and stared like me.
But scruples to prevent, and root
Out every shadow of dispute,
Pomposo, Plausible, and I,
With Fanny, have agreed to try   590
A deep concerted scheme—this night
To fix or to destroy her quite.
If it be true, before we 've done,
We 'll make it glaring as the sun ;
If it be false, admit no doubt
Ere morning's dawn we 'll find it out.
Into the vaulted womb of Death,
Where Fanny now, deprived of breath,
Lies festering, whilst her troubled sprite
Adds horror to the gloom of night,   600
Will we descend, and bring from thence
Proofs of such force to Common-Sense,
Vain triflers shall no more deceive,
And atheists tremble and believe.'
   He said, and ceased ; the chamber rung
With due applause from every tongue :

The mingled sound—(now let me see—   607
Something by way of simile)
Was it more like Strymonian cranes,
Or winds, low murmuring, when it rains,
Or drowsy hum of clustering bees,
Or the hoarse roar of angry seas ?
Or (still to heighten and explain,
For else our simile is vain)
Shall we declare it like all four,
A scream, a murmur, hum, and roar ?
    Let Fancy now, in awful state,
Present this great triumvirate,
(A method which received we find,
In other cases, by mankind)   620
Elected with a joint consent,
All fools in town to represent.
    The clock strikes twelve—Moore starts and swears.
In oaths, we know, as well as prayers,
Religion lies, and a church-brother
May use at will, or one, or t' other ;
Plausible from his cassock drew
A holy manual, seeming new ;
A book it was of private prayer,
But not a pin the worse for wear :   630
For, as we by-the-bye may say,
None but small saints in private pray.
Religion, fairest maid on earth !
As meek as good, who drew her birth
From that bless'd union, when in heaven
Pleasure was bride to Virtue given ;
Religion, ever pleased to pray,
Possess'd the precious gift one day ;
Hypocrisy, of Cunning born,
Crept in and stole it ere the morn ;   640

Whitefield, that greatest of all saints,   641
Who always prays and never faints,
(Whom she to her own brothers bore,
Rapine and Lust, on Severn's shore)
Received it from the squinting dame;
From him to Plausible it came,
Who, with unusual care oppress'd,
Now, trembling, pull'd it from his breast;
Doubts in his boding heart arise,
And fancied spectres blast his eyes,   650
Devotion springs from abject fear,
And stamps his prayers for once sincere.
  Pomposo, (insolent and loud,
Vain idol of a scribbling crowd,
Whose very name inspires an awe,
Whose every word is sense and law,
For what his greatness hath decreed,
Like laws of Persia and of Mede,
Sacred through all the realm of Wit,
Must never of repeal admit;   660
Who, cursing flattery, is the tool
Of every fawning, flattering fool;
Who wit with jealous eye surveys,
And sickens at another's praise;
Who, proudly seized of Learning's throne,
Now damns all learning but his own;
Who scorns those common wares to trade in,
Reasoning, convincing, and persuading,
But makes each sentence current pass
With puppy, coxcomb, scoundrel, ass;   670
For 'tis with him a certain rule,
The folly's proved when he calls fool;
Who, to increase his native strength,
Draws words six syllables in length,

With which, assisted with a frown 675
By way of club, he knocks us down ;
Who 'bove the vulgar dares to rise,
And sense of decency defies ;
For this same decency is made
Only for bunglers in the trade, 680
And, like the cobweb laws, is still
Broke through by great ones when they will) —
Pomposo, with strong sense supplied,
Supported, and confirm'd by Pride,
His comrades' terrors to beguile
'Grinn'd horribly a ghastly smile :'
Features so horrid, were it light,
Would put the Devil himself to flight.

Such were the three in name and worth
Whom Zeal and Judgment singled forth 690
To try the sprite on Reason's plan,
Whether it was of God or man.

Dark was the night ; it was that hour
When Terror reigns in fullest power,
When, as the learn'd of old have said,
The yawning Grave gives up her dead ;
When Murder, Rapine by her side,
Stalks o'er the earth with giant stride ;
Our Quixotes (for that knight of old
Was not in truth by half so bold, 700
Though Reason at the same time cries,
'Our Quixotes are not half so wise,'
Since they, with other follies, boast
An expedition 'gainst a ghost)
Through the dull deep surrounding gloom,
In close array, towards Fanny's tomb [1]

[1] 'Fanny's tomb :' it had been stated that her tomb had been disturbed, and an expedition actually took place to ascertain the truth.

Adventured forth ; Caution before,   707
With heedful step, the lantern bore,
Pointing at graves ; and in the rear,
Trembling, and talking loud, went Fear.
The churchyard teem'd—th' unsettled ground,
As in an ague, shook around ;
While, in some dreary vault confined,
Or riding on the hollow wind,
Horror, which turns the heart to stone,
In dreadful sounds was heard to groan.
All staring, wild, and out of breath,
At length they reach the place of Death.

   A vault it was, long time applied
To hold the last remains of Pride :   720
No beggar there, of humble race,
And humble fortunes, finds a place ;
To rest in pomp as well as ease,
The only way's to pay the fees.
Fools, rogues, and whores, if rich and great,
Proud even in death, here rot in state.
No thieves disrobe the well-dress'd dead ;
No plumbers steal the sacred lead ;
Quiet and safe the bodies lie ;
No sextons sell, no surgeons buy.   730

   Thrice, each the ponderous key applied,
And thrice to turn it vainly tried,
Till taught by Prudence to unite,
And straining with collected might,
The stubborn wards resist no more,
But open flies the growling door.

   Three paces back they fell amazed,
Like statues stood, like madmen gazed ;
The frighted blood forsakes the face,
And seeks the heart with quicker pace ;   740

The throbbing heart its fear declares,   741
And upright stand the bristled hairs ;
The head in wild distraction swims,
Cold sweats bedew the trembling limbs ;
Nature, whilst fears her bosom chill,
Suspends her powers, and life stands still.

    Thus had they stood till now ; but Shame
(An useful, though neglected dame,
By Heaven design'd the friend of man,
Though we degrade her all we can,   750
And strive, as our first proof of wit,
Her name and nature to forget)
Came to their aid in happy hour,
And with a wand of mighty power
Struck on their hearts ; vain fears subside,
And, baffled, leave the field to Pride.

    Shall they, (forbid it, Fame !) shall they
The dictates of vile Fear obey ?
Shall they, the idols of the Town,
To bugbears, fancy-form'd, bow down ?   760
Shall they, who greatest zeal express'd,
And undertook for all the rest,
Whose matchless courage all admire,
Inglorious from the task retire ?
How would the wicked ones rejoice,
And infidels exalt their voice,
If Moore and Plausible were found,
By shadows awed, to quit their ground ?
How would fools laugh, should it appear
Pomposo was the slave of fear ?   770
'Perish the thought ! Though to our eyes,
In all its terrors, Hell should rise ;
Though thousand ghosts, in dread array,
With glaring eyeballs, cross our way ;

Though Caution, trembling, stands aloof,   775
Still we will on, and dare the proof.'
They said ; and, without farther halt,
Dauntless march'd onward to the vault.
    What mortal men, who e'er drew breath,
Shall break into the house of Death,   780
With foot unhallow'd, and from thence
The mysteries of that state dispense,
Unless they, with due rites, prepare
Their weaker sense such sights to bear,
And gain permission from the state,
On earth their journal to relate ?
Poets themselves, without a crime,
Cannot attempt it e'en in rhyme,
But always, on such grand occasion,
Prepare a solemn invocation,   790
A posy for grim Pluto weave,
And in smooth numbers ask his leave.
But why this caution ? why prepare
Rites, needless now ? for thrice in air
The Spirit of the Night hath sneezed,
And thrice hath clapp'd his wings, well-pleased.
    Descend then, Truth, and guard thy side,
My Muse, my patroness, and guide !
Let others at invention aim,
And seek by falsities for fame ;   800
Our story wants not, at this time,
Flounces and furbelows in rhyme ;
Relate plain facts ; be brief and bold ;
And let the poets, famed of old,
Seek, whilst our artless tale we tell,
In vain to find a parallel :
Silent all three went in ; about
All three turn'd, silent, and came out.

Book III.

It was the hour, when housewife Morn
With pearl and linen hangs each thorn ;
When happy bards, who can regale
Their Muse with country air and ale,
Ramble afield to brooks and bowers,
To pick up sentiments and flowers ;
When dogs and squires from kennel fly,
And hogs and farmers quit their sty ;
When my lord rises to the chase,
And brawny chaplain takes his place.   10
   These images, or bad, or good,
If they are rightly understood,
Sagacious readers must allow
Proclaim us in the country now ;
For observations mostly rise
From objects just before our eyes,
And every lord, in critic wit,
Can tell you where the piece was writ ;
Can point out, as he goes along,
(And who shall dare to say he's wrong ?)   20
Whether the warmth (for bards, we know,
At present never more than glow)
Was in the town or country caught,
By the peculiar turn of thought.
   It was the hour,—though critics frown,
We now declare ourselves in Town,
Nor will a moment's pause allow
For finding when we came, or how.
The man who deals in humble prose,
Tied down by rule and method goes ;   30

But they who court the vigorous Muse   31
Their carriage have a right to choose.
Free as the air, and unconfined,
Swift as the motions of the mind,
The poet darts from place to place,
And instant bounds o'er time and space :
Nature (whilst blended fire and skill
Inflame our passions to his will)
Smiles at her violated laws,
And crowns his daring with applause.   40
    Should there be still some rigid few,
Who keep propriety in view,
Whose heads turn round, and cannot bear
This whirling passage through the air,
Free leave have such at home to sit,
And write a regimen for wit ;
To clip our pinions let them try,
Not having heart themselves to fly.
    It was the hour when devotees
Breathe pious curses on their knees ;   50
When they with prayers the day begin
To sanctify a night of sin ;
When rogues of modesty, who roam
Under the veil of night, sneak home,
That, free from all restraint and awe,
Just to the windward of the law,
Less modest rogues their tricks may play,
And plunder in the face of day.
    But hold,—whilst thus we play the fool,
In bold contempt of every rule,   60
Things of no consequence expressing,
Describing now, and now digressing,
To the discredit of our skill,
The main concern is standing still.

In plays, indeed, when storms of rage 65
Tempestuous in the soul engage,
Or when the spirits, weak and low,
Are sunk in deep distress and woe,
With strict propriety we hear
Description stealing on the ear, 70
And put off feeling half an hour
To thatch a cot, or paint a flower ;
But in these serious works, design'd
To mend the morals of mankind,
We must for ever be disgraced
With all the nicer sons of Taste,
If once, the shadow to pursue,
We let the substance out of view.
Our means must uniformly tend
In due proportion to their end, 80
And every passage aptly join
To bring about the one design.
Our friends themselves cannot admit
This rambling, wild, digressive wit ;
No—not those very friends, who found
Their credit on the self-same ground.

    Peace, my good grumbling sir—for once,
Sunk in the solemn, formal dunce,
This coxcomb shall your fears beguile—
We will be dull—that you may smile. 90

    Come, Method, come in all thy pride,
Dulness and Whitehead by thy side ;
Dulness and Method still are one,
And Whitehead is their darling son :
Not he,[1] whose pen, above control,
Struck terror to the guilty soul,

---

[1] 'Not he:' Paul Whitehead, the profligate satirist.

Made Folly tremble through her state,   97
And villains blush at being great ;
Whilst he himself, with steady face,
Disdaining modesty and grace,
Could blunder on through thick and thin,
Through every mean and servile sin,
Yet swear by Philip and by Paul,
He nobly scorn'd to blush at all ;
But he who in the Laureate chair,
By grace, not merit, planted there,
In awkward pomp is seen to sit,
And by his patent proves his wit ;
For favours of the great, we know,
Can wit as well as rank bestow ;   110
And they who, without one pretension,
Can get for fools a place or pension,
Must able be supposed, of course,
(If reason is allow'd due force)
To give such qualities and grace
As may equip them for the place.
    But he—who measures as he goes
A mongrel kind of tinkling prose,
And is too frugal to dispense,
At once, both poetry and sense ;   120
Who, from amidst his slumbering guards,
Deals out a charge to subject bards,
Where couplets after couplets creep
Propitious to the reign of sleep ;
Yet every word imprints an awe,
And all his dictates pass for law
With beaux, who simper all around,
And belles, who die in every sound :

1 ' Laureate :' William Whitehead, the poet laureate.

For in all things of this relation, 129
Men mostly judge from situation,
Nor in a thousand find we one
Who really weighs what's said or done;
They deal out censure, or give credit,
Merely from him who did or said it.
    But he—who, happily serene,
Means nothing, yet would seem to mean;
Who rules and cautions can dispense
With all that humble insolence
Which Impudence in vain would teach,
And none but modest men can reach; 140
Who adds to sentiments the grace
Of always being out of place,
And drawls out morals with an air
A gentleman would blush to wear;
Who, on the chastest, simplest plan,
As chaste, as simple, as the man
Without or character, or plot,
Nature unknown, and Art forgot,
Can, with much raking of the brains,
And years consumed in letter'd pains, 150
A heap of words together lay,
And, smirking, call the thing a play;[1]
Who, champion sworn in Virtue's cause,
'Gainst Vice his tiny bodkin draws,
But to no part of prudence stranger,
First blunts the point for fear of danger.
So nurses sage, as caution works,
When children first use knives and forks,
For fear of mischief, it is known,
To others' fingers or their own, 160

---

[1] 'Play': alluding to Whitehead's comedy of the 'School for Lovers.

To take the edge off wisely choose,   161
Though the same stroke takes off the use.
   Thee, Whitehead, thee I now invoke,
Sworn foe to Satire's generous stroke,
Which makes unwilling Conscience feel,
And wounds, but only wounds to heal.
Good-natured, easy creature, mild
And gentle as a new-born child,
Thy heart would never once admit
E'en wholesome rigour to thy wit;   170
Thy head, if Conscience should comply,
Its kind assistance would deny,
And lend thee neither force nor art
To drive it onward to the heart.
Oh, may thy sacred power control
Each fiercer working of my soul,
Damp every spark of genuine fire,
And languors, like thine own, inspire!
Trite be each thought, and every line
As moral and as dull as thine!   180
   Poised in mid-air—(it matters not
To ascertain the very spot,
Nor yet to give you a relation
How it eluded gravitation)—
Hung a watch-tower, by Vulcan plann'd
With such rare skill, by Jove's command,
That every word which, whisper'd here,
Scarce vibrates to the neighbour ear,
On the still bosom of the air
Is borne and heard distinctly there—   190
The palace of an ancient dame
Whom men as well as gods call Fame.
   A prattling gossip, on whose tongue
Proof of perpetual motion hung,

Whose lungs in strength all lungs surpass,   195
Like her own trumpet made of brass ;
Who with an hundred pair of eyes
The vain attacks of sleep defies ;
Who with an hundred pair of wings
News from the farthest quarters brings,   200
Sees, hears, and tells, untold before,
All that she knows and ten times more.
    Not all the virtues which we find
Concenter'd in a Hunter's[1] mind,
Can make her spare the ranc'rous tale,
If in one point she chance to fail ;
Or if, once in a thousand years,
A perfect character appears,
Such as of late with joy and pride
My soul possess'd, ere Arrow died ;   210
Or such as, Envy must allow,
The world enjoys in Hunter now ;
This hag, who aims at all alike,
At virtues e'en like theirs will strike,
And make faults in the way of trade,
When she can't find them ready made.
    All things she takes in, small and great,
Talks of a toy-shop and a state ;
Of wits and fools, of saints and kings,
Of garters, stars, and leading strings ;   220
Of old lords fumbling for a clap,
And young ones full of prayer and pap ;
Of courts, of morals, and tye-wigs,
Of bears and serjeants dancing jigs ;
Of grave professors at the bar
Learning to thrum on the guitar,

---

[1] 'Hunter:' Miss Hunter, one of Queen Charlotte's maids of honour, eloped on the day of the coronation with the Earl of Pembroke.

Whilst laws are slubber'd o'er in haste,   227
And Judgment sacrificed to Taste ;
Of whited sepulchres, lawn sleeves,
And God's house made a den of thieves :
Of funeral pomps,[1] where clamours hung,
And fix'd disgrace on every tongue,
Whilst Sense and Order blush'd to see
Nobles without humanity ;
Of coronations,[2] where each heart,
With honest raptures, bore a part ;
Of city feasts, where Elegance
Was proud her colours to advance,
And Gluttony, uncommon case,
Could only get the second place ;   240
Of new-raised pillars in the state,
Who must be good, as being great ;
Of shoulders, on which honours sit
Almost as clumsily as wit ;
Of doughty knights, whom titles please,
But not the payment of the fees ;
Of lectures, whither every fool,
In second childhood, goes to school ;
Of graybeards, deaf to Reason's call,
From Inn of Court, or City Hall,   250
Whom youthful appetites enslave,
With one foot fairly in the grave,
By help of crutch, a needful brother,
Learning of Hart [3] to dance with t' other ;
Of doctors regularly bred
To fill the mansions of the dead ;

[1] 'Funeral Pomps:' alluding to certain improprieties at the interment of George the Second, which took place the 11th of November 1760.—[2] 'Coronations:' the coronation of George the Third on the 22d of September 1761. —[3] 'Hart:' a dancing-master of the day.

Of quacks, (for quacks they must be still,   257
Who save when forms require to kill)
Who life, and health, and vigour give
To him, not one would wish to live ;
Of artists who, with noblest view,
Disinterested plans pursue,
For trembling worth the ladder raise,
And mark out the ascent to praise ;
Of arts and sciences, where meet,
Sublime, profound, and all complete,
A set [1] (whom at some fitter time
The Muse shall consecrate in rhyme)
Who, humble artists to out-do,
A far more liberal plan pursue,   270
And let their well-judged premiums fall
On those who have no worth at all ;
Of sign-post exhibitions, raised
For laughter more than to be praised,
(Though, by the way, we cannot see
Why Praise and Laughter mayn't agree)
Where genuine humour runs to waste,
And justly chides our want of taste,
Censured, like other things, though good,
Because they are not understood.   280
    To higher subjects now she soars,
And talks of politics and whores ;
(If to your nice and chaster ears
That term indelicate appears,
Scripture politely shall refine,
And melt it into concubine)
In the same breath spreads Bourbon's league ; [2]
And publishes the grand intrigue ;

[1] 'A set:' an invidious reflection on the Society for the Encouragement of
Arts, Manufactures, and Commerce, founded in the year 1753.—[2] 'Bourbon's
league :' the family compact between France and Spain.

In Brussels or our own Gazette [1]   289
Makes armies fight which never met,
And circulates the pox or plague
To London, by the way of Hague ;
For all the lies which there appear
Stamp'd with authority come here ;
Borrows as freely from the gabble
Of some rude leader of a rabble,
Or from the quaint harangues of those
Who lead a nation by the nose,
As from those storms which, void of art,
Burst from our honest patriot's heart,[2]   300
When Eloquence and Virtue, (late
Remark'd to live in mutual hate)
Fond of each other's friendship grown,
Claim every sentence for their own ;
And with an equal joy recites
Parade amours and half-pay fights,
Perform'd by heroes of fair weather,
Merely by dint of lace and feather,
As those rare acts which Honour taught
Our daring sons where Granby [3] fought,   310
Or those which, with superior skill,
Sackville achieved by standing still.

This hag, (the curious, if they please,
May search, from earliest times to these,
And poets they will always see
With gods and goddesses make free,
Treating them all, except the Muse,
As scarcely fit to wipe their shoes)

---

[1] 'Gazette:' the *Brussels Gazette*, a notorious paper of that time.—
[2] 'Patriot's heart:' Mr Pitt, afterwards Lord Chatham. — [3] 'Granby:' the
Marquis of Granby, distinguished in a conspicuous manner during the seven
years' war, under Prince Ferdinand of Brunswick. See Junius.

Who had beheld, from first to last, 319
How our triumvirate had pass'd
Night's dreadful interval, and heard,
With strict attention, every word,
Soon as she saw return of light,
On sounding pinions took her flight.
　　Swift through the regions of the sky,
Above the reach of human eye,
Onward she drove the furious blast,
And rapid as a whirlwind pass'd,
O'er countries, once the seats of Taste,
By Time and Ignorance laid waste; 330
O'er lands, where former ages saw
Reason and Truth the only law;
Where Arts and Arms, and Public Love,
In generous emulation strove;
Where kings were proud of legal sway,
And subjects happy to obey,
Though now in slavery sunk, and broke
To Superstition's galling yoke;
Of Arts, of Arms, no more they tell,
Or Freedom, which with Science fell, 340
By tyrants awed, who never find
The passage to their people's mind;
To whom the joy was never known
Of planting in the heart their throne;
Far from all prospect of relief,
Their hours in fruitless prayers and grief,
For loss of blessings, they employ,
Which we unthankfully enjoy.
　　Now is the time (had we the will)
T' amaze the reader with our skill, 350
To pour out such a flood of knowledge
As might suffice for a whole college,

Whilst with a true poetic force,   353
We traced the goddess in her course,
Sweetly describing, in our flight,
Each common and uncommon sight,
Making our journal gay and pleasant,
With things long past, and things now present.
Rivers—once nymphs—(a transformation
Is mighty pretty in relation)   360
From great authorities we know
Will matter for a tale bestow :
To make the observation clear,
We give our friends an instance here.
  The day (that never is forgot)
Was very fine, but very hot ;
The nymph (another general rule)
Inflamed with heat, laid down to cool ;
Her hair (we no exceptions find)
Waved careless, floating in the wind ;   370
Her heaving breasts, like summer seas,
Seem'd amorous of the playful breeze :
Should fond Description tune our lays
In choicest accents to her praise,
Description we at last should find,
Baffled and weak, would halt behind.
Nature had form'd her to inspire
In every bosom soft desire ;
Passions to raise, she could not feel,
Wounds to inflict, she would not heal.   380
A god, (his name is no great matter,
Perhaps a Jove, perhaps a Satyr)
Raging with lust, a godlike flame,
By chance, as usual, thither came ;
With gloating eye the fair one view'd,
Desired her first, and then pursued :

She (for what other can she do ?)   387
Must fly—or how can he pursue ?
The Muse (so custom hath decreed)
Now proves her spirit by her speed,
Nor must one limping line disgrace
The life and vigour of the race ;
She runs, and he runs, till at length,
Quite destitute of breath and strength,
To Heaven (for there we all apply
For help, when there's no other nigh)
She offers up her virgin prayer,
(Can virgins pray unpitied there ?)
And when the god thinks he has caught her,
Slips through his hands and runs to water,   400
Becomes a stream, in which the poet,
If he has any wit, may show it.
    A city once for power renown'd
Now levell'd even to the ground,
Beyond all doubt is a direction
To introduce some fine reflection.
    Ah, woeful me ! ah, woeful man !
Ah, woeful all, do all we can !
Who can on earthly things depend
From one to t' other moment's end ?   410
Honour, wit, genius, wealth, and glory,
Good lack ! good lack ! are transitory ;
Nothing is sure and stable found,
The very earth itself turns round :
Monarchs, nay ministers, must die,
Must rot, must stink—ah, me ! ah, why !
Cities themselves in time decay ;
If cities thus—ah, well-a-day !
If brick and mortar have au end,
On what can flesh and blood depend !   420

Ah, woeful me ! ah, woeful man !   42?
Ah, woeful all, do all we can !
   England, (for that's at last the scene,
Though worlds on worlds should rise between,
Whither we must our course pursue)
England should call into review
Times long since past indeed, but not
By Englishmen to be forgot,
Though England, once so dear to Fame,
Sinks in Great Britain's dearer name.
   Here could we mention chiefs of old,   430
In plain and rugged honour bold,
To Virtue kind, to Vice severe,
Strangers to bribery and fear,
Who kept no wretched clans in awe,
Who never broke or warp'd the law ;
Patriots, whom, in her better days,
Old Rome might have been proud to raise ;
Who, steady to their country's claim,
Boldly stood up in Freedom's name,   440
E'en to the teeth of tyrant Pride,
And when they could no more, they died.
   There (striking contrast !) might we place
A servile, mean, degen'rate race ;
Hirelings, who valued naught but gold,
By the best bidder bought and sold ;
Truants from Honour's sacred laws,
Betrayers of their country's cause ;
The dupes of party, tools of power,
Slaves to the minion of an hour ;   450
Lackies, who watch'd a favourite's nod,
And took a puppet for their god.
   Sincere and honest in our rhymes,
How might we praise these happier times !

How might the Muse exalt her lays, 455
And wanton in a monarch's praise !
Tell of a prince, in England born,
Whose virtues England's crown adorn,
In youth a pattern unto age,
So chaste, so pious, and so sage ; 460
Who, true to all those sacred bands,
Which private happiness demands,
Yet never lets them rise above
The stronger ties of public love.
  With conscious pride see England stand,
Our holy Charter in her hand ;
She waves it round, and o'er the isle
See Liberty and Courage smile.
No more she mourns her treasures hurl'd
In subsidies to all the world ; 470
No more by foreign threats dismay'd,
No more deceived with foreign aid,
She deals out sums to petty states,
Whom Honour scorns and Reason hates,
But, wiser by experience grown,
Finds safety in herself alone.
  'Whilst thus,' she cries, 'my children stand
An honest, valiant, native band,
A train'd militia, brave and free,
True to their king, and true to me, 480
No foreign hirelings shall be known,
Nor need we hirelings of our own :
Under a just and pious reign
The statesman's sophistry is vain ;
Vain is each vile, corrupt pretence,
These are my natural defence ;
Their faith I know, and they shall prove
The bulwark of the king they love.'

These, and a thousand things beside,   489
Did we consult a poet's pride,
Some gay, some serious, might be said,
But ten to one they'd not be read ;
Or were they by some curious few,
Not even those would think them true ;
For, from the time that Jubal first
Sweet ditties to the harp rehearsed,
Poets have always been suspected
Of having truth in rhyme neglected,
That bard except, who from his youth
Equally famed for faith and truth,   500
By Prudence taught, in courtly chime
To courtly ears brought truth in rhyme.[1]

But though to poets we allow,
No matter when acquired or how,
From truth unbounded deviation,
Which custom calls Imagination,
Yet can't they be supposed to lie
One half so fast as Fame can fly ;
Therefore (to solve this Gordian knot,
A point we almost had forgot)   510
To courteous readers be it known,
That, fond of verse and falsehood grown,
Whilst we in sweet digression sung,
Fame check'd her flight, and held her tongue,
And now pursues, with double force
And double speed, her destined course,
Nor stops till she the place [2] arrives
Where Genius starves and Dulness thrives ;
Where riches virtue are esteem'd
And craft is truest wisdom deem'd,   520

---

[1] 'Rhyme:' Mallet addressed a contemptible poem, entitled 'Truth in Rhyme,' to the celebrated Lord Chesterfield.—[2] 'Place:' the Royal Exchange.

Where Commerce proudly rears her throne,   521
In state to other lands unknown :
Where, to be cheated and to cheat,
Strangers from every quarter meet ;
Where Christians, Jews, and Turks shake hands,
United in commercial bands :
All of one faith, and that to own
No god but Interest alone.
  When gods and goddesses come down
To look about them here in Town,   530
(For change of air is understood
By sons of Physic to be good,
In due proportions, now and then,
For these same gods as well as men)
By custom ruled, and not a poet
So very dull but he must know it,
In order to remain *incog.*
They always travel in a fog ;
For if we majesty expose
To vulgar eyes, too cheap it grows ;   540
The force is lost, and free from awe,
We spy and censure every flaw ;
But well preserved from public view,
It always breaks forth fresh and new ;
Fierce as the sun in all his pride
It shines, and not a spot 's descried.
  Was Jove to lay his thunder by,
And with his brethren of the sky
Descend to earth, and frisk about,
Like chattering N——[1] from rout to rout,   550
He would be found, with all his host,
A nine days' wonder at the most.

[1] 'N——:' not known.

Would we in trim our honours wear,   553
We must preserve them from the air ;
What is familiar men neglect,
However worthy of respect.
Did they not find a certain friend
In Novelty to recommend,
(Such we, by sad experience, find
The wretched folly of mankind)   560
Venus might unattractive shine,
And Hunter fix no eyes but mine.

But Fame, who never cared a jot
Whether she was admired or not,
And never blush'd to show her face
At any time in any place,
In her own shape, without disguise,
And visible to mortal eyes,
On 'Change exact at seven o'clock
Alighted on the weathercock,   570
Which, planted there time out of mind
To note the changes of the wind,
Might no improper emblem be
Of her own mutability.

Thrice did she sound her trump, (the same
Which from the first belong'd to Fame,
An old ill-favour'd instrument,
With which the goddess was content,
Though under a politer race
Bagpipes might well supply its place)   580
And thrice, awaken'd by the sound,
A general din prevail'd around ;
Confusion through the city pass'd,
And Fear bestrode the dreadful blast.

Those fragrant currents, which we meet
Distilling soft through every street,

Affrighted from the usual course,   587
Ran murmuring upwards to their source.;
Statues wept tears of blood, as fast
As when a Cæsar breathed his last;
Horses, which always used to go
A foot-pace in my Lord Mayor's show,
Impetuous from their stable broke,
And aldermen and oxen spoke.

 Halls felt the force, towers shook around,
And steeples nodded to the ground;
St Paul himself (strange sight!) was seen
To bow as humbly as the Dean;
The Mansion House, for ever placed
A monument of City taste,   600
Trembled, and seem'd aloud to groan
Through all that hideous weight of stone.

 To still the sound, or stop her ears,
Remove the cause or sense of fears,
Physic, in college seated high,
Would anything but med'cine try.
No more in Pewterer's Hall [1] was heard
The proper force of every word;
Those seats were desolate become,
A hapless Elocution dumb.   610
Form, city-born and city-bred,
By strict Decorum ever led,
Who threescore years had known the grace
Of one dull, stiff, unvaried pace,
Terror prevailing over Pride,
Was seen to take a larger stride;
Worn to the bone, and clothed in rags,
See Avarice closer hug his bags;

---

[1] 'Pewterers' Hall:' Macklin's recitations and his lectures on elocution were delivered at Pewterers' Hall, in Lime Street.

With her own weight unwieldy grown,   619
See Credit totter on her throne ;
Virtue alone, had she been there,
The mighty sound, unmoved, could bear.
    Up from the gorgeous bed, where Fate
Dooms annual fools to sleep in state,
To sleep so sound that not one gleam
Of Fancy can provoke a dream,
Great Dulman [1] started at the sound,
Gaped, rubb'd his eyes, and stared around.
Much did he wish to know, much fear,
Whence sounds so horrid struck his ear,   630.
So much unlike those peaceful notes,
That equal harmony, which floats
On the dull wing of City air,
Grave prelude to a feast or fair :
Much did he inly ruminate
Concerning the decrees of Fate,
Revolving, though to little end,
What this same trumpet might portend.
    Could the French—no—that could not be,
Under Bute's active ministry,   640
Too watchful to be so deceived—
Have stolen hither unperceived ?
To Newfoundland,[2] indeed, we know
Fleets of war unobserved may go ;
Or, if observed, may be supposed,
At intervals when Reason dozed,
No other point in view to bear
But pleasure, health, and change of air ;

---

[1] 'Dulman:' Sir Samuel Fludyer, Bart. M.P. for Chippenham, Deputy-Governor of the Bank of England, and Lord Mayor of London for 1761-2.—
[2] 'Newfoundland:' in May 1762 a French squadron escaped out of Brest in a fog, and took the town of St John's in Newfoundland.

But Reason ne'er could sleep so sound   649
To let an enemy be found
In our land's heart, ere it was known
They had departed from their own.
   Or could his súccessor, (Ambition
Is ever haunted with suspicion)
His daring successor elect,
All customs, rules, and forms reject,
And aim,[1] regardless of the crime,
To seize the chair before his time ?
   Or (deeming this the lucky hour,
Seeing his countrymen in power,   660
Those countrymen, who, from the first,
In tumults and rebellion nursed,
Howe'er they wear the mask of art,
Still love a Stuart in their heart)
Could Scottish Charles——
                        Conjecture thus,
That mental *ignis fatuus*,
Led his poor brains a weary dance
From France to England, hence to France,
Till Information (in the shape
Of chaplain learnèd, good Sir Crape,   670
A lazy, lounging, pamper'd priest,
Well known at every city feast,
For he was seen much oftener there
Than in the house of God at prayer ;
Who, always ready in his place,
Ne'er let God's creatures wait for grace,
Though, as the best historians write,
Less famed for faith than appetite ;
His disposition to reveal,
The grace was short, and long the meal ;   680

---

1 'Aim:' Beckford was the Lord Mayor elect for 1762-3.

S

Who always would excess admit,   681
If haunch or turtle came with it,
And ne'er engaged in the defence
Of self-denying Abstinence,
When he could fortunately meet
With anything he liked to eat ;
Who knew that wine, on Scripture plan,
Was made to cheer the heart of man ;
Knew too, by long experience taught,
That cheerfulness was kill'd by thought ;   690
And from those premises collected,
(Which few perhaps would have suspected)
That none who, with due share of sense,
Observed the ways of Providence,
Could with safe conscience leave off drinking
Till they had lost the power of thinking ;
With eyes half-closed came waddling in,
And, having stroked his double chin,
(That chin, whose credit to maintain
Against the scoffs of the profane,   700
Had cost him more than ever state
Paid for a poor electorate,[1]
Which, after all the cost and rout
It had been better much without)
Briefly (for breakfast, you must know,
Was waiting all the while below)
Related, bowing to the ground,
The cause of that uncommon sound ;
Related, too, that at the door
Pomposo, Plausible, and Moore,   710
Begg'd that Fame might not be allow'd
Their shame to publish to the crowd ;

---

[1] ' Electorate : ' the electorate of Hanover.

That some new laws he would provide,   713
(If old could not be misapplied
With as much ease and safety there
As they are misapplied elsewhere)
By which it might be construed treason
In man to exercise his reason ;
Which might ingeniously devise
One punishment for truth and lies,   720
And fairly prove, when they had done,
That truth and falsehood were but one ;
Which juries must indeed retain,
But their effects should render vain,
Making all real power to rest
In one corrupted rotten breast,
By whose false gloss the very Bible
Might be interpreted a libel.

    Moore (who, his reverence to save,
Pleaded the fool to screen the knave,   730
Though all who witness'd on his part
Swore for his head against his heart)
Had taken down, from first to last,
A just account of all that pass'd ;
But, since the gracious will of Fate,
Who mark'd the child for wealth and state
E'en in the cradle, had decreed
The mighty Dulman ne'er should read,
That office of disgrace to bear
The smooth-lipp'd Plausible [1] was there ;   740
From Holborn e'en to Clerkenwell,
Who knows not smooth-lipp'd Plausible ?
A preacher, deem'd of greatest note
For preaching that which others wrote.

---

[1] 'Plausible:' the Rev. W. Sellon in 1763 published a stolen sermon as his own.

Had Dulman now, (and fools, we see,   745
Seldom want curiosity)
Consented (but the mourning shade
Of Gascoyne hasten'd to his aid,
And in his hand—what could he more ?—
Triumphant Canning's picture bore)   750
That our three heroes should advance
And read their comical romance,
How rich a feast, what royal fare,
We for our readers might prepare !
So rich and yet so safe a feast,
That no one foreign blatant beast,
Within the purlieus of the law,
Should dare thereon to lay his paw,
And, growling, cry, with surly tone,
' Keep off—this feast is all my own.'   760
    Bending to earth the downcast eye,
Or planting it against the sky,
As one immersed in deepest thought,
Or with some holy vision caught,
His hands, to aid the traitor's art,
Devoutly folded o'er his heart ;
Here Moore, in fraud well skill'd, should go,
All saint, with solemn step and slow.
Oh, that Religion's sacred name,
Meant to inspire the purest flame,   770
A prostitute should ever be
To that arch-fiend Hypocrisy,
Where we find every other vice
Crown'd with damn'd sneaking cowardice !
Bold sin reclaim'd is often seen ;
Past hope that man, who dares be mean.
    There, full of flesh, and full of grace,
With that fine round unmeaning face

Which Nature gives to sons of earth 779
Whom she designs for ease and mirth,
Should the prim Plausible be seen,
Observe his stiff, affected mien ;
'Gainst Nature, arm'd by Gravity,
His features too in buckle see ;
See with what sanctity he reads,
With what devotion tells his beads !
Now, prophet, show me, by thine art,
What 's the religion of his heart :
Show there, if truth thou canst unfold,
Religion centred all in gold ; 790
Show him, nor fear Correction's rod,
As false to friendship, as to God.

Horrid, unwieldy, without form.
Savage as ocean in a storm,
Of size prodigious, in the rear,
That post of honour, should appear
Pomposo ; fame around should tell
How he a slave to Interest fell ;
How, for integrity renown'd,
Which booksellers have often found, 800
He for subscribers baits his hook,[1]
And takes their cash—but where 's the book ?
No matter where—wise fear, we know,
Forbids the robbing of a foe ;
But what, to serve our private ends,
Forbids the cheating of our friends ?
No man alive, who would not swear
All 's safe, and therefore honest there ;
For, spite of all the learned say,
If we to truth attention pay, 810

---

[1] ' His hook : ' Dr Johnson was in possession of subscriptions for his edition
of Shakspeare for upwards of twenty years ere it appeared.

The word dishonesty is meant   811
For nothing else but punishment.
Fame, too, should tell, nor heed the threat
Of rogues, who brother rogues abet,
Nor tremble at the terrors hung
Aloft, to make her hold her tongue,
How to all principles untrue,
Not fix'd to old friends nor to new,
He damns the pension which he takes
And loves the Stuart he forsakes.   820
Nature (who, justly regular,
Is very seldom known to err,
But now and then, in sportive mood,
As some rude wits have understood,
Or through much work required in haste,
Is with a random stroke disgraced)
Pomposo, form'd on doubtful plan,
Not quite a beast, nor quite a man ;
Like—God knows what—for never yet
Could the most subtle human wit   830
Find out a monster which might be
The shadow of a simile.
    These three, these great, these mighty three,—
Nor can the poet's truth agree,
Howe'er report hath done him wrong,
And warp'd the purpose of his song,
Amongst the refuse of their race,
The sons of Infamy, to place
That open, generous, manly mind,
Which we, with joy, in Aldrich[1] find—   840
These three, who now are faintly shown,
Just sketch'd, and scarcely to be known,

---

[1] 'Aldrich:' the Reverend Stephen Aldrich, Rector of St John's, Clerkenwell, actively contributed to the exposure of the Cock-lane ghost.

If Dulman their request had heard,　　　843
In stronger colours had appear'd,
And friends, though partial, at first view,
Shuddering, had own'd the picture true.
　But had their journal been display'd,
And their whole process open laid,
What a vast unexhausted field
For mirth must such a journal yield !　　　850
In her own anger strongly charm'd,
'Gainst Hope, 'gainst Fear, by Conscience arm'd,
Then had bold Satire made her way,
Knights, lords, and dukes, her destined prey.
But Prudence—ever sacred name
To those who feel not Virtue's flame,
Or only feel it, at the best,
As the dull dupe of Interest !—
Whisper'd aloud (for this we find
A custom current with mankind,　　　860
So loud to whisper, that each word
May all around be plainly heard ;
And Prudence, sure, would never miss
A custom so contrived as this
Her candour to secure, yet aim
Sure death against another's fame)
' Knights, lords, and dukes !—mad wretch, forbear,
Dangers unthought of ambush there ;
Confine thy rage to weaker slaves,
Laugh at small fools, and lash small knaves ;　　870
But never, helpless, mean, and poor,
Rush on, where laws cannot secure ;
Nor think thyself, mistaken youth !
Secure in principles of truth :
Truth ! why shall every wretch of letters
Dare to speak truth against his betters !

Let ragged Virtue stand aloof,   877
Nor mutter accents of reproof ;
Let ragged Wit a mute become,
When Wealth and Power would have her dumb ;
For who the devil doth not know
That titles and estates bestow
An ample stock, where'er they fall,
Of graces which we mental call ?
Beggars, in every age and nation,
Are rogues and fools by situation ;
The rich and great are understood
To be of course both wise and good.
Consult, then, Interest more than Pride,
Discreetly take the stronger side ;   890
Desert, in time, the simple few
Who Virtue's barren path pursue ;
Adopt my maxims—follow me—
To Baal bow the prudent knee ;
Deny thy God, betray thy friend,
At Baal's altars hourly bend,
So shalt thou rich and great be seen ;
To be great now, you must be mean.'
    Hence, Tempter, to some weaker soul,
Which fear and interest control ;   900
Vainly thy precepts are address'd
Where Virtue steels the steady breast ;
Through meanness wade to boasted power,
Through guilt repeated every hour ;
What is thy gain, when all is done,
What mighty laurels hast thou won ?
Dull crowds, to whom the heart's unknown,
Praise thee for virtues not thine own :
But will, at once man's scourge and friend,
Impartial Conscience too commend ?   910

From her reproaches canst thou fly ?   911
Canst thou with worlds her silence buy ?
Believe it not—her stings shall find
A passage to thy coward mind :
There shall she fix her sharpest dart ;
There show thee truly as thou art,
Unknown to those by whom thou 'rt prized,
Known to thyself to be despised.
    The man who weds the sacred Muse,
Disdains all mercenary views,   920
And he, who Virtue's throne would rear   .
Laughs at the phantoms raised by Fear.
Though Folly, robed in purple, shines,
Though Vice exhausts Peruvian mines,
Yet shall they tremble, and turn pale,
When Satire wields her mighty flail ;
Or should they, of rebuke afraid,
With Melcombe[1] seek hell's deepest shade,
Satire, still mindful of her aim,
Shall bring the cowards back to shame.   930
Hated by many, loved by few,
Above each little private view,
Honest, though poor, (and who shall dare
To disappoint my boasting there ?)
Hardy and resolute, though weak,
The dictates of my heart to speak,
Willing I bend at Satire's throne ;
What power I have be all her own.
    Nor shall yon lawyer's specious art,
Conscious of a corrupted heart,   940

[1] 'Melcombe:' George Bubb Doddington, the son of an apothecary at Weymouth, by skilful electioneering, raised himself to the peerage under the title of Lord Melcombe. Thomson addressed to him his ' Summer,' and Young his ' Universal Passion.'

Create imaginary fear 941
To damp us in our bold career.
Why should we fear? and what? The laws?
They all are arm'd in Virtue's cause;
And aiming at the self-same end,
Satire is always Virtue's friend.
Nor shall that Muse, whose honest rage,
In a corrupt degen'rate age,
(When, dead to every nicer sense,
Deep sunk in vice and indolence, 950
The spirit of old Rome was broke
Beneath the tyrant fiddler's yoke)
Banish'd the rose from Nero's cheek,
Under a Brunswick fear to speak.
   Drawn by Conceit from Reason's plan,
How vain is that poor creature, Man!
How pleased is every paltry elf
To prate about that thing, himself!
After my promise made in rhyme,
And meant in earnest at that time, 960
To jog, according to the mode,
In one dull pace, in one dull road,
What but that curse of heart and head
To this digression could have led?
Where plunged, in vain I look about,
And can't stay in, nor well get out.
   Could I, whilst Humour held the quill,
Could I digress with half that skill;
Could I with half that skill return,
Which we so much admire in Sterne, 970
Where each digression, seeming vain,
And only fit to entertain,
Is found, on better recollection,
To have a just and nice connexion,

To help the whole with wondrous art,   975
Whence it seems idly to depart ;
Then should our readers ne'er accuse
These wild excursions of the Muse ;
Ne'er backward turn dull pages o'er
To recollect what went before ;   980
Deeply impress'd, and ever new,
Each image past should start to view,
And we to Dulman now come in,
As if we ne'er had absent been.

    Have you not seen, when danger's near,
The coward cheek turn white with fear ?
Have you not seen, when danger's fled,
The self-same cheek with joy turn red ?
These are low symptoms which we find,
Fit only for a vulgar mind,   990
Where honest features, void of art,
Betray the feelings of the heart ;
Our Dulman with a face was bless'd,
Where no one passion was express'd ;
His eye, in a fine stupor caught,
Implied a plenteous lack of thought ;
Nor was one line that whole face seen in
Which could be justly charged with meaning.

    To Avarice by birth allied,
Debauch'd by marriage into Pride,   1000
In age grown fond of youthful sports,
Of pomps, of vanities, and courts,
And by success too mighty made
To love his country or his trade ;
Stiff in opinion, (no rare case
With blockheads in or out of place)
Too weak, and insolent of soul
To suffer Reason's just control,

But bending, of his own accord,   1009
To that trim transient toy, my lord ;
The dupe of Scots, (a fatal race,
Whom God in wrath contrived to place
To scourge our crimes, and gall our pride,
A constant thorn in England's side ;
Whom first, our greatness to oppose,
He in his vengeance mark'd for foes ;
Then, more to serve his wrathful ends,
And more to curse us, mark'd for friends)
Deep in the state, if we give credit
To him, for no one else e'er said it,   1020
Sworn friend of great ones not a few,
Though he their titles only knew,
And those (which, envious of his breeding,
Book-worms have charged to want of reading)
Merely to show himself polite
He never would pronounce aright ;
An orator with whom a host
Of those which Rome and Athens boast,
In all their pride might not contend ;
Who, with no powers to recommend,   1030
Whilst Jackey Hume, and Billy Whitehead,
And Dicky Glover,[1] sat delighted,
Could speak whole days in Nature's spite,
Just as those able versemen write ;
Great Dulman from his bed arose—
Thrice did he spit—thrice wiped his nose—
Thrice strove to smile—thrice strove to frown—
And thrice look'd up—and thrice look'd down—
Then silence broke—'Crape, who am I ?'
Crape bow'd, and smiled an arch reply.   1040

[1] 'Dicky Glover:' Richard Glover, author of 'Leonidas.'

'Am I not, Crape?   I am, you know,   1041
Above all those who are below.
Have I not knowledge? and for wit,
Money will always purchase it:
Nor, if it needful should be found,
Will I grudge ten or twenty pound,
For which the whole stock may be bought
Of scoundrel wits, not worth a groat.
But lest I should proceed too far,
I'll feel my friend the Minister,   1050
(Great men, Crape, must not be neglected)
How he in this point is affected;
For, as I stand a magistrate,
To serve him first, and next the state,
Perhaps he may not think it fit
To let his magistrates have wit.
    Boast I not, at this very hour,
Those large effects which troop with power?
Am I not mighty in the land?
Do not I sit whilst others stand?   1060
Am I not with rich garments graced,
In seat of honour always placed?
And do not cits of chief degree,
Though proud to others, bend to me?
    Have I not, as a Justice ought,
The laws such wholesome rigour taught,
That Fornication, in disgrace,
Is now afraid to show her face,
And not one whore these walls approaches
Unless they ride in their own coaches?   1070
And shall this Fame, an old poor strumpet,
Without our licence sound her trumpet,
And, envious of our city's quiet,
In broad daylight blow up a riot?

If insolence like this we bear,   1075
Where is our state ? our office where ?
Farewell, all honours of our reign ;
Farewell, the neck-ennobling chain,
Freedom's known badge o'er all the globe ;
Farewell, the solemn-spreading robe ;   1080
Farewell, the sword ; farewell, the mace ;
Farewell, all title, pomp, and place ;
Removed from men of high degree,
(A loss to them, Crape, not to me)
Banish'd to Chippenham or to Frome,
Dulman once more shall ply the loom.'
   Crape, lifting up his hands and eyes,
' Dulman !—the loom !—at Chippenham !'—cries ;
' If there be powers which greatness love,
Which rule below, but dwell above,   1090
Those powers united all shall join
To contradict the rash design.
   Sooner shall stubborn Will[1] lay down
His opposition with his gown ;
Sooner shall Temple leave the road
Which leads to Virtue's mean abode ;
Sooner shall Scots this country quit,
And England's foes be friends to Pitt,
Than Dulman, from his grandeur thrown,
Shall wander outcast and unknown.   1100
Sure as that cane,' (a cane there stood
Near to a table made of wood,
Of dry fine wood a table made,
By some rare artist in the trade,

---

[1] 'Will:' William Beckford, Esq., elected an alderman, June 1752, and
twice Lord Mayor of London, in 1762 and 1769. He was a West India merchant, possessed a princely fortune, and became highly popular by his strenuous
opposition to the court : his son was the author of ' Caliph Vathek.'

Who had enjoy'd immortal praise   1105
If he had lived in Homer's days)
'Sure as that cane, which once was seen
In pride of life all fresh and green,
The banks of Indus to adorn,
Then, of its leafy honours shorn,   1110
According to exactest rule,
Was fashion'd by the workman's tool,
And which at present we behold
Curiously polish'd, crown'd with gold,
With gold well wrought ; sure as that cane
Shall never on its native plain
Strike root afresh, shall never more
Flourish in tawny India's shore,
So sure shall Dulman and his race
To latest times this station grace.'   1120

Dulman, who all this while had kept
His eyelids closed as if he slept,
Now looking steadfastly on Crape,
As at some god in human shape :
'Crape, I protest, you seem to me
To have discharged a prophecy :
Yes—from the first it doth appear
Planted by Fate, the Dulmans here
Have always held a quiet reign,
And here shall to the last remain.   1130

'Crape, they're all wrong about this ghost—
Quite on the wrong side of the post—
Blockheads ! to take it in their head
To be a message from the dead,
For that by mission they design,
A word not half so good as mine.
Crape—here it is—start not one doubt—
A plot—a plot—I 've found it out.'

' O God ! ' cries Crape, ' how bless'd the nation,
Where one son boasts such penetration ! '   1140
    ' Crape, I 've not time to tell you now
When I discover'd this, or how ;
To Stentor [1] go—if he 's not there,
His place let Bully Norton bear—
Our citizens to council call—
Let all meet—'tis the cause of all :
Let the three witnesses attend,
With allegations to befriend,
To swear just so much, and no more,
As we instruct them in before.   1150
    ' Stay, Crape, come back—what ! don't you see
The effects of this discovery ?
Dulman all care and toil endures—
The profit, Crape, will all be yours.
A mitre, (for, this arduous task
Perform'd, they 'll grant whate'er I ask)
A mitre (and perhaps the best) ·
Shall, through my interest, make thee blest :
And at this time, when gracious Fate
Dooms to the Scot the reins of state,   1160
Who is more fit (and for your use
We could some instances produce)
Of England's Church to be the head,
Than you, a Presbyterian bred ?
But when thus mighty you are made,
Unlike the brethren of thy trade,
Be grateful, Crape, and let me not,
Like old Newcastle,[2] be forgot.
    But an affair, Crape, of this size
Will ask from Conduct vast supplies ;   1170

---

[1] ' Stentor' : unknown.—[2] ' Newcastle : ' the Duke of Newcastle, who died
in 1768, had for more than fifty years filled the greatest offices in the state.
See Macaulay's papers on Chatham, and Humphrey Clinker.

It must not, as the vulgar say, 1171
Be done in hugger-mugger way :
Traitors, indeed (and that's discreet)
Who hatch the plot, in private meet ;
They should in public go, no doubt,
Whose business is to find it out.

  To-morrow—if the day appear
Likely to turn out fair and clear—
Proclaim a grand processionade [1] —
Be all the city-pomp display'd ; 1180
Let the Train-bands'—Crape shook his head—
They heard the trumpet, and were fled—
'Well,' cries the Knight, 'if that's the case,
My servants shall supply their place—
My servants—mine alone—no more
Than what my servants did before—
Dost not remember, Crape, that day,
When, Dulman's grandeur to display,
As all too simple and too low,
Our city friends were thrust below, 1190
Whilst, as more worthy of our love,
Courtiers were entertain'd above ?
Tell me, who waited then ? and how ?
My servants—mine : and why not now ?
In haste then, Crape, to Stentor go—
But send up Hart, who waits below ;
With him, till you return again,
(Reach me my spectacles and cane)
I'll make a proof how I advance in
My new accomplishment of dancing.' 1200
  Not quite so fast as lightning flies,
Wing'd with red anger, through the skies ;

---

[1] 'Processionade :' for the purpose of preparing an address to his Majesty
on the conclusion of the peace with France.

T

Not quite so fast as, sent by Jove,   1203
Iris descends on wings of love ;
Not quite so fast as Terror rides
When he the chasing winds bestrides,
Crape hobbled ; but his mind was good—
Could he go faster than he could ?
    Near to that tower, which, as we're told,
The mighty Julius raised of old,   1210
Where, to the block by Justice led,
The rebel Scot hath often bled ;
Where arms are kept so clean, so bright,
'Twere sin they should be soil'd in fight ;
Where brutes of foreign race are shown
By brutes much greater of our own ;
Fast by the crowded Thames, is found
An ample square of sacred ground,
Where artless Eloquence presides,
And Nature every sentence guides.   1220
    Here female parliaments debate
About religion, trade, and state ;
Here every Naïad's patriot soul,
Disdaining foreign base control,
Despising French, despising Erse,
Pours forth the plain old English curse,
And bears aloft, with terrors hung,
The honours of the vulgar tongue.
    Here Stentor, always heard with awe,
In thundering accents deals out law :   1230
Twelve furlongs off each dreadful word
Was plainly and distinctly heard,
And every neighbour hill around
Return'd and swell'd the mighty sound ;
The loudest virgin of the stream,
Compared with him would silent seem ;

Thames, (who, enraged to find his course   1237
Opposed, rolls down with double force,
Against the bridge indignant roars,
And lashes the resounding shores)
Compared with him, at lowest tide,
In softest whispers seems to glide.
   Hither, directed by the noise,
Swell'd with the hope of future joys,
Through too much zeal and haste made lame,
The reverend slave of Dulman came.
   'Stentor'—with such a serious air,
With such a face of solemn care,
As might import him to contain
A nation's welfare in his brain—   1250
'Stentor,' cries Crape, 'I 'm hither sent
On business of most high intent,
Great Dulman's orders to convey ;
Dulman commands, and I obey ;
Big with those throes which patriots feel,
And labouring for the commonweal,
Some secret, which forbids him rest,
Tumbles and tosses in his breast ;
Tumbles and tosses to get free,
And thus the Chief commands by me :   1260
  ' To-morrow, if the day appear
Likely to turn out fair and clear,
Proclaim a grand processionade—
Be all the city pomp display'd—
Our citizens to council call—
Let all meet—'tis the cause of all ! '

Book IV.

Coxcombs, who vainly make pretence
To something of exalted sense
'Bove other men, and, gravely wise,
Affect those pleasures to despise,
Which, merely to the eye confined,
Bring no improvement to the mind,
Rail at all pomp; they would not go
For millions to a puppet-show,
Nor can forgive the mighty crime
Of countenancing pantomime;   10
No, not at Covent Garden, where,
Without a head for play or player,
Or, could a head be found most fit,
Without one player to second it,
They must, obeying Folly's call,
Thrive by mere show, or not at all.
    With these grave fops, who, (bless their brains!)
Most cruel to themselves, take pains
For wretchedness, and would be thought
Much wiser than a wise man ought,   20
For his own happiness, to be;
Who what they hear, and what they see,
And what they smell, and taste, and feel,
Distrust, till Reason sets her seal,
And, by long trains of consequences
Insured, gives sanction to the senses;
Who would not (Heaven forbid it!) waste
One hour in what the world calls Taste,
Nor fondly deign to laugh or cry,
Unless they know some reason why;   30

With these grave fops, whose system seems   31
To give up certainty for dreams,
The eye of man is understood
As for no other purpose good
Than as a door, through which, of course,
Their passage crowding, objects force ;
A downright usher, to admit
New-comers to the court of Wit :
(Good Gravity ! forbear thy spleen ;
When I say Wit, I Wisdom mean)   40
Where (such the practice of the court,
Which legal precedents support)
Not one idea is allow'd
To pass unquestion'd in the crowd,
But ere it can obtain the grace
Of holding in the brain a place,
Before the chief in congregation
Must stand a strict examination.
    Not such as those, who physic twirl,
Full fraught with death, from every curl ;   50
Who prove, with all becoming state,
Their voice to be the voice of Fate ;
Prepared with essence, drop, and pill,
To be another Ward or Hill,[1]
Before they can obtain their ends,
To sign death-warrants for their friends,
And talents vast as theirs employ,
Secundum artem to destroy,
Must pass (or laws their rage restrain)
Before the chiefs of Warwick Lane :[2]   60
Thrice happy Lane ! where, uncontroll'd,
In power and lethargy grown old,

---

[1] 'Ward:' Joshua Ward, a quack of the period.—[2] 'Warwick Lane,' Newgate Street, was the seat of the College of Physicians.

Most fit to take, in this bless'd land,   63
The reins which fell from Wyndham's hand,[1]
Her lawful throne great Dulness rears,
Still more herself, as more in years ;
Where she, (and who shall dare deny
Her right, when Reeves[2] and Chauncy's[3] by ?)
Calling to mind, in ancient time,
One Garth,[4] who err'd in wit and rhyme,   70
Ordains, from henceforth, to admit
None of the rebel sons of Wit,
And makes it her peculiar care
That Schomberg[5] never shall be there.

  Not such as those, whom Folly trains
To letters, though unbless'd with brains,
Who, destitute of power and will
To learn, are kept to learning still ;
Whose heads, when other methods fail,
Receive instruction from the tail,   80
Because their sires,—a common case
Which brings the children to disgrace,—
Imagine it a certain rule
They never could beget a fool,
Must pass, or must compound for, ere
The chaplain, full of beef and prayer,
Will give his reverend permit,
Announcing them for orders fit ;
So that the prelate (what 's a name ?
All prelates now are much the same)   90

---

[1] ' Wyndham : ' Lord Egremont.—[2] ' Reeves : ' Dr Reeves was a physician of some practice in the city.—[3] ' Chauncy : ' Dr Chauncy, descended of a good family, and possessed of a competent estate, did not practise.—[4] ' Garth : ' Sir Samuel Garth, a celebrated poet and physician, author of ' The Dispensary.'—[5] ' Schomberg : ' Dr Isaac Schomberg, a friend of Garrick, and an eminent and learned physician.

May, with a conscience safe and quiet,   91
With holy hands lay on that fiat
Which doth all faculties dispense,
All sanctity, all faith, all sense ;
Makes Madan [1] quite a saint appear,
And makes an oracle of Cheere.
  Not such as in that solemn seat,
Where the Nine Ladies hold retreat,—
The Ladies Nine, who, as we 're told,
Scorning those haunts they loved of old,   100
The banks of Isis now prefer,   •
Nor will one hour from Oxford stir,—
Are held for form, which Balaam's ass
As well as Balaam's self might pass,
And with his master take degrees,
Could he contrive to pay the fees.
  Men of sound parts, who, deeply read,
O'erload the storehouse of the head
With furniture they ne'er can use,
Cannot forgive our rambling Muse   110
This wild excursion ; cannot see
Why Physic and Divinity,
To the surprise of all beholders,
Are lugg'd in by the head and shoulders ;
Or how, in any point of view,
Oxford hath any thing to do.
But men of nice and subtle learning,
Remarkable for quick discerning,
Through spectacles of critic mould,
Without instruction, will behold   120
That we a method here have got
To show what is, by what is not ;

---

[1] 'Madan :' Martin Madan, a celebrated English preacher, many years chaplain to the Lock Hospital. See Cowper's Letters.

And that our drift (parenthesis   123
For once apart) is briefly this:
   Within the brain's most secret cells
A certain Lord Chief-Justice dwells,
Of sovereign power, whom, one and all,
With common voice, we Reason call;
Though, for the purposes of satire,
A name, in truth, is no great matter;   130
Jefferies or Mansfield, which you will—
It means a Lord Chief-Justice still.
Here, so our great projectors say,
The Senses all must homage pay;
Hither they all must tribute bring,
And prostrate fall before their king;
Whatever unto them is brought,
Is carried on the wings of Thought
Before his throne, where, in full state,
He on their merits holds debate,   140
Examines, cross-examines, weighs
Their right to censure or to praise:
Nor doth his equal voice depend
On narrow views of foe and friend,
Nor can, or flattery, or force
Divert him from his steady course;
The channel of Inquiry's clear,
No sham examination's here.
   He, upright justicer, no doubt,
Ad libitum puts in and out,   150
Adjusts and settles in a trice
What virtue is, and what is vice;
What is perfection, what defect;
What we must choose, and what reject;
He takes upon him to explain
What pleasure is, and what is pain;

Whilst we, obedient to the whim, 151
And resting all our faith on him,
True members of the Stoic Weal,
Must learn to think, and cease to feel.
_This glorious system, form'd for man
To practise when and how he can,
If the five Senses, in alliance,
To Reason hurl a proud defiance,
And, though oft conquer'd, yet unbroke,
Endeavour to throw off that yoke,
Which they a greater slavery hold
Than Jewish bondage was of old;
Or if they, something touch'd with shame,
Allow him to retain the name 170
Of Royalty, and, as in sport,
To hold a mimic formal court;
Permitted—no uncommon thing—
To be a kind of puppet king,
And suffer'd, by the way of toy,
To hold a globe, but not employ;
Our system-mongers, struck with fear,
Prognosticate destruction near;
All things to anarchy must run;
The little world of man's undone. 180
    Nay, should the Eye, that nicest sense,
Neglect to send intelligence
Unto the Brain, distinct and clear,
Of all that passes in her sphere;
Should she, presumptuous, joy receive
Without the Understanding's leave,
They deem it rank and daring treason
Against the monarchy of Reason,
Not thinking, though they 're wondrous wise,
That few have reason, most have eyes; 190

So that the pleasures of the mind   191
To a small circle are confined,
Whilst those which to the senses fall
Become the property of all.
Besides, (and this is sure a case
Not much at present out of place)
Where Nature reason doth deny,
No art can that defect supply ;
But if (for it is our intent
Fairly to state the argument)   200
A man should want an eye or two,
The remedy is sure, though new :
The cure's at hand—no need of fear—
For proof—behold the Chevalier ![1]—
As well prepared, beyond all doubt,
To put eyes in, as put them out.
      But, argument apart, which tends
T' embitter foes and separate friends,
(Nor, turn'd apostate from the Nine,
Would I, though bred up a divine,   210
And foe, of course, to Reason's Weal,
Widen that breach I cannot heal)
By his own sense and feelings taught,
In speech as liberal as in thought,
Let every man enjoy his whim ;
What's he to me, or I to him ?
Might I, though never robed in ermine,
A matter of this weight determine,
No penalties should settled be
To force men to hypocrisy,   220
To make them ape an awkward zeal,
And, feeling not, pretend to feel.

[1] 'Chevalier:' the Chevalier John Taylor, a quack oculist.

I would not have, might sentence rest   223
Finally fix'd within my breast,
E'en Annet[1] censured and confined,
Because we 're of a different mind.

    Nature, who, in her act most free,
Herself delights in liberty,
Profuse in love, and without bound,
Pours joy on every creature round ;   230
Whom yet, was every bounty shed
In double portions on our head,
We could not truly bounteous call,
If Freedom did not crown them all.

    By Providence forbid to stray,
Brutes never can mistake their way ;
Determined still, they plod along
By instinct, neither right nor wrong ;
But man, had he the heart to use
His freedom, hath a right to choose ;   240
Whether he acts, or well, or ill,
Depends entirely on his will.
To her last work, her favourite Man,
Is given, on Nature's better plan,
A privilege in power to err.
Nor let this phrase resentment stir
Amongst the grave ones, since indeed
The little merit man can plead
In doing well, dependeth still
Upon his power of doing ill.   250

    Opinions should be free as air ;
No man, whate'er his rank, whate'er
His qualities, a claim can found
That my opinion must be bound,

[1] ' Annet:' Peter Annet, for blasphemy, was sentenced by the court to suffer a year's imprisonment in Bridewell with hard labour, and to stand twice in the pillory.

And square with his ; such slavish chains   255
From foes the liberal soul disdains ;
Nor can, though true to friendship, bend
To wear them even from a friend.
Let those, who rigid judgment own,
Submissive bow at Judgment's throne,   260
And if they of no value hold
Pleasure, till pleasure is grown cold,
Pall'd and insipid, forced to wait
For Judgment's regular debate
To give it warrant, let them find
Dull subjects suited to their mind.
Theirs be slow wisdom ; be my plan,
To live as merry as I can,
Regardless, as the fashions go,
Whether there 's reason for 't or no :   270
Be my employment here on earth
To give a liberal scope to mirth,
Life's barren vale with flowers to adorn,
And pluck a rose from every thorn.
     But if, by Error led astray,
I chance to wander from my way,
Let no blind guide observe, in spite,
I 'm wrong, who cannot set me right.
That doctor could I ne'er endure
Who found disease, and not a cure ;   280
Nor can I hold that man a friend
Whose zeal a helping hand shall lend
To open happy Folly's eyes,
And, making wretched, make me wise :
For next (a truth which can't admit
Reproof from Wisdom or from Wit)
To being happy here below,
Is to believe that we are so.

Some few in knowledge find relief ;   289
I place my comfort in belief.
Some for reality may call ;
Fancy to me is all in all.
Imagination, through the trick
Of doctors, often makes us sick ;
And why, let any sophist tell,
May it not likewise make us well ?
This I am sure, whate'er our view,
Whatever shadows we pursue,
For our pursuits, be what they will,
Are little more than shadows still ;   300
Too swift they fly, too swift and strong,
For man to catch or hold them long ;
But joys which in the fancy live,
Each moment to each man may give :
True to himself, and true to ease,
He softens Fate's severe decrees,
And (can a mortal wish for more ?)
Creates, and makes himself new o'er,
Mocks boasted vain reality,
And is, whate'er he wants to be.   310
    Hail, Fancy !—to thy power I owe
Deliverance from the gripe of Woe ;
To thee I owe a mighty debt,
Which Gratitude shall ne'er forget,
Whilst Memory can her force employ,
A large increase of every joy.
When at my doors, too strongly barr'd,
Authority had placed a guard,[1]
A knavish guard, ordain'd by law
To keep poor Honesty in awe ;   320

---

[1] ' A guard : ' Churchill was often in danger of being arrested for debt.

Authority, severe and stern, 321
To intercept my wish'd return ;
When foes grew proud, and friends grew cool,
And laughter seized each sober fool ;
When Candour started in amaze,
And, meaning censure, hinted praise ;
When Prudence, lifting up her eyes
And hands, thank'd Heaven that she was wise ;
When all around me, with an air
Of hopeless sorrow, look'd despair ; 330
When they, or said, or seem'd to say,
There is but one, one only way:
Better, and be advised by us,
Not be at all, than to be thus ;
When Virtue shunn'd the shock, and Pride,
Disabled, lay by Virtue's side,
Too weak my ruffled soul to cheer,
Which could not hope, yet would not fear ;
Health in her motion, the wild grace
Of pleasure speaking in her face, 340
Dull regularity thrown by,
And comfort beaming from her eye,
Fancy, in richest robes array'd,
Came smiling forth, and brought me aid ;
Came smiling o'er that dreadful time,
And, more to bless me, came in rhyme.
   Nor is her power to me confined ;
It spreads, it comprehends mankind.
When (to the spirit-stirring sound
Of trumpets breathing courage round, 350
And fifes well-mingled, to restrain
And bring that courage down again ;
Or to the melancholy knell
Of the dull, deep, and doleful bell,

Such as of late the good Saint Bride [1]   355
Muffled; to mortify the pride
Of those who, England quite forgot,
Paid their vile homage to the Scot ;
Where Asgill held the foremost place,
Whilst my lord figured at a race)   360
Processions ('tis not worth debate
Whether they are of stage or state)
Move on, so very, very slow,
'Tis doubtful if they move, or no ;
When the performers all the while
Mechanically frown or smile,
Or, with a dull and stupid stare,
A vacancy of sense declare,
Or, with down-bending eye, seem wrought
Into a labyrinth of thought,   370
Where Reason wanders still in doubt,
And, once got in, cannot get out ;
What cause sufficient can we find,
To satisfy a thinking mind,
Why, duped by such vain farces, man
Descends to act on such a plan ?
Why they, who hold themselves divine,
Can in such wretched follies join,
Strutting like peacocks, or like crows,
Themselves and Nature to expose ?   380
What cause, but that (you'll understand
We have our remedy at hand,
That if perchance we start a doubt,
Ere it is fix'd, we wipe it out ;
As surgeons, when they lop a limb,
Whether for profit, fame, or whim,

---

[1] 'Saint Bride:' an address of congratulation on the peace, from the city of London, was accompanied on its way by a muffled peal from St Bride's.

Or mere experiment to try,   387
Must always have a styptic by)
Fancy steps in, and stamps that real,
Which, *ipso facto*, is ideal.
    Can none remember ?—yes, I know,
All must remember that rare show
When to the country Sense went down,
And fools came flocking up to town ;
When knights (a work which all admit
To be for knighthood much unfit)
Built booths for hire ; when parsons play'd,
In robes canonical array'd,
And, fiddling, join'd the Smithfield dance,
The price of tickets to advance :   400
Or, unto tapsters turn'd, dealt out,
Running from booth to booth about,
To every scoundrel, by retail,
True pennyworths of beef and ale,
Then first prepared, by bringing beer in,
For present grand electioneering ;
When heralds, running all about
To bring in Order, turn'd it out ;
When, by the prudent Marshal's care,
Lest the rude populace should stare,   410
And with unhallow'd eyes profane
Gay puppets of Patrician strain,
The whole procession, as in spite,
Unheard, unseen, stole off by night ;
When our loved monarch, nothing loth,
Solemnly took that sacrèd oath,
Whence mutual firm agreements spring
Betwixt the subject and the king,
By which, in usual manner crown'd,
His head, his heart, his hands, he bound,   - 420

Against himself, should passion stir   421
The least propensity to err,
Against all slaves, who might prepare,
Or open force, or hidden snare,
That glorious Charter to maintain,
By which we serve, and he must reign ;
Then Fancy, with unbounded sway,
Revell'd sole mistress of the day,
And wrought such wonders, as might make
Egyptian sorcerers forsake   430
Their baffled mockeries, and own
The palm of magic hers alone.
   A knight, (who, in the silken lap
Of lazy Peace, had lived on pap ;
Who never yet had dared to roam
'Bove ten or twenty miles from home,
Nor even that, unless a guide
Was placed to amble by his side,
And troops of slaves were spread around
To keep his Honour safe and sound ;   440
Who could not suffer, for his life,
A point to sword, or edge to knife ;
And always fainted at the sight
Of blood, though 'twas not shed in fight ;
Who disinherited one son
For firing off an alder gun,
And whipt another, six years old,
Because the boy, presumptuous, bold
To madness, likely to become
A very Swiss, had beat a drum,   450
Though it appear'd an instrument
Most peaceable and innocent,
Having, from first, been in the hands

U

And service of the City bands)   454
Graced with those ensigns, which were meant
To farther Honour's dread intent,
The minds of warriors to inflame,
And spur them on to deeds of fame ;
With little sword, large spurs, high feather,
Fearless of every thing but weather,   460
(And all must own, who pay regard
To charity, it had been hard
That in his very first campaign
His honours should be soil'd with rain)
A hero all at once became,
And (seeing others much the same
In point of valour as himself,
Who leave their courage on a shelf
From year to year, till some such rout
In proper season calls it out)   470
Strutted, look'd big, and swagger'd more
Than ever hero did before ;
Look'd up, look'd down, look'd all around,
Like Mavors, grimly smiled and frown'd ;
Seem'd Heaven, and Earth, and Hell to call
To fight, that he might rout them all,
And personated Valour's style
So long, spectators to beguile,
That, passing strange, and wondrous true,
Himself at last believed it too ;   480
Nor for a time could he discern,
Till Truth and Darkness took their turn,
So well did Fancy play her part,
That coward still was at the heart.
     Whiffle (who knows not Whiffle's name,
By the impartial voice of Fame

Recorded first through all this land   487
In Vanity's illustrious band ?)
Who, by all-bounteous Nature meant
For offices of hardiment,
A modern Hercules at least,
To rid the world of each wild beast,
Of each wild beast which came in view,
Whether on four legs or on two,
Degenerate, delights to prove
His force on the parade of Love,
Disclaims the joys which camps afford,
And for the distaff quits the sword ;
Who fond of women would appear
To public eye and public ear,   500
But, when in private, lets them know
How little they can trust to show ;
Who sports a woman, as of course,
Just as a jockey shows a horse,
And then returns her to the stable,
Or vainly plants her at his table,
Where he would rather Venus find
(So pall'd, and so depraved his mind)
Than, by some great occasion led,
To seize her panting in her bed,   510
Burning with more than mortal fires,
And melting in her own desires ;
Who, ripe in years, is yet a child,
Through fashion, not through feeling, wild ;
Whate'er in others, who proceed
As Sense and Nature have decreed,
From real passion flows, in him
Is mere effect of mode and whim ;
Who laughs, a very common way,
Because he nothing has to say;   520

As your choice spirits oaths dispense   521
To fill up vacancies of sense ;
Who, having some small sense, defies it,
Or, using, always misapplies it ;
Who now and then brings something forth
Which seems indeed of sterling worth ;
Something, by sudden start and fit,
Which at a distance looks like wit,
But, on examination near,
To his confusion will appear,   530
By Truth's fair glass, to be at best
A threadbare jester's threadbare jest;
Who frisks and dances through the street,
Sings without voice, rides without seat,
Plays o'er his tricks, like Æsop's ass,
A gratis fool to all who pass ;
Who riots, though he loves not waste,
Whores without lust, drinks without taste,
Acts without sense, talks without thought,
Does every thing but what he ought ;   540
Who, led by forms, without the power
Of vice, is vicious ; who one hour,
Proud without pride, the next will be
Humble without humility :
Whose vanity we all discern,
The spring on which his actions turn ;
Whose aim in erring, is to err,
So that he may be singular,
And all his utmost wishes mean
Is, though he's laugh'd at, to be seen :   550
Such, (for when Flattery's soothing strain
Had robb'd the Muse of her disdain,
And found a method to persuade
Her art to soften every shade,

Justice, enraged, the pencil snatch'd 555
From her degen'rate hand, and scratch'd
Out every trace ; then, quick as thought,
From life this striking likeness caught)
In mind, in manners, and in mien,
Such Whiffle came, and such was seen 560
In the world's eye ; but (strange to tell !)
Misled by Fancy's magic spell,
Deceived, not dreaming of deceit,
Cheated, but happy in the cheat,
Was more than human in his own.
Oh, bow, bow all at Fancy's throne,
Whose power could make so vile an elf
With patience bear that thing, himself.
　　But, mistress of each art to please,
Creative Fancy, what are these, 570
These pageants of a trifler's pen,
To what thy power effected then ?
Familiar with the human mind,
And swift and subtle as the wind,
Which we all feel, yet no one knows,
Or whence it comes, or where it goes,
Fancy at once in every part
Possess'd the eye, the head, the heart,
And in a thousand forms array'd,
A thousand various gambols play'd. 580
　　Here, in a face which well might ask
The privilege to wear a mask
In spite of law, and Justice teach
For public good t' excuse the breach,
Within the furrow of a wrinkle
'Twixt eyes, which could not shine but twinkle,
Like sentinels i' th' starry way,
Who wait for the return of day,

Almost burnt out, and seem to keep   589
Their watch, like soldiers, in their sleep ;
Or like those lamps, which, by the power
Of law,[1] must burn from hour to hour,
(Else they, without redemption, fall
Under the terrors of that Hall,[2]
Which, once notorious for a hop,
Is now become a justice shop)
Which are so managed, to go out
Just when the time comes round about,
Which yet, through emulation, strive
To keep their dying light alive,   600
And (not uncommon, as we find,
Amongst the children of mankind)
As they grow weaker, would seem stronger,
And burn a little, little longer :
Fancy, betwixt such eyes enshrined,
No brush to daub, no mill to grind,
Thrice waved her wand around, whose force
Changed in an instant Nature's course,
And, hardly credible in rhyme,
Not only stopp'd, but call'd back Time ;   610
The face of every wrinkle clear'd,
Smooth as the floating stream appear'd,
Down the neck ringlets spread their flame,
The neck admiring whence they came ;
On the arch'd brow the Graces play'd ;
On the full bosom Cupid laid ;
Suns, from their proper orbits sent,
Became for eyes a supplement ;
Teeth, white as ever teeth were seen,
Deliver'd from the hand of Green,   620

---

[1] 'Of law:' referring to the punishment of negligent lamplighters.—
[2] 'Hall:' the Westminster Session-house was then held at a house in King Street, which had probably been a low public house.

Started, in regular array, 621
Like train-bands on a grand field day,
Into the gums, which would have fled,
But, wondering, turn'd from white to red ;
Quite alter'd was the whole machine,
And Lady —— —— was fifteen.
    Here she made lordly temples rise
Before the pious Dashwood's eyes,
Temples which, built aloft in air,
May serve for show, if not for prayer ; 630
In solemn form herself, before,
Array'd like Faith, the Bible bore.
There over Melcombe's feather'd head—
Who, quite a man of gingerbread,
Savour'd in talk, in dress, and phiz,
More of another world than this,
To a dwarf Muse a giant page,
The last grave fop of the last age—
In a superb and feather'd hearse,
Bescutcheon'd and betagg'd with verse, 640
Which, to beholders from afar,
Appear'd like a triumphal car,
She rode, in a cast rainbow clad ;
There, throwing off the hallow'd plaid,
Naked, as when (in those drear cells
Where, self-bless'd, self-cursed, Madness dwells)
Pleasure, on whom, in Laughter's shape,
Frenzy had pérfected a rape,
First brought her forth, before her time,
Wild witness of her shame and crime, 650
Driving before an idol band
Of drivelling Stuarts, hand in hand ;
Some who, to curse mankind, had wore
A crown they ne'er must think of more ;

Others, whose baby brows were graced   655
With paper crowns, and toys of paste,
(She jigg'd,) and, playing on the flute,
Spread raptures o'er the soul of Bute.
    Big with vast hopes, some mighty plan,
Which wrought the busy soul of man   660
To her full bent; the Civil Law,
Fit code to keep a world in awe,
Bound o'er his brows, fair to behold,
As Jewish frontlets were of old;
The famous Charter of our land
Defaced, and mangled in his hand;
As one whom deepest thoughts employ,
But deepest thoughts of truest joy,
Serious and slow he strode, he stalk'd;
Before him troops of heroes walk'd,   670
Whom best he loved, of heroes crown'd,
By Tories guarded all around;
Dull solemn pleasure in his face,
He saw the honours of his race,
He saw their lineal glories rise,
And touch'd, or seem'd to touch, the skies;
Not the most distant mark of fear,
No sign of axe or scaffold near,
Not one cursed thought to cross his will
Of such a place as Tower Hill.   680
    Curse on this Muse, a flippant jade,
A shrew, like every other maid
Who turns the corner of nineteen,
Devour'd with peevishness and spleen;
Her tongue (for as, when bound for life,
The husband suffers for the wife,
So if in any works of rhyme
Perchance there blunders out a crime,

Poor culprit bards must always rue it,   689
Although 'tis plain the Muses do it)
Sooner or later cannot fail
To send me headlong to a jail.
Whate'er my theme, (our themes we choose,
In modern days, without a Muse ;
Just as a father will provide
To join a bridegroom and a bride,
As if, though they must be the players,
The game was wholly his, not theirs)
Whate'er my theme, the Muse, who still
Owns no direction but her will,   700
Flies off, and ere I could expect,
By ways oblique and indirect,
At once quite over head and ears
In fatal politics appears.
Time was, and, if I aught discern
Of fate, that time shall soon return,
When, decent and demure at least,
As grave and dull as any priest,
I could see Vice in robes array'd,
Could see the game of Folly play'd   710
Successfully in Fortune's school,
Without exclaiming rogue or fool.
Time was, when, nothing loth or proud,
I lackey'd with the fawning crowd,
Scoundrels in office, and would bow
To cyphers great in place ; but now
Upright I stand, as if wise Fate,
To compliment a shatter'd state,
Had me, like Atlas, hither sent
To shoulder up the firmament,   720
And if I stoop'd, with general crack,
The heavens would tumble from my back.

Time was, when rank and situation   723
Secured the great ones of the nation
From all control ; satire and law
Kept only little knaves in awe ;
But now, Decorum lost, I stand
Bemused, a pencil in my hand,
And, dead to every sense of shame,
Careless of safety and of fame,   730
The names of scoundrels minute down,
And libel more than half the town.
   How can a statesman be secure
In all his villanies, if poor
And dirty authors thus shall dare
To lay his rotten bosom bare ?
Muses should pass away their time
In dressing out the poet's rhyme
With bills, and ribands, and array
Each line in harmless taste, though gay ;   740
When the hot burning fit is on,
They should regale their restless son
With something to allay his rage,
Some cool Castalian beverage,
Or some such draught (though they, 'tis plain,
Taking the Muse's name in vain,
Know nothing of their real court,
And only fable from report)
As makes a Whitehead's Ode go down,
Or slakes the Feverette of Brown :[1]   750
But who would in his senses think,
Of Muses giving gall to drink,

[1] ' Brown :' the Rev. John Brown, D.D., born in 1715, was author, among
other works, of the ' Essay on the Characteristics,' and of an ' Estimate of
the Manners and Principles of the Times.' See Cowper's ' Table-talk.' The
' Estimate ' was extremely popular for a time. He was inordinately vain,
and died at last insane and a suicide.

Or that their folly should afford 753
To raving poets gun or sword ?
Poets were ne'er design'd by Fate
To meddle with affairs of state,
Nor should (if we may speak our thought
Truly as men of honour ought)
Sound policy their rage admit,
To launch the thunderbolts of Wit 760
About those heads, which, when they're shot,
Can't tell if 'twas by Wit or not.
These things well known, what devil, in spite,
Can have seduced me thus to write
Out of that road, which must have led
To riches, without heart or head,
Into that road, which, had I more
Than ever poet had before
Of wit and virtue, in disgrace
Would keep me still, and out of place ; 770
Which, if some judge (you'll understand
One famous, famous through the land
For making law [1]) should stand my friend,
At last may in a pillory end ;
And all this, I myself admit,
Without one cause to lead to it ?
For instance, now—this book—the Ghost—
Methinks I hear some critic Post
Remark most gravely—'The first word
Which we about the Ghost have heard.' 780
Peace, my good sir !—not quite so fast—
What is the first, may be the last,
Which is a point, all must agree,
Cannot depend on you or me.

[1] 'For making law:' alluding to Lord Mansfield's construction of the libel-law.

Fanny, no ghost of common mould,   785
Is not by forms to be controll'd ;
To·keep her state, and show her skill,
She never comes but when she will.
I wrote and wrote, (perhaps you doubt,
And shrewdly, what I wrote about ;   790
Believe me, much to my disgrace,
I, too, am in the self-same case ;)
But still I wrote, till Fanny came
Impatient, nor could any shame
On me with equal justice fall
If she had never come at all.
An underling, I could not stir
Without the cue thrown out by her,
Nor from the subject aid receive
Until she came and gave me leave.   800
So that, (ye sons of Erudition
Mark, this is but a supposition,
Nor would I to so wise a nation
Suggest it as a revelation)
If henceforth, dully turning o'er
Page after page, ye read no more
Of Fanny, who, in sea or air,
May be departed God knows where,
Rail at jilt Fortune ; but agree
No censure can be laid on me ;   810
For sure (the cause let Mansfield try)
Fanny is in the fault, not I.
    But, to return—and this I hold
A secret worth its weight in gold
To those who write, as I write now,
Not to mind where they go, or how,
Through ditch, through bog, o'er hedge and stile,
Make it but worth the reader's while,

And keep a passage fair and plain   819
Always to bring him back again.
Through dirt, who scruples to approach,
At Pleasure's call, to take a coach ?
But we should think the man a clown,
Who in the dirt should set us down.
  But to return—if Wit, who ne'er .
The shackles of restraint could bear,
In wayward humour should refuse
Her timely succour to the Muse,
And, to no rules and orders tied,
Roughly deny to be her guide,   830
She must renounce Decorum's plan,
And get back when, and how she can ;
As parsons, who, without pretext,
As soon as mention'd, quit their text,
And, to promote sleep's genial power,
Grope in the dark for half an hour,
Give no more reason (for we know
Reason is vulgar, mean, and low)
Why they come back (should it befall
That ever they come back at all)   840
Into the road, to end their rout,
Than they can give why they went out.
  But to return—this book—the Ghost—
A mere amusement at the most ;
A trifle, fit to wear away
The horrors of a rainy day ;
A slight shot-silk, for summer wear,
Just as our modern statesmen are,
If rigid honesty permit
That I for once purloin the wit   850
Of him, who, were we all to steal,
Is much too rich the theft to feel :

Yet in this book, where Ease should join   853
With Mirth to sugar every line;
Where it should all be mere chit-chat,
Lively, good-humour'd, and all that;
Where honest Satire, in disgrace,
Should not so much as show her face,
The shrew, o'erleaping all due bounds,
Breaks into Laughter's sacred grounds,   860
And, in contempt, plays o'er her tricks
In science, trade, and politics.
   By why should the distemper'd scold
Attempt to blacken men enroll'd
In Power's dread book, whose mighty skill
Can twist an empire to their will;
Whose voice is fate, and on their tongue
Law, liberty, and life are hung;
Whom, on inquiry, Truth shall find
With Stuarts link'd, time out of mind,   870
Superior to their country's laws,
Defenders of a tyrant's cause;
Men, who the same damn'd maxims hold
Darkly, which they avow'd of old;
Who, though by different means, pursue
The end which they had first in view,
And, force found vain, now play their part
With much less honour, much more art?
Why, at the corners of the streets,
To every patriot drudge she meets,   880
Known or unknown, with furious cry
Should she wild clamours vent? or why,
The minds of groundlings to inflame,
A Dashwood, Bute, and Wyndham name?
Why, having not, to our surprise,
The fear of death before her eyes,

Bearing, and that but now and then,　　　887
No other weapon but her pen,
Should she an argument afford
For blood to men who wear a sword ?
Men, who can nicely trim and pare
A point of honour to a hair—
(Honour !—a word of nice import,
A pretty trinket in a court,
Which my lord, quite in rapture, feels
Dangling and rattling with his seals—
Honour !—a word which all the Nine
Would be much puzzled to define—
Honour !—a word which torture mocks,
And might confound a thousand Lockes—　　　900
Which—for I leave to wiser heads,
Who fields of death prefer to beds
Of down, to find out, if they can,
What honour is, on their wild plan—
Is not, to take it in their way,
And this we sure may dare to say
Without incurring an offence,
Courage, law, honesty, or sense) :
Men, who, all spirit, life, and soul,
Neat butchers of a button-hole,　　　910
Having more skill, believe it true
That they must have more courage too :
Men who, without a place or name,
Their fortunes speechless as their fame,
Would by the sword new fortunes carve,
And rather die in fight than starve
At coronations, a vast field,
Which food of every kind might yield ;
Of good sound food, at once most fit
For purposes of health and wit,　　　920

Could not ambitious Satire rest,   921
Content with what she might digest?
Could she not feast on things of course,
A champion, or a champion's horse?
A champion's horse—no, better say,
Though better figured on that day,[1]
A horse, which might appear to us,
Who deal in rhyme, a Pegasus;
A rider, who, when once got on,
Might pass for a Bellerophon,   930
Dropt on a sudden from the skies,
To catch and fix our wondering eyes,
To witch, with wand instead of whip,
The world with noble horsemanship,
To twist and twine, both horse and man,
On such a well-concerted plan,
That, Centaur-like, when all was done,
We scarce could think they were not one?
Could she not to our itching ears
Bring the new names of new-coin'd peers,   940
Who walk'd, nobility forgot,
With shoulders fitter for a knot
Than robes of honour; for whose sake
Heralds in form were forced to make,
To make, because they could not find,
Great predecessors to their mind?
Could she not (though 'tis doubtful since
Whether he plumber is, or prince)
Tell of a simple knight's advance
To be a doughty peer of France?   950
Tell how he did a dukedom gain,
And Robinson was Aquitain?

---

[1] 'On that day:' alluding to Lord Talbot's horsemanship as high-steward at the coronation.

Tell how her city chiefs, disgraced,   953
Were at an empty table placed,—
A gross neglect, which, whilst they live,
They can't forget, and won't forgive ;
A gross neglect of all those rights
Which march with city appetites,
Of all those canons, which we find
By Gluttony, time out of mind,   960
Establish'd, which they ever hold
Dearer than any thing but gold ?
Thanks to my stars—I now see shore—
Of courtiers, and of courts no more—
Thus stumbling on my city friends,
Blind Chance my guide, my purpose bends
In line direct, and shall pursue
The point which I had first in view,
Nor more shall with the reader sport
Till I have seen him safe in port.   970
Hush'd be each fear—no more I bear
Through the wide regions of the air
The reader terrified, no more
Wild ocean's horrid paths explore.
Be the plain track from henceforth mine—
Cross roads to Allen I resign ;
Allen, the honor of this nation ;
Allen, himself a corporation ;
Allen, of late notorious grown
For writings, none, or all, his own ;   980
Allen, the first of letter'd men,
Since the good Bishop [1] holds his pen;
And at his elbow takes his stand,
To mend his head, and guide his hand.

[1] 'Good Bishop:' Warburton was married on Allen's niece.

X

But hold—once more, Digression hence—   985
Let us return to Common Sense ;
The car of Phœbus I discharge,
My carriage now a Lord Mayor's barge.
    Suppose we now—we may suppose
In verse, what would be sin in prose—   990
The sky with darkness overspread,
And every star retired to bed ;
The gewgaw robes of Pomp and Pride
In some dark corner thrown aside ;
Great lords and ladies giving way
To what they seem to scorn by day,
The real feelings of the heart,
And Nature taking place of Art ;
Desire triumphant through the night,
And Beauty panting with delight ;   1000
Chastity, woman's fairest crown,
Till the return of morn laid down,
Then to be worn again as bright
As if not sullied in the night ;
Dull Ceremony, business o'er,
Dreaming in form at Cottrell's [1] door ;
Precaution trudging all about
To see the candles safely out,
Bearing a mighty master-key,
Habited like Economy,   1010
Stamping each lock with triple seals ;
Mean Avarice creeping at her heels.
    Suppose we too, like sheep in pen,
The Mayor and Court of Aldermen
Within their barge, which through the deep,
The rowers more than half asleep,

---

[1] 'Cottrell:' Sir Clement Cottrell, master of the ceremonies.

Moved slow, as overcharged with state ;   1017
Thames groan'd beneath the mighty weight,
And felt that bauble heavier far
Than a whole fleet of men of war.
Sleep o'er each well-known faithful head
With liberal hand his poppies shed ;
Each head, by Dulness render'd fit
Sleep and his empire to admit.
Through the whole passage not a word,
Not one faint, weak half-sound was heard ;
Sleep had prevail'd to overwhelm
The steersman nodding o'er the helm ;
The rowers, without force or skill,
Left the dull barge to drive at will ;   1030
The sluggish oars suspended hung,
And even Beardmore held his tongue.
Commerce, regardful of a freight
On which depended half her state.
Stepp'd to the helm ; with ready hand
She safely clear'd that bank of sand,
Where, stranded, our west-country fleet
Delay and danger often meet,
Till Neptune, anxious for the trade,
Comes in full tides, and brings them aid.   1040
Next (for the Muses can survey
Objects by night as well as day ;
Nothing prevents their taking aim,
Darkness and light to them the same)
They pass'd that building [1] which of old
Queen-mothers was design'd to hold ;
At present a mere lodging-pen,
A palace turn'd into a den ;

'Building:' the Savoy and Old Somerset House were formerly the
residences of the Queens of England.

To barracks turn'd, and soldiers tread 1049
Where dowagers have laid their head.
Why should we mention Surrey Street,
Where every week grave judges meet
All fitted out with hum and ha,
In proper form to drawl out law,
To see all causes duly tried
'Twixt knaves who drive, and fools who ride ?
Why at the Temple should we stay ?
What of the Temple dare we say ?
A dangerous ground we tread on there,
And words perhaps may actions bear ; 1060
Where, as the brethren of the seas
For fares, the lawyers ply for fees.
What of that Bridge,[1] most wisely made
To serve the purposes of trade,
In the great mart of all this nation,
By stopping up the navigation,
And to that sand bank adding weight,
Which is already much too great ?
What of that Bridge, which, void of sense
But well supplied with impudence, 1070
Englishmen, knowing not the Guild,
Thought they might have a claim to build,
Till Paterson, as white as milk,
As smooth as oil, as soft as silk,
In solemn manner had decreed
That on the other side the Tweed
Art, born and bred, and fully grown,
Was with one Mylne, a man unknown,

---

[1] 'Bridge' referring to a clamour excited by interested persons of all descriptions against the erection of a bridge over the Thames at Blackfriars. It was carried by the exertions of Paterson, an Anti-Wilkite, and built by Mylne, a Scotchman.

But grace, preferment, and renown 1079
Deserving, just arrived in town :
One Mylne, an artist perfect quite
Both in his own and country's right,
As fit to make a bridge as he,
With glorious Patavinity,[1]
To build inscriptions worthy found
To lie for ever under ground.

    Much more worth observation too,
Was this a season to pursue
The theme, our Muse might tell in rhyme :
The will she hath, but not the time ; 1090
For, swift as shaft from Indian bow,
(And when a goddess comes, we know,
Surpassing Nature acts prevail.
And boats want neither oar nor sail)
The vessel pass'd, and reach'd the shore
So quick, that Thought was scarce before.

    Suppose we now our City court
Safely deliver'd at the port,
And, of their state regardless quite,
Landed, like smuggled goods, by night. 1100
The solemn magistrate laid down,
The dignity of robe and gown,
With every other ensign gone,
Suppose the woollen nightcap on ;
The flesh-brush used, with decent state,
To make the spirits circulate,
(A form which, to the senses true,
The lickerish chaplain uses too,
Though, something to improve the plan,
He takes the maid instead of man) 1110

---

[1] 'Patavinity :' the provincial dialect of Padua, in which Livy wrote.

Swathed, and with flannel cover'd o'er,   1111
To show the vigour of threescore,
The vigour of threescore and ten,
Above the proof of younger men,
Suppose, the mighty Dulman led
Betwixt two slaves, and put to bed ;
Suppose, the moment he lies down,
No miracle in this great town,——
The drone as fast asleep as he
Must in the course of nature be,——   1120
Who, truth for our foundation take,
When up, is never half awake.
    There let him sleep, whilst we survey
The preparations for the day ;
That day on which was to be shown
Court pride by City pride outdone.
    The jealous mother sends away,
As only fit for childish play,
That daughter who, to gall her pride,
Shoots up too forward by her side.   1130
    The wretch, of God and man accursed,
Of all Hell's instruments the worst,
Draws forth his pawns, and for the day
Struts in some spendthrift's vain array ;
Around his awkward doxy shine
The treasures of Golconda's mine ;
Each neighbour, with a jealous glare,
Beholds her folly publish'd there.
    Garments well saved, (an anecdote
Which we can prove, or would not quote)   1140
Garments well saved, which first were made
When tailors, to promote their trade,
Against the Picts in arms arose,
And drove them out, or made them clothes ;

Garments immortal, without end,　　　　1145
Like names and titles, which descend
Successively from sire to son ;
Garments, unless some work is done
Of note, not suffer'd to appear
'Bove once at most in every year,　　　　1150
Were now, in solemn form, laid bare,
To take the benefit of air,
And, ere they came to be employ'd
On this solemnity, to void
That scent which Russia's leather gave,
From vile and impious moth to save.
　　Each head was busy, and each heart
In preparation bore a part ;
Running together all about
The servants put each other out,　　　　1160
Till the grave master had decreed,
The more haste ever the worse speed.
Miss, with her little eyes half-closed,
Over a smuggled toilette dosed ;
The waiting-maid, whom story notes
A very Scrub in petticoats,
Hired for one work, but doing all,
In slumbers lean'd against the wall.
Milliners, summon'd from afar,
Arrived in shoals at Temple Bar,　　　　1170
Strictly commanded to import
Cart loads of foppery from Court ;
With labour'd visible design,
Art strove to be superbly fine ;
Nature, more pleasing, though more wild,
Taught otherwise her darling child,
And cried, with spirited disdain,
Be Hunter elegant and plain !

Lo ! from the chambers of the East,   1179
A welcome prelude to the feast,
In saffron-colour'd robe array'd,
High in a car, by Vulcan made,
Who work'd for Jove himself, each steed,
High-mettled, of celestial breed,
Pawing and pacing all the way,
Aurora brought the wish'd-for day,
And held her empire, till out-run
By that brave jolly groom, the Sun.
   The trumpet—hark ! it speaks—it swells
The loud full harmony ; it tells   1190
The time at hand when Dulman, led
By Form, his citizens must head,
And march those troops, which at his call
Were now assembled, to Guildhall,
On matters of importance great,
To court and city, church and state.
   From end to end the sound makes way,
All hear the signal and obey ;
But Dulman, who, his charge forgot,
By Morpheus fetter'd, heard it not ;   1200
Nor could, so sound he slept and fast,
Hear any trumpet, but the last.
   Crape, ever true and trusty known,
Stole from the maid's bed to his own,
Then in the spirituals of pride,
Planted himself at Dulman's side.
Thrice did the ever-faithful slave,
With voice which might have reach'd the grave,
And broke Death's adamantine chain,
On Dulman call, but call'd in vain.   1210
Thrice with an arm, which might have made
The Theban boxer curse his trade,

The drone he shook, who rear'd the head,   1213
And thrice fell backward on his bed.
What could be done ?   Where force hath fail'd,
Policy often hath prevail'd ;
And what—an inference most plain—
Had been, Crape thought might be again.
  Under his pillow (still in mind
The proverb kept, ' fast bind, fast find ')   1220
Each blessed night the keys were laid,
Which Crape to draw away assay'd.
What not the power of voice or arm
Could do, this did, and broke the charm ;
Quick started he with stupid stare,
For all his little soul was there.
  Behold him, taken up, rubb'd down,
In elbow-chair, and morning-gown ;
Behold him, in his latter bloom,
Stripp'd, wash'd, and sprinkled with perfume ; 1230
Behold him bending with the weight
Of robes, and trumpery of state ;
Behold him (for the maxim 's true,
Whate'er we by another do,
We do ourselves ; and chaplain paid,
Like slaves in every other trade,
Had mutter'd over God knows what,
Something which he by heart had got)
Having, as usual, said his prayers,
Go titter, totter to the stairs :   1240
Behold him for descent prepare,
With one foot trembling in the air ;
He starts, he pauses on the brink,
And, hard to credit, seems to think ;
Through his whole train (the chaplain gave
The proper cue to every slave)

At once, as with infection caught,   1247
Each started, paused, and aim'd at thought ;
He turns, and they turn ; big with care,
He waddles to his elbow-chair,
Squats down, and, silent for a season,
At last with Crape begins to reason :
But first of all he made a sign,
That every soul, but the divine,
Should quit the room ; in him, he knows,
He may all confidence repose.
    ' Crape—though I 'm yet not quite awake—
Before this awful step I take,
On which my future all depends,
I ought to know my foes and friends.   1260
My foes and friends—observe me still—
I mean not those who well or ill
Perhaps may wish me, but those who
Have 't in their power to do it too.
Now if, attentive to the state,
In too much hurry to be great,
Or through much zeal,—a motive, Crape,
Deserving praise,—into a scrape
I, like a fool, am got, no doubt
I, like a wise man, should get out :   1270
Note that remark without replies ;
I say that to get out is wise,
Or, by the very self-same rule,
That to get in was like a fool.
The marrow of this argument
Must wholly rest on the event,
And therefore, which is really hard,
Against events too I must guard.
    Should things continue as they stand,
And Bute prevail through all the land   1280

Without a rival, by his aid 1281
My fortunes in a trice are made ;
Nay, honours on my zeal may smile,
And stamp me Earl of some great Isle : [1]
But if, a matter of much doubt,
The present minister goes out,
Fain would I know on what pretext
I can stand fairly with the next ?
For as my aim, at every hour,
Is to be well with those in power, 1290
And my material point of view,
Whoever's in, to be in too,
I should not, like a blockhead, choose
To gain these, so as those to lose :
'Tis good in every case, you know,
To have two strings unto our bow.'
 As one in wonder lost, Crape view'd
His lord, who thus his speech pursued :
 ' This, my good Crape, is my grand point ;
And as the times are out of joint, 1300
The greater caution is required
To bring about the point desired.
What I would wish to bring about
Cannot admit a moment's doubt ;
The matter in dispute, you know,
Is what we call the *Quomodo*.
That be thy task.'—The reverend slave,
Becoming in a moment grave,
Fix'd to the ground and rooted stood,
Just like a man cut out of wood, 1310
Such as we see (without the least
Reflection glancing on the priest)

[1] ' Isle : ' alluding to the insignificant size of the Isle of Bute.

One or more, planted up and down,   1313
Almost in every church in town ;
He stood some minutes, then, like one
Who wish'd the matter might be done,
But could not do it, shook his head,
And thus the man of sorrow said :
   ' Hard is this task, too hard I swear,
By much too hard for me to bear ;   1320
Beyond expression hard my part,
Could mighty Dulman see my heart,
When he, alas ! makes known a will
Which Crape 's not able to fulfil.
Was ever my obedience barr'd
By any trifling nice regard
To sense and honour ?   Could I reach
Thy meaning without help of speech,
At the first motion of thy eye
Did not thy faithful creature fly ?   1330
Have I not said, not what I ought,
But what my earthly master taught ?
Did I e'er weigh, through duty strong,
In thy great biddings, right and wrong ?
Did ever Interest, to whom thou
Canst not with more devotion bow,
Warp my sound faith, or will of mine
In contradiction run to thine ?
Have I not, at thy table placed,
When business call'd aloud for haste,   1340
Torn myself thence, yet never heard
To utter one complaining word,
And had, till thy great work was done,
All appetites, as having none ?
Hard is it, this great plan pursued
Of voluntary servitude ;

Pursued without or shame, or fear,　　　1347
Through the great circle of the year,
Now to receive, in this grand hour,
Commands which lie beyond my power,
Commands which baffle all my skill,
And leave me nothing but my will :
Be that accepted ; let my lord
Indulgence to his slave afford:
This task, for my poor strength unfit,
Will yield to none but Dulman's wit.'
　　With such gross incense gratified,
And turning up the lip of pride,
'Poor Crape'—and shook his empty head—
'Poor puzzled Crape!' wise Dulman said,　　1360
'Of judgment weak, of sense confined,
For things of lower note design'd ;
For things within the vulgar reach,
To run of errands, and to preach ;
Well hast thou judged, that heads like mine
Cannot want help from heads like thine ;
Well hast thou judged thyself unmeet
Of such high argument to treat ;
'Twas but to try thee that I spoke,
And all I said was but a joke.　　　1370
　　Nor think a joke, Crape, a disgrace,
Or to my person, or my place ;
The wisest of the sons of men
Have deign'd to use them now and then.
The only caution, do you see,
Demanded by our dignity,
From common use and men exempt,
Is that they may not breed contempt.
Great use they have, when in the hands
Of one like me, who understands,　　　1380

Who understands the time and place,   1381
The person, manner, and the grace,
Which fools neglect ; so that we find,
If all the requisites are join'd,
From whence a. perfect joke must spring,
A joke's a very serious thing.

   But to our business—my design,
Which gave so rough a shock to thine,
To my capacity is made
As ready as a fraud in trade ;   1390
Which, like broad-cloth, I can, with ease,
Cut out in any shape I please.

   Some, in my circumstance, some few,
Aye, and those men of genius too,
Good men, who, without love or hate,
Whether they early rise or late,
With names uncrack'd, and credit sound,
Rise worth a hundred thousand pound,
By threadbare ways and means would try
To bear their point—so will not I.   1400
New methods shall my wisdom find
To suit these matters to my mind ;
So that the infidels at court,
Who make our city wits their sport,
Shall hail the honours of my reign,
And own that Dulman bears a brain.

   Some, in my place, to gain their ends,
Would give relations up, and friends ;
Would lend a wife, who, they might swear
Safely, was none the worse for wear ;   1410
Would see a daughter, yet a maid,
Into a statesman's arms betray'd ;
Nay, should the girl prove coy, nor know
What daughters to a father owe,

Sooner than schemes so nobly plann'd   1415
Should fail, themselves would lend a hand ;
Would vote on one side, whilst a brother,
Properly taught, would vote on t' other ;
Would every petty band forget ;
To public eye be with one set,   1420
In private with a second herd,
And be by proxy with a third ;
Would, (like a queen,[1] of whom I read,
The other day—her name is fled—
In a book,—where, together bound,
'Whittington and his Cat' I found—
A tale most true, and free from art,
Which all Lord Mayors should have by heart ;
A queen oh!—might those days begin
Afresh, when queens would learn to spin—   1430
Who wrought, and wrought, but for some plot,
The cause of which I've now forgot,
During the absence of the sun
Undid what she by day had done)
Whilst they a double visage wear,
What's sworn by day, by night unswear.
    Such be their arts, and such, perchance,
May happily their ends advance ;
From a new system mine shall spring,
A *locum tenens* is the thing.   1440
That 's your true plan.   To obligate
The present ministers of state,
My shadow shall our court approach,
And bear my power, and have my coach ;
My fine state-coach, superb to view,
A fine state-coach, and paid for too.

---

[1] 'A queen :'. Penelope, in the Odyssey.

To curry favour, and the grace   1447
Obtain of those who 're out of place ;
In the mean time I—that's to say,
I proper, I myself—here stay.
    But hold—perhaps unto the nation,
Who hate the Scot's administration,
To lend my coach may seem to be
Declaring for the ministry,
For where the city-coach is, there
Is the true essence of the Mayor :
Therefore (for wise men are intent
Evils at distance to prevent,
Whilst fools the evils first endure,
And then are plagued to seek a cure)   1460
No coach—a horse—and free from fear,
To make our Deputy appear,
Fast on his back shall he be tied,
With two grooms marching by his side ;
Then for a horse—through all the land,
To head our solemn city-band,
Can any one so fit be found
As he who in Artillery-ground,
  • Without a rider, (noble sight !)
Led on our bravest troops to fight ?   1470
    But first, Crape, for my honour's sake—
A tender point—inquiry make
About that horse, if the dispute
Is ended, or is still in suit :
For whilst a cause, (observe this plan
Of justice) whether horse or man
The parties be, remains in doubt,
Till 'tis determined out and out,
That power must tyranny appear
Which should, prejudging, interfere,   1480

And weak, faint judges overawe,   1481
To bias the free course of law.
   You have my will—now quickly run,
And take care that my will be done.
In public, Crape, you must appear,
Whilst I in privacy sit here ;
Here shall great Dulman sit alone,
Making this elbow-chair my throne,
And you, performing what I bid,
Do all, as if I nothing did.'   1490
   Crape heard, and speeded on his way ;
With him to hear was to obey ;
Not without trouble, be assured,
A proper proxy was procured
To serve such infamous intent,
And such a lord to represent ;
Nor could one have been found at all
On t' other side of London Wall.
   The trumpet sounds—solemn and slow
Behold the grand procession go,   1500
All moving on, cat after kind,
As if for motion ne'er design'd.
   Constables, whom the laws admit
To keep the peace by breaking it ;
Beadles, who hold the second place
By virtue of a silver mace,
Which every Saturday is drawn,
For use of Sunday, out of pawn ;
Treasurers, who with empty key
Secure an empty treasury ;   1510
Churchwardens, who their course pursue
In the same state, as to their pew
Churchwardens of St Margaret's go,
Since Peirson taught them pride and show,

Y

Who in short transient pomp appear,   1515
Like almanacs changed every year ;
Behind whom, with unbroken locks,
Charity carries the poor's box,
Not knowing that with private keys
They ope and shut it when they please :   1520
Overseers, who by frauds ensure
The heavy curses of the poor ;
Unclean came flocking, bulls and bears,
Like beasts into the ark, by pairs.
    Portentous, flaming in the van,
Stalk'd the professor, Sheridan,
A man of wire, a mere pantine,
A downright animal machine;
He knows alone, in proper mode,
How to take vengeance on an ode,   1530
And how to butcher Ammon's son
And poor Jack Dryden both in one :
On all occasions next the chair
He stands, for service of the Mayor,
And to instruct him how to use
His A's and B's, and P's and Q's :
O'er letters, into tatters worn,
O'er syllables, defaced and torn,.
O'er words disjointed, and o'er sense,
Left destitute of all defence,   1540
He strides, and all the way he goes
Wades, deep in blood, o'er Criss-cross-rows :
Before him every consonant
In agonies is seen to pant ;
Behind, in forms not to be known,
The ghosts of tortured vowels groan.
    Next Hart and Duke, well worthy grace
And city favour, came in place ;

No children can their toils engage,   1549
Their toils are turn'd to reverend age ;
When a court dame, to grace his brows
Resolved, is wed to city-spouse,
Their aid with madam's aid must join,
The awkward dotard to refine,
And teach, whence truest glory flows,
Grave sixty to turn out his toes.
Each bore in hand a kit ; and each
To show how fit he was to teach
A cit, an alderman, a mayor,
Led in a string a dancing bear.   1560
   Since the revival of Fingal,
Custom, and custom's all in all,
Commands that we should have regard,
On all high seasons, to the bard.
Great acts like these, by vulgar tongue
Profaned, should not be said, but sung.
This place to fill, renown'd in fame,
The high and mighty Lockman [1] came,
And, ne'er forgot in Dulman's reign,
With proper order to maintain   1570
The uniformity of pride,
Brought Brother Whitehead by his side.   .
   On horse, who proudly paw'd the ground,
And cast his fiery eyeballs round,
Snorting, and champing the rude bit,
As if, for warlike purpose fit,
His high and generous blood disdain'd,
To be for sports and pastimes rein'd,
Great Dymock, in his glorious station,
Paraded at the coronation.   1580

---

[1] ' John Lockman :' secretary to the British Herring Fishery Board.

Not so our city Dymock came,   1581
Heavy, dispirited, and tame ;
No mark of sense, his eyes half-closed,
He on a mighty dray-horse dozed :
Fate never could a horse provide
So fit for such a man to ride,
Nor find a man with strictest care,
So fit for such a horse to bear.
Hung round with instruments of death,
The sight of him will stop the breath   1590
Of braggart Cowardice, and make
The very court Drawcansir[1] quake ;
With dirks, which, in the hands of Spite,
Do their damn'd business in the night,
From Scotland sent, but here display'd
Only to fill up the parade ;
With swords, unflesh'd, of maiden hue,
Which rage or valour never drew ;
With blunderbusses, taught to ride
Like pocket-pistols, by his side,   1600
In girdle stuck, he seem'd to be
A little moving armoury.
One thing much wanting to complete
The sight, and make a perfect treat,
Was, that the horse, (a courtesy
In horses found of high degree)
Instead of going forward on,
All the way backward should have gone.
Horses, unless they breeding lack,
Some scruple make to turn their back,   1610
Though riders, which plain truth declares,
No scruple make of turning theirs.

_____

[1] 'Drawcansir:' Lord Talbot.

Far, far apart from all the rest,   1618
Fit only for a standing jest,
The independent, (can you get
A better suited epithet ?)
The independent Amyand came,[1]
All burning with the sacred flame
Of Liberty, which well he knows
On the great stock of Slavery grows ;   1620
Like sparrow, who, deprived of mate,
Snatch'd by the cruel hand of Fate,
From spray to spray no more will hop,
But sits alone on the house-top ;
Or like himself, when all alone
At Croydon he was heard to groan,
Lifting both hands in the defence
Of interest, and common sense ;
Both hands, for as no other man
Adopted and pursued his plan,   1630
The left hand had been lonesome quite,
If he had not held up the right ;
Apart he came, and fix'd his eyes
With rapture on a distant prize,
On which, in letters worthy note,
There 'twenty thousand pounds' was wrote.
False trap, for credit sapp'd is found
By getting twenty thousand pound :
Nay, look not thus on me, and stare,
Doubting the certainty—to swear   1640
In such a case I should be loth—
But Perry Cust [2] may take his oath.
   In plain and decent garb array'd,
With the prim Quaker, Fraud, came Trade ;

---

[1] 'Amyand:' George and Claudius Amyand were eminent merchants.—
[2] 'Perry Cust:' a London merchant.

Connivance, to improve the plan,   1645
Habited like a juryman,
Judging as interest prevails,
Came next, with measures, weights, and scales ;
Extortion next, of hellish race
A cub most damn'd, to show his face   1650
Forbid by fear, but not by shame,
Turn'd to a Jew, like Gideon[1] came ;
Corruption, Midas-like, behold
Turning whate'er she touch'd to gold ;
Impotence, led by Lust, and Pride,
Strutting with Ponton[2] by her side ;
Hypocrisy, demure and sad,
In garments of the priesthood clad,
So well disguised, that you might swear,
Deceived, a very priest was there ;   1660
Bankruptcy, full of ease and health,
And wallowing in well-saved wealth,
Came sneering through a ruin'd band,
And bringing B—— in her hand ;
Victory, hanging down her head,
Was by a Highland stallion led ;
Peace, clothed in sables, with a face
Which witness'd sense of huge disgrace,
Which spake a deep and rooted shame
Both of herself and of her name,   1670
Mourning creeps on, and, blushing, feels
War, grim War, treading on her heels ;
Pale Credit, shaken by the arts
Of men with bad heads and worse hearts,
Taking no notice of a band
Which near her were ordain'd to stand,

[1] 'Gideon:' Sampson Gideon, a wealthy Jew broker.—[2] 'Ponton:' Daniel Ponton, a gentleman of fortune, and a friend of the administration, was a magistrate for the county of Surrey.

Well-nigh destroy'd by sickly fit,   1677
Look'd wistful all around for Pitt ;
Freedom—at that most hallow'd name
My spirits mount into a flame,
Each pulse beats high, and each nerve strains,
Even to the cracking ; through my veins
The tides of life more rapid run,
And tell me I am Freedom's son—
Freedom came next, but scarce was seen,
When the sky, which appear'd serene
And gay before, was overcast ;
Horror bestrode a foreign blast,
And from the prison of the North,
To Freedom deadly, storms burst forth.   1690
   A car like those, in which, we 're told,
Our wild forefathers warr'd of old,
Loaded with death, six horses bear
Through the blank region of the air.
Too fierce for time or art to tame,
They pour'd forth mingled smoke and flame
From their wide nostrils ; every steed
Was of that ancient savage breed
Which fell Gerýon nursed ; their food
The flesh of man, their drink his blood.   1700
   On the first horses, ill-match'd pair,
This fat and sleek, that lean and bare,
Came ill-match'd riders side by side,
And Poverty was yoked with Pride ;
Union most strange it must appear,
Till other unions make it clear.
   Next, in the gall of bitterness,
With rage which words can ill express,
With unforgiving rage, which springs
From a false zeal for holy things,   1710

Wearing such robes as prophets wear,   1711
False prophets placed in Peter's chair,
(On which, in characters of fire,
Shapes antic, horrible, and dire
Inwoven flamed, where, to the view,
In groups appear'd a rabble crew
Of sainted devils ; where, all round,
Vile relics of vile men were found,
Who, worse than devils, from the birth
Perform'd the work of hell on earth,   1720
Jugglers, Inquisitors, and Popes,
Pointing at axes, wheels, and ropes,
And engines, framed on horrid plan,
Which none but the destroyer, Man,
Could, to promote his selfish views,
Have head to make or heart to use,)
Bearing, to consecrate her tricks,
In her left hand a crucifix,
'Remembrance of our dying Lord,'
And in her right a two-edged sword,   1730
Having her brows, in impious sport,
Adorn'd with words of high import,
'On earth peace, amongst men good will,
Love bearing and forbearing still,'
All wrote in the hearts' blood of those
Who rather death than falsehood chose :
On her breast, (where, in days of yore,
When God loved Jews, the High Priest wore
Those oracles which were decreed
To instruct and guide the chosen seed)   1740
Having with glory clad and strength,
The Virgin pictured at full length,
Whilst at her feet, in small pourtray'd,
As scarce worth notice, Christ was laid,—

Came Superstition, fierce and fell, 1745
An imp detested, e'en in hell ;
Her eye inflamed, her face all o'er
Foully besmear'd with human gore,
O'er heaps of mangled saints she rode ;
Fast at her heels Death proudly strode, 1750
And grimly smiled, well pleased to see
Such havoc of mortality ;
Close by her side, on mischief bent,
And urging on each bad intent
To its full bearing, savage, wild,
The mother fit of such a child,
Striving the empire to advance
Of Sin and Death, came Ignorance.
    With looks where dread command was placed,
And sovereign power by pride disgraced, 1760
Where, loudly witnessing a mind
Of savage, more than human kind,
Not choosing to be loved, but fear'd,
Mocking at right, Misrule appear'd
    With eyeballs glaring fiery red,
Enough to strike beholders dead,
Gnashing his teeth, and in a flood
Pouring corruption forth and blood
From his chafed jaws ; without remorse
Whipping and spurring on his horse, 1770
Whose sides, in their own blood embay'd,
E'en to the bone were open laid,
Came Tyranny, disdaining awe,
And trampling over Sense and Law ;
One thing, and only one, he knew,
One object only would pursue ;
Though less (so low doth passion bring)
Than man, he would be more than king.

With every argument and art   1779
Which might corrupt the head and heart,
Soothing the frenzy of his mind,
Companion meet, was Flattery join'd ;
Winning his carriage, every look
Employed, whilst it conceal'd a hook ;
When simple most, most to be fear'd ;
Most crafty, when no craft appear'd ;
His tales, no man like him could tell ;
His words, which melted as they fell,
Might even a hypocrite deceive,
And make an infidel believe,   1790
Wantonly cheating o'er and o'er
Those who had cheated been before :—
Such Flattery came, in evil hour,
Poisoning the royal ear of Power,
And, grown by prostitution great,
Would be first minister of state.
    Within the chariot, all alone,
High seated on a kind of throne,
With pebbles graced, a figure came,
Whom Justice would, but dare not name.   1800
Hard times when Justice, without fear,
Dare not bring forth to public ear
The names of those who dare offend
'Gainst Justice, and pervert her end !
But, if the Muse afford me grace,
Description shall supply the place.
    In foreign garments he was clad ;
Sage ermine o'er the glossy plaid
Cast reverend honour ; on his heart,
Wrought by the curious hand of Art,   1810
In silver wrought, and brighter far
Than heavenly or than earthly star,

Shone a White Rose, the emblem dear   1813
Of him he ever must revere ;
Of that dread lord, who, with his host
Of faithful native rebels lost,
Like those black spirits doom'd to hell,
At once from power and virtue fell :
Around his clouded brows was placed
A bonnet, most superbly graced   1820
With mighty thistles, nor forgot
The sacred motto—' Touch me not.'
   In the right hand a sword he bore
Harder than adamant, and more
Fatal than winds, which from the mouth
Of the rough North invade the South ;
The reeking blade to view presents
The blood of helpless innocents,
And on the hilt, as meek become
As lamb before the shearers dumb,   1830
With downcast eye, and solemn show
Of deep, unutterable woe,
Mourning the time when Freedom reign'd,
Fast to a rock was Justice chain'd.
   In his left hand, in wax impress'd,
With bells and gewgaws idly dress'd,
An image, cast in baby mould,
He held, and seem'd o'erjoy'd to hold ·
On this he fix'd his eyes ; to this,
Bowing, he gave the loyal kiss,   1840
And, for rebellion fully ripe,
Seem'd to desire the antitype.
What if to that Pretender's foes
His greatness, nay, his life, he owes ;
Shall common obligations bind,
And shake his constancy of mind ?

Scorning such weak and petty chains,   1847
Faithful to James [1] he still remains,
Though he the friend of George appear:
Dissimulation's virtue here.
 Jealous and mean, he with a frown
Would awe, and keep all merit down,
Nor would to Truth and Justice bend,
Unless out-bullied by his friend:
Brave with the coward, with the brave
He is himself a coward slave:
Awed by his fears, he has no heart
To take a great and open part:
Mines in a subtle train he springs,
And, secret, saps the cars of kings;   1860
But not e'en there continues firm
'Gainst the resistance of a worm:
Born in a country, where the will
Of one is law to all, he still
Retain'd th' infection, with full aim
To spread it wheresoe'er he came;
Freedom he hated, Law defied,
The prostitute of Power and Pride;
Law he with ease explains away,
And leads bewilder'd Sense astray;   1870
Much to the credit of his brain,
Puzzles the cause he can't maintain;
Proceeds on most familiar grounds,
And where he can't convince, confounds;
Talents of rarest stamp and size,
To Nature false, he misapplies,
And turns to poison what was sent
For purposes of nourishment.

---

[1] 'Faithful to James:' alluding to the Earl of Mansfield's original pre-
dilection for the Pretender.

Paleness, not such as on his wings   1879
The messenger of Sickness brings,
But such as takes its coward rise
From conscious baseness, conscious vice,
O'erspread his cheeks ; Disdain and Pride,
To upstart fortunes ever tied,
Scowl'd on his brow ; within his eye,
Insidious, lurking like a spy,
To Caution principled by Fear,
Not daring open to appear,
Lodged covert Mischief ; Passion hung
On his lip quivering ; on his tongue   1890
Fraud dwelt at large ; within his breast
All that makes villain found a nest ;
All that, on Hell's completest plan,
E'er join'd to damn the heart of man.
    Soon as the car reach'd land, he rose,
And, with a look which might have froze
The heart's best blood, which was enough
Had hearts been made of sterner stuff
In cities than elsewhere, to make
The very stoutest quail and quake,   1900
He cast his baleful eyes around :
Fix'd without motion to the ground,
Fear waiting on Surprise, all stood,
And horror chill'd their curdled blood ;
No more they thought of pomp, no more
(For they had seen his face before)
Of law they thought ; the cause forgot,
Whether it was or ghost, or plot,
Which drew them there : they all stood more
Like statues than they were before.   1910
    What could be done ?   Could Art, could Force,
Or both, direct a proper course

To make this savage monster tame,   1913
Or send him back the way he came ?
    What neither art, nor force, nor both,
Could do, a Lord of foreign growth,
A Lord to that base wretch allied
In country, not in vice and pride,
Effected ; from the self-same land,
(Bad news for our blaspheming band   1920
Of scribblers, but deserving note)
The poison came and antidote.
Abash'd, the monster hung his head,
And like an empty vision fled ;
His train, like virgin snows, which run,
Kiss'd by the burning bawdy sun,
To love-sick streams, dissolved in air ;
Joy, who from absence seem'd more fair,
Came smiling, freed from slavish Awe ;
Loyalty, Liberty, and Law,   1930
Impatient of the galling chain,
And yoke of Power, resumed their reign ;
And, burning with the glorious flame
Of public virtue, Mansfield came.

THE CANDIDATE.

This poem was written in 1764, on occasion of the contest between the Earls of Hardwicke and Sandwich for the High-stewardship of the University of Cambridge, vacant by the death of the Lord Chancellor Hardwicke. The spirit of party ran high in the University, and no means were left untried by either candidate to obtain a majority. The election was fixed for the 30th of March, when, after much altercation, the votes appearing equal, a scrutiny was demanded ; whereupon the Vice-Chancellor adjourned the senate *sine die.* On appeal to the Lord High-Chancellor, he determined in favour of the Earl of Hardwicke, and a mandamus issued accordingly.

ENOUGH of Actors—let them play the player, 1
And, free from censure, fret, sweat, strut, and stare ;
Garrick [1] abroad, what motives can engage
To waste one couplet on a barren stage ?
Ungrateful Garrick ! when these tasty days,
In justice to themselves, allow'd thee praise ;
When, at thy bidding, Sense, for twenty years,
Indulged in laughter, or dissolved in tears ;
When in return for labour, time, and health,
The town had given some little share of wealth, 10
Couldst thou repine at being still a slave ?
Dar'st thou presume t' enjoy that wealth she gave ?
Couldst thou repine at laws ordain'd by those
Whom nothing but thy merit made thy foes ?
Whom, too refined for honesty and trade,
By need made tradesmen, Pride had bankrupts made ;
Whom Fear made drunkards, and, by modern rules,
Whom Drink made wits, though Nature made them fools ;
With such, beyond all pardon is thy crime,
In such a manner, and at such a time, 20
To quit the stage ; but men of real sense,
Who neither lightly give, nor take offence,
Shall own thee clear, or pass an act of grace,
Since thou hast left a Powell in thy place.
　　Enough of Authors—why, when scribblers fail,
Must other scribblers spread the hateful tale ?
Why must they pity, why contempt express,
And why insult a brother in distress ?
Let those, who boast th' uncommon gift of brains
The laurel pluck, and wear it for their pains ; 30
Fresh on their brows for ages let it bloom,
And, ages past, still flourish round their tomb.

---

[1] ' Garrick abroad :' Garrick, in September 1763, in order to make his value
more appreciated after his return, resolved to visit the continent.

Let those who without genius write, and write,　　33
Versemen or prosemen, all in Nature's spite,
The pen laid down, their course of folly run
In peace, unread, unmention'd, be undone.
Why should I tell, to cross the will of Fate,
That Francis once endeavour'd to translate?
Why, sweet oblivion winding round his head,
Should I recall poor Murphy from the dead?　　40
Why may not Langhorne,[1] simple in his lay,
Effusion on effusion pour away;
With friendship and with fancy trifle here,
Or sleep in pastoral at Belvidere?
Sleep let them all, with Dulness on her throne,
Secure from any malice but their own.
　　Enough of Critics—let them, if they please,
Fond of new pomp, each month pass new decrees;
Wide and extensive be their infant state,
Their subjects many, and those subjects great,　　50
Whilst all their mandates as sound law succeed,
With fools who write, and greater fools who read.
What though they lay the realms of Genius waste,
Fetter the fancy and debauch the taste;
Though they, like doctors, to approve their skill,
Consult not how to cure, but how to kill;
Though by whim, envy, or resentment led,
They damn those authors whom they never read;
Though, other rules unknown, one rule they hold,
To deal out so much praise for so much gold:　　60
Though Scot with Scot, in damnèd close intrigues,
Against the commonwealth of letters leagues;
Uncensured let them pilot at the helm,
And rule in letters, as they ruled the realm:

---

[1] 'Langhorne:' John Langhorne, D.D., the translator of Plutarch.

Ours be the curse, the mean tame coward's curse,   65
(Nor could ingenious Malice make a worse,
To do our sense and honour deep despite)
To credit what they say, read what they write.
    Enough of Scotland—let her rest in peace ;
The cause removed, effects of course should cease ;   70
Why should I tell, how Tweed, too mighty grown,
And proudly swell'd with waters not his own,
Burst o'er his banks, and, by Destruction led,
O'er our fair England desolation spread,
Whilst, riding on his waves, Ambition, plumed
In tenfold pride, the port of Bute assumed,
Now that the river god, convinced, though late,
And yielding, though reluctantly, to Fate,
Holds his fair course, and with more humble tides,
In tribute to the sea, as usual, glides?   80
    Enough of States, and such like trifling things ;
Enough of kinglings, and enough of kings ;
Henceforth, secure, let ambush'd statesmen lie,
Spread the court web, and catch the patriot fly ;
Henceforth, unwhipt of Justice, uncontroll'd
By fear or shame, let Vice, secure and bold,
Lord it with all her sons, whilst Virtue's groan
Meets with compassion only from the throne.
    Enough of Patriots—all I ask of man
Is only to be honest as he can :   90
Some have deceived, and some may still deceive ;
'Tis the fool's curse at random to believe.
Would those, who, by opinion placed on high,
Stand fair and perfect in their country's eye,
Maintain that honour, let me in their ear
Hint this essential doctrine—Persevere.
Should they (which Heaven forbid) to win the grace
Of some proud courtier, or to gain a place,

z

Their king and country sell, with endless shame   99
Th' avenging Muse shall mark each traitorous name ;
But if, to Honour true, they scorn to bend,
And, proudly honest, hold out to the end,
Their grateful country shall their fame record,
And I myself descend to praise a lord.

    Enough of Wilkes—with good and honest men '
His actions speak much stronger than my pen,
And future ages shall his name adore,
When he can act and I can write no more.
England may prove ungrateful and unjust,
But fostering France [1] shall ne'er betray her trust :   110
'Tis a brave debt which gods on men impose,
To pay with praise the merit e'en of foes.
When the great warrior of Amilcar's race
Made Rome's wide empire tremble to her base,
To prove her virtue, though it gall'd her pride,
Rome gave that fame which Carthage had denied.

    Enough of Self—that darling luscious theme,
O'er which philosophers in raptures dream ;
Of which with seeming disregard they write,
Then prizing most, when most they seem to slight ;   120
Vain proof of folly tinctured strong with pride !
What man can from himself, himself divide ?
For me, (nor dare I lie) my leading aim
(Conscience first satisfied) is love of fame ;
Some little fame derived from some brave few,
Who, prizing Honour, prize her votaries too.
Let all (nor shall resentment flush my cheek)
Who know me well, what they know, freely speak,
So those (the greatest curse I meet below)
Who know me not, may not pretend to know.   130

    [1] ' France:' Wilkes had fled to France to escape the prosecutions entered against him.

Let none of those whom, bless'd with parts above   131
My feeble genius, still I dare to love,
Doing more mischief than a thousand foes,
Posthûmous nonsense to the world expose,
And call it mine ; for mine though never known,
Or which, if mine, I living blush'd to own.
Know all the world, no greedy heir shall find,
Die when I will, one couplet left behind.
Let none of those, whom I despise, though great,
Pretending friendship to give malice weight,   140
Publish my life ; let no false sneaking peer,[1]
(Some such there are) to win the public ear,
Hand me to shame with some vile anecdote,
Nor soul-gall'd bishop[2] damn me with a note.
Let one poor sprig of bay around my head
Bloom whilst I live, and point me out when dead ;
Let it (may Heaven, indulgent, grant that prayer !)
Be planted on my grave, nor wither there ;
And when, on travel bound, some rhyming guest
Roams through the churchyard, whilst his dinner's dress'd,
Let it hold up this comment to his eyes—   151
'Life to the last enjoy'd, here Churchill lies ; '
Whilst (oh, what joy that pleasing flattery gives !)
Reading my works, he cries—' Here Churchill lives.'
    Enough of Satire—in less harden'd times
Great was her force, and mighty were her rhymes.
I've read of men, beyond man's daring brave,
Who yet have trembled at the strokes she gave ;
Whose souls have felt more terrible alarms
From her one line, than from a world in arms.   160
When in her faithful and immortal page
They saw transmitted down from age to age

---

[1] 'Sneaking peer:' John Boyle, Earl of Cork and Orrery, was the author of severe 'Observations on the Life of Swift.'—[2] 'Bishop:' Bishop Warburton.

Recorded villains, and each spotted name   163
Branded with marks of everlasting shame,
Succeeding villains sought·her as a friend,
And, if not really mended, feign'd to mend;
But in an age, when actions are allow'd
Which strike all honour dead, and crimes avow'd
Too terrible to suffer the report,   ⸱
Avow'd and praised by men who stain a court,   170
Propp'd by the arm of Power ; when Vice, high
          born,
High-bred, high-station'd, holds rebuke in scorn ;
When she is lost to every thought of fame,
And, to all virtue dead, is dead to shame ;
When Prudence a much easier task must hold
To make a new world, than reform the old,
Satire throws by her arrows on the ground,
And if she cannot cure, she will not wound.
    Come, Panegyric—though the Muse disdains,
Founded on truth, to prostitute her strains   180
At the base instance of those men, who hold
No argument but power, no god but gold,
Yet, mindful that from Heaven she drew her birth,
She scorns the narrow maxims of this earth ;
Virtuous herself, brings Virtue forth to view,
And loves to praise, where praise is justly due.
    Come, Panegyric—in a former hour,
My soul with pleasure yielding to thy power,
Thy shrine I sought, I pray'd—but wanton air,
Before it reach'd thy ears, dispersed my prayer ;   190
E'en at thy altars whilst I took my stand,
The pen of Truth and Honour in my hand,
Fate, meditating wrath 'gainst me and mine,
Chid my fond zeal, and thwarted my design,

Whilst, Hayter [1] brought too quickly to his end,   195
I lost a subject and mankind a friend.
   Come, Panegyric—bending at thy throne,
Thee and thy power my soul is proud to own
Be thou my kind protector, thou my guide,
And lead me safe through passes yet untried.   200
Broad is the road, nor difficult to find,
Which to the house of Satire leads mankind ;
Narrow and unfrequented are the ways,
Scarce found out in an age, which lead to praise.
   What though no theme I choose of vulgar note,
Nor wish to write as brother bards have wrote,
So mild, so meek in praising, that they seem
Afraid to wake their patrons from a dream ;
What though a theme I choose, which might demand
The nicest touches of a master's hand ;   - 210
Yet, if the inward workings of my soul
Deceive me not, I shall attain the goal,
And Envy shall behold, in triumph raised,
The poet praising, and the patron praised.
   What patron shall I choose ?   Shall public voice,
Or private knowledge, influence my choice ?
Shall I prefer the grand retreat of Stowe,
Or, seeking patriots, to friend Wildman's [2] go ?
   'To Wildman's !' cried Discretion, (who had heard,
Close standing at my elbow, every word)   220
'To Wildman's ! Art thou mad ? Canst thou be sure
One moment there to have thy head secure ?
Are they not all, (let observation tell)
All mark'd in characters as black as Hell,
In Doomsday book, by ministers set down,
Who style their pride the honour of the crown ?

---

[1] ' Hayter : ' Dr Thomas Hayter, Bishop of Norwich, and next of London,
died prematurely.—[2] ' Wildman's : ' a tavern in Albemarle Street.

Make no reply—let Reason stand aloof—   227
Presumptions here must pass as solemn proof.
That settled faith, that love which ever springs
In the best subjects, for the best of kings,
Must not be measured now by what men think,
Or say, or do ;—by what they eat and drink,
Where, and with whom, that question's to be tried,
And statesmen are the judges to decide ;
No juries call'd, or, if call'd, kept in awe ;
They, facts confess'd, in themselves vest the law.
Each dish at Wildman's of sedition smacks ;
Blasphemy may be gospel at Almacks.'[1]

   Peace, good Discretion ! peace—thy fears are vain ;
Ne'er will I herd with Wildman's factious train ;   240
Never the vengeance of the great incur,
Nor, without might, against the mighty stir.
If, from long proof, my temper you distrust,
Weigh my profession, to my gown be just ;
Dost thou one parson know so void of grace
To pay his court to patrons out of place ?
   If still you doubt (though scarce a doubt remains)
Search through my alter'd heart, and try my reins ;
There, searching, find, nor deem me now in sport,
A convert made by Sandwich to the court.   250
Let madmen follow error to the end,
I, of mistakes convinced, and proud to mend,
Strive to act better, being better taught,
Nor blush to own that change which Reason wrought :
For such a change as this, must Justice speak ;
My heart was honest, but my head was weak.
   Bigot to no one man, or set of men,
Without one selfish view, I drew my pen ;

---

[1] ' Almacks :' Old Almacks, a noted Tory club-house in Pall Mall.

My country ask'd, or seem'd to ask, my aid,   259
Obedient to that call, I left off trade ;
A side I chose, and on that side was strong,
Till time hath fairly proved me in the wrong :
Convinced, I change, (can any man do more ?)
And have not greater patriots changed before ?
Changed, I at once, (can any man do less ?)
Without a single blush, that change confess ;
Confess it with a manly kind of pride,
And quit the losing for the winning side,
Granting, whilst virtuous Sandwich holds the rein,
What Bute for ages might have sought in vain.   270

    Hail, Sandwich !—nor shall Wilkes resentment show,
Hearing the praises of so brave a foe—
Hail, Sandwich !—nor, through pride, shalt thou refuse
The grateful tribute of so mean a Muse—
Sandwich, all hail !—when Bute with foreign hand,
Grown wanton with ambition, scourged the land ;
When Scots, or slaves to Scotsmen, steer'd the helm ;
When peace, inglorious peace, disgraced the realm,
Distrust, and general discontent prevail'd ;
But when, (he best knows why) his spirits fail'd ;   280
When, with a sudden panic struck, he fled,
Sneak'd out of power, and hid his recreant head ;
When, like a Mars, (Fear order'd to retreat)
We saw thee nimbly vault into his seat,
Into the seat of power, at one bold leap,
A perfect connoisseur in statesmanship ;
When, like another Machiavel, we saw
Thy fingers twisting, and untwisting law,
Straining, where godlike Reason bade, and where
She warranted thy mercy, pleased to spare ;   290
Saw thee resolved, and fix'd (come what, come might)
To do thy God, thy king, thy country right ;

All things were changed, suspense remain'd no more,
Certainty reign'd where Doubt had reign'd before :   294
All felt thy virtues, and all knew their use,
What virtues such as thine must needs produce.
   Thy foes (for Honour ever meets with foes)
Too mean to praise, too fearful to oppose,
In sullen silence sit ; thy friends (some few,
Who, friends to thee, are friends to Honour too)   300
Plaud thy brave bearing, and the Commonweal
Expects her safety from thy stubborn zeal.
A place amongst the rest the Muses claim,
And bring this freewill-offering to thy fame ;
To prove their virtue, make thy virtues known,
And, holding up thy fame, secure their own.
   From his youth upwards to the present day,
When vices, more than years, have mark'd him gray ;
When riotous Excess, with wasteful hand,
Shakes life's frail glass, and hastes each ebbing sand, 310
Unmindful from what stock he drew his birth,
Untainted with one deed of real worth,
Lothario, holding honour at no price,
Folly to folly added, vice to vice,
Wrought sin with greediness, and sought for shame
With greater zeal than good men seek for fame.
   Where (Reason left without the least defence)
Laughter was mirth, obscenity was sense :
Where Impudence made Decency submit ;
Where noise was humour, and where whim was wit ; 320
Where rude, untemper'd license had the merit
Of liberty, and lunacy was spirit ;
Where the best things were ever held the worst,
Lothario was, with justice, always first.
   To whip a top, to knuckle down at taw,
To swing upon a gate, to ride a straw,

To play at push-pin with dull brother peers,   327
To belch.out catches in a porter's ears,
To reign the monarch of a midnight cell,
To be the gaping chairman's oracle ;
Whilst, in most blessèd union, rogue and whore
Clap hands, huzza, and hiccup out, 'Encore ;'
Whilst gray Authority, who slumbers there
In robes of watchman's fur, gives up his chair ;
With midnight howl to bay the affrighted moon,
To walk with torches through the streets at noon ;
To force plain Nature from her usual way,
Each night a vigil, and a blank each day ;
To match for speed one feather 'gainst another,
To make one leg run races with his brother ;   340
'Gainst all the rest to take the northern wind,
Bute to ride first, and he to ride behind ;
To coin newfangled wagers, and to lay 'em,
Laying to lose, and losing not to pay 'em ;
Lothario, on that stock which Nature gives,
Without a rival stands, though March yet lives.
   When Folly, (at that name, in duty bound,
Let subject myriads kneel, and kiss the ground,
Whilst they who, in the presence, upright stand,
Are held as rebels through the loyal land)   350
Queen every where, but most a queen in courts,
Sent forth her heralds, and proclaim'd her sports ;
Bade fool with fool on her behalf engage,
And prove her right to reign from age to age,
Lothario, great above the common size,
With all engaged, and won from all the prize ;
Her cap he wears, which from his youth he wore,
And every day deserves it more and more.
   Nor in such limits rests his soul confined ;
Folly may share but can't engross his mind ;   ·   360

Vice, bold substantial Vice, puts in her claim,   361
And stamps him perfect in the books of Shame.
Observe his follies well, and you would swear
Folly had been his first, his only care ;
Observe his vices, you'll that oath disown,
And swear that he was born for vice alone.

    Is the soft nature of some hapless maid,
Fond, easy, full of faith, to be betray'd ?
Must she, to virtue lost, be lost to fame,
And he who wrought her guilt declare her shame ?   370
Is some brave friend, who, men but little known,
Deems every heart as honest as his own,
And, free himself, in others fears no guile,
To be ensnared, and ruin'd with a smile ?
Is Law to be perverted from her course ?
Is abject fraud to league with brutal force ?
Is Freedom to be crush'd, and every son
Who dares maintain her cause, to be undone ?
Is base Corruption, creeping through the land,
To plan, and work her ruin, underhand,   380
With regular approaches, sure, though slow ?
Or must she perish by a single blow ?
Are kings, who trust to servants, and depend
In servants (fond, vain thought !) to find a friend,
To be abused, and made to draw their breath
In darkness thicker than the shades of death ?
Is God's most holy name to be profaned,
His word rejected, and his laws arraign'd,
His servants scorn'd, as men who idly dream'd,
His service laugh'd at, and his Son blasphemed ?   390
Are debauchees in morals to preside ?
Is Faith to take an Atheist for her guide ?
Is Science by a blockhead to be led ?
Are States to totter on a drunkard's head ?

To answer all these purposes, and more, 395
More black than ever villain plann'd before,
Search earth, search hell, the Devil cannot find
An agent like Lothario to his mind.

    Is this nobility, which, sprung from kings,
Was meant to swell the power from whence it springs ;
Is this the glorious produce, this the fruit, 401
Which Nature hoped for from so rich a root ?
Were there but two, (search all the world around)
Were there but two such nobles to be found,
The very name would sink into a term
Of scorn, and man would rather be a worm
Than be a lord : but Nature, full of grace,
Nor meaning birth and titles to be base,
Made only one, and having made him, swore,
In mercy to mankind, to make no more : 410
Nor stopp'd she there, but, like a generous friend,
The ills which Error caused, she strove to mend,
And having brought Lothario forth to view,
To save her credit, brought forth Sandwich too.

    Gods ! with what joy, what honest joy of heart,
Blunt as I am, and void of every art,
Of every art which great ones in the state   .
Practise on knaves they fear, and fools they hate,
To titles with reluctance taught to bend,
Nor prone to think that virtues can descend, 420
Do I behold (a sight, alas ! more rare
Than Honesty could wish) the noble wear
His father's honours, when his life makes known
They 're his by virtue, not by birth alone ;
When he recalls his father from the grave,
And pays with interest back that fame he gave :
Cured of her splenetic and sullen fits,
To such a peer my willing soul submits,

And to such virtue is more proud to yield   229
Than 'gainst ten titled rogues to keep the field.
Such, (for that truth e'en Envy shall allow) .
Such Wyndham was, and such is Sandwich now.
    O gentle Montague! in blessed hour
Didst thou start up, and climb the stairs of power ;
England of all her fears at once was eased,   ᒥ
Nor, 'mongst her many foes, was one displeased :
France heard the news, and told it cousin Spain ;   ,
Spain heard, and told it cousin France again ;
The Hollander relinquish'd his design
Of adding spice to spice, and mine to mine ;   440
Of Indian villanies he thought no more,
Content to rob us on our native shore :
Awed by thy fame, (which winds with open mouth
Shall blow from east to west, from north to south)
The western world shall yield us her increase,
And her wild sons be soften'd into peace ;
Rich eastern monarchs shall exhaust their stores,
And pour unbounded wealth on Albion's shores ;
Unbounded wealth, which from those golden scenes,
And all acquired by honourable means,   450
Some honourable chief shall hither steer,
To pay our debts, and set the nation clear.
    Nabobs themselves, allured by thy renown,
Shall pay due homage to the English crown ;
Shall freely as their king our king receive—
Provided the Directors give them leave.
    Union at home shall mark each rising year,
Nor taxes be complain'd of, though severe ;
Envy her own destroyer shall become,
And Faction with her thousand mouths be dumb :   460
With the meek man thy meekness shall prevail,
Nor with the spirited thy spirit fail :

Some to thy force of reason shall submit,   463
And some be converts to thy princely wit :
Reverence for thee shall still a nation's cries,
A grand concurrence crown a grand excise ;
And unbelievers of the first degree,
Who have no faith in God, have faith in thee.
    When a strange jumble, whimsical and vain,
Possess'd the region of each heated brain ;   470
When some were fools to censure, some to praise,
And all were mad, but mad in different ways ;
When commonwealthsmen, starting at the shade
Which in their own wild fancy had been made,
Of tyrants dream'd, who wore a thorny crown,
And with state bloodhounds hunted Freedom down ;
When others, struck with fancies not less vain,
Saw mighty kings by their own subjects slain,
And, in each friend of Liberty and Law,
With horror big, a future Cromwell saw,   480
Thy manly zeal stept forth, bade discord cease,
And sung each jarring atom into peace ;
Liberty, cheer'd by thy all-cheering eye,
Shall, waking from her trance, live and not die ;
And, patronised by thee, Prerogative
Shall, striding forth at large, not die, but live ;
Whilst Privilege, hung betwixt earth and sky,
Shall not well know whether to live or die.
    When on a rock which overhung the flood,
And seem'd to totter, Commerce shivering stood ;   490
When Credit, building on a sandy shore,
Saw the sea swell, and heard the tempest roar,
Heard death in every blast, and in each wave
Or saw, or fancied that she saw her grave ;
When Property, transferr'd from hand to hand,
Weaken'd by change, crawl'd sickly through the land ;

When mutual confidence was at an end,   497
And man no longer could on man depend ;
Oppress'd with debts of more than common weight,
When all men fear'd a bankruptcy of state ;
When, certain death to honour, and to trade,
A sponge was talk'd of as our only aid ;
That to be saved we must be more undone,
And pay off all our debts, by paying none ;
Like England's better genius, born to bless,
And snatch his sinking country from distress,
Didst thou step forth, and, without sail or oar,
Pilot the shatter'd vessel safe to shore :
Nor shalt thou quit, till, anchor'd firm and fast,
She rides secure, and mocks the threatening blast !   510
    Born in thy house, and in thy service bred,
Nursed in thy arms, and at thy table fed,
By thy sage counsels to reflection brought,
Yet more by pattern than by precept taught,
Economy her needful aid shall join
To forward and complete thy grand design,
And, warm to save, but yet with spirit warm,
Shall her own conduct from thy conduct form.
Let friends of prodigals say what they will,
Spendthrifts at home, abroad are spendthrifts still.   520
In vain have sly and subtle sophists tried
Private from public justice to divide ;
For credit on each other they rely,
They live together, and together die,
'Gainst all experience 'tis a rank offence,
High treason in the eye of Common-sense,
To think a statesman ever can be known
To pay our debts, who will not pay his own :
But now, though late, now may we hope to see
Our debts discharged, our credit fair and free,   530

Since rigid Honesty (fair fall that hour !)   531
Sits at the helm, and Sandwich is in power.
With what delight I view thee, wondrous man,
With what delight survey thy sterling plan,
That plan which all with wonder must behold,
And stamp thy age the only age of Gold.
    Nor rest thy triumphs here—that Discord fled,
And sought with grief the hell where she was bred ;
That Faction, 'gainst her nature forced to yield,
Saw her rude rabble scatter'd o'er the field,   540
Saw her best friends a standing jest become,
Her fools turn'd speakers, and her wits struck dumb ;
That our most bitter foes (so much depends
On men of name) are turn'd to cordial friends ;
That our offended friends (such terror flows
From men of name) dare not appear our foes ;
That Credit, gasping in the jaws of Death,
And ready to expire with every breath,
Grows stronger from disease ; that thou hast saved
Thy drooping country ; that thy name, engraved   550
On plates of brass, defies the rage of Time ;
Than plates of brass more firm, that sacred rhyme
Embalms thy memory, bids thy glories live,
And gives thee what the Muse alone can give :—
These heights of Virtue, these rewards of Fame,
With thee in common other patriots claim.
    But, that poor sickly Science, who had laid
And droop'd for years beneath Neglect's cold shade,
By those who knew her purposely forgot,
And made the jest of those who knew her not :   560
Whilst Ignorance in power, and pamper'd pride,
' Clad like a priest, pass'd by on t' other side,'
Recover'd from her wretched state, at length
Puts on new health, and clothes herself with strength,

To thee we owe, and to thy friendly hand   565
Which raised, and gave her to possess the land :
This praise, though in a court, and near a throne,
· This praise is thine, and thine, alas ! alone.
    With what fond rapture did the goddess smile,
What blessings did she promise to this isle,   570
What honour to herself, and length of reign,   ).
Soon as she heard that thou didst not disdain
To be her steward ; but what grief, what shame,
What rage, what disappointment, shook her frame,
When her proud children dared her will dispute,
When Youth was insolent,[1] and Age was mute !
    That young men should be fools, and some wild few,
To Wisdom deaf, be deaf to Interest too,
Moved not her wonder ; but that men, grown gray
In search of wisdom ; men who own'd the sway   580
Of Reason ; men who stubbornly kept down
Each rising passion ; men who wore the gown ;
That they should cross her will, that they should dare
Against the cause of Interest to declare ;
That they should be so abject and unwise,
Having no fear of loss before their eyes,   .
Nor hopes of gain ; scorning the ready means
Of being vicars, rectors, canons, deans,
With all those honours which on mitres wait,
And mark the virtuous favourites of state ;   590
That they should dare a Hardwicke to support,
And talk, within the hearing of a court,
Of that vile beggar, Conscience, who, undone,
And starved herself, starves every wretched son ;
This turn'd her blood to gall, this made her swear
No more to throw away her time and care

---

[1] ' Youth was insolent : ' the younger members of the University were unanimous in favour of Lord Hardwicke, and incurred the censure of their superiors.

On wayward sons who scorn'd her love, no more   597
To hold her courts on Cam's ungrateful shore.
Rather than bear such insults, which disgrace
Her royalty of nature, birth, and place,
Though Dulness there unrivall'd state doth keep,
Would she at Winchester with Burton [1] sleep ;
Or, to exchange the mortifying scene
For something still more dull, and still more mean,
Rather than bear such insults, she would fly
Far, far beyond the search of English eye,
And reign amongst the Scots : to be a queen
Is worth ambition, though in Aberdeen.
Oh, stay thy flight, fair Science ! what though some,
Some base-born children, rebels are become ?   610
All are not rebels ; some are duteous still,
Attend thy precepts, and obey thy will ;
Thy interest is opposed by those alone
Who either know not, or oppose their own.

   Of stubborn virtue, marching to thy aid,
Behold in black, the livery of their trade,
Marshall'd by Form, and by Discretion led,
A grave, grave troop, and Smith [2] is at their head,
Black Smith of Trinity ; on Christian ground
For faith in mysteries none more renown'd.   620
Next, (for the best of causes now and then
Must beg assistance from the worst of men)
Next (if old story lies not) sprung from Greece,
Comes Pandarus, but comes without his niece :
Her, wretched maid ! committed to his trust,
To a rank letcher's coarse and bloated lust
The arch, old, hoary hypocrite had sold,
And thought himself and her well damn'd for gold.

---

[1] ' Burton :' Dr John Burton, head master of Winchester school.—[2] ' Smith :'
Dr Smith, master of Trinity College, Cambridge, a mechanical and musical
genius.

But (to wipe off such traces from the mind,   629
And make us in good humour with mankind)
Leading on men, who, in a college bred,
No woman knew, but those which made their bed ;
Who, planted virgins on Cam's virtuous shore,
Continued still male virgins at threescore,
Comes Sumner,[1] wise, and chaste as chaste can be,
With Long,[2] as wise, and not less chaste than he.

   Are there not friends, too, enter'd in thy cause
Who, for thy sake, defying penal laws,
Were, to support thy honourable plan,
Smuggled from Jersey, and the Isle of Man ?   640
Are there not Philomaths of high degree
Who, always dumb before, shall speak for thee ?
Are there not Proctors, faithful to thy will,
One of full growth, others in embryo still,
Who may, perhaps, in some ten years, or more,
Be ascertain'd that two and two make four,
Or may a still more happy method find,
And, taking one from two, leave none behind ?

   With such a mighty power on foot, to yield
Were death to manhood ; better in the field   650
To leave our carcases, and die with fame,
Than fly, and purchase life on terms of shame.
Sackvilles [3] alone anticipate defeat,
And ere they dare the battle, sound retreat.

   But if persuasions ineffectual prove,
If arguments are vain, nor prayers can move,
Yet in thy bitterness of frantic woe
Why talk of Burton ? why to Scotland go ?
Is there not Oxford ? she, with open arms,
Shall meet thy wish, and yield up all her charms :   660

---

[1] ' Sumner : ' the Rev. Dr Humphrey Sumner, Vice Chancellor of the University of Cambridge.—[2] ' Long : ' Roger Long, D.D., professor of Astronomy, Cambridge.—[3] ' Sackville : ' Sir George, who behaved scandalously at the battle of Minden.

Shall for thy love her former loves resign,   661
And jilt the banish'd Stuarts to be thine.

Bow'd to the yoke, and, soon as she could read,
Tutor'd to get by heart the despot's creed,
She, of subjection proud, shall knee thy throne,
And have no principles but thine alone ;
She shall thy will implicitly receive,
Nor act, nor speak, nor think, without thy leave.
Where is the glory of imperial sway
If subjects none but just commands obey ?   670
Then, and then only, is obedience seen,
When by command they dare do all that's mean :
Hither, then, wing thy flight, here fix thy stand,
Nor fail to bring thy Sandwich in thy hand.

Gods! with what joy, (for Fancy now supplies,
And lays the future open to my eyes)
Gods! with what joy I see the worthies meet,
And Brother Litchfield [1] Brother Sandwich greet !
Blest be your greetings, blest each dear embrace ;
Blest to yourselves, and to the human race.   680
Sickening at virtues, which she cannot reach,
Which seem her baser nature to impeach,
Let Envy, in a whirlwind's bosom hurl'd,
Outrageous, search the corners of the world,
Ransack the present times, look back to past,
Rip up the future, and confess at last,
No times, past, present, or to come, could e'er
Produce, and bless the world with such a pair.

Phillips,[2] the good old Phillips, out of breath,
Escaped from Monmouth, and escaped from death,   690

---

[1] 'Brother Litchfield:' the last Earl of Litchfield succeeded the Earl of Westmoreland as Chancellor of the University of Oxford, in 1762, through Lord Bute's influence.—[2] 'Phillips:' Sir John Phillips, a barrister and active member of the House of Commons, a defender of the rebellion in 1745.

Shall hail his Sandwich with that virtuous zeal,   691
That glorious ardour for the commonweal,
Which warm'd his loyal heart and bless'd his tongue,
When on his lips the cause of rebels hung ;
Whilst Womanhood, in habit of a nun,
At Medenham [1] lies, by backward monks undone ;
A nation's reckoning, like an alehouse score,
Whilst Paul, the agèd, chalks behind a door,
Compell'd to hire a foe to cast it up,
Dashwood shall pour, from a communion cup,   700
Libations to the goddess without eyes,
And hob or nob in cider and excise.

From those deep shades, where Vanity, unknown,
Doth penance for her pride, and pines alone,
Cursed in herself, by her own thoughts undone,
Where she sees all, but can be seen by none ;
Where she, no longer mistress of the schools,
Hears praise loud pealing from the mouths of fools,
Or hears it at a distance, in despair
To join the crowd, and put in for a share,   710
Twisting each thought a thousand different ways,
For his new friends new-modelling old praise ;
Where frugal sense so very fine is spun,
It serves twelve hours, though not enough for one,
King [2] shall arise, and, bursting from the dead,
Shall hurl his piebald Latin at thy head.

Burton (whilst awkward affectation hung
In quaint and labour'd accents on his tongue,
Who 'gainst their will makes junior blockheads speak,
Ignorant of both, new Latin and new Greek,   720

---

[1] 'Medenham:' or as it was commonly called, Mednam Abbey, was a very large house on the banks of the Thames, near Marlow, in Bucks, where infamous doings went on under the auspices of Sir F. Dashwood, Lord Sandwich, and others.—[2] 'King:' Dr William King, LL.D., Principal of St Mary's Hall.

Not such as was in Greece and Latium known,   721
But of a modern cut, and all his own ;
Who threads, like beads, loose thoughts on such a string,
They 're praise and censure ; nothing, every thing ;
Pantomime thoughts, and style so full of trick,
They even make a Merry Andrew sick ;
Thoughts all so dull, so pliant in their growth,
They 're verse, they 're prose, they 're neither, and
      they 're both)
Shall (though by nature ever loth to praise)
Thy curious worth set forth in curious phrase ;   730
Obscurely stiff, shall press poor Sense to death,
Or in long periods run her out of breath ;
Shall make a babe, for which, with all his fame,
Adam could not have found a proper name,
Whilst, beating out his features to a smile,
He hugs the bastard brat, and calls it Style.

Hush'd be all Nature as the land of Death ;
Let each stream sleep, and each wind hold his breath ;
Be the bells muffled, nor one sound of Care,
Pressing for audience, wake the slumbering air ;   740
Browne [1] comes—behold how cautiously he creeps—
How slow he walks, and yet how fast he sleeps—
But to thy praise in sleep he shall agree ;
He cannot wake, but he shall dream of thee.

Physic, her head with opiate poppies crown'd,
Her loins by the chaste matron Camphire bound ;
Physic, obtaining succour from the pen
Of her soft son, her gentle Heberden,[2]
If there are men who can thy virtue know,
Yet spite of virtue treat thee as a foe,   750

---

[1] 'Browne :' Dr William Browne, Lord Litchfield's Vice-Chancellor of the University of Oxford from 1759 to 1769.—[2] 'Heberden :' Dr William Heberden, the celebrated physician, the first who used the wet-sheet.

Shall, like a scholar, stop their rebel breath,   751
And in each recipe send classic death.
    So deep in knowledge, that few lines can sound
And plumb the bottom of that vast profound,
Few grave ones with such gravity can think,
Or follow half so fast as he can sink;
With nice distinctions glossing o'er the text,
Obscure with meaning, and in words perplex'd,
With subtleties on subtleties refined,
Meant to divide and subdivide the mind,   760
Keeping the forwardness of youth in awe,
The scowling Blackstone[1] bears the train of law.
    Divinity, enrobed in college fur,
In her right hand a new Court Calendar,
Bound like a book of prayer, thy coming waits
With all her pack, to hymn thee in the gates.
    Loyalty, fix'd on Isis' alter'd shore,
A stranger long, but stranger now no more,
Shall pitch her tabernacle, and, with eyes
Brimful of rapture, view her new allies;   770
Shall, with much pleasure and more wonder, view
Men great at court, and great at Oxford too.
    O sacred Loyalty! accursed be those
Who, seeming friends, turn out thy deadliest foes,
Who prostitute to kings thy honour'd name,
And soothe their passions to betray their fame;
Nor praised be those, to whose proud nature clings
Contempt of government, and hate of kings,
Who, willing to be free, not knowing how,
A strange intemperance of zeal avow,   780
And start at Loyalty, as at a word
Which without danger Freedom never heard.

---

[1] 'Blackstone:' Dr Blackstone, afterwards Sir William Blackstone, Solicitor-General, and a Judge of the Court of Common Pleas.

Vain errors of vain men—wild both extremes.   783
And to the state not wholesome, like the dreams,
Children of night, of Indigestion bred,
Which, Reason clouded, seize and turn the head ;
Loyalty without Freedom is a chain
Which men of liberal notice can't sustain ;
And Freedom without Loyalty, a name
Which nothing means, or means licentious shame.   790
   Thine be the art, my Sandwich, thine the toil,
In Oxford's stubborn and untoward soil
To rear this plant of union, till at length,
Rooted by time, and foster'd into strength,
Shooting aloft, all danger it defies,
And proudly lifts its branches to the skies ;
Whilst, Wisdom's happy son but not her slave,
Gay with the gay, and with the grave ones grave,
Free from the dull impertinence of thought,
Beneath that shade, which thy own labours wrought 800
And fashion'd into strength, shalt thou repose,
Secure of liberal praise, since Isis flows,
True to her Tame, as duty hath decreed,
Nor longer, like a harlot, lust for Tweed,
And those old wreaths, which Oxford once dared twine
To grace a Stuart brow, she plants on thine.

THE FAREWELL.

P. FAREWELL to Europe, and at once farewell
To all the follies which in Europe dwell ;
To Eastern India now, a richer clime,
Richer, alas ! in everything but rhyme,

The Muses steer their course ; and, <u>fond of change,</u>   5
At large, in other worlds, desire to range ;
Resolved, at least, since they the fool must play,
To do it in a different place, and way.
   F. What whim is this, what error of the brain,
What madness worse than in the dog-star's reign ?   10
Why into foreign countries would you roam,
Are there not knaves and fools enough at home ?
If satire be thy object—and thy lays
As yet have shown no talents fit for praise—
If satire be thy object, search all round,
Nor to thy purpose can one spot be found
Like England, where, to rampant vigour grown,
Vice chokes up every virtue ; where, self-sown,
The seeds of folly shoot forth rank and bold,
And every seed brings forth a hundredfold.   20
   P. No more of this—though Truth, (the more our shame,
The more our guilt) though Truth perhaps may claim,
And justify her part in this, yet here,
For the first time, e'en Truth offends my ear ;
Declaim from morn to night, from night to morn,
Take up the theme anew, when day 's new-born,
I hear, and hate—be England what she will,
With all her faults, she is my country still.
   F. Thy country ! and what then ? Is that mere word
Against the voice of Reason to be heard ?   30
Are prejudices, deep imbibed in youth,
To counteract, and make thee hate the truth ?
'Tis sure the symptom of a narrow soul
To draw its grand attachment from the whole,
And take up with a part ; men, not confined
Within such paltry limits, men design'd
Their nature to exalt, where'er they go,
Wherever waves can roll, and winds can blow,

Where'er the blessed sun, placed in the sky   39
To watch this subject world, can dart his eye,
Are still the same, and, prejudice outgrown,
Consider every country as their own ;
At one grand view they take in Nature's plan,
Not more at home in England than Japan.

   P. My good, grave Sir of Theory, whose wit,
Grasping at shadows, ne'er caught substance yet,
'Tis mighty easy o'er a glass of wine
On vain refinements vainly to refine,
To laugh at poverty in plenty's reign,
To boast of apathy when out of pain,   50
And in each sentence, worthy of the schools,
Varnish'd with sophistry, to deal out rules
Most fit for practice, but for one poor fault
That into practice they can ne'er be brought.

   At home, and sitting in your elbow-chair,
You praise Japan, though you was never there :
But was the ship this moment under sail,
Would not your mind be changed, your spirits fail ?
Would you not cast one longing eye to shore,
And vow to deal in such wild schemes no more ?   60
Howe'er our pride may tempt us to conceal
Those passions which we cannot choose but feel,
There 's a strange something, which, without a brain,
Fools feel, and which e'en wise men can't explain,
Planted in man to bind him to that earth,
In dearest ties, from whence he drew his birth.

   If Honour calls, where'er she points the way
The sons of Honour follow, and obey ;
If need compels, wherever we are sent
'Tis want of courage not to be content ;   70
But, if we have the liberty of choice,
And all depends on our own single voice,

To deem of every country as the same   · 73
Is rank rebellion 'gainst the lawful claim
Of Nature, and such dull indifference
May be philosophy, but can't be sense.
     F. Weak and unjust distinction, strange design,
Most peevish, most perverse, to undermine
Philosophy, and throw her empire down
By means of Sense, from whom she holds her crown. 80
Divine Philosophy! to thee we owe
All that is worth possessing here below ;
Virtue and wisdom consecrate thy reign,
Doubled each joy, and pain no longer pain.
     When, like a garden, where, for want of toil
And wholesome discipline, the rich, rank soil
Teems with incumbrances ; where all around,
Herbs, noxious in their nature, make the ground,
Like the good mother of a thankless son,
Curse her own womb, by fruitfulness undone ;   .   90
Like such a garden, when the human soul,
Uncultured, wild, impatient of control,
Brings forth those passions of luxuriant race,
Which spread, and stifle every herb of grace ;
Whilst Virtue, check'd by the cold hand of Scorn,
Seems withering on the bed where she was born,
Philosophy steps in ; with steady hand,
She brings her aid, she clears the encumber'd land ;
Too virtuous to spare Vice one stroke, too wise
One moment to attend to Pity's cries—   100
See with what godlike, what relentless power
She roots up every weed !
     P.   And every flower.
Philosophy, a name of meek degree,   ·
Embraced, in token of humility,

By the proud sage, who, whilst he strove to hide, 105
In that vain artifice reveal'd his pride ;
Philosophy, whom Nature had design'd
To purge all errors from the human mind,
Herself misled by the philosopher,
At once her priest and master, made us err : 110
Pride, pride, like leaven in a mass of flour,
Tainted her laws, and made e'en Virtue sour.
　Had she, content within her proper sphere,
Taught lessons suited to the human ear,
Which might fair Virtue's genuine fruits produce,
Made not for ornament, but real use,
The heart of man, unrivall'd, she had sway'd,
· Praised by the good, and by the bad obey'd ;
But when she, overturning Reason's throne,
Strove proudly in its place to plant her own ; 120
When she with apathy the breast would steel,.
And teach us, deeply feeling, not to feel ;
When she would wildly all her force employ,
Not to correct our passions, but destroy ;
When, not content our nature to restore,
As made by God, she made it all new o'er ;
When, with a strange and criminal excess,
To make us more than men, she made us less ;
The good her dwindled power with pity saw,
The bad with joy, and none but fools with awe. 130
　Truth, with a simple and unvarnish'd tale,
E'en from the mouth of Norton might prevail,
Could she get there ; but Falsehood's sugar'd strain
Should pour her fatal blandishments in vain,
Nor make one convert, though the Siren hung,
Where she too often hangs, on Mansfield's.tongue.
Should all the Sophs, whom in his course the sun
Hath seen, or past, or present, rise in one ;

Should he, whilst pleasure in each sentence flows,   139
Like Plato, give us poetry in prose ;
Should he, full orator, at once impart
Th' Athenian's genius with the Roman's art ;
Genius and Art should in this instance fail,
Nor Rome, though join'd with Athens, here prevail.
'Tis not in man, 'tis not in more than man,
To make me find one fault in Nature's plan.
Placed low ourselves, we censure those above,
And, wanting judgment, think that she wants love ;
Blame, where we ought in reason to commend,
And think her most a foe when most a friend.   150
Such be philosophers—their specious art,
Though Friendship pleads, shall never warp my heart,
Ne'er make me from this breast one passion tear,
Which Nature, my best friend, hath planted there.
   F. Forgiving as a friend, what, whilst I live,
As a philosopher I can't forgive,
In this one point at last I join with you,
To Nature pay all that is Nature's due ;
But let not clouded Reason sink so low,
To fancy debts she does not, cannot owe :   160
Bear, to full manhood grown, those shackles bear,
Which Nature meant us for a time to wear,
As we wear leading-strings, which, useless grown,
Are laid aside, when we can walk alone ;
But on thyself, by peevish humour sway'd,
Wilt thou lay burdens Nature never laid ?
Wilt thou make faults, whilst Judgment weakly errs,
And then defend, mistaking them for hers ?
Dar'st thou to say, in our enlighten'd age,
That this grand master passion, this brave rage,   170
Which flames out for thy country, was impress'd
And fix'd by Nature in the human breast ?

If you prefer the place where you were born,   173
And hold all others in contempt and scorn,
On fair comparison ; if on that land
With liberal, and a more than equal hand,
Her gifts, as in profusion, Plenty sends ;
If Virtue meets with more and better friends ;
If Science finds a patron 'mongst the great ;
If Honesty is minister of state ;   180
If Power, the guardian of our rights design'd,
Is to that great, that only end, confined ;
If riches are employ'd to bless the poor ;
If Law is sacred, Liberty secure ;
Let but these facts depend on proofs of weight,
Reason declares thy love can't be too great,
And, in this light could he our country view,
A very Hottentot must love it too.
    But if, by Fate's decrees, you owe your birth
To some most barren and penurious earth,   190
Where, every comfort of this life denied,
Her real wants are scantily supplied ;
Where Power is Reason, Liberty a joke,
Laws never made, or made but to be broke ;
To fix thy love on such a wretched spot,
Because in Lust's wild fever there begot ;
Because, thy weight no longer fit to bear,
By chance, not choice, thy mother dropp'd thee there,
Is folly, which admits not of defence ;
It can't be Nature, for it is not sense.   200
By the same argument which here you hold,
(When Falsehood's insolent, let Truth be told)
If Propagation can in torments dwell,
A devil must, if born there, love his Hell.
    P. Had Fate, to whose decrees I lowly bend,
And e'en in punishment confess a friend,

Ordain'd my birth in some place yet untried,   207
On purpose made to mortify my pride,
Where the sun never gave one glimpse of day,
Where Science never yet could dart one ray,
Had I been born on some bleak, blasted plain
Of barren Scotland, in a Stuart's reign,
Or in some kingdom, where men, weak, or worse,
Turn'd Nature's every blessing to a curse ;
Where crowns of freedom, by the fathers won,
Dropp'd leaf by leaf from each degenerate son ;
In spite of all the wisdom you display,
All you have said, and yet may have to say,
My weakness here, if weakness I confess,
I, as my country, had not loved her less.   220
    Whether strict Reason bears me out in this,
Let those who, always seeking, always miss
The ways of Reason, doubt with precious zeal ;
Theirs be the praise to argue, mine to feel.
Wish we to trace this passion to the root,
We, like a tree, may know it by its fruit ;
From its rich stem ten thousand virtues spring,
Ten thousand blessings on its branches cling ;
Yet in the circle of revolving years
Not one misfortune, not one vice, appears.   230
Hence, then, and what you Reason call, adore ;
This, if not Reason, must be something more.
    But (for I wish not others to confine ;
Be their opinions unrestrain'd as mine)
Whether this love 's of good or evil growth,
A vice, a virtue, or a spice of both,
Let men of nicer argument decide ;
If it is virtuous, soothe an honest pride
With liberal praise ; if vicious, be content,
It is a vice I never can repent ;   240

A vice which, weigh'd in Heaven, shall more avail   241
Than ten cold virtues in the other scale.

F. This wild, untemper'd zeal (which, after all,
We, candour unimpeach'd, might madness call)
Is it a virtue ? That you scarce pretend ;
Or can it be a vice, like Virtue's friend,
Which draws us off from and dissolves the force
Of private ties, nay, stops us in our course
To that grand object of the human soul,
That nobler love which comprehends the whole ?   250
Coop'd in the limits of this petty isle,
This nook, which scarce deserves a frown or smile,
Weigh'd with Creation, you, by whim undone,
Give all your thoughts to what is scarce worth one.
The generous soul, by Nature taught to soar,
Her strength confirm'd in philosophic lore,
At one grand view takes in a world with ease,
And, seeing all mankind, loves all she sees.

P. Was it most sure, which yet a doubt endures,
Not found in Reason's creed, though found in yours, 260
That these two services, like what we 're told,
And know, of God's and Mammon's, cannot hold
And draw together ; that, however loth,
We neither serve, attempting to serve both,
I could not doubt a moment which to choose,
And which in common reason to refuse.

Invented oft for purposes of art,
Born of the head, though father'd on the heart,
This grand love of the world must be confess'd
A barren speculation at the best.   270
Not one man in a thousand, should he live
Beyond the usual term of life, could give,
So rare occasion comes, and to so few,
Proof whether his regards are feign'd, or true.

The love we bear our country is a root   275
Which never fails to bring forth golden fruit ;
'Tis in the mind an everlasting spring
Of glorious actions, which become a king,
Nor less become a subject ; 'tis a debt
Which bad men, though they pay not, can't forget ;   280
A duty, which the good delight to pay,   )
And every man can practise every day.
   Nor, for my life (so very dim my eye,
Or dull your argument) can I descry
What you with faith assert, how that dear love,
Which binds me to my country, can remove,
And make me of necessity forego,
That general love which to the world I owe. '
Those ties of private nature, small extent,
In which the mind of narrow cast is pent,   290
Are only steps on which the generous soul   )
Mounts by degrees till she includes the whole.
That spring of love, which, in the human mind,
Founded on self, flows narrow and confined,
Enlarges as it rolls, and comprehends
The social charities of blood and friends,
Till, smaller streams included, not o'erpast,
It rises to our country's love at last ;
And he, with liberal and enlargèd mind,
Who loves his country, cannot hate mankind.   300
   F. Friend, as you would appear, to Common Sense,
Tell me, or think no more of a defence,
Is it a proof of love by choice to run
A vagrant from your country ?
   P.   Can the son
(Shame, shame on all such sons !) with ruthless eye,
And heart more patient than the flint, stand by,

And by some ruffian, from all shame divorced,
All virtue, see his honour'd mother forced ?
Then—no, by Him that made me ! not e'en then,
Could I with patience, by the worst of men,
Behold my country plunder'd, beggar'd, lost
Beyond redemption, all her glories cross'd,
E'en when occasion made them ripe, her fame
Fled like a dream, while she awakes to shame.

   F. Is it not more the office of a friend,
The office of a patron, to defend
Her sinking state, than basely to decline
So great a cause, and in despair resign ?

   P. Beyond my reach, alas ! the grievance lies,
And, whilst more able patriots doubt, she dies.   320
From a foul source, more deep than we suppose,
Fatally deep and dark, this grievance flows.
'Tis not that peace our glorious hopes defeats :
'Tis not the voice of Faction in the streets ;
'Tis not a gross attack on Freedom made ;
'Tis not the arm of Privilege display'd,
Against the subject, whilst she wears no sting
To disappoint the purpose of a king ;
These are no ills, or trifles, if compared
With those which are contrived, though not declared.

   Tell me, Philosopher, is it a crime   331
To pry into the secret womb of Time ;
Or, born in ignorance, must we despair
To reach events, and read the future there ?
Why, be it so—still 'tis the right of man,
Imparted by his Maker, where he can,
To former times and men his eye to cast,
And judge of what's to come, by what is past.

   Should there be found, in some not distant year,
(Oh, how I wish to be no prophet here !)   340

Amongst our British Lords should there be found   341
Some great in power, in principles unsound,
Who look on Freedom with an evil eye,
In whom the springs of Loyalty are dry ;
Who wish to soar on wild Ambition's wings,
Who hate the Commons, and who love not Kings ;
Who would divide the people and the throne,
To set up separate interests of their own ;
Who hate whatever aids their wholesome growth,
And only join with, to destroy them both ;   350
Should there be found such men in after-times,
May Heaven, in mercy to our grievous crimes,
Allot some milder vengeance, nor to them,
And to their rage, this wretched land condemn.

    Thou God above, on whom all states depend,
Who knowest from the first their rise, and end,
If there's a day mark'd in the book of Fate,
When ruin must involve our equal state ;
When law, alas ! must be no more, and we,
To freedom born, must be no longer free ;   360
Let not a mob of tyrants seize the helm,
Nor titled upstarts league to rob the realm ;
Let not, whatever other ills assail,
A damnèd aristocracy prevail.
If, all too short, our course of freedom run,
'Tis thy good pleasure we should be undone,
Let us, some comfort in our griefs to bring,
Be slaves to one, and be that one a king.

    F. Poets, accustom'd by their trade to feign,
Oft substitute creations of the brain   370
For real substance, and, themselves deceived,
Would have the fiction by mankind believed.
Such is your case—but grant, to soothe your pride,
That you know more than all the world beside,

Why deal in hints, why make a moment's doubt ? 375
Resolved, and like a man, at once speak out ;
Show us our danger, tell us where it lies,
And, to ensure our safety, make us wise.
 P. Rather than bear the pain of thought, fools
  stray ;
The proud will rather lose than ask their way : 380
To men of sense what needs it to unfold,
And tell a tale which they must know untold ?
In the bad, interest warps the canker'd heart,
The good are hoodwink'd by the tricks of art ;
And, whilst arch, subtle hypocrites contrive
To keep the flames of discontent alive ;
Whilst they, with arts to honest men unknown,
Breed doubts between the people and the throne,
Making us fear, where Reason never yet
Allow'd one fear, or could one doubt admit, 390
Themselves pass unsuspected in disguise,
And 'gainst our real danger seal our eyes.
 F. Mark them, and let their names recorded stand
On Shame's black roll, and stink through all the land.
 P. That might some courage, but no prudence be ;
No hurt to them, and jeopardy to me.
 F. Leave out their names.
 P.   For that kind caution, thanks ;
But may not judges sometimes fill up blanks ?
 F. Your country's laws in doubt then you reject ?
 P. The laws I love, the lawyers I suspect. 401
Amongst twelve judges may not one be found
(On bare, bare possibility I ground
This wholesome doubt) who may enlarge, retrench,
Create, and uncreate, and from the bench,
With winks, smiles, nods, and such like paltry arts,
May work and worm into a jury's hearts ?

Or, baffled there, may, turbulent of soul,   408
Cramp their high office, and their rights control ;
Who may, though judge, turn advocate at large,
And deal replies out by the way of charge,
Making Interpretation all the way,
In spite of facts, his wicked will obey,
And, leaving Law without the least defence,
May damn his conscience to approve his sense ?
   F. Whilst, the true guardians of this charter'd land,
In full and perfect vigour, juries stand,
A judge in vain shall awe, cajole, perplex.
   P. Suppose I should be tried in Middlesex ?
   F. To pack a jury they will never dare.   420
   P. There's no occasion to pack juries there.[1]
   F. 'Gainst prejudice all arguments are weak';
Reason herself without effect must speak.
Fly then thy country, like a coward fly,
Renounce her interest, and her laws defy.
But why, bewitch'd, to India turn thine eyes ?
Cannot our Europe thy vast wrath suffice ?
Cannot thy misbegotten Muse lay bare
Her brawny arm, and play the butcher there ?
   P. Thy counsel taken, what should Satire do ?   430
Where could she find an object that is new ?
Those travell'd youths, whom tender mothers wean,
And send abroad to see, and to be seen ;
With whom, lest they should fornicate, or worse,
A tutor's sent by way of a dry nurse ;
Each of whom just enough of spirit bears
To show our follies, and to bring home theirs,
Have made all Europe's vices so well known,
They seem almost as natural as our own.

---

[1] 'Juries there:' alluding to the then recent acquittal from the charge of perjury, by the petty jury, of Mr Philip Carteret Webb, solicitor to the Treasury, who had sworn against Wilkes.

F. Will India for thy purpose better do ?	440
P. In one respect, at least—there 's something new.
F. A harmless people, in whom Nature speaks
Free and untainted, 'mongst whom Satire seeks,
But vainly seeks, so simply plain their hearts,
One bosom where to lodge her poison'd darts.
	P. From knowledge speak you this ? or, doubt on
		doubt
Weigh'd and resolved, hath Reason found it out ?
Neither from knowledge, nor by Reason taught,
You have faith every where, but where you ought.
India or Europe—what 's there in a name ?	450
Propensity to vice in both the same,
Nature alike in both works for man's good,
Alike in both by man himself withstood.
Nabobs, as well as those who hunt them down,
Deserve a cord much better than a crown,
And a Mogul can thrones as much debase
As any polish'd prince of Christian race.
	F. Could you,—a task more hard than you sup-
		pose,—
Could you, in ridicule whilst Satire glows,
Make all their follies to the life appear,	460
'Tis ten to one you gain no credit here ;
Howe'er well drawn, the picture, after all,
Because we know not the original,
Would not find favour in the public eye.
	P. That, having your good leave, I mean to try :
And if your observations sterling hold,
If the piece should be heavy, tame, and cold,
To make it to the side of Nature lean,
And meaning nothing, something seem to mean :
To make the whole in lively colours glow,	470
To bring before us something that we know,

And from all honest men applause to win,   472
I'll group the Company,[1] and put them in.

  F. Be that ungenerous thought by shame suppress'd,
Add not distress to those too much distress'd ;
Have they not, by blind zeal misled, laid bare
Those sores which never might endure the air ?
Have they not brought their mysteries so low,
That what the wise suspected not, fools know ?
From their first rise e'en to the present hour,   480
Have they not proved their own abuse of power,
Made it impossible, if fairly view'd,
Ever to have that dangerous power renew'd,
Whilst, unseduced by ministers, the throne
Regards our interests, and knows its own ?

  P. Should every other subject chance to fail,
Those who have sail'd, and those who wish'd to sail
In the last fleet, afford an ample field,
Which must beyond my hopes a harvest yield.

  F. On such vile food Satire can never thrive.   490
  P. She cannot starve, if there was only Clive.[2]

THE TIMES.

THE time hath been, a boyish, blushing time,
When modesty was scarcely held a crime ;
When the most wicked had some touch of grace,
And trembled to meet Virtue face to face ;
When those, who, in the cause of Sin grown gray,
Had served her without grudging day by day,
Were yet so weak an awkward shame to feel,
And strove that glorious service to conceal :

<hr/>

[1] ' Company :' East Indian Co.—[2] ' Clive :' See Macaulay's Essay.

We, better bred, and than our sires more wise, 9
Such paltry narrowness of soul despise :
To virtue every mean pretence disclaim,
Lay bare our crimes, and glory in our shame.
Time was, ere Temperance had fled the realm,
Ere Luxury sat guttling at the helm
From meal to meal, without one moment's space
Reserved for business or allow'd for grace ;
Ere Vanity had so far conquer'd Sense
To make us all wild rivals in expense,
To make one fool strive to outvie another,
And every coxcomb dress against his brother ; 20
Ere banish'd Industry had left our shores,
And Labour was by Pride kick'd out of doors ;
Ere Idleness prevail'd sole queen in courts,
Or only yielded to a rage for sports ;
Ere each weak mind was with externals caught,
And dissipation held the place of thought ;
Ere gambling lords in vice so far were gone
To cog the die, and bid the sun look on ;
Ere a great nation, not less just than free,
Was made a beggar by economy ; 30
Ere rugged Honesty was out of vogue ;
Ere Fashion stamp'd her sanction on the rogue ;
Time was, that men had conscience, that they made
Scruples to owe what never could be paid.
Was one then found, however high his name,
So far above his fellows damn'd to shame,
Who dared abuse, and falsify his trust,
Who, being great, yet dared to be unjust,
Shunn'd like a plague, or but at distance view'd,
He walk'd the crowded streets in solitude, 40
Nor could his rank and station in the land
Bribe one mean knave to take him by the hand.

Such rigid maxims (Oh ! might such revive   43
To keep expiring Honesty alive)
Made rogues, all other hopes of fame denied,
Not just through principle, be just through pride.
    Our times, more polish'd, wear a different face ;
Debts are an honour, payment a disgrace.
Men of weak minds, high-placed on Folly's list,   '
May gravely tell us trade cannot subsist,   50
Nor all those thousands who 're in trade employ'd,
If faith 'twixt man and man is once destroy'd.
Why—be it so—we in that point accord ;
But what are trade, and tradesmen, to a lord ?
    Faber, from day to day, from year to year,
Hath had the cries of tradesmen in his ear,
Of tradesmen by his villany betray'd,
And, vainly seeking justice, bankrupts made.
What is 't to Faber ? Lordly as before,
He sits at ease, and lives to ruin more :   60
Fix'd at his door, as motionless as stone,
Begging, but only begging for their own,
Unheard they stand, or only heard by those,
Those slaves in livery, who mock their woes.
What is 't to Faber ? He continues great,
Lives on in grandeur, and runs out in state.
The helpless widow, wrung with deep despair,
In bitterness of soul pours forth her prayer,
Hugging her starving babes with streaming eyes,
And calls down vengeance, vengeance from the skies. 70
What is 't to Faber ? He stands safe and clear,
Heaven can commence no legal action here ;
And on his breast a mighty plate he wears,
A plate more firm than triple brass, which bears
The name of Privilege, 'gainst vulgar awe ;
He feels no conscience, and he fears no law.

Nor think, acquainted with small knaves alone,   77
Who have not shame outlived, and grace outgrown,
The great world hidden from thy reptile view,
That on such men, to whom contempt is due,
Contempt shall fall, and their vile author's name
Recorded stand through all the land of shame.
No—to his porch, like Persians to the sun,
Behold contending crowds of courtiers run ;
See, to his aid what noble troops advance,
All sworn to keep his crimes in countenance ;
Nor wonder at it—they partake the charge,
As small their conscience, and their debts as large.
  Propp'd by such clients, and without control
From all that's honest in the human soul ;   90
In grandeur mean, with insolence unjust,
Whilst none but knaves can praise, and fools will trust,
Caress'd and courted, Faber seems to stand
A mighty pillar in a guilty land.
And (a sad truth, to which succeeding times
Will scarce give credit, when 'tis told in rhymes)
Did not strict Honour with a jealous eye
Watch round the throne, did not true Piety
(Who, link'd with Honour for the noblest ends,
Ranks none but honest men amongst her friends)   100
Forbid us to be crush'd with such a weight,
He might in time be minister of state.
  But why enlarge I on such petty crimes ?
They might have shock'd the faith of former times,
But now are held as nothing—we begin
Where our sires ended, and improve in sin,
Rack our invention, and leave nothing new
In vice and folly for our sons to do.
  Nor deem this censure hard ; there's not a place
Most consecrate to purposes of Grace,   110

Which Vice hath not polluted; none so high,   111
But with bold pinion she hath dared to fly,
And build there for her pleasure; none so low
But she hath crept into it, made it know
And feel her power; in courts, in camps, she reigns,
O'er sober citizens, and simple swains;
E'en in our temples she hath fix'd her throne,
And 'bove God's holy altars placed her own.
   More to increase the horror of our state,
To make her empire lasting as 'tis great;   120
To make us, in full-grown perfection, feel
Curses which neither Art nor Time can heal;
All shame discarded, all remains of pride,
Meanness sits crown'd, and triumphs by her side:
Meanness, who gleans out of the human mind
Those few good seeds which Vice had left behind,
Those seeds which might in time to virtue tend,
And leaves the soul without a power to mend;
Meanness, at sight of whom, with brave disdain,
The breast of Manhood swells, but swells in vain;   130
Before whom Honour makes a forced retreat,
And Freedom is compell'd to quit her seat;
Meanness, which, like that mark by bloody Cain
Borne in his forehead for a brother slain,
God, in his great and all-subduing rage,
Ordains the standing mark of this vile age.
   The venal hero trucks his fame for gold,
The patriot's virtue for a place is sold;
The statesman bargains for his country's shame,
And, for preferment, priests their God disclaim;   140
Worn out with lust, her day of lechery o'er,
The mother trains the daughter whom she bore
In her own paths; the father aids the plan,
And, when the innocent is ripe for man,

Sells her to some old lecher for a wife,   145
And makes her an adulteress for life ;
Or in the papers bids his name appear,
And advertises for a L—— :
Husband and wife (whom Avarice must applaud)
Agree to save the charge of pimp and bawd ;   150
Those parts they play themselves, a frugal pair,
And share the infamy, the gain to share ;
Well pleased to find, when they the profits tell,
That they have play'd the whore and rogue so well.
 Nor are these things (which might imply a spark
Of shame still left) transacted in the dark :
No—to the public they are open laid,
And carried on like any other trade :
Scorning to mince damnation, and too proud
To work the works of darkness in a cloud,   160
In fullest vigour Vice maintains her sway ;
Free are her marts, and open at noonday.
Meanness, now wed to Impudence, no more
In darkness skulks, and trembles, as of yore,
When the light breaks upon her coward eye ;
Boldly she stalks on earth, and to the sky
Lifts her proud head, nor fears lest time abate,
And turn her husband's love to canker'd hate,
Since Fate, to make them more sincerely one,
Hath crown'd their loves with Montague their son ; 170
A son so like his dam, so like his sire,
With all the mother's craft, the father's fire,
An image so express in every part,
So like in all bad qualities of heart,
That, had they fifty children, he alone
Would stand as heir apparent to the throne.
 With our own island vices not content,
We rob our neighbours on the Continent ;

Dance Europe round, and visit every court,   179
To ape their follies, and their crimes import :
To different lands for different sins we roam,
And, richly freighted, bring our cargo home,
Nobly industrious to make Vice appear
In her full state, and perfect only here.

To Holland, where politeness ever reigns,
Where primitive sincerity remains,
And makes a stand ; where Freedom in her course
Hath left her name, though she hath lost her force
In that as other lands ; where simple Trade
Was never in the garb of Fraud array'd ;   190
Where Avarice never dared to show his head ;
Where, like a smiling cherub, Mercy, led
By Reason, blesses the sweet-blooded race,
And Cruelty could never find a place ;
To Holland for that charity we roam,
Which happily begins and ends at home.

France, in return for peace and power restored,
For all those countries which the hero's sword
Unprofitably purchased, idly thrown
Into her lap, and made once more her own ;   200
France hath afforded large and rich supplies
Of vanities full trimm'd ; of polish'd lies ;
Of soothing flatteries, which through the ears
Steal to, and melt the heart ; of slavish fears
Which break the spirit, and of abject fraud—
For which, alas ! we need not send abroad.

Spain gives us Pride—which Spain to all the earth
May largely give, nor fear herself a dearth—
Gives us that Jealousy, which, born of Fear
And mean Distrust, grows not by Nature here—   210
Gives us that Superstition, which pretends
By the worst means to serve the best of ends—

That Cruelty, which, stranger to the brave, 213
Dwells only with the coward and the slave ;
That Cruelty, which led her Christian bands
With more than savage rage o'er savage lands,
Bade her, without remorse, whole countries thin,
And hold of naught, but Mercy, as a sin.
Italia, nurse of every softer art,
Who, feigning to refine, unmans the heart ; 220
Who lays the realms of Sense and Virtue waste ;
Who mars while she pretends to mend our taste ;
Italia, to complete and crown our shame,
Sends us a fiend, and Legion is his name.
The farce of greatness without being great,
Pride without power, titles without estate,
Souls without vigour, bodies without force,
Hate without cause, revenge without remorse,
Dark, mean revenge, murder without defence,
Jealousy without love, sound without sense, 230
Mirth without humour, without wit grimace,
Faith without reason, Gospel without Grace,
Zeal without knowledge, without nature art,
Men without manhood, women without heart ;
Half-men, who, dry and pithless, are debarr'd
From man's best joys—no sooner made than marr'd—
Half-men, whom many a rich and noble dame,
To serve her lust, and yet secure her fame,
Keeps on high diet, as we capons feed,
To glut our appetites at last decreed ; 240
Women, who dance in postures so obscene,
They might awaken shame in Aretine ;
Who when, retired from the day's piercing light,
They celebrate the mysteries of Night,
Might make the Muses, in a corner placed
To view their monstrous lusts, deem Sappho chaste ;

These, and a thousand follies rank as these,   247
A thousand faults, ten thousand fools, who please
Our pall'd and sickly taste, ten thousand knaves,
Who serve our foes as spies, and us as slaves,
Who, by degrees, and unperceived, prepare
Our necks for chains which they already wear,
Madly we entertain, at the expense
Of fame, of virtue, taste, and common sense.

    Nor stop we here—the soft luxurious East,
Where man, his soul degraded, from the beast
In nothing different but in shape we view,
They walk on four legs, and he walks on two,
Attracts our eye ; and flowing from that source,
Sins of the blackest character, sins worse   260
Than all her plagues, which truly to unfold,
Would make the best blood in my veins run cold,
And strike all manhood dead, which but to name,
Would call up in my cheeks the marks of shame :
Sins, if such sins can be, which shut out grace,
Which for the guilty leave no hope, no place,
E'en in God's mercy ; sins 'gainst Nature's plan
Possess the land at large, and man for man
Burns, in those fires, which Hell alone could raise
To make him more than damn'd ; which, in the days
Of punishment, when guilt becomes her prey,   271
With all her tortures she can scarce repay.

    Be grace shut out, be mercy deaf, let God
With tenfold terrors arm that dreadful nod
Which speaks them lost, and sentenced to despair ;
Distending wide her jaws, let Hell prepare,
For those who thus offend amongst mankind,
A fire more fierce, and tortures more refined.
On earth, which groans beneath their monstrous weight,
On earth, alas ! they meet a different fate ;   280

And whilst the laws, false grace, false mercy shown, 281
Are taught to wear a softness not their own,
Men, whom the beasts would spurn, should they appear
Amongst the honest herd, find refuge here.
No longer by vain fear or shame controll'd,
From long, too long, security grown bold,
Mocking rebuke, they brave it in our streets,
And Lumley e'en at noon his mistress meets :
So public in their crimes, so daring grown,
They almost take a pride to have them known, 290
And each unnatural villain scarce endures
To make a secret of his vile amours.
Go where we will, at every time and place,
Sodom confronts, and stares us in the face ;
They ply in public at our very doors,
And take the bread from much more honest whores.
Those who are mean high paramours secure,
And the rich guilty screen the guilty poor ;
The sin too proud to feel from reason awe,
And those who practise it, too great for law. 300
Woman, the pride and happiness of man,
Without whose soft endearments Nature's plan
Had been a blank, and life not worth a thought ;
Woman, by all the Loves and Graces taught,
With softest arts, and sure, though hidden skill,
To humanise, and mould us to her will ;
Woman, with more than common grace form'd here,
With the persuasive language of a tear
To melt the rugged temper of our isle,
Or win us to her purpose with a smile ; 310
Woman, by Fate the quickest spur decreed,
The fairest, best reward of every deed
Which bears the stamp of honour ; at whose name
Our ancient heroes caught a quicker flame,

And dared beyond belief, whilst o'er the plain,   315
Spurning the carcases of princes slain,
Confusion proudly strode, whilst Horror blew
The fatal trump, and Death stalk'd full in view ;
Woman is out of date, a thing thrown by,
As having lost its use : no more the eye,   320
With female beauty caught, in wild amaze,
Gazes entranced, and could for ever gaze ;
No more the heart, that seat where Love resides,
Each breath drawn quick and short, in fuller tides
Life posting through the veins, each pulse on fire,
And the whole body tingling with desire,
Pants for those charms, which Virtue might engage,
To break his vow, and thaw the frost of Age,
Bidding each trembling nerve, each muscle strain,
And giving pleasure which is almost pain.   330
Women are kept for nothing but the breed ;
For pleasure we must have a Ganymede,
A fine, fresh Hylas, a delicious boy,
To serve our purposes of beastly joy.
     Fairest of nymphs, where every nymph is fair,
Whom Nature form'd with more than common care,
With more than common care whom Art improved,
And both declared most worthy to be loved,
—— neglected wanders, whilst a crowd
Pursue and consecrate the steps of —— ;   340
She, hapless maid, born in a wretched hour,
Wastes life's gay prime in vain, like some fair flower,
Sweet in its scent, and lively in its hue,
Which withers on the stalk from whence it grew,
And dies uncropp'd ; whilst he, admired, caress'd,
Beloved, and everywhere a welcome guest,
With brutes of rank and fortune plays the whore,
For their unnatural lust a common sewer.

Dine with Apicius—at his sumptuous board 349
Find all, the world of dainties can afford—
And yet (so much distemper'd spirits pall
The sickly appetite) amidst them all
Apicius finds no joy, but, whilst he carves
For every guest, the landlord sits and starves.

    The forest haunch, fine, fat, in flavour high,
Kept to a moment, smokes before his eye,
But smokes in vain ; his heedless eye runs o'er
And loathes what he had deified before :
The turtle, of a great and glorious size,
Worth its own weight in gold, a mighty prize 360
For which a man of taste all risks would run,
Itself a feast, and every dish in one ;
The turtle in luxurious pomp comes in,
Kept, kill'd, cut up, prepared, and dress'd by Quin ; [1]
In vain it comes, in vain lies full in view ;
As Quin hath dress'd it, he may eat it too ;
Apicius cannot.   When the glass goes round,
Quick-circling, and the roofs with mirth resound,
Sober he sits, and silent—all alone
Though in a crowd, and to himself scarce known : 370
On grief he feeds : nor friends can cure, nor wine
Suspend his cares, and make him cease to pine.

    Why mourns Apicius thus ? Why runs his eye,
Heedless, o'er delicates, which from the sky
Might call down Jove ?   Where now his generous wish,
That, to invent a new and better dish,
The world might burn, and all mankind expire,
So he might roast a phœnix at the fire ?
Why swims that eye in tears, which, through a race
Of sixty years, ne'er show'd one sign of grace ? 380

---

[1] ' Quin : ' was a great voluptuary.

2 c

Why feels that heart, which never felt before ?   381
Why doth that pamper'd glutton eat no more,
Who only lived to eat, his stomach pall'd,
And drown'd in floods of sorrow ? Hath Fate call'd
His father from the grave to second life ?
Hath Clodius on his hands return'd his wife ?
Or hath the law, by strictest justice taught,
Compell'd him to restore the dow'r she brought ?
Hath some bold creditor, against his will,
Brought in, and forced him to discharge, a bill,   390
Where eating had no share ? Hath some vain wench
Run out his wealth, and forced him to retrench ?
Hath any rival glutton got the start,
And beat him in his own luxurious art—
Bought cates for which Apicius could not pay,
Or dress'd old dainties in a newer way ?
Hath his cook, worthy to be slain with rods,
Spoil'd a dish fit to entertain the gods ?
Or hath some varlet, cross'd by cruel Fate,
Thrown down the price of empires in a plate ?   400
    None, none of these—his servants all are tried :
So sure, they walk on ice, and never slide ;
His cook, an acquisition made in France,
Might put a Chloe [1] out of countenance ;
Nor, though old Holles still maintains his stand,
Hath he one rival glutton in the land.
Women are all the objects of his hate ;
His debts are all unpaid, and yet his state
In full security and triumph held,
Unless for once a knave should be expell'd :   410
His wife is still a whore, and in his power,
The woman gone, he still retains the dower ;

---

[1] 'Chloe:' M. St Clouet, or Chloe, cook to Holles, Duke of Newcastle.

Sound in the grave (thanks to his filial care   413
Which mix'd the draught, and kindly sent him there)
His father sleeps, and, till the last trump shake
The corners of the earth, shall not awake.
    Whence flows this sorrow, then ?   Behind his chair,
Didst thou not see, deck'd with a solitaire,
Which on his bare breast glittering play'd, and graced
With nicest ornaments, a stripling placed,   420
A smooth, smug stripling, in life's fairest prime ?
Didst thou not mind, too, how from time to time,
The monstrous lecher, tempted to despise
All other dainties, thither turn'd his eyes ?
How he seem'd inly to reproach us all,
Who strove his fix'd attention to recall,
And how he wish'd, e'en at the time of grace,
Like Janus, to have had a double face ?
His cause of grief behold in that fair boy;
Apicius dotes, and Corydon is coy.   430
    Vain and unthinking stripling ! when the glass
Meets thy too curious eye, and, as you pass,
Flattering, presents in smiles thy image there,
Why dost thou bless the gods, who made thee fair ?
Blame their large bounties, and with reason blame ;
Curse, curse thy beauty, for it leads to shame ;
When thy hot lord, to work thee to his end,
Bids showers of gold into thy breast descend,
Suspect his gifts, nor the vile giver trust ;
They 're baits for virtue, and smell strong of lust.   440
On those gay, gaudy trappings, which adorn
The temple of thy body, look with scorn ;
View them with horror ; they pollution mean,
And deepest ruin : thou hast often seen
From 'mongst the herd, the fairest and the best
Carefully singled out, and richly dress'd,

With grandeur mock'd, for sacrifice decreed,   447
Only in greater pomp at last to bleed.
Be warn'd in time, the threaten'd danger shun,
To stay a moment is to be undone.
What though, temptation proof, thy virtue shine,
Nor bribes can move, nor arts can undermine ?
All other methods failing, one resource
Is still behind, and thou must yield to force.
Paint to thyself the horrors of a rape,
Most strongly paint, and, while thou canst, escape.
Mind not his promises—they 're made in sport—
Made to be broke—was he not bred at court ?
Trust not his honour, he 's a man of birth :
Attend not to his oaths—they 're made on earth,   460
Not register'd in heaven—he mocks at Grace,
And in his creed God never found a place ;
Look not for Conscience—for he knows her not,
So long a stranger, she is quite forgot ;
Nor think thyself in law secure and firm,
Thy master is a lord, and thou a worm,
A poor mean reptile, never meant to think,
Who, being well supplied with meat and drink,
And suffer'd just to crawl from place to place,
Must serve his lusts, and think he does thee grace.   470
    Fly then, whilst yet 'tis in thy power to fly ;
But whither canst thou go ? on whom rely
For wish'd protection ? Virtue 's sure to meet
An armèd host of foes in every street.
What boots it, of Apicius fearful grown,
Headlong to fly into the arms of Stone ?
Or why take refuge in the house of prayer
If sure to meet with an Apicius there ?
Trust not old age, which will thy faith betray ;
Saint Socrates is still a goat, though gray :   480

Trust not green youth ; Florio will scarce go down, 481
And, at eighteen, hath surfeited the town :
Trust not to rakes—alas ! 'tis all pretence—
They take up raking only as a fence
'Gainst common fame—place H—— in thy view,
He keeps one whore, as Barrowby kept two :
Trust not to marriage—T—— took a wife,
Who chaste as Dian might have pass'd her life,
Had she not, far more prudent in her aim,
(To propagate the honours of his name, 490
And save expiring titles) taken care,
Without his knowledge, to provide an heir :
Trust not to marriage, in mankind unread ;
S——'s a married man, and S—— new wed.

 Wouldst thou be safe ? Society forswear,
Fly to the desert, and seek shelter there ;
Herd with the brutes—they follow Nature's plan—
There 's not one brute so dangerous as man
In Afric's wilds—'mongst them that refuge find
Which Lust denies thee here among mankind : 500
Renounce thy name, thy nature, and no more
Pique thy vain pride on Manhood : on all four
Walk, as you see those honest creatures do,
And quite forget that once you walk'd on two.

 But, if the thoughts of solitude alarm,
And social life hath one remaining charm ;
If still thou art to jeopardy decreed
Amongst the monsters of Augusta's[1] breed,
Lay by thy sex, thy safety to procure ;
Put off the man, from men to live secure ; 510
Go forth a woman to the public view,
And with their garb assume their manners too.

---

[1] 'Augusta :' London.

Had the light-footed Greek[1] of Chiron's school   513
Been wise enough to keep this single rule,
The maudlin hero, like a puling boy
Robb'd of his plaything, on the plains of Troy
Had never blubber'd at Patroclus' tomb,
And placed his minion in his mistress' room.
Be not in this than catamites more nice,
Do that for virtue, which they do for vice.   520
Thus shalt thou pass untainted life's gay bloom,
Thus stand uncourted in the drawing-room ;
At midnight thus, untempted, walk the street,
And run no danger but of being beat.

   Where is the mother, whose officious zeal,
Discreetly judging what her daughters feel
By what she felt herself in days of yore,
Against that lecher man makes fast the door ?
Who not permits, e'en for the sake of prayer,
A priest, uncastrated, to enter there,   530
Nor (could her wishes, and her care prevail)
Would suffer in the house a fly that 's male ?
Let her discharge her cares, throw wide her doors,
Her daughters cannot, if they would, be whores ;
Nor can a man be found, as times now go,
Who thinks it worth his while to make them so.

   Though they more fresh, more lively than the morn,
And brighter than the noonday sun, adorn
The works of Nature ; though the mother's grace
Revives, improved, in every daughter's face,   540
Undisciplined in dull Discretion's rules,
Untaught and undebauch'd by boarding-schools,
Free and unguarded let them range the town,
Go forth at random, and run Pleasure down,

---

[1] 'Light-footed Greek :' Achilles, who was left at Scyros, dressed in female attire.

Start where she will; discard all taint of fear,   545
Nor think of danger, when no danger's near.
Watch not their steps—they're safe without thy care,
Unless, like jennets, they conceive by air,
And every one of them may die a nun,   550
Unless they breed, like carrion, in the sun.
Men, dead to pleasure, as they're dead to grace,
Against the law of Nature set their face,
The grand primeval law, and seem combined
To stop the propagation of mankind ;
Vile pathics read the Marriage Act with pride,
And fancy that the law is on their side.   •

  Broke down, and strength a stranger to his bed,
Old L——[1], though yet alive, is dead ;
T—— lives no more, or lives not to our isle ;
No longer bless'd with a Cz——'s [2] smile ;   560
T—— is at P——[3] disgraced,
And M—— grown gray, perforce grows chaste ;
Nor to the credit of our modest race,
Rises one stallion to supply their place.
A maidenhead, which, twenty years ago,
In mid December the rank fly would blow,
Though closely kept, now, when the Dog-star's heat
Inflames the marrow, in the very street
May lie untouch'd, left for the worms, by those
Who daintily pass by, and hold their nose ;   570
Poor, plain Concupiscence is in disgrace,
And simple Lechery dares not show her face,
Lest she be sent to bridewell ; bankrupts made,   •
To save their fortunes, bawds leave off their trade,
Which first had left off them ; to Wellclose Square
Fine, fresh, young strumpets (for Dodd [4] preaches there)

---

[1] 'L——:' Ligonier.—[2] 'Cz——'s :' Czarina's.—[3] 'P—— :' Petersburg.
—[4] 'Dodd:' the Rev. Dr William Dodd, the unfortunate divine, afterwards
hanged for forgery. See Boswell.

Throng for subsistence ; pimps no longer thrive,   577
And pensions only keep L—— alive.
  Where is the mother, who thinks all her pain,
And all her jeopardy of travail, gain
When a man-child is born ; thinks every prayer
Paid to the full, and answer'd in an heir ?
Short-sighted woman ! little doth she know
What streams of sorrow from that source may flow :
Little suspect, while she surveys her boy,
Her young Narcissus, with an eye of joy
Too full for continence, that Fate could give
Her darling as a curse ; that she may live,
Ere sixteen winters their short course have run,
In agonies of soul, to curse that son.   590
  Pray then for daughters, ye wise mothers, pray ;
They shall reward your love, nor make ye gray
Before your time with sorrow ; they shall give
Ages of peace, and comfort ; whilst ye live
Make life most truly worth your care, and save,
In spite of death, your memories from the grave.
  That sense with more than manly vigour fraught,
That fortitude of soul, that stretch of thought,
That genius, great beyond the narrow bound
Of earth's low walk, that judgment perfect found   600
When wanted most, that purity of taste,
Which critics mention by the name of chaste ;
Adorn'd with elegance, that easy flow
Of ready wit, which never made a foe ;
That face, that form, that dignity, that ease,
Those powers of pleasing, with that will to please,
By which Lepel,[1] when in her youthful days,
E'en from the currish Pope extorted praise,

---

[1] 'Lepel:' Mary, daughter of Brigadier-General Le Pell, married in 1720
to John Lord Hervey.

We see, transmitted, in her daughter shine,   609
And view a new Lepel in Caroline.[1]
   Is a son born into this world of woe ?
In never-ceasing streams let sorrow flow ;
Be from that hour the house with sables hung,
Let lamentations dwell upon thy tongue ;
E'en from the moment that he first began
To wail and whine, let him not see a man ;
Lock, lock him up, far from the public eye ;
Give him no opportunity to buy,
Or to be bought ; B——, though rich, was sold,
And gave his body up to shame for gold.   620
   Let it be bruited all about the town,
That he is coarse, indelicate, and brown,
An antidote to lust ; his face deep scarr'd
With the small-pox, his body maim'd and marr'd ;
Ate up with the king's evil, and his blood
Tainted throughout, a thick and putrid flood,
Where dwells Corruption, making him all o'er,
From head to foot, a rank and running sore.
Shouldst thou report him, as by Nature made,
He is undone, and by thy praise betray'd ;   630
Give him out fair, lechers, in number more,
More brutal and more fierce, than throng'd the door
Of Lot in Sodom, shall to thine repair,
And force a passage, though a God is there.
   Let him not have one servant that is male ;
Where lords are baffled, servants oft prevail.
Some vices they propose to all agree ;
H—— was guilty, but was M—— free ?
   Give him no tutor—throw him to a punk,
Rather than trust his morals to a monk—   640

---

[1] 'Caroline:' Lady Caroline Hervey was the youngest daughter of John
Lord Hervey.

Monks we all know—we, who have lived at home,   641
From fair report, and travellers, who roam,
More feelingly ;—nor trust him to the gown,
'Tis oft a covering in this vile town
For base designs : ourselves have lived to see
More than one parson in the pillory.
Should he have brothers, (image to thy view
A scene, which, though not public made, is true)
Let not one brother be to t' other known,
Nor let his father sit with him alone.   650
Be all his servants female, young and fair ;
And if the pride of Nature spur thy heir
To deeds of venery, if, hot and wild,
He chance to get some score of maids with child,
Chide, but forgive him ; whoredom is a crime
Which, more at this than any other time,
Calls for indulgence, and, 'mongst such a race,
To have a bastard is some sign of grace.
     Born in such times, should I sit tamely down,
Suppress my rage, and saunter through the town   660
As one who knew not, or who shared these crimes ?
Should I at lesser evils point my rhymes,
And let this giant sin, in the full eye
Of observation, pass unwounded by ?
Though our meek wives, passive obedience taught,
Patiently bear those wrongs, for which they ought,
With the brave spirit of their dams possess'd,
To plant a dagger in each husband's breast,
To cut off male increase from this fair isle,
And turn our Thames into another Nile ;   670
Though, on his Sunday, the smug pulpiteer,
Loud 'gainst all other crimes, is silent here,
And thinks himself absolved, in the pretence
Of decency, which, meant for the defence

Of real virtue, and to raise her price,   675
Becomes an agent for the cause of vice ;
Though the law sleeps, and through the care they take
To drug her well, may never more awake ;
Born in such times, nor with that patience cursed
Which saints may boast of, I must speak or burst.   680
    But if, too eager in my bold career,
Haply I wound the nice, and chaster ear ;
If, all unguarded, all too rude, I speak,
And call up blushes in the maiden's cheek,
Forgive, ye fair—my real motives view,
And to forgiveness add your praises too.
For you I write—nor wish a better plan,
The cause of woman is most worthy man—
For you I still will write, nor hold my hand
Whilst there 's one slave of Sodom in the land.   690
    Let them fly far, and skulk from place to place,
Not daring to meet manhood face to face,
Their steps I'll track, nor yield them one retreat
Where they may hide their heads, or rest their feet,
Till God, in wrath, shall let his vengeance fall,
And make a great example of them all,
Bidding in one grand pile this town expire,
Her towers in dust, her Thames a lake of fire ;
Or they (most worth our wish) convinced, though late,
Of their past crimes, and dangerous estate,   700
Pardon of women with repentance buy,
And learn to honour them, as much as I.

INDEPENDENCE.

HAPPY the bard (though few such bards we find)
Who, 'bove controlment, dares to speak his mind ;
Dares, unabash'd, in every place appear,
And nothing fears, but what he ought to fear :
Him Fashion cannot tempt, him abject Need
Cannot compel, him Pride cannot mislead
To be the slave of Greatness, to strike sail
When, sweeping onward with her peacock's tail,
Quality in full plumage passes by ;
He views her with a fix'd, contemptuous eye,   10
And mocks the puppet, keeps his own due state,
And is above conversing with the great.
     Perish those slaves, those minions of the quill,
Who have conspired to seize that sacred hill
Where the Nine Sisters pour a genuine strain,
And sunk the mountain level with the plain ;
Who, with mean, private views, and servile art,
No spark of virtue living in their heart,
Have basely turn'd apostates; have debased
Their dignity of office ; have disgraced,   20
Like Eli's sons, the altars where they stand,
And caused their name to stink through all the land ;
Have stoop'd to prostitute their venal pen
For the support of great, but guilty men ;
Have made the bard, of their own vile accord,
Inferior to that thing we call a lord.
     What is a lord ?   Doth that plain simple word
Contain some magic spell ?   As soon as heard,
Like an alarum bell on Night's dull ear,
Doth it strike louder, and more strong appear   30

Than other words ?   Whether we will or no,   31
Through Reason's court doth it unquestion'd go
E'en on the mention, and of course transmit
Notions of something excellent ; of wit
Pleasing, though keen ; of humour free, though chaste ;
Of sterling genius, with sound judgment graced ;
Of virtue far above temptation's reach,
And honour, which not malice can impeach ?
Believe it not—'twas Nature's first intent,
Before their rank became their punishment,   40
They should have pass'd for men, nor blush'd to prize
The blessings she bestow'd ; she gave them eyes,   .
And they could see ; she gave them ears—they heard ;
The instruments of stirring, and they stirr'd ;
Like us, they were design'd to eat, to drink,
To talk, and (every now and then) to think ;
Till they, by Pride corrupted, for the sake
Of singularity, disclaim'd that make ;
Till they, disdaining Nature's vulgar mode,
Flew off, and struck into another road,   50
More fitting Quality, and to our view
Came forth a species altogether new,
Something we had not known, and could not know,
Like nothing of God's making here below ;
Nature exclaim'd with wonder—' Lords are things,
Which, never made by me, were made by kings.'
    A lord (nor let the honest and the brave,
The true old noble, with the fool and knave
Here mix his fame ; cursed be that thought of mine,
Which with a B——[1] and F——[2] should Grafton [3] join),
A lord (nor here let Censure rashly call   61
My just contempt of some, abuse of all,

[1] ' B—— :' Bute.—[2] ' F——- :' Fox.—[3] ' Grafton :' see Junius, *passim*.

And, as of late, when Sodom was my theme,   63
Slander my purpose, and my Muse blaspheme,
Because she stops not, rapid in her song,
To make exceptions as she goes along,
Though well she hopes to find, another year,
A whole minority exceptions here),
A mere, mere lord, with nothing but the name,
Wealth all his worth, and title all his fame,   70
Lives on another man, himself a blank,
Thankless he lives, or must some grandsire thank
For smuggled honours, and ill-gotten pelf;
A bard owes all to Nature, and himself.

    Gods! how my soul is burnt up with disdain,
When I see men, whom Phœbus in his train
Might view with pride, lackey the heels of those
Whom Genius ranks among her greatest foes!
And what's the cause? Why, these same sons of Scorn,
No thanks to them, were to a title born,   80
And could not help it; by chance hither sent,
And only deities by accident.
Had Fortune on our getting chanced to shine,
Their birthright honours had been yours or mine.
'Twas a mere random stroke; and should the Throne
Eye thee with favour, proud and lordly grown,
Thou, though a bard, might'st be their fellow yet:
But Felix never can be made a wit.
No, in good faith—that's one of those few things
Which Fate hath placed beyond the reach of kings: 90
Bards may be lords, but 'tis not in the cards,
Play how we will, to turn lords into bards.

    A bard!—a lord!—why, let them, hand in hand,
Go forth as friends, and travel through the land;
Observe which word the people can digest
Most readily, which goes to market best,

Which gets most credit, whether men will trust 97
A bard, because they think he may be just,
Or on a lord will chose to risk their gains,
Though privilege in that point still remains.

A bard!—a lord!—let Reason take her scales,
And fairly weigh those words, see which prevails,·
Which in the balance lightly kicks the beam,
And which, by sinking, we the victor deem.

'Tis done, and Hermes, by command of Jove,
Summons a synod in the sacred grove,
Gods throng with gods to take their chairs on high,
And sit in state, the senate of the sky,
Whilst, in a kind of parliament below,
Men stare at those above, and want to know 110
What they're transacting : Reason takes her stand
Just in the midst, a balance in her hand,
Which o'er and o'er she tries, and finds it true :
From either side, conducted full in view,
A man comes forth, of figure strange and queer ;
We now and then see something like them here.

The first [1] was meagre, flimsy, void of strength,
But Nature kindly had made up in length
What she in breadth denied ; erect and proud,
A head and shoulders taller than the crowd, 120
He deem'd them pigmies all ; loose hung his skin
O'er his bare bones ; his face so very thin,
So very narrow, and so much beat out,
That physiognomists have made a doubt,
Proportion lost, expression quite forgot,
Whether it could be call'd a face or not ;
At end of it, howe'er, unbless'd with beard,
Some twenty fathom length of chin appear'd ;

---

[1] 'First :' Lyttelton.

With legs, which we might well conceive that Fate   129
Meant only to support a spider's weight,
Firmly he strove to tread, and with a stride,
Which show'd at once his weakness and his pride,
Shaking himself to pieces, seem'd to cry,
' Observe, good people, how I shake the sky.'

    In his right hand a paper did he hold,
On which, at large, in characters of gold,
Distinct, and plain for those who run to see,
Saint Archibald[1] had wrote L, O, R, D.
This, with an air of scorn, he from afar
Twirl'd into Reason's scales, and on that bar,   140
Which from his soul he hated, yet admired,
Quick turn'd his back, and, as he came, retired.
The judge to all around his name declared ;
Each goddess titter'd, each god laugh'd, Jove stared,
And the whole people cried, with one accord,
' Good Heaven bless us all, is that a Lord !'

    Such was the first—the second[2] was a man
Whom Nature built on quite a different plan ;
A bear, whom, from the moment he was born,
His dam despised, and left unlick'd in scorn ;   150
A Babel, which, the power of Art outdone,
She could not finish when she had begun ;
An utter Chaos, out of which no might,
But that of God, could strike one spark of light.

    Broad were his shoulders, and from blade to blade
A H—— might at full length have laid ;
Vast were his bones, his muscles twisted strong ;
His face was short, but broader than 'twas long ;
His features, though by Nature they were large,
Contentment had contrived to overcharge,   160

---

[1] ' Archibald :' Archibald Bower, the infamous author of ' Lives of the Popes,' patronised at first by Lyttelton, but detected and exposed by Dr Douglas.—
[2] ' Second :' Churchill himself.

And bury meaning, save that we might spy   161
Sense lowering on the penthouse of his eye ;
His arms were two twin oaks ; his legs so stout
That they might bear a Mansion-house about ;
Nor were they, look but at his body there,
Design'd by Fate a much less weight to bear.

O'er a brown cassock, which had once been black,
Which hung in tatters on his brawny back,
A sight most strange, and awkward to behold,
He threw a covering of blue and gold.   170
Just at that time of life, when man, by rule,
The fop laid down, takes up the graver fool,
He started up a fop, and, fond of show,
Look'd like another Hercules turn'd beau,
A subject met with only now and then,
Much fitter for the pencil than the pen ;
Hogarth would draw him (Envy must allow)
E'en to the life, was Hogarth [1] living now.

With such accoutrements, with such a form,
Much like a porpoise just before a storm,   180
Onward he roll'd ; a laugh prevail'd around ;
E'en Jove was seen to simper ; at the sound
(Nor was the cause unknown, for from his youth
Himself he studied by the glass of Truth)
He joined their mirth ; nor shall the gods condemn,
If, whilst they laugh at him, he laugh'd at them.
Judge Reason view'd him with an eye of grace,
Look'd through his soul, and quite forgot his face,
And, from his hand received, with fair regard
Placed in her other scale the name of Bard.   190
Then, (for she did as judges ought to do,
She nothing of the case beforehand knew,

---

[1] 'Hogarth :' here satirically represented as dead, lived four weeks after
this poem was published, and died nine days before Churchill.

2 D

Nor wish'd to know ; she never stretch'd the laws,   193
Nor, basely to anticipate a cause,
Compell'd solicitors, no longer free,
To show those briefs she had no right to see)
Then she with equal hand her scales held out,
Nor did the cause one moment hang in doubt ;
She held her scales out fair to public view,
The Lord, as sparks fly upwards, upwards flew,   200
More light than air, deceitful in the weight ;
The Bard, preponderating, kept his state ;
Reason approved, and with a voice, whose sound
Shook earth, shook heaven, on the clearest ground
Pronouncing for the Bards a full decree,
Cried—' Those must honour them, who honour me ;
They from this present day, where'er I reign,
In their own right, precedence shall obtain ;
Merit rules here : be it enough that Birth
Intoxicates, and sways the fools of earth.'   210
     Nor think that here, in hatred to a lord,
I've forged a tale, or alter'd a record ;
Search when you will, (I am not now in sport)
You'll find it register'd in Reason's court.
     Nor think that Envy here hath strung my lyre,
That I depreciate what I most admire,
And look on titles with an eye of scorn,
Because I was not to a title born.
By Him that made me, I am much more proud,
More inly satisfied to have a crowd   220
Point at me as I pass, and cry—' That's he—
A poor but honest bard, who dares be free
Amidst corruption,' than to have a train
Of flickering levee slaves, to make me vain
Of things I ought to blush for ; to run, fly,
And live but in the motion of my eye ;

When I am less than man, my faults to adore,   227
And make me think that I am something more.
  Recall past times, bring back the days of old,
When the great noble bore his honours bold,
And in the face of peril, when he dared
Things which his legal bastard, if declared,
Might well discredit ; faithful to his trust,
In the extremest points of justice, just,
Well knowing all, and loved by all he knew,
True to his king, and to his country true ;
Honest at court, above the baits of gain,
Plain in his dress, and in his manners plain ;
Moderate in wealth, generous, but not profuse,
Well worthy riches, for he knew their use ;   240
Possessing much, and yet deserving more,
Deserving those high honours which he wore
With ease to all, and in return gain'd fame
Which all men paid, because he did not claim.
When the grim war was placed in dread array,
Fierce as the lion roaring for his prey,
Or lioness of royal whelps foredone ;
In peace, as mild as the departing sun,
A general blessing wheresoe'er he turn'd,
Patron of learning, nor himself unlearn'd ;   250
Ever awake at Pity's tender call,
A father of the poor, a friend to all ;
Recall such times, and from the grave bring back
A worth like this, my heart shall bend, or crack,
My stubborn pride give way, my tongue proclaim,
And every Muse conspire to swell his fame,
Till Envy shall to him that praise allow
Which she cannot deny to Temple now.
  This justice claims, nor shall the bard forget,
Delighted with the task, to pay that debt,   260

To pay it like a man, and in his lays,   261
Sounding such worth, prove his own right to praise.
But let not pride and prejudice misdeem,
And think that empty titles are my theme ;
Titles, with me, are vain, and nothing worth ;
I reverence virtue, but I laugh at birth.
Give me a lord that 's honest, frank, and brave,
I am his friend, but cannot be his slave ;
Though none, indeed, but blockheads would pretend
To make a slave, where they may make a friend ;   270
I love his virtues, and will make them known,
Confess his rank, but can't forget my own.
Give me a lord, who, to a title born,
Boasts nothing else, I 'll pay him scorn with scorn.
What ! shall my pride (and pride is virtue here)
Tamely make way if such a wretch appear ?
Shall I uncover'd stand, and bend my knee
To such a shadow of nobility,
A shred, a remnant ? he might rot unknown
For any real merit of his own,   280
And never had come forth to public note
Had he not worn, by chance, his father's coat.
To think a M——[1] worth my least regards,
Is treason to the majesty of bards.
     By Nature form'd (when, for her honour's sake,
She something more than common strove to make,
When, overlooking each minute defect,
And all too eager to be quite correct,
In her full heat and vigour she impress'd
Her stamp most strongly on the favour'd breast)   290
The bard, (nor think too lightly that I mean
Those little, piddling witlings, who o'erween
Of their small parts, the Murphys of the stage,
The Masons and the Whiteheads of the age,

---

[1] ' M——:' Melcombe.

Who all in raptures their own works rehearse, 295
And drawl out measured prose, which they call verse)
The real bard, whom native genius fires,
Whom every maid of Castaly inspires,
Let him consider wherefore he was meant,
Let him but answer Nature's great intent, 300
And fairly weigh himself with other men,
Would ne'er debase the glories of his pen,
Would in full state, like a true monarch, live,
Nor bate one inch of his prerogative.

Methinks I see old Wingate[1] frowning here,
(Wingate may in the season be a peer,
Though now, against his will, of figures sick,
He's forced to diet on arithmetic,
E'en whilst he envies every Jew he meets,
Who cries old clothes to sell about the streets) 310
Methinks (his mind with future honours big,
His Tyburn bob turn'd to a dress'd bag wig)
I hear him cry—'What doth this jargon mean?
Was ever such a damn'd dull blockhead seen?
Majesty!—Bard!—Prerogative!—Disdain
Hath got into, and turn'd the fellow's brain:
To Bethlem with him—give him whips and straw—
I'm very sensible he's mad in law.
A saucy groom, who trades in reason, thus
To set himself upon a par with us; 320
If this *here's* suffered, and if that *there* fool,
May, when he pleases, send us all to school,
Why, then our only business is outright
To take our caps, and bid the world good night.
I've kept a bard myself this twenty years,
But nothing of this kind in him appears;

---

[1] 'Wingate:' the purse-proud upstarts of the day are here designated by the generic name of Wingate, an eminent arithmetician, who lived early in the seventeenth century.

He, like a thorough true-bred spaniel, licks   327
The hand which cuffs him, and the foot which kicks ;
He fetches and he carries, blacks my shoes,
Nor thinks it a discredit to his Muse ;
A creature of the right chameleon hue,
He wears my colours, yellow or true blue,
Just as I wear them : 'tis all one to him
Whether I change through conscience, or through whim.
Now this is something like ; on such a plan
A bard may find a friend in a great man ;
But this proud coxcomb—zounds, I thought that all
Of this queer tribe had been like my old Paul.' [1]

   Injurious thought ! accursèd be the tongue
On which the vile insinuation hung,   340
The heart where 'twas engender'd ; cursed be those,
Those bards, who not themselves alone expose,
But me, but all, and make the very name
By which they're call'd a standing mark of shame.

   Talk not of custom—'tis the coward's plea,
Current with fools, but passes not with me ;
An old stale trick, which Guilt hath often tried
By numbers to o'erpower the better side.
Why tell me then that from the birth of Rhyme,
No matter when, down to the present time,   350
As by the original decree of Fate,
Bards have protection sought amongst the great ;
Conscious of weakness, have applied to them
As vines to elms, and, twining round their stem,
Flourish'd on high ; to gain this wish'd support
E'en Virgil to Mæcenas paid his court ?
As to the custom, 'tis a point agreed,
But 'twas a foolish diffidence, not need,

---

[1] 'Old Paul :' Paul Whitehead, a contemptible sycophant as well as profligate.

From which it rose ; had bards but truly known   359
That strength, which is most properly their own,
Without a lord, unpropp'd they might have stood,
And overtopp'd those giants of the wood.
     But why, when present times my care engage,
Must I go back to the Augustan age ?
Why, anxious for the living, am I led
Into the mansions of the ancient dead ?
Can they find patrons nowhere but at Rome,
And must I seek Mæcenas in the tomb ?
Name but a Wingate, twenty fools of note
Start up, and from report Mæcenas quote ;   370
Under his colours lords are proud to fight,
Forgetting that Mæcenas was a knight :
They mention him, as if to use his name
Was, in some measure, to partake his fame,
Though Virgil, was he living, in the street
Might rot for them, or perish in the Fleet.
See how they redden, and the charge disclaim—
Virgil, and in the Fleet !—forbid it, Shame !
Hence, ye vain boasters ! to the Fleet repair,
And ask, with blushes ask, if Lloyd is there !   380
     Patrons in days of yore were men of sense,
Were men of taste, and had a fair pretence
To rule in letters—some of them were heard
To read off-hand, and never spell a word ;
Some of them, too, to such a monstrous height
Was learning risen, for themselves could write,
And kept their secretaries, as the great
Do many other foolish things, for state.
     Our patrons are of quite a different strain,
With neither sense nor taste ; against the grain   390
They patronise for Fashion's sake—no more—
And keep a bard, just as they keep a whore.

Melcombe (on such occasions I am loth   393
To name the dead) was a rare proof of both.
Some of them would be puzzled e'en to read,
Nor could deserve their clergy by their creed ;
Others can write, but such a Pagan hand,
A Willes [1] should always at our elbow stand :
Many, if begg'd, a Chancellor,[2] of right,
Would order into keeping at first sight.   400
Those who stand fairest to the public view
Take to themselves the praise to others due,
They rob the very spital, and make free
With those, alas ! who 've least to spare.   We see
—— hath not had a word to say,
Since winds and waves bore Singlespeech [3] away.

Patrons, in days of yore, like patrons now,
Expected that the bard should make his bow
At coming in, and every now and then
Hint to the world that they were more than men ;   410
But, like the patrons of the present day,
They never bilk'd the poet of his pay.
Virgil loved rural ease, and, far from harm,
Mæcenas fix'd him in a neat, snug farm,
Where he might, free from trouble, pass his days
In his own way, and pay his rent in praise.
Horace loved wine, and, through his friend at court,
Could buy it off the quay in every port :
Horace loved mirth, Mæcenas loved it too ;
They met, they laugh'd, as Goy [4] and I may do,   420

---

[1] 'Willes :' Dr Edward Willes, Bishop of Bath and Wells.—[2] 'Chancellor :'
the Lord High Chancellor is intrusted with the custody of all idiots and luna-
tics.—[3] 'Singlespeech :' the Right Honourable William Gerrard Hamilton.
See Boswell, who describes him as a man of great talent ; others have ascribed
his single speech to the aid of Burke.—[4] 'Goy :' M. Pierre Goy, a Frenchman
of brilliant accomplishments.

Nor in those moments paid the least regard   421
To which was minister, and which was bard.
  Not so our patrons—grave as grave can be,
They know themselves, they keep up dignity ;
Bards are a forward race, nor is it fit
That men of fortune rank with men of wit :
Wit, if familiar made, will find her strength—
'Tis best to keep her weak, and at arm's length.
'Tis well enough for bards, if patrons give,
From hand to mouth, the scanty means to live.   430
Such is their language, and their practice such ;
They promise little, and they give not much.
Let the weak bard, with prostituted strain,
Praise that proud Scot whom all good men disdain ;
What's his reward ? Why, his own fame undone,
He may obtain a patent for the run
Of his lord's kitchen, and have ample time,
With offal fed, to court the cook in rhyme ;
Or (if he strives true patriots to disgrace)
May at the second table get a place ;   440
With somewhat greater slaves allow'd to dine,
And play at crambo o'er his gill of wine.
  And are there bards, who, on creation's file,
Stand rank'd as men, who breathe in this fair isle
The air of freedom, with so little gall,
So low a spirit, prostrate thus to fall
Before these idols, and without a·groan
Bear wrongs might call forth murmurs from a stone ?
Better, and much more noble, to abjure
The sight of men, and in some cave, secure   450
From all the outrages of Pride, to feast
On Nature's salads, and be free at least.
Better, (though that, to say the truth, is worse
Than almost any other modern curse)

Discard all sense, divorce the thankless Muse,   455
Critics commence, and write in the Reviews ;
Write without tremor,'Griffiths [1] cannot read ;
No fool can fail, where Langhorne can succeed.
    But (not to make a brave and honest pride
Try those means first, she must disdain when tried) 460
There are a thousand ways, a thousand arts,
By which, and fairly, men of real parts
May gain a living, gain what Nature craves ;
Let those, who pine for more, live, and be slaves.
Our real wants in a small compass lie,
But lawless appetite, with eager eye,
Kept in a constant fever, more requires,
And we are burnt up with our own desires.
Hence our dependence, hence our slavery springs ;
Bards, if contented, are as great as kings.   470
Ourselves are to ourselves the cause of ill ;
We may be independent, if we will.
The man who suits his spirit to his state
Stands on an equal footing with the great ;
Moguls themselves are not more rich, and he
Who rules the English nation, not more free.
Chains were not forged more durable and strong
For bards than others, but they 've worn them long,
And therefore wear them still ; they've quite forgot
What Freedom is, and therefore prize her not.   480
Could they, though in their sleep, could they but know
The blessings which from Independence flow ;
Could they but have a short and transient gleam
Of Liberty, though 'twas but in a dream,
They would no more in bondage bend their knee,
But, once made freemen, would be always free.

[1] 'Griffiths:' Ralph Griffiths, a bookseller, who, in 1749, published the first number of the ' Monthly Review.'

The Muse, if she one moment freedom gains, 487
Can nevermore submit to sing in chains.
Bred in a cage, far from the feather'd throng,
The bird repays his keeper with his song ;
But if some playful child sets wide the door,
Abroad he flies, and thinks of home no more,
With love of liberty begins to burn,
And rather starves than to his cage return.

Hail, Independence !—by true reason taught,
How few have known, and prized thee as they ought !
Some give thee up for riot ; some, like boys,
Resign thee, in their childish moods, for toys ;
Ambition some, some avarice, misleads,
And in both cases Independence bleeds. 500
Abroad, in quest of thee, how many roam,
Nor know they had thee in their reach at home ;
Some, though about their paths, their beds about,
Have never had the sense to find thee out :
Others, who know of what they are possess'd,
Like fearful misers, lock thee in a chest,
Nor have the resolution to produce,
In these bad times, and bring thee forth for use.
Hail, Independence !—though thy name's scarce known,
Though thou, alas ! art out of fashion grown, 510
Though all despise thee, I will not despise,
Nor live one moment longer than I prize
Thy presence, and enjoy : by angry Fate
Bow'd down, and almost crush'd, thou cam'st, though
    late,
Thou cam'st upon me, like a second birth,
And made me know what life was truly worth.
Hail, Independence !—never may my cot,
Till I forget thee, be by thee forgot :

Thither, oh! thither, oftentimes repair ;   519
Cotes,[1] whom thou lovest too, shall meet thee there.
All thoughts but what arise from joy give o'er,
    Peace dwells within, and law shall guard the door.
O'erweening Bard! Law guard thy door! What law?
The law of England.   To control and awe
Those saucy hopes, to strike that spirit dumb,
Behold, in state, Administration come!
    Why, let her come, in all her terrors too ;
I dare to suffer all she dares to do.
I know her malice well, and know her pride,
I know her strength, but will not change my side.   530
This melting mass of flesh she may control
With iron ribs—she cannot chain my soul.
No—to the last resolved her worst to bear,
I 'm still at large, and independent there.
    Where is this minister? where is the band
Of ready slaves, who at his elbow stand
To hear, and to perform his wicked will?
Why, for the first time, are they slow to ill?
When some grand act 'gainst law is to be done,
Doth —— sleep ; doth blood-hound —— run   540
To L——, and worry those small deer,
When he might do more precious mischief here?
Doth Webb turn tail? doth he refuse to draw
Illegal warrants, and to call them law?
Doth ——, at Guildford kick'd, from Guildford run,
With that cold lump of unbaked dough, his son,
And, his more honest rival Ketch to cheat,
Purchase a burial-place where three ways meet?
Believe it not ; —— is —— still,
And never sleeps, when he should wake to ill :   550

---

[1] 'Cotes:' Humphrey Cotes, a staunch supporter of Wilkes.

—— doth lesser mischiefs by the by,   551
The great ones till the term in *petto* lie :
—— lives, and, to the strictest justice true,
Scorns to defraud the hangman of his due.
    O my poor Country !—weak, and overpower'd
By thine own sons—ate to the bone—devour'd
By vipers, which, in thine own entrails bred,
Prey on thy life, and with thy blood are fed,
With unavailing grief thy wrongs I see,
And, for myself not feeling, feel for thee.   560
I grieve, but can't despair—for, lo ! at hand
Freedom presents a choice, but faithful band
Of loyal patriots ; men who greatly dare
In such a noble cause ; men fit to bear
The weight of empires ; Fortune, Rank, and Sense,
Virtue and Knowledge, leagued with Eloquence,
March in their ranks ; Freedom from file to file
Darts her delighted eye, and with a smile
Approves her honest sons, whilst down her cheek,
As 'twere by stealth, (her heart too full to speak)   570
One tear in silence creeps, one honest tear,
And seems to say, Why is not Granby [1] here ?'
    O ye brave few, in whom we still may find
A love of virtue, freedom, and mankind !
Go forth—in majesty of woe array'd,
See at your feet your Country kneels for aid,
And, (many of her children traitors grown)
Kneels to those sons she still can call her own ;
Seeming to breathe her last in every breath,
She kneels for freedom, or she begs for death—   580
Fly, then, each duteous son, each English chief,
And to your drooping parent bring relief.

---

[1] ' Granby : ' the Marquis of Granby, in 1766, was appointed Commander-in-Chief of all his Majesty's land forces in Great Britain. See Junius.

Go forth—nor let the siren voice of Ease   583
Tempt ye to sleep, whilst tempests swell the seas ;
Go forth—nor let Hypocrisy, whose tongue
With many a fair, false, fatal art is hung,
Like Bethel's fawning prophet, cross your way,
When your great errand brooks not of delay ;
Nor let vain Fear, who cries to all she meets,
Trembling and pale, ' A lion in the streets,'   590
Damp your free spirits ; let not threats affright,
Nor bribes corrupt, nor flatteries delight :
Be as one man—concord success ensures—
There 's not an English heart but what is yours.
Go forth—and Virtue, ever in your sight,
Shall be your guide by day, your guard by night—
Go forth—the champions of your native land,
'And may the battle prosper in your hand—
It may, it must—ye cannot be withstood—
Be your hearts honest, as your cause is good!   600

THE JOURNEY.[1]

SOME of my friends (for friends I must suppose
All, who, not daring to appear my foes,
Feign great good will, and, not more full of spite
Than full of craft, under false colours fight),
Some of my friends (so lavishly I print),
As more in sorrow than in anger, hint
(Though that indeed will scarce admit a doubt)
That I shall run my stock of genius out,

---

[1] ' Journey : ' a posthumous publication.

My no great stock, and, publishing so fast,   9
Must needs become a bankrupt at the last.
  'The husbandman, to spare a thankful soil,
Which, rich in disposition, pays his toil
More than a hundredfold, which swells his store
E'en to his wish, and makes his barns run o'er,
By long Experience taught, who teaches best,
Foregoes his hopes a while, and gives it rest :
The land, allow'd its losses to repair,
Refresh'd, and full in strength, delights to wear
A second youth, and to the farmer's eyes
Bids richer crops, and double harvests rise.   20
  'Nor think this practice to the earth confined,
It reaches to the culture of the mind.
The mind of man craves rest, and cannot bear,
Though next in power to God's, continual care.
Genius himself (nor here let Genius frown)
Must, to ensure his vigour, be laid down,
And fallow'd well : had Churchill known but this,
Which the most slight observer scarce could miss,
He might have flourish'd twenty years or more,
Though now, alas ! poor man ! worn out in four.'[1]   30
  Recover'd from the vanity of youth,
I feel, alas ! this melancholy truth,
Thanks to each cordial, each advising friend,
And am, if not too late, resolved to mend,
Resolved to give some respite to my pen,
Apply myself once more to books and men ;
View what is present, what is past review,
And, my old stock exhausted, lay in new.
For twice six moons (let winds, turn'd porters, bear
This oath to Heaven), for twice six moons, I swear,   40

'In four :' he did not complete the fourth.

No Muse shall tempt me with her siren lay,   41
Nor draw me from Improvement's thorny way.
Verse I abjure, nor will forgive that friend,
Who, in my hearing, shall a rhyme commend.
     It cannot be—whether I will, or no,
Such as they are, my thoughts in measure flow.
Convinced, determined, I in prose begin,
But ere I write one sentence, verse creeps in,
And taints me through and through ; by this good light,
In verse I talk by day, I dream by night!   50
If now and then I curse, my curses chime,
Nor can I pray, unless I pray in rhyme.
E'en now I err, in spite of Common Sense,
And my confession doubles my offence.
     Rest then, my friends ;—spare, spare your precious
         breath,
And be your slumbers not less sound than death ;
Perturbèd spirits rest, nor thus appear,
To waste your counsels in a spendthrift's ear ;
On your grave lessons I cannot subsist,
Nor even in verse become economist.   60
Rest then, my friends ; nor, hateful to my eyes,
Let Envy, in the shape of Pity, rise
To blast me ere my time ; with patience wait,
('Tis no long interval) propitious Fate
Shall glut your pride, and every son of phlegm
Find ample room to censure and condemn.
Read some three hundred lines (no easy task,
But probably the last that I shall ask),
And give me up for ever ; wait one hour,
Nay not so much, revenge is in your power,   70
And ye may cry, ere Time hath turn'd his glass,
Lo! what we prophesied is come to pass.

Let those, who poetry in poems claim,   73
Or not read this, or only read to blame ;
Let those who are by Fiction's charms enslaved,
Return me thanks for half-a-crown well saved ;
Let those who love a little gall in rhyme
Postpone their purchase now, and call next time ;
Let those who, void of Nature, look for Art,
Take up their money, and in peace depart ;   80
Let those who energy of diction prize,
For Billingsgate quit Flexney,[1] and be wise :
Here is no lie, no gall, no art, no force,
Mean are the words, and such as come of course ;
The subject not less simple than the lay ;
A plain, unlabour'd Journey of a Day.
  Far from me now be every tuneful maid,
I neither ask, nor can receive their aid.
Pegasus turn'd into a common hack,
Alone I jog, and keep the beaten track,   90
Nor would I have the Sisters of the hill
Behold their bard in such a dishabille.
Absent, but only absent for a time,
Let them caress some dearer son of Rhyme ;
Let them, as far as decency permits,
Without suspicion, play the fool with wits,
'Gainst fools be guarded ; 'tis a certain rule,
Wits are safe things ; there's danger in a fool.
  Let them, though modest, Gray more modest woo ;
Let them with Mason bleat, and bray, and coo ;   100
Let them with Franklin,[2] proud of some small Greek,
Make Sophocles, disguised, in English speak ;
Let them, with Glover,[3] o'er Medea doze ;
Let them, with Dodsley, wail Cleone's[4] woes,

---

[1] 'Flexney:' the publisher of his poems. — [2] 'Franklin:' Dr Franklin, author of a translation of Sophocles. — [3] 'Glover:' Dr Glover in his tragedy of Medea. — [4] 'Cleone:' a tragedy by Robert Dodsley.

Whilst he, fine feeling creature, all in tears,   105
Melts as they melt, and weeps with weeping peers ;
Let them, with simple Whitehead[1] taught to creep
Silent and soft, lay Fontenelle asleep ;
Let them with Browne,[2] contrive, no vulgar trick,
To cure the dead, and make the living sick ;   110
Let them, in charity, to Murphy give
Some old French piece, that he may steal and live ;
Let them with antic Foote, subscriptions get,
And advertise a summer-house of wit.

    Thus, or in any better way they please,
With these great men, or with great men like these,
Let them their appetite for laughter feed ;
I on my Journey all alone proceed.

    If fashionable grown, and fond of power,
With humorous Scots let them disport their hour,   120
Let them dance, fairy like, round Ossian's tomb ;
Let them forge lies and histories for Hume ;
Let them with Home, the very prince of verse,
Make something like a tragedy in Erse ;
Under dark Allegory's flimsy veil,
Let them, with Ogilvie,[3] spin out a tale
Of rueful length ; let them plain things obscure,
Debase what's truly rich, and what is poor
Make poorer still by jargon most uncouth ;
With every pert, prim prettiness of youth,   130
Born of false taste, with Fancy (like a child
Not knowing what it cries for) running wild,
With bloated style, by Affectation taught,
With much false colouring, and little thought,

---

[1] ' Whitehead : ' Whitehead dedicated his ' School for Lovers ' to the memory of Fontenelle. — [2] ' Browne : ' ' The Cure of Saul, ' a sacred ode by Dr Browne, was set to music. — [3] ' Ogilvie : ' John Ogilvie, A.M., was the author of ' Providence,' an allegorical poem.

With phrases strange, and dialect decreed 135
By Reason never to have pass'd the Tweed,
With words, which Nature meant each other's foe,
Forced to compound whether they will or no ;
With such materials, let them, if they will,
To prove at once their pleasantry and skill, 140
Build up a bard to war 'gainst Common Sense,
By way of compliment to Providence ;
Let them, with Armstrong,[1] taking leave of Sense,
Read musty lectures on Benevolence,
Or con the pages of his gaping Day,
Where all his former fame was thrown away,
Where all, but barren labour, was forgot,
And the vain stiffness of a letter'd Scot ;
Let them, with Armstrong, pass the term of light,
But not one hour of darkness: when the night 150
Suspends this mortal coil, when Memory wakes,
When for our past misdoings, Conscience takes
A deep revenge, when, by Reflection led,
She draws his curtains, and looks Comfort dead,
Let every Muse be gone ; in vain he turns,
And tries to pray for sleep ; an Ætna burns,
A more than Ætna, in his coward breast,
And Guilt, with vengeance arm'd, forbids him rest :
Though soft as plumage from young Zephyr's wing,
His couch seems hard, and no relief can bring ; 160
Ingratitude hath planted daggers there
No good man can deserve, no brave man bear.
　　Thus, or in any better way they please,
With these great men, or with great men like these,
Let them their appetite for laughter feed ;
I on my Journey all alone proceed.

[1] ' Armstrong: ' Dr John Armstrong, author of that beautiful poem, ' The
Art of Preserving Health,' also of one entitled ' Day,' in which he reflected on
Churchill, who had been his friend.

DEDICATION

TO CHURCHILL'S SERMONS.

The manuscript of this unfinished poem was found among the few papers
Churchill left behind him.

HEALTH to great Glo'ster!—from a man unknown,
Who holds thy health as dearly as his own,
Accept this greeting—nor let modest fear
Call up one maiden blush—I mean not here
To wound with flattery ; 'tis a villain's art,
And suits not with the frankness of my heart.
Truth best becomes an orthodox divine,
And, spite of Hell, that character is mine :
To speak e'en bitter truths I cannot fear ;
But truth, my lord, is panegyric here.   10
    Health to great Glo'ster!—nor, through love of ease,
Which all priests love, let this address displease.
I ask no favour, not one *note* I crave,
And when this busy brain rests in the grave,
(For till that time it never can have rest)
I will not trouble you with one bequest.
Some humbler friend, my mortal journey done,
More near in blood, a nephew or a son,
In that dread hour executor I 'll leave,
For I, alas! have many to receive ;   20
To give, but little.—To great Glo'ster health !
Nor let thy true and proper love of wealth
Here take a false alarm—in purse though poor.
In spirit I 'm right proud, nor can endure
The mention of a bribe—thy pocket 's free :
I, though a dedicator, scorn a fee.
Let thy own offspring all thy fortunes share ;
I would not Allen rob, nor Allen's heir.

Think not,—a thought unworthy thy great soul,   29
Which pomps of this world never could control,
Which never offer'd up at Power's vain shrine,—
Think not that pomp and power can work on mine.
'Tis not thy name, though that indeed is great,
'Tis not the tinsel trumpery of state,
'Tis not thy title, Doctor though thou art,
'Tis not thy mitre, which hath won my heart.
State is a farce ; names are but empty things,
Degrees are bought, and, by mistaken kings,
Titles are oft misplaced ; mitres, which shine
So bright in other eyes, are dull in mine,   40
Unless set off by virtue ; who deceives
Under the sacred sanction of lawn sleeves
Enhances guilt, commits a double sin ;
So fair without, and yet so foul within.
'Tis not thy outward form, thy easy mien,
Thy sweet complacency, thy brow serene,
Thy open front, thy love-commanding eye,
Where fifty Cupids, as in ambush, lie,
Which can from sixty to sixteen impart
The force of Love, and point his blunted dart ;   50
'Tis not thy face, though that by Nature's made
An index to thy soul ; though there display'd
We see thy mind at large, and through thy skin
Peeps out that courtesy which dwells within ;
'Tis not thy birth, for that is low as mine,
Around our heads no lineal glories shine—
But what is birth,—when, to delight mankind,
Heralds can make those arms they cannot find,
When thou art to thyself, thy sire unknown,
A whole Welsh genealogy alone ?   60
No ; 'tis thy inward man, thy proper worth,
Thy right just estimation here on earth,

Thy life and doctrine uniformly join'd,   63
And flowing from that wholesome source, thy mind ;
Thy known contempt of Persecution's rod,
Thy charity for man, thy love of God,
Thy faith in Christ, so well approved 'mongst men,
Which now give life and utterance to my pen.
Thy virtue, not thy rank, demands my lays ;
'Tis not the Bishop, but the Saint, I praise :   70
Raised by that theme, I soar on wings more strong,
And burst forth into praise withheld too long.
    Much did I wish, e'en whilst I kept those sheep
Which, for my curse, I was ordain'd to keep,—
Ordain'd, alas ! to keep, through need, not choice,
Those sheep which never heard their shepherd's voice,
Which did not know, yet would not learn their way,
Which stray'd themselves, yet grieved that I should stray ;
Those sheep which my good father (on his bier
Let filial duty drop the pious tear)   80
Kept well, yet starved himself, e'en at that time
Whilst I was pure and innocent of rhyme,
Whilst, sacred Dulness ever in my view,
Sleep at my bidding crept from pew to pew,—
Much did I wish, though little could I hope,
A friend in him who was the friend of Pope.
    His hand, said I, my youthful steps shall guide,
And lead me safe where thousands fall beside ;
His temper, his experience, shall control,
And hush to peace the tempest of my soul ;   90
His judgment teach me, from the critic school,
How not to err, and how to err by rule ;
Instruct me, mingle profit with delight,
Where Pope was wrong, where Shakspeare was not right ;
Where they are justly praised, and where, through whim,
How little 's due to them, how much to him.

Raised 'bove the slavery of common rules,   97
Of common-sense, of modern, ancient schools,
Those feelings banish'd which mislead us all,
Fools as we are, and which we Nature call,
He by his great example might impart
A better something, and baptize it Art ;
He, all the feelings of my youth forgot,
Might show me what is taste by what is not ;
By him supported, with a proper pride,
I might hold all mankind as fools beside ;
He (should a world, perverse and peevish grown,
-Explode his maxims and assert their own)
Might teach me, like himself, to be content,
And let their folly be their punishment ;   110
Might, like himself, teach his adopted son,
'Gainst all the world, to quote a Warburton.

Fool that I was ! could I so much deceive
My soul with lying hopes ? could I believe
That he, the servant of his Maker sworn,
The servant of his Saviour, would be torn
From their embrace, and leave that dear employ,
The cure of souls, his duty and his joy,
For toys like mine, and waste his precious time,
On which so much depended, for a rhyme ?   120
Should he forsake the task he undertook,
Desert his flock, and break his pastoral crook ?
Should he (forbid it, Heaven !) so high in place,
So rich in knowledge, quit the work of grace,
And, idly wandering o'er the Muses' hill,
Let the salvation of mankind stand still ?

Far, far be that from thee—yes, far from thee
Be such revolt from grace, and far from me
The will to think it—guilt is in the thought—
Not so, not so, hath Warburton been taught,   130

Not so learn'd Christ. Recall that day, well known, 131
When (to maintain God's honour, and his own)
He call'd blasphemers forth ; methinks I now
See stern Rebuke enthroned on his brow,
And arm'd with tenfold terrors—from his tongue,
Where fiery zeal and Christian fury hung,
Methinks I hear the deep-toned thunders roll,
And chill with horror every sinner's soul,
In vain they strive to fly—flight cannot save,
And Potter trembles even in his grave—   140
With all the conscious pride of innocence,
Methinks I hear him, in his own defence,
Bear witness to himself, whilst all men knew,
By gospel rules his witness to be true.
     O glorious man ! thy zeal I must commend,
Though it deprived me of my dearest friend ;
The real motives of thy anger known,
Wilkes must the justice of that anger own ;
And, could thy bosom have been bared to view,
Pitied himself, in turn had pitied you.   150
Bred to the law, you wisely took the gown,
Which I, like Demas, foolishly laid down ;
Hence double strength our Holy Mother drew,
Me she got rid of, and made prize of you.
I, like an idle truant fond of play,
Doting on toys, and throwing gems away,
Grasping at shadows, let the substance slip ;
But you, my lord, renounced attorneyship
With better purpose, and more noble aim,
And wisely played a more substantial game :   160
Nor did Law mourn, bless'd in her younger son,
For Mansfield does what Glo'ster would have done.
     Doctor ! Dean ! Bishop ! Glo'ster ! and My Lord !
If haply these high titles may accord

With thy meek spirit; if the barren sound   165
Of pride delights thee, to the topmost round
Of Fortune's ladder got, despise not one
For want of smooth hypocrisy undone,
Who, far below, turns up his wondering eye,
And, without envy, sees thee placed so high: 170
Let not thy brain (as brains less potent might)
Dizzy, confounded, giddy with the height,
Turn round, and lose distinction, lose her skill
And wonted powers of knowing good from ill,
Of sifting truth from falsehood, friends from foes;
Let Glo'ster well remember how he rose,
Nor turn his back on men who made him great;
Let him not, gorged with power, and drunk with state,
Forget what once he was, though now so high,
How low, how mean, and full as poor as I.   180

Cætera desunt.

LINES WRITTEN IN WINDSOR PARK.

These verses appeared with Churchill's name to them in the London
Magazine for 1763, and there is no reason to doubt their being genuine.

WHEN Pope to Satire gave its lawful way,
And made the Nimrods of Mankind his prey;
When haughty Windsor heard through every wood
Their shame, who durst be great, yet not be good;

2 F

Who, drunk with power, and with ambition blind,   5
Slaves to themselves, and monsters to mankind,
Sinking the man, to magnify the prince,
Were heretofore, what Stuarts have been since :
Could he have look'd into the womb of Time,
How might his spirit in prophetic rhyme,
Inspired by virtue, and for freedom bold,
Matters of different import have foretold !
How might his Muse, if any Muse's tongue
Could equal such an argument, have sung
One William,[1] who makes all mankind his care,
And shines the saviour of his country there !
One William, who to every heart gives law ;
The son of George, the image of Nassau !

[1] ' William :' Duke of Cumberland—the Whig hero.

THE END.

BALLANTYNE AND COMPANY, PRINTERS, EDINBURGH.

www.ingramcontent.com/pod-product-compliance
Lightning Source LLC
Chambersburg PA
CBHW022014110726
47901CB00006B/1518